Titles by Todd Borg

THE WILDERNESS THRILLER SERIES:

WILDERNESS VACATION
WILDERNESS JUSTICE
WILDERNESS PUNISHMENT
WILDERNESS THREAT

THE TAHOE MYSTERY SERIES:

TAHOE DEATHFALL
TAHOE BLOWUP
TAHOE ICE GRAVE
TAHOE KILLSHOT
TAHOE SILENCE
TAHOE AVALANCHE
TAHOE NIGHT
TAHOE HEAT
TAHOE HIJACK
TAHOE TRAP
TAHOE CHASE
TAHOE GHOST BOAT
TAHOE BLUE FIRE
TAHOE DARK
TAHOE PAYBACK
TAHOE SKYDROP
TAHOE DEEP
TAHOE HIT
TAHOE JADE
TAHOE MOON
TAHOE FLIGHT
TAHOE RESCUE

WILDERNESS JUSTICE

Josie Strong
A Dark Road Suspense
Book 2

by

TODD BORG

THRILLER PRESS

Thriller Press First Edition, August 2024

ISBN: 978-1-931296-76-2

Manufactured in the United States of America

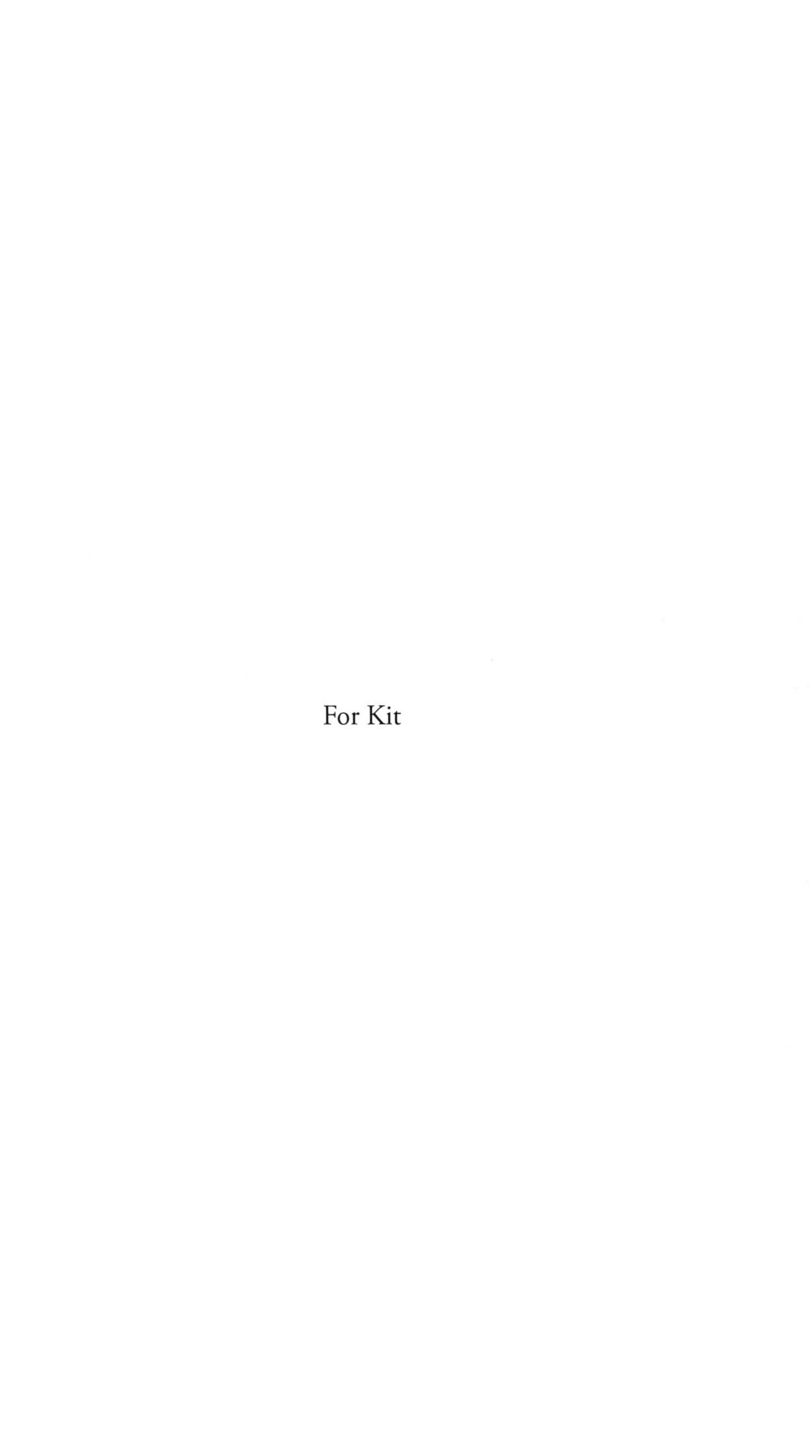

For Kit

ACKNOWLEDGMENTS

I owe a great deal to my editors, Liz Johnston, Eric Berglund, Christel Hall, and my wife Kit. They find and fix countless mistakes. They make much-needed suggestions for improvements. If my book reads well, they get the credit.

Graphic maestro Keith Carlson produced a spectacular new look for this new series. So beautiful I want to keep staring at them. I can't thank him enough.

Kit also serves as initial reader, story coach, last reader. She has an unerring ability to find and take out my misjudgments. I can't thank her enough.

ONE

Josie Strong had just gotten home from an afternoon walk with their dog when the phone rang.

"Hello, my name is Theo Mosconi," the man on the phone said. "I'm an agent with California's Bureau of Investigation. May I please speak to Professor Josephine Strong?"

"Speaking," Josie said.

"I'm calling about your daughter Samantha. We have a situation."

Josie felt her heart thump. "What's wrong? Is there some kind of problem?"

"She was detained at the San Ysidro Customs station."

"I don't understand. She's on a school field trip to Tijuana."

"She was, yes. I'm sorry to tell you she was observed passing a package to someone after the bus came back over the border into California."

Josie couldn't breathe. "What are you saying?"

"Your daughter is being held as a drug trafficking suspect."

"What?! That can't be!" Josie felt like she'd been punched in the gut.

She leaned one hand on the kitchen counter.

"The school bus made several stops in Tijuana. Your daughter claims that when they were in a restaurant, she was approached by someone she knows. That man gave her a small backpack to carry back over the border. The bag contained drugs."

"That's crazy! Samantha knows never to carry any items other than her own. She would never smuggle drugs. She hates drugs. And she knows it's a major crime to smuggle them. I can't believe this."

Josie's heart hurt with each rapid beat, sending throbbing pains from the center of her chest up into her neck. Josie and

Samantha's rescue dog, Unknown, walked over and pushed her nose against Josie's leg, a concerned look on her face. No doubt she picked up on Josie's stress.

"Actually, she admits it all," the man said. "The man who gave her drugs is the older brother of a girl she knows from her school. The brother has lived in Tijuana for two years."

"Then how did he convince my daughter to carry something back to the States?!"

"Samantha claims he told her he'd recently been back stateside visiting his mother in San Diego. When he headed back to Mexico, he took a bag of clothes his mother had set aside for him and put it in his backpack. But when he got to Tijuana, he claimed he'd gotten the wrong bag. The clothes in the bag belonged to his mother, apparently a costume she was to wear in an upcoming play. We're told the woman acts in a community theater in San Diego. The mother was supposedly very upset that her son had taken the wrong clothes. She said that not having the costume would ruin the play. Your daughter was sympathetic about this."

"That's the way Samantha is. Caring about everything."

The man on the phone continued. "Nevertheless, after the school bus went through customs back on the U.S. side, it waited so the students could use the rest room. The man's mother came to meet your daughter. Your daughter gave the woman the bag. It turns out that the woman has been under surveillance by the Bureau of Investigation. As she drove away, policemen attempted to pull the woman over, and the woman tried to escape, driving at high speed. There was an accident. The woman was apprehended. But one of the cops pursuing her was killed."

Josie felt sick. To have Samantha connected to a deadly accident, however remote, was horrifying.

"I'm very sorry to hear that. But my daughter didn't cause that accident. She's just a fourteen-year-old kid."

"We recovered the backpack your daughter carried over the border and gave to the woman. It had fifty grams of methamphetamine sewn into the lining."

"Didn't you hear me? She's just a kid."

"I'm sorry to face you with a difficult reality. But kids can be tried as adults. If convicted, she could be punished by a sentence up to life in prison and a fine up to ten million dollars."

Josie inhaled. "I… I can't believe..." Josie was speechless.

"Furthermore, California law provides that anyone connected to a crime that involves the death of a law enforcement officer can be charged with felony murder. Intent is not necessary."

Josie was hyperventilating.

The man continued, "I agree that it is almost unbelievable. In your daughter's defense, the costume in the backpack was clean. The drugs were well-hidden in the backpack lining. It was a good setup for smuggling. Perhaps, the law will show some leniency. But I want you to know the seriousness of the situation."

Josie felt she was about to be sick.

"We need you to come to the Bureau of Investigation," the man said.

Josie felt paralyzed by fear. She managed to say, "Where?"

"The sooner the better. We're holding your daughter." The man gave her the address. "We're in the annex to the side of the main Bureau of Investigation building. We will be waiting."

TWO

Josie couldn't think. She turned around as if looking for something, searching, trying to focus. All she knew was she had to save her daughter. She went to the door of their condo. Realized she didn't have her keys or purse.

Unknown stood at the door and looked up at her. The dog's brow was furrowed. No anticipation of a walk. The dog knew something was wrong.

Josie thought of bringing her. For comfort. For companionship. But she didn't know what the parking situation was. She couldn't risk leaving the dog in the sun, and they might not let her bring Unknown inside. She briefly rubbed the dog's nose, said goodbye, and left.

She drove east from Santa Monica on the 10. Ninety minutes later, Josie was escorted down a hallway in the Bureau of Investigation annex building on West Temple Street in Los Angeles. Josie had to walk slowly. She'd been shot a month before as she tracked her daughter's kidnapper. The bullet wound in her calf had largely healed, but it left her calf muscle very tight and prone to spasms. Every time she walked any distance, her leg began to throb. She still had a perceptible limp.

The young man directing her made two knocks on a door, turned the knob, and pushed the door open.

"Please have a seat. Someone will be with you in a moment." He left and shut the door behind him.

Josie looked around the empty room. It was just large enough for a rectangular table with six chairs, three on each side. There were no windows, no decor. The room seemed like a stage set where the designer wanted to communicate something about the color white. White walls, white table, white chairs.

The ceiling and the floor tiles were white. As a black woman, Josie felt like she stood out. She didn't mind. But she noticed.

Josie pulled out one of the chairs and sat. Her right eyelid twitched incessantly. She had a powerful headache as if someone were sitting on her head. The muscles between her shoulder blades burned with a muscle cramp. She was so nauseated, she worried she would vomit. She got out her phone and tried calling Samantha. She'd already tried the number three times. But her call was again routed to Samantha's voicemail.

A minute later, the door opened and two men walked in. They looked to be in their early forties—not much younger than Josie—and they wore gray suits and white shirts. They had similar builds and similar eyebrows, almost like brothers. The biggest difference between them was that one had a navy tie, and one maroon. Both had short haircuts. Both were pale white guys who looked like they worked in Maine instead of Los Angeles. The most notable thing about the men was that they were nondescript. Josie doubted she'd be able to recognize them if she saw them wearing jeans and baseball caps at the supermarket.

The man with the maroon tie spoke.

"Josephine Strong?"

"Yes."

"I'm Agent Theo Mosconi. Sorry to meet you under such stressful circumstances."

The two men sat next to each other, across the table from Josie.

"This is Agent José Rodriguez," the first man said. "He is one of our detail men. Keeps track of everything the rest of us forget."

Rodriguez made a little nod, then unlatched his briefcase and pulled out a folder. He set the folder on the table, opened it, spread out several papers, and slid them over in front of the man named Mosconi. Rodriguez pulled one more item out of his briefcase and set it on the table, close to him and out of reach of Josie.

Josie could see the little skull-and-crossbones sticker on it. It was Samantha's cell phone!

"That's Sam's phone!" Josie said. "She's here? I want to see her!"

"Soon," Mosconi said. "Very soon. First we have to go over some things."

"You need to understand that my daughter would never intentionally smuggle drugs! It was obviously a mistake on her part. A terrible mistake. But she was taken advantage of. The drugs were planted."

The man nodded. "First, let me explain. Smuggling drugs is a crime whether you do it on purpose or as an ignorant mule."

"Please don't retreat behind a cliché," Josie said. "Give me a reasonable explanation for why you are holding a fourteen-year-old child!"

The man made a big sigh, clearly frustrated at having to explain. "We don't make the laws. Your daughter has been arrested. But she hasn't been arraigned. The law is strict because that is how the political process works." He looked down at one of the papers in front of him. "It says here you are a professor at UCLA."

Josie nodded. "Yes."

"As a professor, you must know that the specifics of laws are not always written in a way that makes the most sense for society. Often, the details are intended to please a group of voters or a union or other group that can influence voters. The bottom line with this law is that if a cop is killed in the line of duty, everyone two steps removed can still be charged with felony murder. Is that reasonable? You obviously won't think so. The spouse of the dead cop probably does. And politicians always benefit from a tough-on-crime approach."

Josie put her elbows on the table and leaned her head forward into her hands. A wave of nausea made her swallow. She took a deep breath and held it.

"As a result, your daughter is in a grave situation," the man continued, even though Josie wasn't looking at him. "However, the Bureau of Investigation has some latitude regarding how we proceed. With your cooperation, we can mitigate these charges."

Josie felt like she was choking. It took some time before she could speak. "I want to call my lawyer."

"Yes, of course. And it's your right to do so. However, we are prepared to offer you an alternative. You will want to hear what I have to say before you call your lawyer." He paused.

Josie looked at him. She made a small nod.

"Due to the sensitive nature of this situation, that alternative will be off the table if you get legal representation. Lawyers talk, and they manipulate situations to their advantage, not to the benefit of law enforcement. Telling your lawyer would compromise our mission. We simply can't have public attention focused on our work."

Josie lifted her head and looked at the man. "I don't understand what that means," Josie said. "I have a constitutional right to consult an attorney. What does that have to do with this alternative, or whatever it is?"

"We're offering you a way out that avoids charges against your daughter. A way out by means of a quid pro quo."

Josie was suspicious. "How? And why?"

The man named Mosconi seemed frustrated at having to explain what was probably routine for him even though confusing to a lay person. The other man, Rodriguez, still hadn't spoken.

Mosconi said, "As part of the California Attorney General's External Investigations Task Force, our job is to find creative solutions to some of our most intractable crimes. As such, our success depends on the details of our operation not being subject to the scrutiny of the media and attorneys and the like."

"I'm sorry," Josie said, shaking her head, wiping tears from her eyes. "You are talking conceptually. Please tell me what you mean. And when will I see Samantha?"

"In time. Please be patient while I explain. Our most-wanted criminals have eluded traditional law enforcement. Under instructions from the Attorney General and as authorized by the California Legislature, the Task Force operates outside of traditional law enforcement structure. We rarely work with sheriff's offices or police departments or any of the more familiar federal agencies such as the FBI or the Drug Enforcement Administration. Among other projects, we research unusual law enforcement success stories, identify the people involved, and then consider enticing them to help us with other crimes. If outside attorneys learned of the Task Force operations, they would blow our cover."

"Why would you not want to work with other law enforcement agencies?" Josie asked.

"For all the standard reasons. A regrettable but common example would be if a law enforcement agency has a member working in concert with criminals. Once our methods are exposed, our effectiveness is destroyed."

"So what is your quid pro quo?"

"We want you to help us catch a criminal who has eluded us to date. In exchange, the San Diego County District Attorney won't charge your daughter with any crime."

"You're blackmailing me," Josie said.

"We prefer to think of it as a simple exchange of favors. It happens a thousand times a day in law enforcement. The version you are probably most familiar with is when a suspect in a crime is asked to testify against another suspect in return for a reduced sentence. It is a classic you-help-us-we-help-you situation."

Josie sensed her blood pressure pounding in her ears. She shut her eyes, took a deep breath, and let it out slowly.

"Okay," she said. "What on Earth could I do to help you catch a criminal?"

"We're hoping you can answer that question. A month ago, you caught the murderer of a young girl named Clarice Angel. The police had found no leads and no suspects despite a great deal of effort. As you know, the girl's murder made national headlines. When you were able to catch the killer, that also made headlines and brought you to our attention. We especially noticed your tenacity in pursuing a killer who ended up trying to kill you. You thwarted his effort in the most extreme way possible."

Josie knew he was referring to the fact that she killed the

murderer's accomplice, gave the murderer severe, permanent injuries, and made it so law enforcement will be able to put him away for life.

Mosconi continued. "In the process of capturing this killer, you took an unusual approach, choosing to use non-traditional weapons to your creative advantage."

Although Josie could barely get her mind off an imagined picture of her daughter in some degrading prison cell, she nevertheless was amazed at how dense these men seemed. "I'm sorry," she said, "but I only used medieval weapons because I know nothing about other weapons. It wasn't a clever choice. It was a necessity. Someone was trying to kill us. We merely did whatever we could to stop him."

Agent Theo Mosconi made a little dismissive wave of his hand. "Be that as it may. We're not talking to you because you know medieval weapons. We're talking to you because you were creative. That same creativity could serve you well in tracking and catching another criminal who has been difficult to apprehend. If you agree to help us find and capture this criminal, we will release your daughter."

Josie felt as if a fog of confusion was preventing her from thinking clearly. She was so worried about Samantha that she could barely function. She tried to force the worry from her mind. "Let me be sure I understand you correctly. You're saying that you will let Samantha go free today if I agree to help you find a criminal."

"Yes. You will both have to sign an agreement to that effect. As long as we believe you are actively helping us find a particular criminal, we will leave you alone."

"What if I'm not successful?"

"We believe you will be. But if we believe you are no longer trying to find him, then we would have no choice but to recommend to the San Diego County DA that she charge your daughter."

"Finding this criminal might take a long time. What if the process approaches the statute of limitations on drug smuggling?"

"The statute of limitations on drug trafficking is three years. We'll monitor the situation. However, felony murder has no statute of limitations. After three years, you will still have the motivation to help us. Although, the reality is that if this criminal hasn't been caught in three years, he will likely be dead, and we'll have no more interest in your services."

"And if I succeed at finding this person, I would have your word that you won't come after Samantha?"

"It's in the contract. Even if you don't succeed, your good effort is all we ask."

Once again, Josie had the impulse to say no and call her attorney. But she glanced again at Samantha's cell phone. If she said no, these men would probably take Samantha away without even letting Josie talk to her.

Josie tried to shut out that fear.

"What I don't understand," she said, "is that District Attorneys don't operate at the whim of anyone in law enforcement or government. I'm no legal scholar, but I know that DAs are autonomous. You can't tell them who to prosecute or not to prosecute."

The man gave Josie a long look and didn't immediately respond.

Josie continued. "You're saying my daughter was picked up at a customs facility in San Diego County. The county District Attorney wouldn't be directly involved with the California Bureau of Investigation. How could you pressure that DA to follow your wishes?"

Mosconi sighed. "Like all members of law enforcement agencies, District Attorneys often look at the big picture." He sounded very impatient. "If San Diego County holds back while you help us capture a bigger prize than your daughter, then we'll be more inclined to help them in the future. The DA knows that and will respond accordingly."

He hooked the tip of his little finger in his tie and loosened it a tiny bit.

"You've maybe heard of the San Diego County DA. She's quite well known. She goes by SGP, short for Selena Guadalupe

Peralta. Perhaps you've heard about her track record in drug trafficking convictions. It is ninety-eight percent. You don't want her coming after your daughter."

Josie had heard of Peralta. The woman was considered a ferocious warrior. No one wanted to be Peralta's target.

Josie took another deep breath and tried to look at the larger picture.

What stood out was that this man's proposal included a proscription against letting her talk to a lawyer. That seemed a clear red-flag warning, and it suggested to her that there were aspects to this that were unethical or even illegal. Yet here she was in the California Bureau of Investigation building where her daughter was being held.

Josie stared at Samantha's cellphone.

The man spoke. "I realize this is a lot to think about. But you merely have a choice to make. Either you accept our offer, or you decline it. If you decline, the San Diego DA will look at the circumstances and evidence, see an easy drug-trafficking conviction of your daughter, and possibly a felony murder conviction as well."

THREE

Josie looked from one man to the other. So far, only Agent Mosconi, the one with the maroon tie, had spoken.

"How could I look for a criminal when I teach full time?" she asked.

"You would have to prevail on the dean or others who control your schedule and ask for time off. You could use your weekends. Maybe take a sabbatical or something. Either way, we would expect you to devote much effort to this situation."

"You'd be taking over my life," Josie said. "My daughter's life, too."

"It will be a small adjustment for you compared to if she is convicted of a felony and put in prison. For what it's worth, we will help. You will have access to our resources. Any time you want, you can call on us for information."

Josie shut her eyes, trying to calm herself.

"Okay," she said. "Tell me about this criminal you want me to find."

"There's a man who has killed two Mariposa County Sheriff's deputies. He shot them to death with a thirty-aught-six. We don't know who he is. We only have a vague description, which we got from an employee of a hunting store in Merced. From our interviews, we believe the suspect escaped into Yosemite Park and is hiding in the mountain wilderness."

"I suppose I should ask questions as I think of them, otherwise I might miss important information. What is a thirty-aught-six?"

Mosconi turned to Rodriguez. "You want to answer that? You're the gun expert."

Rodriguez hesitated as if unsure that he had the authority to speak directly. "I'm a criminologist, not a hunter," he said. "But the thirty-aught-six label refers to a size of the bullet cartridge."

Josie said, "Maybe I don't need to know this, but just so I'm clear, not all rifles shoot that size bullet?"

"Correct." Rodriguez said.

"What difference does it make?"

Rodriguez shrugged. "A thirty-aught-six is made for hunting large game. Deer and such."

Josie said, "So the shooter you want me to find has a rifle for shooting big game, and I know nothing about rifles or game. Yet you think I can find this killer?"

"That is our hope, yes," Mosconi said.

"But I'm not a tracker."

"We realize that."

"You can see by looking at me that I'm out of shape. So I'm obviously not a mountain climber. Nor am I a mountain biker or hiker."

He nodded. "Understood."

"Then why me? You'd do so much better if you contacted a wilderness expert."

Mosconi shook his head. "We don't think so. First of all, the Mariposa Sheriff's Office has already tried to find this killer. They've consulted wilderness experts. They've seen no sign of him despite a major search effort. By that alone, we have reason to believe that this killer is savvy about law enforcement. He may have even worked as a law enforcement officer in the past. He probably knows how law enforcement agencies respond, how they have pursued him. He probably knows that the sheriff's office as well as state agencies have already done as you've suggested, hired trackers and climbers and hikers and wilderness experts. So either he's in a hiding place that is very difficult to find, or he's seen the searchers coming from a long way off, and he just moves on and stays ahead of them."

"What about search dogs?"

"They've tried that as well. The problem is they have no specific scent of the man to give a dog. Without a scent, a dog can't distinguish one human from another. A popular park like Yosemite has a flood of human scents wafting on the breeze."

Mosconi paused, then resumed talking.

"But unlike with professional searchers, if you and your daughter approach, he won't pay any attention. In fact, he won't notice you at all. He'll just think you are tourists, inexperienced travelers from Los Angeles, there to see the various waterfalls and experience the mountains. You will have access to his realm without him paying any attention."

Josie couldn't believe what he was saying. Mosconi wanted to send her and her daughter to confront someone who'd killed multiple times.

"What do you mean when you refer to his realm? Just Yosemite Park?"

"Territory he's comfortable with. Having successfully eluded capture, he obviously has wilderness skills, finding and hunting food, staying warm during cold nights, hiding in a manner that searchers don't see, leaving no signs of his passage through the forest. Those parameters would work well in Yosemite. Of course, the whole world knows the famous valley and rock walls and waterfalls. But the reality is that most of the park is wilderness, mountains and forests that are largely unknown even to the hikers who travel the remote trails. The forests of Yosemite are dense. Even the bear remain hidden until they choose to come and raid the campsites for food. We think our suspect is like that, completely hidden and only coming out to steal food. And if he thinks that missing food would be noticed, then he need only make a mess before he leaves, and everyone will assume they were visited by a bear. For a careful man, hiding in Yosemite would be very easy."

"Do you think this fugitive is planning to live in the Yosemite forest forever?"

"No. Logic would suggest he simply lays low for a year or two until the search for him winds down. Then he could reemerge, perhaps cleaned up and wearing fresh clothes stolen piece by piece from campers."

"But I don't know how to track someone hiding in the wilderness."

"We see that as an advantage. First, you'll no doubt take an approach that traditional trackers would never think of. Thus you may have better luck finding this guy than they would. Second, with no traditional tracking skills, you won't be recognized by the killer as a tracker."

"Okay, let's say some miracle happens and I can actually find this guy. What happens next? Will I call your number and you'll send in a team of officers to bring him in?"

"That is one approach we'll support. However, if this man senses that cops are approaching, he will likely disappear as he has in the past. Or, worse, he'll kill them and then disappear." Mosconi paused. "After observing this man's elusive nature, you may decide that the best approach is to do what you did last month and take him yourself."

"You've got to be kidding."

"No, I'm serious. We'll deputize you, and give you handcuffs, shackles, and an arrest warrant." He paused. "I realize that seems ludicrous to someone like you. However, the Bureau has done this in the past with civilians who have special skills. We don't talk about the practice simply because of its irregularity and the difficulty in presenting the approach to society at large. Think of it as a mark of effective law enforcement, looking beyond traditional approaches. With only a little bit of research, I could give you many examples of deputizing civilians going back dozens of years."

"I'm sorry, sir, but this seems like a joke. I'm a professor with no useful physical skills. Arresting this man is a task for law enforcement."

"After we deputize you, you will officially be part of law enforcement."

"You'd be sending me and my daughter to our deaths."

"We don't think so. Last month, it was the exact opposite. You caught killers, not the other way around."

Josie found herself staring at the man.

Mosconi said, "Part of your advantage is the very lack of skills you refer to. That is what forced you to take a different approach. We think this killer is so wily that a different approach may be the only way to find and catch him."

Josie was dumbfounded. The idea was absurd. Then she had a separate thought. It was a dark idea, but it made sense.

She said, "Could it be that you don't want to send traditional law enforcement after this guy because the only way to take him is to kill him and not try to arrest him? And you don't want to put a cop in that situation? You want me to do it? Club him with my war hammer? Or shoot him with my crossbow?" Even though Josie had killed someone, it still felt shocking to say the words.

Mosconi's gaze didn't waver.

Josie said, "If I were to kill the man, that would solve your problem without putting any law enforcement officer at risk of being killed."

Again, Mosconi didn't speak.

Josie continued, "But it would put my daughter and myself at great risk."

"I think the greater risk," Mosconi said slowly, "is if your daughter is prosecuted by DA Peralta's office."

Josie raised her hands to her face and breathed through her fingers.

At that moment, Josie felt hate for the man. She'd never been subject to such an awful decision. Yet he held Samantha, so he had infinite power over her.

FOUR

Josie shut her eyes. She focused on what Mosconi said about Samantha and his offer.

The risk of not accepting his offer was that Samantha's life would be effectively destroyed. Even so, Josie couldn't go into this agreement blind. Maybe chasing some murderer for the Bureau of Investigation would be even worse for Samantha than prison.

"Tell me what you know about this killer," Josie said.

"There isn't much to tell. We don't know his name. Two months ago, he was pulled over for speeding on Highway Forty-One near Fish Camp. He was driving a two-thousand-twelve, dark gray Chevy pickup with tinted windows. The sheriff's vehicle had two deputies. The driver stayed with the patrol unit while the other got out. The driver in the patrol unit radioed that the suspect opened up a small sliding window at the rear of the pickup cab, pointed a rifle out, and fired at the approaching cop. Then the cop on the radio went silent. It turned out that the shooter shot him next.

"The pickup was later found abandoned north of Fish Camp in an area with easy access to Yosemite park. The pickup turned out to have been stolen in Merced three days before. The sheriff's office later found a partial, torn receipt under the passenger seat. The business name on the receipt had been torn off. But the receipt had a sales number on it, and it was traced to the Big West Hunting and Fishing store in Merced. Interviews with employees revealed that one of their customers was a Caucasian male, thirty-five to forty years old, about six feet two inches, two hundred pounds, brown hair in a mop cut, brown eyes, and missing a tooth on the upper left side. He had no significant facial hair but had a three-day stubble. The employee who spoke with him said he was a smart and focused prepper."

"What's a prepper?" Josie asked.

"Preppers are survivalists who believe the world is coming to a violent end, most likely at the hands of what they think of as our evil government. They prepare for doomsday by stocking up on survival gear, including weapons and ammunition, and they stockpile food and water and other supplies in anticipation of having to live for long periods without a functioning society."

"Like we're going back to the Early Middle Ages in Europe," Josie said.

"What's that?"

"The fifth through the tenth century. Sometimes called the Dark Ages. The rapid decline of civilization, a shrinking population, the loss of a high-functioning state." Josie realized she'd slipped into professor mode. She stopped talking.

"Yeah, I guess that's what the preppers are all about."

"No idea of the man's name?" Josie asked.

"No. After the Bureau of Investigation got involved, we had a police artist do a sketch of the suspect based on the hunting store employee's description. We've circulated the sketch, but with no positive result."

"Is there anything else you know about this guy that would be good for me to know?"

José looked at Mosconi. It was a moment before Mosconi spoke. "There's just one thing that will make you extra cautious."

Josie waited. It seemed that Mosconi was thinking carefully about how he should speak.

"After the sheriff's deputies were shot, the sheriff's office did a careful analysis of tire tracks and determined that the deputies had stopped their patrol vehicle farther back from the pickup than is normal."

"Why?" Josie asked.

"We don't know. Perhaps the deputy driving sensed danger and subconsciously wanted to keep his distance."

"What's the implication?"

"It suggests that the man they pulled over was a remarkably

good shot. He placed his round in the center of each deputy's forehead. That's especially difficult with a victim sitting in the driver's seat of a vehicle. The reflections on the patrol car windshield make a precise shot extremely difficult, let alone how the windshield glass would alter a bullet's path."

Josie felt a sense of bleakness crowding in on her. "That's really creepy. This guy is a real sharpshooter."

"Yes. Worse, after the driver of the patrol unit pulled the pickup over, he stayed in the vehicle and spoke on the radio. It was his partner who got out and walked toward the pickup."

"What's the significance of that?"

"The cop's partner was a woman. She was small and—for lack of better words—her female form was obvious at a distance. Some men, even some really ruthless killers, hesitate when it comes to shooting a woman. Yet this killer had no reluctance."

Josie swallowed. She couldn't understand why Mosconi had told her these details, as they made her more reluctant to help them. The only explanation she could come up with was that Mosconi wanted to make her uncomfortable. Maybe he liked to make all women uncomfortable.

After half a minute, Mosconi said, "Having said that, I don't think he shot the woman cop for any reason having to do with her gender. I think his animosity was only because she was a cop."

"Why do you think that?" Josie asked.

"Call it a hunch. With you two showing up in Yosemite, he will think you are tourists. Nothing more."

"You think I should bring Samantha with me? Put her in such a risky situation?"

Mosconi paused. "The two of you together would raise even less suspicion than just you."

Josie took her time thinking about it. "If I agree to do this, when will my daughter be released? And where do I go to pick her up?"

"We have her in a room down the hall. If you give us your word you'll do this for us, I'll go get her."

"Okay. I accept."

FIVE

Agent Mosconi pushed back his chair, stood, and walked out the door.

Josie stood as well.

"You stay here with Agent Rodriguez," Mosconi said.

After the door clicked shut, Agent Rodriguez spoke to Josie, his voice soft. "Sorry my boss is brusque. He's under a lot of pressure. But that's also his personality, if you want to know the truth. I've learned just to focus on doing what he wants. That way we get along much better."

A minute later, the door opened. Samantha rushed in and hugged Josie like she was holding onto everything that mattered in life.

"Mama! I didn't know! I was set up! I was framed! I'm so sorry!"

Josie's arms completely wrapped around Samantha's skinny body. Josie hugged her as if to never let go. Samantha's head towered over Josie's.

"I know, Sam, I know. We've both learned a valuable lesson."

"I'll never do anything like that again, Mama!"

"I believe you."

"They said a cop died! I can't bear to think I was involved in something that led to that! It makes me choke and cry. I'm so sorry!"

"You didn't cause the car accident," Josie said.

They held each other for a long time.

"You two can talk about all this at home," Agent Mosconi said. "Right now we have business to attend to. Please take a seat."

"Can't we go home, now?" Samantha said.

"Not yet, Sam," Josie said. "Because of what happened, these men can file serious charges against you. Or I should say, the San Diego District Attorney can file the charges. But these men apparently have the ability to make the District Attorney hold off on those charges." Josie glanced at Mosconi. "But we have to help them," she added.

"I don't understand, Mama. I just want to go home. I'm never going over the border again."

Josie explained some of the details of the Bureau's offer.

"We don't have a choice?" Samantha said. "We have to help capture this killer? We have to do what the man says, or I go to prison?"

"Maybe," Josie said.

Mosconi was looking impatient.

Samantha looked at the men. Josie could see her natural suspicion.

Josie sat down and pulled on Samantha's sleeve to get her to do the same. They sat in adjacent chairs across from the two men.

Rodriguez, who seemed to watch Mosconi as if worried about Mosconi's temper, spread out some pages. Mosconi took them, looked them over, then turned them around to face Josie and Samantha.

"This is what we need you to sign, an agreement between Josephine and Samantha Strong and the Bureau's External Investigations Task Force. There are two pages, which you can read, if you want. Basically, it says what I've already told you. You agree to help us track and apprehend an unnamed suspect who may or may not be hiding in Yosemite Park. The agreement explains that satisfactory performance of your duties means you will make a concerted effort to find this criminal, and that you will continue your effort until either you find the man or until we say that you've made sufficient effort."

Mosconi looked at both Josie and Samantha in turn. Rodriguez looked down at the papers.

"There is one more aspect to this that I forgot to mention," Mosconi said. "The last paragraph of this contract is a nondisclosure agreement. Neither of you is allowed to mention this agreement to anyone at any time. That includes friends and acquaintances, media, other employees of any California agency, or any legal counsel. Should you ever tell an attorney about this contract, you will be in breach of its terms. And we can decide to use that to move forward on arraignment and prosecution of Samantha on the charges we've discussed."

The man looked up from the papers.

"You're locking us into a corner," Josie said. "We have no rights under this contract. We have no alternatives, no options."

Mosconi and Rodriguez gave them placid stares that Josie found infuriating.

Eventually, Mosconi said, "We're not forcing you into this agreement. We're only enticing you. If you don't want to sign this, we will send Samantha back to District Attorney Peralta."

Josie shut her eyes and counted to ten. She turned to Samantha.

"Do you understand what this means? These men basically own us. We have no choice but to do what they want or else we'll face a legal system that may put you away for many years."

Samantha took hold of Josie's hands. "Is this all because we caught the killer of my friend Clarice?" Samantha glanced at the men, then looked back at Josie. "So they think we can find other killers?"

Josie nodded.

"And if we don't sign, I'll have to go to court, right?"

"Probably," Josie said. "Maybe a judge takes pity on you. Maybe they'll offer us a decent plea bargain. But we can't count on it. If it goes to trial, the same applies to a jury. They may be sympathetic and vote to acquit. Or, they may make you the poster girl for drug-smuggling kids undermining the security of our borders."

Samantha made a slow nod. "What do you think my chances will be?"

Josie thought about it. "A young defense attorney hoping to make a name for himself or herself would try to put it into positive light. A more experienced attorney would probably be unwilling to even make a phone call until they were paid in full."

"That's because a more experienced attorney would know just how bad my situation is, right?" Samantha said. "I was caught doing the crime, whether I was framed or not."

Josie felt like crying as she watched Samantha trying to assess the depth of her problems. Her daughter looked across at the two men. Then she turned to Josie.

"Let's sign it. I don't even know what prison would be like. But I'm not willing to take that chance if there is something that will keep it from happening. Even if it's not guaranteed."

Josie looked at Mosconi. She reached for the papers.

Mosconi took out a pen and made two Xs where they needed to sign and date the agreement.

Josie skimmed the pages and saw that they said exactly what Mosconi described. She signed and dated it first, then she slid the paper to Samantha.

Samantha complied, and then, like her mother before her, dropped her head to her hands, her forehead making a noise as it struck her palms.

SIX

Agent Mosconi took the papers and put them in his briefcase.

"Don't I get a copy?" Josie asked.

"No. Too much danger that someone would find it. Even an accidental revelation of this agreement would be a breach of contract. We can't take that chance."

"But how will I know that you won't change what I signed? How can I trust you?"

Mosconi made a slight shake of his head. "I thought I already made the situation clear. While I know that I can be trusted, technically, there is no way for you to know that. I'm sorry to say that you have to take me at my word because you have no choice." He glanced at Samantha, then turned his gaze back to Josie. "Because of your daughter's transgressions, your future is dependent on whether you try to help us. But we've shown good faith. We've returned your daughter to you and are letting you walk out of here."

Josie felt Samantha tense beside her. Josie knew that one of the biggest struggles she would have in the near future was to not overreact to Samantha's mistake. She'd have to continuously try to measure her words when her temper flared or when she pondered the situation that Samantha had created. Even thinking about it now made Josie clench her hands into fists. Josie reminded herself that Samantha hadn't thought she was doing anything wrong. She thought she was helping a friend get misplaced belongings back to his mother. It was a misguided and naive move. But it wasn't a devious move.

Neither Mosconi nor Rodriguez showed any reaction while Josie was trying to settle her emotions.

"Okay," Josie said. She turned to them. "How do we get

whatever info you've got on this criminal? Can you give me some printouts or something?"

"No printouts. No paper of any kind. We need you both to adopt the utmost level of security in how you pursue this or even how you think about it. If you ask someone a question, it has to be phrased so that it doesn't point toward the killer's possible identity or your interest in the situation. If you talk about the case among yourselves, you have to always be certain that no one can overhear you. If this killer should ever get the idea that you are searching for him, he would likely come after you. This guy may be a garden-variety idiot. Or he could be the worst combination of smarts and evil intentions. The fact that this killer has eluded us despite a long, extensive manhunt shows how wily he is. For example, if he were to see you more than just once or twice in the most casual of circumstances, we would expect him to respond. If he gets suspicious of you and decides that you are a cop, he might kill you. But I think you're safe posing as tourists."

Mosconi paused. It seemed to Josie that he was trying to decide if he should tell them what he knew.

"Over the last many months, there have been several bank robberies. We suspect, but don't know, that this man was the perpetrator."

"If you won't give us any printed information on the man we're after, how will we learn about him?"

Agent Rodriguez pulled an old iPhone and an old-style charger out of his briefcase.

Mosconi said, "This phone has been wiped, and its cell and wifi connectibility have been destroyed. It is now a basic computer with no apps. Its battery can be charged, but you can't plug it into anything else. The phone has been loaded with everything we know—or think we know—about this guy and his crimes. The phone has maps of Yosemite, the police artist sketch, a list of the stuff the killer bought at the hunting store. There's lots of other stuff on there as well. Three hundred some pages."

"Like a book about this man," Josie said. "Like a Kindle

book."

"Yes. But if someone saw you look at a Kindle reader while you're hiking down a wilderness trail, that would be slightly unusual. Whereas if someone sees you looking at a phone, that is what nearly everybody does all the time anyway. It won't stand out."

The man handed Josie the phone and the charging cord.

"The phone is password protected." He stuck a Post-it note on the phone. It had the number 26252 on it. "Think of it as an equation. Twenty-six times two equals fifty-two. Memorize it." He waited a moment. "Ready?"

Josie and Samantha nodded.

"Good," Mosconi said. He took the Post-it and put it in his pocket.

Josie pressed the button on the phone and entered the password. The phone opened to a page of writing. It looked a bit like a table of contents. She handed the phone to Samantha.

Samantha pressed the button. "The only app symbols are the built-in stuff that doesn't connect to any carrier," she said. "Calculator. Clock. Camera. Compass. The four Cs."

Josie didn't know if Samantha was being flip or if she was talking about some standard nomenclature for apps that started with the letter C.

"There's nothing else here but pages," Samantha said. "I can swipe them up or down." She glanced at Mosconi. "You could have put all the stuff in here on a memory stick. That would take up a lot less space."

"Sure. But a memory stick has to be plugged into something. And all of those somethings are connected. This phone is a closed system. You can't connect it to any other device, and you can't download any info off it. All you can do is read what's on it. And you need the password to do that. Even if you lose it, it's worthless to anyone else. It's one of the safest ways to protect information. Put it on its own dedicated and isolated device."

"But we still have to use our own phones," Josie said. "If we're posing as tourists in Yosemite, we'd naturally look at the map in our phones just to see where the trails are."

"Sure. But be very careful. A simple map of Yosemite on your phone won't raise any alarm bells. Main trails and waterfalls and campsites and where to eat, et cetera. But in the event this guy is tech savvy, if you're searching on the most secluded places to hide in the park, that could cause a problem. A paper map is better. And never use any wifi. This guy you're after is probably smart. He's evaded us for a long time, so that shows he's smart. He could have his friends set up a free-access wifi in a spot where people are delighted to use it. They think it's connected to something official or a Starbucks. But if you do use it, it gives them access to everything in your phone or computer."

Josie looked at Samantha.

"Fine, Mama," she said, easily perceiving Josie's disapproval. "I get the picture."

Josie turned to Mosconi. "What do we do now?"

"We deputize you."

"You're serious?" Samantha was amazed.

"Not you," Mosconi said. "You're too young."

He turned to Josie. "Put your hand over your heart and repeat after me."

She hesitated, wondering if the man was really serious. This was ludicrous.

The man was waiting.

Eventually, Josie raised her hand and held it across her chest.

Mosconi put his own hand over his chest. "On my honor," he said, "I will never betray my badge, my integrity, my character, or the public trust. I will always have the courage to hold myself and others accountable for our actions. I will always uphold the Constitution, my community, and the agency I serve."

Josie repeated each sentence.

When she finished, Mosconi said, "I now pronounce you a deputy of the California Bureau of Investigation External Investigations Task Force. Your term will last until we terminate it."

Mosconi turned to Rodriguez. "You brought her gear?"

Rodriguez nodded. He reached into the briefcase and pulled

out a plastic card the size of a driver's license, a small blue-and-gold badge with a pin on the back, and two pairs of handcuffs, one normal size and one larger. The larger cuffs were connected with a chain that was about two feet long.

"This is your Bureau of Investigation lapel badge," Mosconi said, handing it to her, carefully putting it in her palm and closing her fingers over it as if it were very precious. "You need not wear it. But you must have it on you at all times. And this is your deputy ID. It already has your photo on it."

"You were so confident I'd agree to this," Josie said. She looked at the photo. It was her UCLA faculty photo. To her knowledge, that was a secure photo, unavailable to anyone without high-level UCLA administrative access.

Mosconi didn't respond to her comment. He said, "The badge and the ID give you the power to act as a deputy on behalf of the California Bureau of Investigation. This power extends statewide but only applies to this particular External Investigations Task Force activity. In law enforcement terminology, you are not an agent with power. You are a deputy acting on behalf of our organization."

"Why give me an ID and badge if everything about this is secret? You said I can tell no one about this."

"We demand secrecy, yes. But we're not brutal for the simple reason that we want you to succeed at this. So if you should be picked up by local law enforcement on some petty charge, we want you to have some cover. You are not allowed to explain the details of what you're doing or your relationship to us, but they could call us. We could then consider the situation and decide how to proceed."

Josie was speechless.

Mosconi picked up the cuffs. "The small ones are handcuffs, obviously. The larger ones with the chain are ankle cuffs. Here are the keys, two of each. Don't lose them."

Mosconi handed Josie a business card. "When you have taken your prisoner, call the number on this card. Identify yourself as Deputy Josephine Strong of the External Investigations Task Force."

Josie shook her head. "I can't believe what you just said. 'When I have my prisoner...' It seems ridiculous that I… that we could find and capture this suspect when no professional has."

Mosconi looked at her for a long moment. He finally spoke. "You found and captured your last suspects, severely wounding one and killing the other. And you did it with no help from any law enforcement."

Mosconi stood. Rodriguez followed suit.

"Good luck, Deputy Strong," Mosconi said. "We'll wait for you to contact us."

SEVEN

As they drove away from the Bureau of Investigations, Samantha once again apologized profusely for the situation she'd created. "I'm so sorry, Mama."

"I understand," Josie said. "Let's try to focus on what's to come rather than mistakes in the past."

"Did the man say who this killer murdered?"

"Yes. He shot two sheriff's deputies who stopped him for speeding after he robbed a bank."

"And now he's hiding in Yosemite Park? How could we find this killer?" Samantha sounded despondent. "What they want is ridiculous. We're just… a mom and a kid."

"I have no idea how to find him. But it's not 'we.' It should be me alone. You should stay home. You can sleep at a friend's house."

"No, absolutely not," Samantha said. In Josie's peripheral vision, she could see Samantha shaking her head. "I won't have you going off to try to fix a mistake I made," Samantha said.

"I appreciate that. But I can't put you at risk."

"You're not putting me at risk. I am. It's my decision. We're a team. We'll do this together."

"Samantha, think about what you're saying. Our task is to find a killer. Someone who murders police."

"I understand that. You know I understand that."

"But I'm your parent. I have the responsibility to make important decisions for you."

"I also have the responsibility to make important decisions for me. If you take this away from me, it will be a very bad thing between us. You have to trust that I have a good ability to decide what's right for me."

Josie found herself gripping the steering wheel as if to crush the plastic. She didn't know what to say.

Samantha said, "California has a law that allows for kids to become legally emancipated starting at the age of fourteen."

"What?" Josie was astonished. "Where did you hear that?"

"In our Visiting Experts class, a lawyer talked about Family Law."

"It seems like a strange subject to talk about with students. And what does that have to do with me protecting you from unnecessary danger?"

"I just mention it because the law indicates that kids aren't stupid about being responsible for themselves. Maybe I do a lot of dumb stuff, but I'm a pretty good judge of what's good for me."

Josie felt exasperated. She eventually said, "I'll think about it and sleep on it."

Samantha said, "I feel safer when I'm with you, Mama. And I'll try to stay out of danger. I won't do anything that makes you worry."

They rode in silence for a few minutes.

Samantha blurted out, "I can never forgive myself for being involved in something where a policeman was killed!" Samantha's voice was choked with tears. "How could I be so stupid?"

Josie reached over and rubbed her leg. "It's very sad, Sam. I'm also very sorry for the cop's family. And I'm also sorry you have to go through this. The best thing I can say is that you were trying to be helpful in returning clothes to your friend's mother. You had good intentions. You didn't cause the accident that killed the police officer. The woman who tried to escape was the primary cause."

"But someone died. And it started with my stupid mistake."

"Yes. And that's very unfortunate. But consider a hypothetical someone who wanted another person to die. That would be much worse, right?"

"Yeah."

"In some situations, we say intentions don't matter, only actions count. But in other situations, intentions do matter.

This is one of those situations where it matters that you didn't mean harm. We have to focus on that."

They drove the rest of the way without talking.

When Josie and Samantha got home to their Santa Monica condo, Samantha sat down on the floor and held Unknown, running her fingers over the dog's head. Josie sat at her desk and began writing on a yellow pad of paper. When she was done, she handed the pad to Samantha. Before Samantha could react, Josie put her finger to her lips.

She watched as Samantha read the note, which said, 'Sam, first, don't say anything. I wrote this so that we could communicate without worry of being monitored. Agent Mosconi had your phone. Maybe I'm paranoid, but what if Mosconi is monitoring us? (I know, I've seen too many movies.)'

Samantha read the note and looked horrified.

Josie wrote more words. 'The phone that he gave us could also be a monitoring device. It might be recording everything we say. Leave your phone here. Take everything out of your pockets. Let's go walk on the beach. We can talk in private there.'

Samantha paused, then made a small nod.

Josie took the piece of paper, folded it and put it in her purse.

Josie went into the kitchen. She called out in a loud voice that would be easily heard by anyone listening in. "Hey, Sam," she said as she walked to Samantha's bedroom door and looked in. "Maybe we should get takeout." Josie gave Samantha an obvious wink.

"Yeah. It's never too early for Chinese," Samantha said. She sounded listless. She hung her head.

Josie had never seen Samantha depressed. Unhappy, sad, frustrated when things were a struggle. But not depression.

"Just the thought of food makes my stomach growl," Josie said. Samantha didn't comment.

Josie watched Samantha do a perfunctory check of her pockets for anything she might have missed. She put her phone on the kitchen counter.

Josie took her purse, which Mosconi hadn't touched, and

Samantha put the leash on Unknown. They went down the stairs and were walking toward the beach when Josie remembered the phone, badge, and ID card Mosconi had given her. Josie once again held her finger to her lips to signal Samantha, and they went back home.

Josie pulled the items out of her purse and set them in a kitchen drawer. She added Samantha's phone. Then she realized that even though her phone hadn't been out of her possession, it could possibly have been hacked from afar. So she left it with the other electronics. Josie double checked her purse, and, satisfied that there was nothing she'd overlooked, they went back to the beach walk and headed south from the Santa Monica pier.

Samantha was carrying the dog backpack. She stopped and got Unknown into the pack so they could walk out on the beach.

The sand was deep and soft up near the street, and much less so near the waves, its structure firmed up by periodic soakings from waves.

"I don't know that we're being monitored," Josie said as they walked. "But I think it's good to be careful. When we're at home, we should probably only say the most basic stuff that doesn't reveal any suspicions about the Bureau of Investigation people. Just in case."

"Just in case," Samantha repeated. "Do you have suspicions about the bureau?"

"Nothing specific. Let me ask you this. When you were picked up at the border, where did they take you?"

"After I gave the backpack to my friend's mom, she took it and jogged away. I was sort of puzzled, and I stood there watching her as she got into a car and drove off. Then I saw a cop car race after her, its lights flashing. Almost at the same time, two cops grabbed my arms and told me I was under arrest for drug trafficking. They pushed me up against a building, patted me down, and handcuffed me behind my back." Samantha paused. "Maybe they read those Miranda words first. I don't know. I was so upset, my memory is all jumbled. I remember they took everything out of my pockets. I hated the way the cop patted me down, putting his hands all over me. Then they put me in the back of a cop car."

"Who were they?"

"I don't know."

"Customs agents? Policemen?"

"They had on green uniforms. At least one of the uniforms I saw said Police on the back. And there were other cops. I don't know what kind they were."

"What did the patrol car look like, the one they put you in?"

"It was white with green doors. It said Border Patrol on it."

"And where did that car take you?"

"To a building. It had writing on it. San Diego something. Sheriff, I think. I'm sorry I can't remember the details. They drove around back to these metal doors. Like service doors where truck deliveries would go. They brought me inside and told me I was being charged with smuggling. Mama, I've never been so scared in my life! Then they locked me in a small room. I had to wait there a long time. Then two women came and said I was being transferred. They took me back out the metal doors, took my handcuffs off, and put me in the back of another car."

"What did that car look like?"

"It was black with white doors. But it was an SUV. It also had one of those metal grids separating the front and back seats."

"Is that the car that took you to the California Bureau of Investigation building?"

"Yes. When we got to the Bureau building, the men locked me in another room where I stayed until they brought me to see you."

"It sounds like Theo Mosconi had already been intending to contact me about helping them. Maybe he put a notice or something in the law enforcement computer systems. When you were arrested, that must have triggered a phone call or some other communication from the San Diego DA's Office to the California Bureau of Investigation. They worked out a deal, and the San Diego Sheriff's Office had you brought to the CBI building."

They walked down the beach walk.

"So back to your question about whether I'm suspicious of the CBI, that all seems legitimate," Josie said. "Or at least somewhat legitimate. The fact that the CBI had the power to get you out of the grasp of the San Diego police and District Attorney makes them seem legitimate. But I guess my natural suspicions kicked in when they did the whole secrecy thing. Not being able to call an attorney… That doesn't seem right."

"No," Samantha said. "Even when they physically abuse the suspect in the movies, he still gets to call a lawyer eventually."

Josie nodded.

"That was good what you said in our condo, Mama," Samantha said. "About getting takeout. It's like when we were in the Canadian wilderness and you had us make the perfect little sleeping hideaway, but then had us sleep in a different place. Now you make like we're getting takeout, but we're doing something completely different."

"Maybe we'll get takeout, too."

Samantha spoke to the dog in the pack on her back. "Okay, Unknown, Chinese is on the way."

Josie still noticed Samantha's depressed tone. Normally, Samantha would have sounded enthusiastic about Chinese takeout.

"What's this called?" Samantha asked. "This thing we're doing, where we talk one way in our condo for Agent Mosconi's benefit, and we talk another way when we're in private out here on the beach. I can't make the word come to my mouth."

"Misdirection?" Josie said.

Samantha nodded. "That's it."

"I learned about misdirection a long time ago."

Samantha looked at Josie. "How?"

"Years ago, I saw a talk by James Randi, the magician who demonstrated that most so-called paranormal claims are merely magic tricks done by magicians who try to present their magic as something grander."

Samantha frowned. "Randi doesn't like that kind of magic?"

"He loves magic. But he wants magicians to admit the truth about it."

"So paranormal stuff isn't real?"

"Not in his opinion. Not in mine, either. Certainly, the kind that Randi focused on isn't real. It's because of Randi that I started thinking about misdirection. Did anyone ever show you how a magic trick worked?" Josie asked.

"Sure, Mama. We've got this kid at school, Azriel Levy. He's always doing tricks. Cards mostly. When Mr. Minori had us do our personal-skills show and tell, Azriel showed us how to do a card trick. First he did it like normal, and none of us figured it out. Then he showed us how it worked."

"When you learned how the trick worked, what did you think?"

"It was… pretty cool, I guess. I mean, you'd have to practice it to be good. But it was amazing how we didn't notice the trick the first time."

"That's the essence of misdirection," Josie said. "The magician distracts you with something that has nothing to do with the trick."

"And that's what you're doing," Samantha said. "And this is coming from a history professor. I never would have thought you were like that, Mama. It's just like when we were in the Quetico Wilderness last month."

"Once you pay attention to it, you learn that people in many professions practice misdirection. Pediatricians distract children before they give them a shot so the shot doesn't hurt as much. University administrators get professors to focus on grand goals so they don't notice their tawdry, stuffy offices and the policies that punish innovation. Politicians are the worst. When things go really wrong, they make up some phony achievement and present it in such a positive light that the major problems seem like no big deal compared to their phony accomplishments. Some politicians are so good at the smoke and mirrors that only the most perceptive voters realize they're being taken."

"Politicians are spin masters," Samantha said.

"Exactly. So that's what taught me about misdirection. Now

we're going to do it with Agent Mosconi."

"Are you saying we won't really help him?"

"No. We need to help him to keep him and his people off your case, to get you free from the smuggling charge. But I don't trust him. So we're going to use misdirection. We'll get him thinking we're doing things the way he wants. But we'll be independent. We'll do things our way. And if he doesn't know what we're doing, there's less chance that he can manipulate us or interfere with our efforts."

"Do you think he's actually listening to us in our condo?"

"Maybe. Maybe not. But he did take your phone away from you. And you probably gave him your passcode."

"I had to. He said I would go to prison if I didn't do everything he said."

"I understand. He could have loaded malware onto your phone. Or had some hacker program it to record whenever someone talks. Then it could transmit the information to Mosconi without you ever realizing it."

Samantha seemed disturbed. "He took away my purse and brought it back later."

"What things were in your purse?"

"Just the normal stuff. My phone. My wallet. Hairbrush. Makeup. Breath mints. That little coin pouch you gave me."

"We should go over everything in it to make certain they didn't—I don't know—change anything."

Samantha nodded. "So what is our plan now?"

"Do you remember the tall kid who helped me find you at that cabin up in Topanga Canyon?"

"Yeah. Cumberland something. Real handsome and real strange."

"Cumberland Durand. And you shouldn't judge people by appearances. Only by their actions, and only over a long time frame."

"I'm not judging. I'm just saying what is. You have to admit Cumberland's strange."

"How about different?"

"Okay."

"I think Cumberland may be able to help us find this bad guy that Agent Mosconi wants us to find. I'll call him and see if we can visit. If so, we'll leave everything at our condo and take the bus to his place."

"Can Unknown come?" Samantha asked.

"Cumberland was fine with her when we rescued you at the cabin. I'm pretty sure he would be okay with her at his house." Josie felt troubled.

"What's wrong, Mama?"

"I just realized that if Mosconi is monitoring our phones, it's hard to even contact Cumberland to ask if we can stop by."

"You need a burner phone."

"I've never even seen one," Josie said.

"You probably have and just didn't know it. You can buy them at lots of stores. They're called prepaid, no-contract phones."

"How do you know this?"

"Basic life info at the movies, of course."

"Maybe I can get one at Amazon."

"No, Mama! The whole point of a burner is to not be traced. So you can't buy it with a credit card anywhere. You have to pay cash. And to have the most privacy, you have to get your cash from a place that's a long way from where you spend it."

"Right, of course," Josie said. "I want my actions to stay incognito."

"With a burner phone, they sort of will," Samantha said. "But not forever."

"What do you mean?"

"Let's say you use the burner to call me on my phone. If someone is monitoring my phone, your call to me would be a clue to who you are, right? And if you call other people who know you, it creates a pattern that points to you. Pretty soon, they know who owns the burner. But if you don't use it for calling your regular contacts, it's pretty anonymous."

"You learn this from the movies, too?"

"It's just simple logic," Samantha said. "But yeah, movies are good for that."

"Basic life info," Josie said.

Samantha turned and looked at her. "You're making fun of me."

"No, Cap'n. I'm learning from you. I'm your first mate, right?"

Samantha started laughing. "Just like in the Quetico Wilderness."

Josie joined in laughing.

"Oh, Mama. That feels good. It's been a long time since I laughed like that."

"Yes, me too."

They turned around and walked north.

"Do you know where I can get one of those phones?" Josie asked.

"There's a store in the Third Street Promenade that sells them."

"Let's go."

They left the beach.

Samantha got Unknown out of the pack and back on her leash. They walked across the street.

"First we have to get cash," Josie said.

"Which means we go the opposite direction." Samantha turned about-face.

"Right," Josie followed.

They walked south to an ATM, then northeast to the shopping center. Twenty minutes later, they'd found two phone models. Samantha looked them over. "No smarts or computer in these phones. It's just a phone. All you can do with them is make calls and receive messages."

"Imagine that," Josie said. Josie hefted one in her hand. "This is smallest. That suits me."

"No, get the other one, Mama."

"Why? It's longer."

"But thinner and more rounded edges. It would be more comfortable to carry in your bra."

"What are you saying, girl?! You think I'm going to carry a phone in my bra? Where do you get these ideas?"

"This is about being incognito. A phone tucked between your boobs won't be found in most pat-downs."

"Sam, I'm not intending to get frisked."

"Right. But what if you do? You've got the cleavage. May as well put it to good use. Although some of your bras probably won't work. You know, wrong shape. We'll have to do a bra phone test. You can be like a model going down the runway. It'll make a fun evening! Unknown and I will be the judges and see if we can tell when you've got the phone and when you don't."

"Sam, I don't believe this. You're talking about my, my..."

"Equipment, Mama. Be proud. Skinny girls like me can only buy those kinds of assets."

"Sam! Stop it. You're embarrassing me."

They bought the thin phone, left the store, and headed back to their condo.

"Remember, only small talk once we're inside," Josie said in a low voice. "We'll get Cumberland's number, come back outside and call him."

"And I still won't have my phone."

"No. We're safest that way."

"Maybe Cumberland could turn off any tracking stuff in my phone?"

"Maybe. But that would reveal our intent to prevent Agent Mosconi from tracking us. We want him to think everything is normal. So we should probably leave both our phones as they currently are. Whenever we want privacy, we'll leave them at home and talk on the beach. But if Cumberland could tell us whether or not people were listening, I'd like to know that."

Back home, Josie flipped through her old-fashioned address book and found Cumberland's number. She wrote it down on a Post-it note, grateful again for the privacy afforded by old-fashioned paper that couldn't easily be hacked from the outside.

Once again, they walked with Unknown over to the beach.

Josie dialed Cumberland's number.

"Hello?" The kid's voice made a croaking noise and sounded to Josie like he was under water.

"Cumberland? This is Josie Strong calling."

"Oh. Professor Strong."

"I have a situation I need help with. I'm wondering if I can hire you."

"I'm not, you know, for hire in the normal way. But I'm happy to help you."

"Okay, we'll talk about that later. I'd like to make an appointment with you. I'm free pretty much any day after my classes are over. Two p.m. or later. But I don't want to meet at my office."

"Um, you could come to my house. It doesn't matter when."

"I don't want to interfere with your life. I only want you to help when it's convenient."

"I don't have a life. So any time is convenient."

"Would tomorrow afternoon work?"

"Any time," he said again.

"How about three o'clock?"

"I'll see you whenever you get here."

Josie repeated the conversation to Samantha.

"Cumberland is some name," Samantha said. "Kind of… Cumbersome."

"I've heard other kids call him that," Josie said. "Now, what about that takeout?"

"Yes, definitely."

The next day, when Samantha got home from school, they left all their electronic gear at the condo, got on a bus, rode a couple of miles, transferred, rode the next bus as close as it went to Cumberland's house, and got off. From there, they walked.

The streets went up, and Josie was soon breathing hard.

"This Cumberland guy lives in Beverly Hills?"

"Yeah."

"Is he rich?"

"Maybe. Or possibly his mom or dad is. But I've never heard him mention his father."

"What does Cumberland do?"

Josie was breathing too hard to answer in continuous sentences.

"He goes to college at UCLA. But his main focus is hacking."

"He's a computer nerd?"

"More than that. He gets hired to break into the computer systems of the big high-tech companies. When he learns how to exploit security flaws and tells the companies, they can fix the flaws. They pay him rewards for his work. A quarter million dollars last year, from what I read in an article about him."

Samantha gasped. "That guy makes big bucks? Wow!"

"Indeed. He always reminds me of that joke about how you should always be nice to nerds because you'll probably end up working for one someday."

Josie had to slow further, she was breathing so hard. The streets seemed steeper.

"What do you want him to do for us?" Samantha asked.

"I'd like him to show us how not to be tracked by Agent Mosconi or anyone else. I also want to ask if he has any ideas about how to find the killer who's supposedly hiding in Yosemite. But we have to remember the secrecy agreement we signed."

"So we'll have to be vague or something?"

"Yes," Josie said. "But Cumberland might be very good at keeping secrets."

"You think he can help us by using computers? How would he do that?"

"I have no idea. But I want to ask."

They walked in silence, Josie trying to get enough air.

"Did it go okay at school today?"

"Yes. The kids had seen me get arrested. So they had lots of questions. So I did that thing you told me about. About omission and commission."

"The sin of omission is less than the sin of commission."

"That's it. I told them the truth but left out some stuff. I said that a guy I sort of knew gave me a pack in Tijuana, and he wanted me to give it to his mother. I said I didn't realize how stupid I was to take it and that the cops were upset but that it looked like everything was now okay. All true. Pretty much, anyway."

"You told me he was Malaiya's brother, right?"

"Yes."

"Did you mention her when the kids asked about your arrest?"

"No. I didn't think that would be right. She didn't do anything wrong."

"That was smart. A little discipline can prevent so much malicious gossip. It sounds like you handled it well," Josie said. "A selective truth was a good approach."

Josie went back to her heavy breathing. The only other sounds were the occasional car and the birds singing from the lush gardens that grew unseen behind thick hedges.

Josie gestured when they came to the drive of the house where Cumberland lived with his mother. She was too out of breath to speak.

"Whoa, some sugar mama got major deep pockets," Samantha said when she looked at the house.

Josie looked at her daughter. "Is that basic life talk?"

"Nope. That's basic sugar mama talk."

Samantha skipped away from Josie like a little kid. It was the first act of normalcy from her since her arrest. Unknown trotted next to her. Samantha went up to the large stone entrance and pressed the doorbell. The door opened as Josie finally approached.

EIGHT

"Oh, hi," Cumberland said after he opened the door. He wore baggy jeans with no belt and an oversized T-shirt covered in strange, brightly-colored patterns. His sneakers were coming apart where the fabric met the soles. His hair was an unruly tangle. Yet he still looked model-handsome.

"You're Samantha, the, um, girl we found in the woods," he said. "Topanga Canyon."

"And you're the warrior with the war hammer."

Despite the shade from the overhang, Josie could see Cumberland blush.

"It's right there." He pointed to the long, scary weapon that leaned in a corner by the door. "Professor Strong wanted me to keep it. Maybe I'll, you know, use it to defend the castle."

"Let me know when," Samantha said. "I'll come watch."

The words made Josie grin and Cumberland turn redder. His skin looked extra pink next to Samantha's brown complexion.

Unknown walked up to Cumberland, sniffed his feet. She wagged slowly, recognizing him from the night they rescued Samantha.

Cumberland bent down and gave her a single touch on her head. He turned and took them through the house. When they came to the windows that overlooked the pool, Samantha stared. Cumberland turned down the stairs. Unknown followed him first. He led them into his basement bedroom studio. It had even more glowing lights and humming equipment than Josie remembered from before.

Cumberland perched on a tall stool. He didn't suggest that Josie or Samantha sit. Josie knew his lack of social decorum was simply his awkward manner, a possible autism component of the young man's genius.

Unknown made a circuit of the room, sniffing the floor, furniture, equipment. Samantha followed the dog, stepping past Cumberland's small bed, looking at the racks of electronic gear. "This is, like, where the secret alchemy happens, right?"

Josie was surprised to hear her daughter use the word. She was a smart girl, but she was still only 14 years old. Alchemy was an example of the kid growing up.

Cumberland made a small awkward grin. "Yeah, I Frankenstein computer code together. Sometimes, my project is DOA. Sometimes I create a monster that can't be killed." He said it like it was a joke, but he didn't grin. Cumberland turned to Josie. "What do you want me to do?"

Josie thought again about whether Cumberland could be very discreet. She decided he could.

"First, I need to say that everything I tell you is secret. I have to ask you to agree to never tell anyone about this. Secrecy is so important, we left our phones at home in case someone may have hacked into them."

"Smart," Cumberland said. "You must be working as a spy. For the government, I suppose. 'Cept they would have given you hack-resistant phones. So maybe you're working for a... you know, a rogue arm of the government. A group that's underfunded."

Josie was surprised at how perceptive Cumberland was. She decided not to explain but to just dive in.

"We've been asked to help find a killer who is supposedly hiding in Yosemite."

"Why would he do that?" Cumberland asked.

"Hide in Yosemite? Why not?" Josie was confused.

"Because the woods are a bad place to hide. It's too easy to be found. Much easier to hide in a big city."

"Are you saying that you know how to find someone in the woods? This man is apparently a survivalist, knows the backcountry well. He would be far off the regular trails."

Cumberland paused. "I've never searched for someone in the woods. And I've never worked with mapping software. But certain principles are simple."

Josie frowned. She could not think of any simple principle that would apply to finding someone well hidden in the woods. Josie looked at Samantha. Samantha was frowning, too.

"Data mapping and related analytics can be complicated," Cumberland said. "But a man in the woods…" Cumberland was staring at the far wall, seeing something else entirely. "Pretend you want to find—I don't know—an ant. Not just any ant, but a particular ant. Someone tells you the ant is, um, somewhere in a large area with relatively few other ants. And there are a bunch of leaves and stuff scattered around. What do you do? Program a computer to scan the area and look for movement of any small item. Subject to the limits of your scanner and computer, it won't take long to find a small moving item when it comes out from under a leaf, and when you do, there's a chance it will be an ant. Once your computer finds several ants, there's a decent chance one of them will be your ant."

Cumberland seemed to think about what he'd said.

He continued, "Now what if your ant is in the jungle and there are millions of other ants running around. Finding your ant would be much harder."

"A city full of people versus a forest with very few people," Samantha said.

Cumberland nodded. "If we scan Yosemite, there won't be many people compared to the size of the park. If we tell our computer to ignore the trails and parking lots and, um, the waterfalls and only look in the most secluded part of the forest, it will be easy to spot a person."

Cumberland looked over toward his bed. Unknown was sitting on the floor, her body against the side of the bed.

"You can lie on the bed," Cumberland said, looking at her.

Unknown didn't move. If she understood, she didn't act on it.

Cumberland walked over and patted the bed. His movements were stiff and awkward. "It's okay," he said.

Unknown looked over at Samantha, then jumped up on the bed and lay down.

Josie felt uncomfortable. She didn't let Unknown on their

beds. Maybe this would be bad for Unknown's discipline. Then she remembered seeing some of Unknown's fur on Samantha's bed. And Samantha slept with her bedroom door closed. Josie suddenly realized that Samantha probably let Unknown sleep on her bed every night. Maybe this was another example of how Josie was so much more uptight than other people. Would she ever relax?

Josie realized she'd lost her train of thought.

"How would you scan the woods?" Josie asked.

"You've seen the Google Earth photos where you get a picture from space?"

"Yes," Josie said.

"Those pictures are assembled from lots of sources. Satellites, airplanes, and even some drones. The satellites are owned by several different companies, but they all do the same thing. They take thousands of pictures of the ground. The Google computers assemble them into searchable databases."

"Are the satellite photos good enough to see a person?" Josie asked.

"Some are. I read about the new Geo-Eye-One, a commercial satellite that has a resolution of a half meter per pixel. Good enough to spot a person. There are also some high resolution images that Google doesn't get to use for a variety of reasons. Some satellite owners don't sell their highest resolution images to Google."

"Like the military," Josie said. "They probably wouldn't share."

"Yeah." Cumberland was nodding. "The thing is, resolution isn't everything. In fact, it isn't even the main thing."

"I don't get it," Samantha said. "If you can't focus on something, you can't really see it, right?"

"Well… Imagine I have my camera looking at the area where my ant is hiding, and my camera picks up a dark spot. The spot is too fuzzy to make out what it is. But my camera keeps taking pictures. The dark spot moves. Sometimes faster, sometimes slower. Sometimes it stays in one place for a long time. The computer compares the movement pattern to everything in its memory and decides the spot moves like an ant. The camera can't really see the ant, but it nevertheless picked up enough information about movement that the dark spot was identified as an ant."

"But even if you could get enough satellite images of Yosemite, you'd still have to see through the trees," Josie said. "The forest canopy can be pretty opaque."

Samantha said, "In the Quetico Wilderness, in the thickest woods, we could always look up through the branches and see a little sky someplace. So it makes sense that a satellite could see down through the trees. Sort of, anyway."

"I've never seen that." Cumberland sounded stressed.

Samantha frowned. "You've never been in the thick woods? You don't get out much."

Josie winced. She hoped Samantha wouldn't make Cumberland feel uncomfortable.

Cumberland nodded. "I just don't like the woods, so I never go there. Almost my only first-hand experience was when Professor Strong and I went to find you when the killer kidnapped you."

Josie said, "I remember you told me your friend got a severe case of poison oak and that put you off the woods."

"Yeah. He looked like some creature they'd create in the makeup department at the USC film school."

"I'm actually kind of scared of the woods," Samantha said. "I didn't used to be."

Cumberland looked at her, genuine concern on his face. "Why? Oh, wait, don't answer that. All that bad stuff happened to you in the Canadian wilderness. And here in the California woods."

Samantha said, "What if the person we're trying to find stays where there's total tree cover?"

Cumberland seemed to think about it. "So, um, if I look down from above and I don't have normal viewing holes to look through, I still might see a person moving around. There are some ways to see through the tree canopy."

"How?" Josie said.

"Infrared is one way. A heat signature from a person might still come through cool leaves."

"What's infrared?" Samantha asked.

"Part of the electromagnetic spectrum, just like visible light. Our eyes don't pick it up. Infrared is emitted by warm surfaces."

"Human bodies," Samantha said. "Of course."

"How would you do this… I don't know what to call it," Josie said.

"Infrared imaging?" Cumberland said.

"Right. Is there special software for that?"

"I don't know." Cumberland stared off again, seeing something other than the basement room. "I remember reading about astronomers. They take a zillion pictures of the stars. But a lot of the time they don't use visible light. I could learn about that."

"Then you look for the moving ant," Samantha said. "How do you do that? Especially if you're not using visible light, whatever that means."

"Astronomers often focus on just one part of the sky. The photos reveal uncountable points of light. Every night they take more pictures of the same patch of sky. Then they use software that compares the pictures and looks for any differences. The process has led to the discovery of many objects that seem to move in comparison to the background image. Asteroids, comets…" he trailed off. "Maybe I could do that with Yosemite. And I can probably find satellites that will image with infrared light or other ways. Military satellites might use stuff other than visible light."

"I assume military satellite images would be off limits to non-military people," Josie said.

"Yeah, probably."

Samantha widened her eyes and grinned. "Just because they're off limits doesn't mean you can't get them. Hacking's your job, after all."

"But hacking into a military computer would be a serious crime," Josie said. "You can't take that risk. They could put you away forever."

Cumberland turned to Samantha. "I can tell this is something important."

Samantha shifted position so she could look at Cumberland without even seeing Josie. "I'm in very serious trouble, and the only way out of it is to help the authorities catch a killer."

"Samantha!" Josie exclaimed.

"I didn't say any details, Mama. Just the principle."

Cumberland spoke to Samantha, "The most important thing I've ever done in my life was to help your mother save you last month. This would be like that. The risk I get caught is small. And I wouldn't be putting any good person in harm's way, correct? And if I help you catch another bad guy..."

Josie shut her eyes and put her fingertips to her temples, rubbing them, wondering how far she had strayed from her intentions now that Cumberland suggested doing something highly illegal.

"You say the risk from hacking into military satellites would be small," Josie said. "How could you possibly do this and only have it be a small risk?"

Cumberland didn't answer for a long moment. "Think of a mouse wanting to get into your house. It can fit through tiny spaces and climb vertical walls and dig through hard soil and chew through wood. No matter how carefully your house was built, a really determined mouse can probably find a way in. And while the mouse is looking for a tiny opening, it might also find that you've left a door open."

"You're the mouse," Samantha said.

Cumberland nodded.

"You don't look like a mouse." Samantha said it in a way that made Cumberland blush again. She added, "And I never saw a mouse swing a war hammer the way you did."

"That's enough, Sam," Josie said. The words were innocent enough. But she was uncomfortable with her 14-year-old daughter flirting in front of her. "Let's focus on the task at hand. I'm still not comfortable with you breaking into a military computer. Can't they tell when their security has been breached?"

Cumberland shrugged. "Depends."

"How do you keep from getting caught?" Josie asked.

"I usually use an anonymizing proxy tool, and TOR, and other stuff like that. Sometimes you can even brute-force your way in and still leave no trace. The kids tweaking open-source hacking tools are often ahead of the security experts who are trying to keep them out of their companies. And I've done some work designing honeypots, so I usually recognize one when I get close."

"What's a honeypot?"Samantha asked.

"It's a trap set up to attract hackers and then get enough information from them or about their approach to make it easier to track them down."

"What exactly is hacking?" Samantha asked.

"It's just breaking into computer systems that you don't have normal access to. Some kids do it for the fun of causing trouble. Like digital vandalism. For the professionals, it's just about making money. A lot of the pros make money by stealing info. They're called black-hat hackers. Some focus on small-time theft, like draining your bank account. Others get into big banking systems where banks and big corporations send huge sums of money over the internet. The hackers can sometimes hijack those payments and reroute them to their own secret accounts."

"But how do hackers do that?"

Cumberland shrugged. "Mostly it's about finding an opening, like a mouse looking to get inside your house."

"You're not one of the hackers who steals information," Samantha said as if it were a statement of fact.

"No. I find computer vulnerabilities and tell companies what they need to do to be more secure. The stuff I do is legal. I'm a white-hat hacker."

"And they pay you for that," Samantha said.

"Yeah."

"It would be pretty cool to do your job and get paid for it," Samantha said.

"It's not really cool. It's hard work. Hacking is tedious."

"What if you want to get into a computer system and there are no security flaws?" Josie asked. "What if there are no holes big enough for a mouse?"

Cumberland made a face that Josie couldn't interpret.

"There's pretty much always a hole big enough for a mouse," he said.

After a pause he said, "Anyway, I'll look around. If I can learn something that might help, I'll call you."

Josie sighed. She worried that she'd made a terrible mistake. But she realized that she couldn't go back. She had to move forward. "You can only call me on this new burner phone." She pulled it out and showed it to Cumberland.

He nodded. "Smart." He tapped on the phone, waited, tapped again, then wrote on a Post-it note.

"What are you writing?" Samantha asked.

"The burner phone number," he said.

"How did you find it?"

"It's just..." Cumberland paused.

"Basic life info?" Samantha said, grinning.

"Yeah." Cumberland didn't grin.

Josie said, "I'd like you to come to our condo and look at our regular phones and a third phone that supposedly has no apps and only contains a file with a great deal of information on the killer we're trying to track. We were told that phone can't be connected."

Cumberland looked at Josie. "You think the phone is actually live and phoning home."

"See, Mama, phoning home is a technical term," Samantha said.

"I'm sure it is. Could you do that sometime?" Josie asked.

"How about now?" Cumberland said.

NINE

Cumberland went through his studio/bedroom and gathered supplies. Josie couldn't tell what they were. She saw Samantha watching carefully. Samantha was an enthusiastic user of technology. But she obviously had no idea of what Cumberland was collecting.

A little black box, cables, a red device with two miniature screens on the front and wires that came out of the back, and two items that were similar to a TV remote. The only devices Josie recognized for certain were his phone and a laptop computer. He put everything in a small backpack.

The three of them and Unknown walked from Cumberland's house in Beverly Hills, down the lush streets toward the bus stop. Josie sensed movement behind them. She turned around as a car pulled out from a parking place up the street. It rolled very slowly after them. After Josie watched it for a bit, it turned down a side street and disappeared.

Samantha said, "When we get to our place, we can't say anything about this project, right?"

Josie thought it perceptive of Samantha to phrase it as if she were reminding herself of the concern and not instructing Cumberland.

"They could be listening," Josie said.

"Microphones are always listening," Cumberland said. He pointed up to a street light pole that had a small camera mounted near the top. "Cameras are always watching, too."

Josie said, "Sometimes I wonder if my impulse to question means I'm paranoid."

"It's not paranoia," Cumberland said. "We live in a surveillance state. Our government isn't very good at using the surveillance equipment. And most people are not that competent using it either. But the equipment and technology are there."

"Politicians might not know this stuff," Samantha said. "But they could hire people like you, right?"

Cumberland said, "Yeah, but most people like me aren't real good at taking orders from the kind of people who are bosses. Plus, working for the government doesn't pay well."

They walked in silence for a minute.

"Those cameras you pointed to," Samantha said. "Those are traffic cams, right?"

"Most of them are, yes. And most of them are public and can be accessed by anyone."

"If they're public, does that mean I could use my phone to watch what a traffic cam sees?"

"Sure."

"Is there, like, an access code or something?"

"Not for most. Do you want me to show you?"

Samantha nodded.

Cumberland tapped on his phone, swiped, tapped some more, swiped again. Waited. "I'll just Google 'traffic cam' and put in this street." He tapped again. He handed his phone to Samantha, then pointed up at a street light. The phone had a picture that was looking down at a street. Cumberland pointed at the picture on his phone. "Do you recognize those people?"

"Oh, my God. Mama. That's us." She looked back up at the light pole and its camera. "I can't believe we're looking at us." Samantha handed the phone to Josie. "Do you recognize us? You can easily tell Unknown here." She pointed.

"This is really creepy," Josie said. She gave the phone back to Cumberland. "Who runs that webcam?"

He tapped on his phone and brought up the website address. "Here's the website. I don't know who put up the webcam. Probably the city of Los Angeles. I don't know exactly what they use it for. It's probably an ALPRS cam."

"What's that?" Samantha asked.

"Oh, sorry. Automatic License Plate Recognition System. They're everywhere. I think they justify the expense by saying the webcam is on a public street and the video is free to the public. Anyone can use the webcam. But the real purpose is so the cops can know whose cars go by any traffic cam."

"Can the traffic cams recognize people?"

"Yeah." He looked again at the picture on his phone. "It doesn't look like you can see us very well. But the webcams can read license plates on cars, so the resolution is there."

"The movies always show cops looking at security tapes. That would be the worst job," Samantha said.

"Actually, that's pretty rare. It's computers that look at video. But they don't show that in the movies because there's nothing to look at. No action. Anyway, if a company logs onto these cams and applies facial recognition software, then they will be able to tell who we are. Same for government."

"But the image is blurry."

"Doesn't matter," he said. "The artificial intelligence software doesn't need a very clear image."

"AI," Samantha said, as if clarifying to herself.

Cumberland looked down the street. "Where are we going?"

"Our condo is in Santa Monica," Josie said. She gave him the number and street.

Cumberland nodded. He pulled out his phone, held it with one hand, and tapped and swiped with his thumb. He walked behind Josie as he worked his phone. Samantha walked next to him, watching him.

"Here's the bus stop," Josie said after they'd gone a distance.

"Let's go to this other stop," Cumberland said. "Five blocks that way." He pointed.

"But that's…" Josie stopped. "Oh, of course. Obfuscation."

"There's another bus line that will work better for a transfer. More confusing to anyone who's looking," Cumberland said without elaborating.

"We could get soft hats that can be rolled up," Samantha said. "One with a broad brim, one like a baseball cap. When we go indoors, we could change our hats before we go back out."

"Unfortunately, nowadays, the new software will still figure out who you are. CV is very thorough."

"CV," Samantha said.

"CV means computer vision."

"So how does a computer recognize people from a webcam?" Samantha asked.

"The AI has gotten very sophisticated. If it can see your face, it can recognize it. It looks at a lot of variables, but especially the placement and width of your eyes, the shape and position of your nose, and the shape of your forehead. It especially looks at the area where your eyes, nose, and forehead come together."

"So is there any way to fool it?" Josie asked.

"Nothing sure fire. The best approach is to keep the camera from seeing your face. Wear the broad brimmed hat Samantha mentioned. Wear a scarf. Keep your head turned away from the cameras if you can. If you can't do that, you can wear a shirt like this." He looked down at his chest. The colored shapes were brilliant in the sunshine.

"I don't get it," Samantha said. "That's just a bunch of colored shapes."

"Artificial intelligence software doesn't see faces like we do. It sees patterns it translates into algorithms. To facial AI, this shirt looks like several faces. Those faces are so arresting to the software that it doesn't even notice my face above the shirt."

"You're kidding," Samantha said. Her eyes were wide as she stared at Cumberland's shirt.

"No, I'm not," he said, his voice earnest.

"Oh, sorry, I was just using a… What's it called, Mama?"

"Figure of speech?"

Cumberland nodded like he understood.

But Josie thought that at some emotional level, he didn't understand much of human interaction, especially joking and teasing.

Samantha said, "If we all wore those shirts, our faces wouldn't be recognized?"

"Right. Not by computers. At least until the next iteration of AI is available."

"How does a computer system find out what we look like?" Samantha asked.

"You tell them," Cumberland said.

Samantha frowned. "What do you mean?"

"Do you ever take selfies and upload them to Facebook or send them to your friends?"

"Oh, my God. I do that all the time."

"You've created a large database of what you look like. Probably in every mood and at every angle and when you're wearing every kind of clothing. And any time you post a picture with other people in it, then you've given the AI photographic information about them, too."

Samantha looked at Josie. "I'm so sorry, Mama. I never knew."

Cumberland continued, "It becomes very easy for the software to match up a webcam photo to you. A computer can watch a thousand web cams at once. It can memorize thousands of Facebook pages a minute. If you want privacy, taking the bus is way better than driving your own car, but the computer can still figure out where you go and who you are. I learned a phrase that comes from some famous book. Big Brother is watching you."

"George Orwell's Nineteen Eighty-Four," Josie said. "It was published in the late nineteen forties, and it painted a disturbing picture of an imaginary surveillance state. Thirty years after it was published, the fictional concept came to exist in the real world. Seventy years later, the surveillance state is ubiquitous."

Cumberland nodded.

Samantha leaned toward him. "You know she's a professor, right? She talks like that all the time."

He nodded again. "I took medieval history from her at UCLA."

The bus came.

Two transfers and a short walk later, they were at the entrance to the building where Josie and Samantha lived. As they went inside, Josie looked down the street. Was the car in the distance the same one she saw near Cumberland's house? She couldn't tell. The car turned down a side street.

TEN

They walked up the stairs to the third floor. It was Josie's only regular exercise beyond basic walking. As always, it left her panting.

Once inside their door, Josie pulled out the phone Mosconi had given her, then wrote on the yellow pad.

'This is the phone that is supposedly disconnected and can only be used to read the file on the person we're supposed to find.'

Cumberland read it and nodded. He opened his pack, pulled out his gear, and carefully arranged it on the table. He set the items down carefully. It didn't seem that he was being gentle to prevent jarring his equipment. It was more as if he wanted to stay very quiet.

He plugged the red device into his laptop computer. Then he typed on the keyboard. An image came up that looked like a graph. The little screens of the red device showed moving lines that looked like old-fashioned meters.

Cumberland picked up Josie's pen and wrote on the pad, his letters a nearly-illegible scrawl.

'Enter the passcode on the phone.'

Josie hit the phone's button, entered the passcode, and did the swipe move on the little slider.

Cumberland stared at the meters and at his computer. Nothing happened. Then the meter needles jumped and wavered, one at the top of the dial and the other turned over to the far right side. The graph on the computer filled with bars of varying heights. After a time, the bar height wavered, and the meter needles changed position.

Cumberland wrote, 'Show me the file on the phone.'

Josie clicked an icon, and a page appeared. It was nothing

but sentences describing the Mariposa Sheriff's investigation of the two cops who were killed.

Cumberland reached over and dragged his finger on the screen to move the pages. He watched the bar graph and meter reading. Each time he dragged his finger, the positions changed. He used his thumb and forefinger to press both of the phone's buttons at once to turn the phone off.

When the phone was off, the meter needles rotated to the zero position, and the bars on the computer graph disappeared.

He wrote on the pad. 'Did the man give you anything else?'

Josie wrote, 'A photo ID and a lapel badge with the bureau emblem.' She opened the kitchen drawer, pulled out the badge and ID.

Cumberland picked up the badge as if it were a fragile gem that would shatter if dropped. He turned it over, then held it sideways as if to gauge its thickness. He set it down and held his finger to his lips just like Josie had done.

'Anything else?' he wrote.

'Just the ID card.' She pointed to it.

He took one of the TV remote look-alikes and passed it over both the badge and the ID card. A little red light on the remote flashed like a strobe when it was near the ID card.

Cumberland picked up the other remote look-alike, plugged it into his laptop, and held the remote near the badge. Cumberland typed on the computer. A page of numbers came up in groups of five. In the second group, the numbers changed in a fast sequence. Cumberland watched for awhile, then unplugged his equipment.

He wrote, 'You said they got Samantha's phone and passcode. But not your phone.'

Josie nodded.

He turned to Samantha, then wrote. 'Put a Post-it note or tape over the camera lenses on your phone.'

Her eyes got wide. She nodded, and went to her room. She came back a minute later. She'd cut little rectangles of Post-it note and put them over the lenses.

Cumberland wrote, 'Enter passcode.'

She did, then handed Cumberland the phone.

He carried it into the living room and sat down on the couch. He started tapping on the screen, swiping with his finger, typing with his thumbs.

Samantha looked at Josie and drew a large question mark in the air.

Josie shrugged and mouthed the words, 'I don't know.'

They waited for 15 minutes while Cumberland probed the phone.

Josie realized they should be making small talk.

She turned and faced toward the bedrooms. "Are you done in there, yet?"

"Almost," Samantha said, facing the other way, making it sound like she was talking from her bedroom.

"Is a peanut butter sandwich okay?"

"Yeah. I can eat more later when we feed Unknown." Samantha paused. Then, as if to add believability, she bent down to the dog and pet her and said, "Isn't that right, baby? Walk first, feast later, huh, girl?"

Josie worried that if the Bureau of Investigation agents were monitoring Samantha's phone, they would notice the unusual things that Cumberland was doing to it. However, she didn't dare say anything. All she could do was hope Cumberland knew of the risk and was taking appropriate steps.

Cumberland walked up, powered off Samantha's phone, then wrote on the pad.

'Has a vet checked if the dog has a chip?'

Josie wrote. 'Yes, she checked. No chip.'

Cumberland seemed to think about it. He picked up one of his devices, then bent down and gently touched Unknown as he passed the device over and around the dog.

Cumberland walked over to the TV, looked behind it, traced the cable back to the wall. He looked at the DVD player beneath the TV.

He wrote on the pad. 'Do you stream any TV or movies?'

Josie wrote, 'Yes, we get streaming from Netflix.'

Cumberland wrote, 'Do you have a digital assistant from Amazon or Google or any other kind like Alexa, Echo, or Nest?'

Josie shook her head.

Samantha wrote on the pad, 'I use Apple's Siri. Is that like what you're looking for?'

Cumberland wrote, 'I already found that on your phone. Do you have a smart TV or a doorbell camera or voice-activated movie or music streaming, or any wifi-connected appliances, or any other digital device? A new refrigerator? A wifi-connected gas grill?'

Josie wrote, 'We don't have any "smart" stuff. Only dumb stuff.'

Josie thought her comment was amusing. But Cumberland didn't smile. He just nodded his approval.

He wrote, 'How old is your car?'

Josie wrote, '2012 Prius.'

He nodded. It seemed to Josie like a nod of approval. Old was good.

He stood up and wrote, 'Talk outside. Bring nothing that could have electronics. No phones, no badge or IDs. No wallets. No watches. Check that all pockets are empty. Just the dog and the house key.'

Despite Cumberland's statement about talking outside, Josie was confident they could still make small talk that might make them seem more normal if anyone were listening.

"You grab Unknown's leash," Josie called out. "I'll bring the sandwiches."

As Samantha picked up Unknown's leash, Cumberland took it and examined it from one end to the other. The handle was a woven loop of imitation leather. He checked it with his remote, then handed it to Samantha.

Cumberland gathered his gear and replaced it in his backpack. He put the pack on, and they all left.

ELEVEN

Only when they got to the beach did Cumberland speak.

"You two are hot."

Samantha grinned. "There's more than one kind of hot."

"I meant wired," Cumberland said with no amusement in his voice. "Think of your life as being on the stage. Everything you do is being monitored and recorded."

"They hacked my phone?" Samantha said.

"Yeah. They're also recording through Professor Strong's badge."

"How?" Josie asked.

RFID technology. It's passive in the ID, like a credit card chip. But it's active in the badge."

"So they're listening to everything we do?"

"On the old iPhone, yes. On the badge, also. But not in real time on the badge. The passive chip in the ID merely registers your presence every time you go near one of their readers. The active RFID in the badge is battery powered. It probably records your conversation, maybe stuff about your location. It keeps a time log of all activity. It saves all the info then uploads it in bursts whenever it's near a reader."

"Where are the readers?" Samantha asked.

"Lot of places. Do you have anything like a toll booth account or garage account where you just drive in and you get charged whenever you use it?"

"Sure," Josie said. "We have a FasTrak toll account. And I have my garage account at UCLA."

"When your car drives through the entrance gate, it's an RFID reader that logs your passage. There are readers at many webcam locations. Shopping center entrances. Most government buildings. Lots of private companies. Parking garages. Airports. The Bureau of Investigation probably has access to lots of those readers. So you get near one and, bam, they learn who you are, where you are, what you've said, where you've been. They have an audio record of your phone calls, the movies you've watched, everything. Let me guess. The guy who gave you the lapel badge and ID probably told you to bring it with you all the time."

"He did. He said that it would give me some cover in case I got picked up by local law enforcement while I was looking for the target. But now it seems like the real reason is that having them with me makes it so they can keep tabs on me."

Cumberland nodded.

Josie felt a shiver go through her body. "How long do the batteries on these things last?"

"The ID chip is like a credit card. There's no battery. It's read by the way radio waves bounce off it. If you get close to a reader, it registers your presence. But the badge is active. They say those batteries last three to five years. But I've heard that it's more like only two years."

"What about Sam's phone?"

"They're in it." He turned to Samantha. "They can see who you text and what you say. If you send a friend a photo, they get that, too. They can look at your phone call records. Have you used your phone for emails since this happened?"

"Yeah."

"Then they have your email password. You're an open book to them."

Josie stopped walking, stood still, and stared at Cumberland. "This is terrifying," Josie said. "What do you recommend we do?"

"You should compartmentalize your life. You should live in two worlds. The normal world and the private world. In the normal world you bring your phone and ID and badge with you and you do all the regular stuff each day. That way they don't suspect you're aware of what they're doing. But you never talk about sensitive stuff except when you want them to think you're working on their problem. Then you figure out the best stuff to say."

"What about turning off our phones completely?" Samantha asked. "Doesn't that make it so a hacker can't use it as a listening device?"

"No. Powering down your phone mostly just slows down your phone's transmissions and makes it so your battery charge lasts longer. Most phones, most of the time, still phone home using their backup battery. Your phone still pings off the nearest cell tower every few minutes, so the monitoring computers can tell where you are. When you think you might want privacy, you have to leave your phones and the other electronics with RFID chips at home and go somewhere else. Another problem is that turning off your phone is a break in pattern. If software monitoring you notices a change in your signal, they might think you're onto them."

"Oh, yeah!" Samantha said. "Like in the movies when the security guard is watching the bank of screens and one of them suddenly goes dark. It means someone has covered up a camera someplace."

"Right. The lack of signal is hugely obvious. When you're doing private-world stuff, it's best to leave your phone on like normal. But leave it at home. Same with the lapel badge. Maybe put them both within range of some noise. Leave the TV on. The Artificial Intelligence that companies use for monitoring isn't very good at distinguishing between a TV sound track and real people talking. It's not a great disguise, but it helps. And remember, you still have to keep your phones and badge with you most of the time. The more normal world signal you give them, the less likely they are to suspect that you also have a private world. Also, while you have a dumb car, and that's good, it's very easy for them to put a monitor on it. The simplest type is a GPS broadcast. They stick it underneath where no one will ever find it. Then they can tell where you drive."

Samantha said, "Can't you use your fancy electronics to test the car the way you tested our other stuff?"

"Sure. But if it comes up clean, that doesn't mean they won't bug it tonight. So you have to always be in your normal world when you're driving. Because they've gone to so much effort already, I'm sure they'll be watching your car eventually."

"Can we talk inside of the car when we're driving?" Josie asked. "The road noise would cover, right?"

Cumberland shook his head.

Josie turned to Samantha. "Does that seem clear to you?"

"Got it, Mama. It's already capitalized in my brain. Normal World and Private World." She said to Cumberland, "We can't always get to the beach, right? We could get stuck in some motel with no nearby place to talk." She paused. "Oh, of course. We do like in the movies. Put all our gear on the bed, then go into the bathroom, turn on the shower, and talk in there."

Cumberland nodded. He looked at his watch, a large garish device that looked like it was designed for playing video games. "I should go. I can find my way home. If I find out something useful, I'll call your burner. But keep its ringer off when you're in your normal world. We don't want the monitors to hear an unidentified phone ringing."

"Thanks, Cumberland," Josie said.

He didn't seem to hear her. He bent down and pet Unknown. "Bye, dog." He straightened up and left, never looking at Josie or Samantha in the eye.

TWELVE

Josie and Samantha went through the rest of their walk discussing how to sound normal yet never say anything they didn't want heard. When they got home, they practiced writing messages to each other on paper. Josie watched as Samantha used her phone to text her friends with benign messages.

When they spoke, it felt very strange, self-editing before each statement so that their communication would sound like a normal amount of stress and worry, but would not communicate anything about their efforts to engage Cumberland or any other aspect of the subjects they didn't want monitored.

Josie felt like Cumberland was their secret weapon. If Mosconi and Rodriguez suspected that Josie had told Cumberland anything about their mission, it would mean a breach of contract, and they could take Samantha back into custody.

Josie found it difficult to not sound so stilted and awkward that it would communicate that they were aware their handlers were listening to them. They came up with generic things to say about the task of searching Yosemite, things that wouldn't suggest that they'd engaged someone like Cumberland.

As evening came, they went out for pizza, brought it home, and ate in their condo while they watched a comedy with Will Smith. They cut up some pizza into pieces and mixed them into Unknown's dog food.

Later, they sat in the dark, looking out toward the partial view they had of the ocean and the lights of the Santa Monica pier. Josie poured a glass of Chardonnay. She also added a little seltzer water to it. She knew that horrified her fellow professors with their snobby attitudes about wine. But she was in the privacy of her own home. No one would know about her philistine tendencies, except the Bureau of Investigation people listening in, who would hear the pop of the wine cork and then the fizzy sound of pouring seltzer.

"You can drink this stuff straight, right?" Samantha said, lifting up the seltzer bottle.

"Yes. Much better for you than the sugar drinks you like. Give it a try."

Samantha poured a glass, brought it back to the couch, and sat next to Josie. She took a sip.

"Yow, that ain't for me."

Josie hadn't heard Yow before. It would soon be just another word in the long line of different words that Samantha experimented with. "You'll get used to it. Some adults drink seltzer plain. Others use it as a mixer." Josie knew that comment was a bit of psychological persuasion. The technique of referencing adult behaviors had been successful in the past. Samantha was desperate to grow up, and she was quickly adopting behaviors that made her seem more like an adult and less like a kid. Josie also hoped that when Samantha found herself in social situations where there was pressure to drink, she could feel comfortable drinking seltzer.

"Do you think we'll be able to find this bad guy in Yosemite?" Samantha asked.

"I don't know, Sam. But we'll give it a try. We'll do whatever it takes to keep the DA's office from charging you with smuggling."

The first call from Cumberland came the next day after Samantha and Josie both came home from their respective schools. Josie and Samantha had shed all of the potential tracking gear and were on their Private World beach walk with Unknown when Josie's burner phone rang.

"I'm calling for two reasons," Cumberland said in Josie's ear.

"Okay."

"One, I think I've figured out a way to put surveillance

on Yosemite from some land-mapping satellites in low-Earth orbit."

"Do I want to know the details?"

"Maybe not. It's boring."

"What's the other thing?"

"I'm wondering if you are planning to go to Yosemite. For research or whatever."

"I don't have a specific plan about that, but I assume we'll go there."

"Okay. Then I'll print up some maps of Yosemite. If I find out anything about this bad guy, I can make location notes to give you. I'll call when I have stuff to show you."

"Sounds good," Josie said.

They said goodbye.

THIRTEEN

After Josie disconnected from Cumberland, she and Samantha and Unknown continued south toward Venice and Marina Del Rey.

"How do you see this playing out, Mama?" Samantha asked. "Going to Yosemite?"

"I don't know, Sam. But I have a wild idea."

"What is it?"

"Before we even get close to trying to find him, we could fool him from a distance."

"How, Mama?"

Josie thought about her answer, something that seemed almost ridiculous.

"How?" Samantha repeated.

"I'm still thinking."

They stopped. Samantha got Unknown into her dog pack and up on her back, so they could walk down on the sand. The sun was lowering over the ocean, its rays becoming a deeper orange and casting everything on the beach in a golden light. The waves were large and rhythmic, crashing loud and heavy and sending huge arcs of foam up the sloped beach.

After a few minutes, Josie said, "You know how you get so wrapped up in stories…"

"What do you mean, Mama? I don't read that many books. Do you mean movies?"

"Any kind of stories. Books, TV shows, movies, the stories your friends pass along at school."

"Yeah, okay, stories are cool."

"Killers get wrapped up in stories, too," Josie said.

"They watch movies, sure. But why does it matter?"

"We all love stories. So I'm contemplating that we'll create a story that will grab the killer."

"And then what?"

"If we can pull the killer into a story, we can manipulate him."

Samantha stopped walking and looked at Josie. "How?"

"I don't know. I need your help on this."

Samantha scoffed. "I can't give advice about psycho killers."

"Sure you can," Josie said. "You're a huge fan of stories. You know how they work."

"No I don't. I just watch them. Sometimes I read them."

"Tell me why you watch movies. What makes them so compelling?"

"I'm not sure. Let me think." Samantha started walking again, moving faster than before. Unknown nearly bounced in the pack on Samantha's back. Josie hustled along at her side, trying to keep up.

After five minutes of walking, they were getting close to Venice Beach.

Samantha once again stopped. "Here's what I think. In every story there's a hero or heroine that we care about. Someone we worry about, right? The heroine is in trouble, right? Bad trouble. And the guy who causes all that trouble is really evil. So we keep reading or watching to see if our heroine can kick the bad guy's butt and get out of trouble. That's why stories grab us."

"Good point. Or wait, what was that word you were using? Yow. So here's my question. What kind of story would grab the killer in Yosemite?"

They walked in silence again. Josie didn't want to interrupt Samantha's thoughts. She believed that Samantha might come up with a way to understand the killer and what he wanted. And that might give them an approach of how to go after him.

After another long march of silence, Samantha said. "Okay, here's an idea. Pretend our bad guy is in trouble just like the hero in a normal story. There's some evil dude who has him all bent out of shape. Maybe the evil dude is even worse than our bad guy. So our bad guy needs to shake the evil dude off his tail."

Josie thought about it as she walked. "You know what, Sam? I think you've got it."

"No, I don't. Even if that kind of story would interest our killer, what good does it do us?"

"If we can tell the kind of story you're talking about, we can interest the killer. If we can get his attention, maybe we can manipulate him one way or another. Or at least distract him."

"Gimme a break, Mama. He's a killer. He's totally focused on being a bad dude. What could we possibly do to manipulate him?"

"I don't know. My turn to think."

They walked ahead, getting closer to Venice Beach. The sun's glow was more golden. The evening beach walkers were more numerous. People had their phones out, planning their sunset photos. Far out to sea were two ships. One heading south toward Mexico, one heading north toward San Francisco or maybe Portland or Seattle. The ships crossed paths in the evening light.

Josie pulled Samantha to a stop. Samantha's stop brought Unknown to a stop as well.

"I have an idea," Josie said.

She turned Samantha.

"Let me take Unknown out of her chariot, and we'll go back to dog walking."

Samantha took off her pack, made the changes, and they started walking the beach walk back toward Santa Monica. They'd come a long way, and the Santa Monica pier was very distant. But they'd be back before dusk.

Josie said, "Here's a basic idea. Bare-bones stuff. But with your help, we can make it good."

"Okay, Mama, what is it?"

"There's an ancient story about an evil monster named Grendel. Grendel was in a poem called Beowulf."

"What did Grendel do?"

"He tore people into pieces and ate them."

Samantha raised her eyebrows. "I guess that qualifies as totally evil."

"So what if we write a new story about Grendel? We act as if it's journalism. Something scientists and professors have studied. And we make it look as if reporters have discovered this story. They're excited, so they write stories about this story, and they publish it on websites and maybe in some newspapers and magazines."

"Wait," Samantha said. "Is our story a real story? Or is it a made-up story?"

"It's made up. But it's based on existing made-up stories, so it takes on a sense of reality."

Samantha shook her head. "Listen to yourself, Mama. A made-up story about a monster that's based on an existing made-up story?"

"Exactly," Josie said as if ignoring Samantha. "And we do that to frighten the killer. If we can scare him, he'll make mistakes and maybe get caught."

"You're basically saying that we could get the killer to believe in monsters?"

"Yes."

"No offense, Mama, but that's ridiculous."

"Is it? Do you believe in monsters?"

"Of course not." Samantha shook her head as she looked at Josie.

"That's what I would say, too. But sometimes I get creeped out. Don't you ever get creeped out?" Josie was thinking about the two men she'd shot with her medieval crossbow the month before.

"Sure," Samantha said. "After I see a scary movie with a really bad villain, I sometimes think I hear a noise in the middle of the night. Then I lie there wondering. You know… like could a bad guy like that be in our condo."

"So bad people can creep you out. But what about that horror movie you told me about a week ago, the one you saw at Sienna's house. I think it was about an alien creature."

"Oh yeah. That really scared me. The tentacle creature was in this country house where three girls were staying, and they could hear it moving at night. But they never knew where it was or saw any signs of it. They could only hear it. So they figured it had to just be a figment of their imaginations. Then one night, when the girls went to sleep, it was under one of the girls' beds. She woke up in the middle of the night, and it had its slimy tentacles around her neck strangling her, and it was feeling her eyeballs and poking into her ears! And one really long tentacle was under her pajamas, going under her armpit and down her stomach. The movie totally freaked me out. I still have bad dreams about it. I wake up and I want to look under the bed to be sure it's not there. But I'm afraid to."

"Do you believe alien creatures like that exist? That they're here among us?"

"No way. They're just, like, movie aliens."

"But you still get creeped out."

Samantha nodded. "I see what you mean. One part of your mind knows they don't exist. The other part of your mind wants to check under the bed."

"That's the power of story. That's what I want to do with the man who shot the sheriff's deputies."

"Creep him out?" Samantha said.

"Yes. Let me run an idea by you," Josie said. "But you have to promise not to make fun of me. This is just a starting point."

"Promise," Samantha said. "So what's the real made-up story?"

"A thousand years ago, someone wrote the epic poem called Beowulf."

"Grendel was in the poem," Samantha said.

"Yes. The poem was set in Scandinavia. The king of the Danes was called Hrothgar, and his kingdom was being plagued by the monster Grendel. Grendel attacked the men, ripped their arms and legs off, and ate them."

"Talk about yow," Samantha said.

"So a warrior named Beowulf went to help Hrothgar. He went into battle and attacked Grendel. The monster was amazingly strong, but Beowulf managed to slay him."

"All this was in a poem?" Samantha said.

Josie nodded. "It was. Not a simple rhyming poem. But

a long-story poem with a complex structure. There are many aspects to the story. But my idea is this. What if the monster Grendel didn't really die?"

"Wait," Samantha said. "You just said that he dies in the poem."

"Right. So let's take some artistic license. What if some kind of ghost of Grendel lives on? Maybe this surviving Grendel isn't so evil. Maybe he lives on through the centuries and keeps killing. But he changes his MO and only kills humans who murder other humans."

Samantha was looking at the sand as she walked. "What's the point?"

"Because it would mean that our new Grendel is more discriminating with his victims than the old version. And maybe it would make the Yosemite killer feel unsettled."

Unknown stopped to sniff a piece of driftwood lying in the sand at the edge of the walkway. Samantha waited a bit, then tugged on the leash to get her walking again.

"We make it seem like Grendel is alive in the forests of Yosemite. And the killer will find signs of Grendel. I don't know exactly what. Maybe something as simple as the letter G."

"Okay. But how would we make the killer believe that the signs actually come from Grendel?" Samantha asked.

"I don't know," Josie said. "I'll have to think about it."

"And what would the killer do if he started to believe that Grendel was coming to eat him?"

"I don't know that, either," Josie said. "Become frightened and careless? Maybe come out of his hiding place?"

"I know how you're going to find out," Samantha said.

Josie looked at her.

"You're going to do the professor thing. What are the three Rs you talk about? Research, Ruminate, and Reflect. And then, for the fourth R, you Right it all down." Samantha made a short laugh at her joke.

Josie noticed that it wasn't the hearty laugh that was so common to Samantha. But it was something.

"Back to Private Mode," Samantha said in a soft voice as

they climbed the three flights of stairs.

When they got back inside their condo, Samantha unclipped Unknown's leash while Josie hung up her windbreaker. Josie turned toward the kitchen and stopped.

The drawer where they put their phones and the RFID badge was open an inch. Josie stared at it, trying to remember what she'd done just before they'd left on their walk. Had either of them shut it before they left? She walked over and looked without touching. She could see both phones through the narrow opening.

On the counter nearby was the pad of paper where they wrote notes to each other when they were in Private Mode. Was it in the same place? The last note she'd written was still on the pad. The pen lay on top.

Josie flipped over the sheet and wrote on the next one.

'Sam, do you remember either of us shutting the kitchen drawer? We put our phones in, but the drawer is open a little.'

Josie made a waving motion that caught Samantha's eye. She beckoned Samantha over, held her finger to her lips, pointed at the drawer, and then at her note.

Samantha walked over, read the note, frowned, then wrote, 'I don't remember. You think someone was in our condo?!'

'I think I just have jumpy nerves.'

Samantha looked worried, which made Josie feel much worse. Josie was thinking that if Agent Mosconi had some way to send a burglar to inspect their condo, he would now know that Josie and Samantha were evading him, leaving their phones behind. It would be a breach of trust on Josie's part but nowhere near as bad as Mosconi breaking the law and sending someone to enter their home.

Josie decided she was imagining things.

FOURTEEN

The next day, Josie hoped that Cumberland would call with information. When there was no word, she felt frustrated but knew she could not expect anything.

That evening, on their Private World beach walk, she once again talked to Samantha about her Grendel idea.

“Do you think it’s a crazy notion?” she asked.

“Kinda, Mama. But the next time I feel like I should check under my bed for the tentacle creature, it won’t seem crazy at all. Maybe you should run your idea by someone else. Maybe one of those eggheads at UCLA will have a useful opinion.”

“Eggheads?” Josie said. “You call us eggheads?”

“Not you, Mama.”

Josie turned and gave Samantha her strongest stare.

“Okay, maybe a little bit you. It’s just a name for super smart people. It sounds kind of rude, but the truth is regular people know that we’d be screwed if we didn’t have super smart people in the world. Professors are like nerds. We all depend on smart people.”

That night, lying in bed, trying unsuccessfully to sleep, Josie worried about the passage of time. She needed to provide some indication to Agent Mosconi that she was working on a plan to pursue the killer in Yosemite. But the only way she could think of to do that was to travel to Yosemite. And she couldn’t travel until she had a viable plan.

Josie stared at the ceiling as she went over her story idea. She thought she might talk to a sometime friend who taught creative writing in the English Department, someone who knew the power of story and understood how it worked.

The next morning after Samantha went to school, Josie

carried her burner phone to the beach and called the woman. The woman's voicemail message said she was on sabbatical. Josie left a polite response and hung up. She thought for some time, going over the people she knew who might be able to help her. Nothing came to mind until she opened up the PDF directory of UCLA academic offerings and scrolled down. When she got to Psychology, it made sense.

There was a man whom she'd once met at a faculty soiree. Manfred Gronsky taught and also ran a clinical practice. It seemed unlikely that he could help her. But she reminded herself that there was no harm in asking a question.

He actually answered his phone, and Josie asked if they might meet for lunch. They picked a vegetarian restaurant just off Wilshire at 1:00 p.m. Josie was there early.

Gronsky came in, they shook hands, sat down, and made some small talk. They both ordered the daily special. After the waiter left, Gronsky asked how he could be of help.

Josie said, "I'm not sure how to describe this thing I'm working on. I want to create an outlandish historical idea, a complete fabrication, and see who would believe it."

"Interesting!" Gronsky said. "That sounds like a blend of psychological and historical experiment."

"Yes, I suppose it is," Josie said.

"Let me guess your intention. You want to establish whether or not your students are rigorous thinkers."

Josie once again chastised herself for engaging with someone without having anticipated the obvious questions. "Not quite. I'm wondering if you can give me a sense of why people will believe something that is not only fictional but appears to be fictional in the extreme."

"That's a question that psychologists have spent time on, usually in regard to conspiracy theories, many of which would seem to really stretch credulity."

"That would probably apply to my project," Josie said.

Gronsky nodded. "As you know, lots of people believe conspiracy theories, even ones that seem especially wacko to me and, probably, to you. And of course psychologists have many theories about that!" He laughed.

"This is exactly what I need for my project," Josie said. "If I know why people believe strange things, I can make my crazy fabrication more believable. Any tips you have will be greatly appreciated."

"Okay. First tip. People think and believe things because of their feelings, not because of their knowledge. If it feels right, then it is right. Facts don't matter at all except when they reinforce what people already feel. Some psychologists call this motivated reasoning. Let's say my life is messed up. I'm destabilized and unhappy. A rational explanation might just be that I've had a run of bad luck. Or, that I've made a series of bad decisions. So, rather than realistically looking at my own possible failings, I have a possible motive for finding a culprit to blame for my discontent. When a huckster comes along selling a conspiracy story just like the way they sell snake oil or magic pills, I'm susceptible. If I can think some other person or group is responsible for my sorry state, I might feel a little better because then it's not all my fault."

The waiter came and brought Josie's iced tea and Gronsky's beer. He took a sip.

"Now let's say," he said, "I read something about a certain secret group in the government. It seems like they're out to get me and people like me. Or, they've been working on an objective, the fallout from which—as far as I can tell—has ruined my life. They are to blame. Never mind that a rational person can point to many reasons that suggest this secret group doesn't exist, or, if it does, it would find it nearly impossible to implement its goals working in the government, which is a huge organization bedeviled by incompetence at every level. When a person with strong motivated reasoning finds a current conspiracy focus on which to blame their troubles, they forget that every organization they've ever experienced, from their workplace to the local school board, struggles to get anything done. Yet they assign amazing effectiveness to their emotional enemy."

Josie said, "So basically, motivated reasoning is about finding someone else to blame for your problems."

"Sometimes it is."

"This is great." Josie took a small pad out of her purse and scribbled some notes. She scanned her writing. "You referred to this as your First tip. That people go with their feelings, not with their knowledge. Is there a Second tip?"

"There is. When you fabricate your story, don't just put in aliens. Make certain they're green."

Josie was taken aback. "I don't think I understand."

"Meaning," Gronsky said, "You'll draw more attention to your story if every aspect of it is extreme or outrageous. It sounds like I'm being flip. But I'm being sincere."

"But outrageous aspects to my fiction would make it even less believable."

"Only for some, only for those of us who are especially rational. And even we who will think your story's excesses are ridiculous will nevertheless notice it more. Think about the supermarket checkout magazines."

"They're all weird," Josie said.

"Right. That's what you and I think. But they sell well. Mostly to believers but a little bit to nonbelievers, too, who probably just want something funny to laugh at."

"I can't imagine buying or reading one," Josie said.

"Yet you are going to write a similar story and try it out on your students."

"Yes, I guess that's the height of irony, isn't it? I'm trying to create a story I wouldn't believe myself."

"Maybe tell me about your idea, and I can comment on it directly."

Josie thought about it. "Okay. But don't laugh at me."

"Promise."

They both laughed.

"And I'm sorry to do this," Josie said, "but I have to ask that you don't tell anyone about this if you end up seeing this story someplace. There's actually a serious side to this project, and I don't want the wrong people to get hurt."

"Cross my heart, hope to die," Manfred Gronsky said in a

serious voice.

"Thank you. I'm thinking of creating a modern-day version of the monster Grendel."

"From Beowulf," Gronsky said.

For a moment, Josie was surprised that this man would know about Beowulf and Grendel. Then she remembered that he had a Ph.D. from UCLA. Of course, he would know.

"Right," Josie said. "In my story, Grendel has come back to life. He's hiding in the forest of Yosemite. In a change from his earlier incarnation, he no longer kills innocent men. Instead, he only kills murderers and other serious criminals."

"Ah, a vigilante Grendel. Maybe you're going to test this on your students. But based on what I've read about a recent case where you tracked down and caught a murderer, I'm thinking you want to unnerve a killer who's hiding in Yosemite."

Josie was surprised, maybe even shocked, at Gronsky's perceptiveness. She wondered how to respond.

"You're too smart," she finally said. "Yes, I'm trying to draw out the killer, a man no one has seen, a man who may be nowhere near Yosemite. The evidence suggests he exists and he simply has a very good hiding place. A law enforcement agency has asked me to help them."

"Your story will give the killer bad dreams," Gronsky said. He drank more beer. "If he's given to believe non-rational stories, he may completely fall for it. And if he doesn't succumb to the influence of such stories, he'll still be very curious. The more outrageous your story, the more he'll notice. He may even sense that the story is aimed at ruffling his feathers. Either way, he might come out of hiding to investigate."

"Wow, why am I doing this project?" Josie said. "This is your area of expertise."

Gronsky made a small, tight smile, more, Josie thought, like a smile of tolerance than enthusiasm.

The waiter came back with black bean soup and fresh hot corn bread for both of them.

"My advice is still the same," Gronsky said as he blew on a spoonful of soup to cool it off. "Punch up your story to ridiculous levels. Make this Grendel the monster to end all monsters. Every murderer who remains at large will have bad dreams about this."

"Do you think I need to apply any medieval background to give this credibility?"

"Like I say, credibility doesn't matter. If your target has heard of Grendel, fine. If not, the story may have even more of an effect."

"What kinds of outrageous ideas would you think of?"

Gronsky looked off toward the windows.

"Well, Grendel is green, of course," he said as he slurped a spoonful of soup. "And he doesn't just eat his victims, he rips them apart in fits of unimaginable violence. And Grendel hides near his victim's house, or, in your case, the victim's campsite, so that he can pounce on the victim at any odd point. If the victim just walks outside, or even goes to the bathroom in the middle of the night, Grendel is there to bite his head off. And when Grendel bites down on the head, brains squish out."

Josie found herself wincing and panting. "That is… That might be a little too extreme for me."

"I can see," Manfred Gronsky said, "that you're having trouble breathing. You are rational, yet even you are prone to find resonance in the actions of a terrible monster."

Josie sat up straight in her chair, trying to breathe better. Her heart pounded. Something about Gronsky's vision of a monster leaping out reminded her of the moment a month before, when the killer in the Quetico Wilderness grabbed her daughter Samantha.

Gronsky said, "Do you want me to help with your fabrication?"

Josie took another breath. Calmed herself. "I don't think I need that. My notion is fairly clear to me. I was primarily wondering how far I could push it before people would think it's completely nuts. But it seems that you've answered that."

"Right. There are no limits on how outlandish your idea can be. In fact, the wilder your concept is, the more likely certain people are to believe it."

"Why do you think that is?"

"I don't have an explanation of why. But I know it's true. For example, there are people who believe that little green aliens in flying saucers come to our planet, then adopt a human disguise and walk among us."

"Right. But people who believe that are rare, right?"

"Maybe. But there are also people who believe the Earth is flat, and the moon landing was faked, and Bigfoot is alive and well, and divining rods will tell you what's beneath the Earth's surface, and there are faeries and elves and hobbits all over the forest, and a medium can hold a seance and help you communicate with the dead."

"Wow, you are quite conversant with such ideas."

"I hear them every day in my practice. Many, many people believe irrational thoughts."

"Because it fits with their feelings," Josie said.

"Right. Whether or not our feelings are corroborated by factual knowledge is not that important."

They both sat in silence and ate. After a minute, Gronsky said, "Does this give you a sense of the direction to take your story?"

"Yes. Thank you very much."

FIFTEEN

That evening on their Private World beach walk, Josie told Samantha what the psychologist Manfred Gronsky had told her. That any story, no matter how fantastic, can find believers.

Samantha said, "The people who check under their bed for the tentacle creature."

"Right," Josie said, laughing.

Samantha bent down and patted Unknown. "Be good, Unknown, so the tentacle creature stays away." She turned to Josie. "What else happens in this story?"

"First, this new Grendel leaves signs of his presence."

"Yeah. A G brand! Burned into the victim!"

"Right, that's a great idea!" Josie said. "When those signs of Grendel start appearing, a reporter writes about them. The reporter interviews some people who visited Yosemite and finds someone who describes a loud groaning, moaning sound coming from the forest in the middle of the night. That visitor went out the next morning and found the G brand. Maybe it was burned into the trunk of a tree." Josie paused, running through her imaginary scenario. "Then a professor from Oxford University in England contacts the reporter. He's heard about the story and is intrigued because it matches what he's been studying, which is references to deadly attacks on humans, attacks that were horrifically violent. The attacks were usually isolated incidents that took place hundreds of miles apart from each other. And they also took place over hundreds of years. But the thing that links them are how violent they are—arms and legs torn off the victims—and the common background of the victims."

"What's that background?"

"That they were murderers who hadn't been caught."

"And they were killed by Grendel," Samantha said.

"Yes, exactly. So the Oxford professor travels to Yosemite to investigate. And he believes the medieval monster Grendel has left Europe and reappeared in America in contemporary times."

"The professor makes the whole story more believable," Samantha said. "Because he's kind of like you. All serious and academic."

"That's my hope." Josie walked along, thinking about what Samantha had said. "I'm visualizing our man hiding out in the wilderness. He learns of the story that suggests that Grendel lives on and may be in the wilds of Yosemite. It's been written about by scholars, especially the Oxford professor. Eventually, our Yosemite killer learns that this Grendel only kills killers."

Samantha said, "So, if any regular person in Yosemite hears about this new Grendel, they just laugh and think it's a quirky story, right? It doesn't creep them out because they're not murderers. But if the real killer hears about this new Grendel who seems to have survived through the ages, he would take notice. At least a little bit, anyway."

"What if people find multiple signs of Grendel?"

"More G brands?" Samantha seemed more interested.

"Sure. The letter G could be burned into tree trunks." Josie paused. "It would be gross, but maybe someone dies and the body has a letter G branded into it, and when the investigators pursue it, it turns out the dead person was a murderer."

"But where would you get a dead body?"

"We make it up," Josie said. "We create the story, give it some background and bona fides, and the local paper writes about it."

"So there really isn't a dead body."

"Right. It's just a story."

Samantha narrowed her eyes as she slowed to a stop on the beach walk, her stare focused on the sand. Unknown pulled gently on the leash. Samantha resumed walking. "Talk about the power of story. The killer we're chasing might think it's real."

Josie nodded.

"And the local news media would do follow-up stories about the Oxford professor who has been researching the Beowulf poem about the monster Grendel and how signs of Grendel had appeared over the centuries. And now that professor has been looking into reports of a new Grendel in Yosemite. And this Grendel is finding murderers and killing them."

"What should we do next?" Samantha asked.

"First, we write the stories. They would be articles that could be on news websites. Maybe the closest newspaper to Yosemite has one. Then it only makes sense that a UCLA professor of medieval history would want to go up to Yosemite and investigate what she'd read in those same articles."

"That's you."

"Right," Josie said. "You'd come, too. We'd hike around and investigate. Ask questions. Talk about the Grendel monster."

"Which would create its own kind of, what's it called, credibility." Samantha was enthusiastic.

"The more people hear about something, whether it's real or not, the more they believe it. If various people all over Yosemite start talking about the vigilante monster that kills murderers, eventually our man is going to hear about it. And that will make our presence more believable, too."

"There's a problem with this, Mama."

"What?"

"If the killer thinks we're too connected to this Grendel business, he might target us."

"Maybe," Josie said. "But if so, he would just be looking for more information about the monster. He wouldn't want us to notice him. He's in hiding after all."

"And," Samantha said, "while we're tromping around in the woods, we'll probably discover signs of Grendel. The letter G burned into cabin walls." She looked off, thinking. "But how would those brand marks actually get there?"

Josie grinned. "We create them when no one is looking. Then we'd act as if we just discovered them."

"Wow, Mama. The Josie Strong I never knew."

SIXTEEN

An extra-large wave crashed as they walked, the foamy water rushing up the beach. They paused and watched from the dry safety of the beach walk. Josie thought of what the artist Shulu Ojai told her a month ago, that the Chumash Indians believed that huge crashing waves were a warning of some kind.

Samantha said, "You think the signs of Grendel will gradually creep out the murderer. That makes sense to me. But how will that help us find him?"

"I'm not sure. He'll be a bit like the rest of us. Distracted. Glancing behind himself. Wondering about it when he might otherwise be focusing on staying hidden. Checking under his bed."

Samantha said, "That idea kind of represents a lot of things."

"Yes, it certainly does. Checking under your bed is a useful metaphor."

"The other stuff you talked about, the details about the Oxford professor, do you know such a guy? Or would he be made up?"

"He would be fictional."

"What about the Grendel signs?"

"You thought of a branding iron. That's a great idea. Maybe we could have a blacksmith create a branding iron in the shape of a capital G, and we could use it to burn the G shape into trees."

"Do you think that would seem silly?" Samantha asked.

"Maybe. But it would probably be effective at getting attention."

"The Yosemite killer would read about this stuff in a story?

How's he gonna find where to read about it? Does he even read stuff? Or maybe he sees it on TV? Maybe he has a laptop with a cell connection. So, when he sees a G burned into something like a tree or a deer carcass, he Googles 'G burned into a tree' and up comes a website article about Grendel and the Oxford professor who's researching it."

"Sam, that's great. That's inspired."

"And you will write the article?" Samantha said.

"We will," Josie said.

"How does it get on the website?"

Josie thought about it. "Cumberland could figure that out. In fact, maybe he could make a new website that is all about the Grendel monster."

"And I could post about it on Facebook. And tweet about it. It could go viral."

"I think we need to keep this to ourselves for the time being. We can post it, but only anonymously."

Samantha said, "So this whole Grendel thing is part of our Private World?"

"I can see it both ways. We want the Bureau of Investigation to see that we're actively working on the problem. So it might be good if they eavesdrop on our plans to some extent. On the other hand, if they have their own leaks, some of our plan might get back to the killer, which would negate the whole point of doing it. And it could put us at great risk."

"Leaks at the Bureau of Investigation? You mean like they could have a bad egg in their system?"

"I don't know. Would this bad egg be an egghead?"

"I was joking, Mama."

Josie nodded. "I'm thinking we should first work out our concept when we're in our Private World, like we are now. After we've considered all the pros and cons of each thing we do, we'll decide what we're able to talk about in our Normal World."

"In the meantime, how do we keep the Bureau guys thinking we're working on the case in a normal way and not creating the whole Grendel thing?"

"We'll plan a trip to Yosemite. We can talk about that in our

Normal World."

"When we're at home near our phones and your Bureau badge."

"Right."

"Here's a question," Samantha said. "Yosemite is in the mountains, right? It's already October. Does that mean there'll be snow there?"

"I don't know. Maybe. I think the main valley floor is around four thousand feet. I've seen pictures of Yosemite with snow on the valley floor. But I'm guessing that the valley floor won't have much or any snow at the end of October. But, of course, the high mountains can have lots of snow. In some ways, a blanket of snow higher up would make our life easier."

"Why is that?"

"Because the murderer can't move in the snow without leaving tracks. So, as the snow comes, he probably isn't able to hide out in the high country. He'll have to move down to lower elevations in order to move freely without being tracked."

"I never would have thought of that. You're a natural tracker."

Josie laughed. "Half the time I can't even track my car keys."

"That's because professors are naturally absent-minded. You're always thinking about big stuff. And catching a murderer is big stuff."

"Keeping you out of prison is big stuff."

Samantha was quiet for a moment. "Yeah, it sure is."

Josie felt bad she'd brought up the subject of prison. She wanted to take it back. "I've been thinking about the articles we'll write to create the Grendel character," she said. "Everything we normally write goes into our cloud storage files, right?"

"Yeah."

"Is there a way to turn that off? To go back to the old days?"

"You mean so no one could hack into what we're writing," Samantha said.

"Right."

"I'm sure there's a way. But I don't know. Oh, wait, I do know! Let's get a cheap laptop that isn't connected online and use that."

"There's a Best Buy over by the Four O Five freeway."

An hour later, they'd picked out a laptop, then decided to get two of them so they could both work simultaneously. When Josie explained to the sales clerk that they didn't want their computers to connect to the internet, that they only wanted them to write and then store a copy of the writing in the computer's memory or on a memory stick, he frowned and gave Samantha an imploring look as if to ask for help dealing with a ridiculous older woman. He said the whole point of the computer would be negated by refusing to be online. He said it was like buying a dumb TV. They were ignoring the most useful aspect of the computer.

Josie was firm, and he eventually backed off and explained how to disable the wifi connection and use the computer without ever logging on to the internet. They left the store with the computers and a pack of memory sticks.

When they walked into their condo, a phone was ringing. Samantha ran to the kitchen drawer and pulled out her phone.

"Mama, it's not my phone that's ringing," she said. "It's yours."

Josie looked at her phone. The readout said 'Theo Mosconi.'

Josie's chest and body clenched with dread.

SEVENTEEN

It took Josie a moment to adjust to the idea of talking to Theo Mosconi, the man who'd so thoroughly disrupted their lives. Josie picked up her phone. She struggled to breathe. She tapped the answer button. "Hello?"

"This is Agent Theo Mosconi calling."

"Yes, Mr. Mosconi," she said.

"I'm calling to check on your progress. We are, of course, trying not to intrude unnecessarily in your lives. But we also want to know that you are moving forward on our agreement. It is very important that you stay focused."

"Yes, we are."

"Have you developed a plan for how to find this man we're after?"

Josie thought he sounded just like a patronizing teacher she remembered from her childhood.

"Yes, we think we have."

"Are you planning to go to Yosemite?"

"Soon, yes. We still have to get a couple of things figured out first. But I believe you can look forward to us finding your murderer. I'll let you know when that happens."

"Okay. Keep me informed. You have a lot riding on this."

"Yes, I know." Josie clicked off without saying goodbye.

Samantha wrote on the pad of paper. 'Mama, it seems like you just hung up on Mr. Mosconi.'

Josie wrote, 'Yes, I suppose I did. He was patronizing, acting as if he had to check up on wayward children.'

Samantha wrote, 'I'm sorry, Mama. Let's focus on something better. The articles we're going to write.'

Samantha started unboxing one of the laptops. Then wrote, 'With two identical computers, how will we tell them apart?'

Josie hesitated. Then scrawled, 'I suppose I'll just look for the skull-and-crossbones sticker on yours.'

Samantha blurted out, "Mama, I might be done with that phase."

"I didn't mean to sound judgmental," Josie said, aware that Mosconi might be listening on any of several devices. But for the moment she didn't care.

"You're supposed to sound at least a little judgmental. That's the job of a mother, right?"

"I don't know, Sam. I don't know anything." She picked up the pen and wrote, 'This man has me very upset. I'm trying very hard on this thing. You are, too.'

Samantha gave Josie a hug, then rubbed her back. She wrote, 'Don't let him get to you, Mama. We'll get through this. We'll buck each other up.'

Josie sat down on the couch.

Samantha went back to unboxing the computers. When she had them out, she plugged in the charging cords. She picked up the pad of paper and wrote, 'These computers are Private World?'

Josie thought about it, then reached for the pad. She wrote, 'Private World for the time being. Coffee shop. We'll see where it goes.'

They plugged in the computers to charge, left their phones, the RFID photo ID, lapel badge, and walked with Unknown to the local coffee shop. They brought only pens and pads of paper The barrista they'd come to know was working.

"Hi, Amelia," Josie said. "You look stressed. Are you okay?"

Josie and Samantha had come to know Amelia Lopez as a 19-year-old immigrant from Peru who was always charming, always friendly, and who, despite crooked teeth, had a spectacular smile.

"I'm a little worried. Our landlord is going to sell the house where my roommates and I live. He has given us an eviction notice."

"I'm so sorry," Josie said. "Do you have a place to stay?"

Amelia shrugged. "I can't go back to my family in Bakersfield.

They are too angry with me for leaving farming. They think I'm crazy for wanting to start my own business."

"Oh? What business is that?"

Amelia took a furtive look at her surroundings. She leaned closer and spoke in a quiet voice. "I want to start a coffee business. Roasting, and coffee shop too. But mi padre thinks men run businesses and women raise families."

"And you know women can do both," Josie said.

"Yes. Business first. Family later."

Samantha was quiet. Josie was glad for their recent friendship with Amelia. The young woman didn't have Samantha's economic privilege, but she radiated ambition. Josie thought she was a good influence on Samantha. Perhaps even a role model.

"Have you found a place to live?"

"Not yet."

Josie hesitated, then said, "If you need to, maybe you could stay with us for awhile."

"Oh, professor. You are too kind! I'm sure I will find someplace."

"Okay. But keep it in mind."

Amelia took their order for cappucinos, Samantha's favorite as she learned to drink coffee.

Later, sitting at a table with their pens and paper, Samantha rubbed Unknown. "These articles we're going to write. How do we do it?"

"I don't have a clear idea," Josie said. "This is what fiction writers do. They have to create characters and a story line for them. There's a woman I went to school with at UC Davis. Her name is Tyla Beaumont, and she writes romance novels. A few years ago, she came to UCLA and gave a talk. She said that fiction writers have to dream up characters and a story line, and they have to put them all in some kind of believable world. Tyla called it world building. She said that when you build a fictional world, it has to have the same kind of things that the real world has. Only then will readers believe the fictional characters."

"So that's what we need to do? World building?"

"Yes, I think so."

"How do we start?"

Josie was so glad to see Samantha's interest. The project immediately seemed to engage her in a more active way than when she watched movies.

"Let's start with characters. We'll create some characters and make notes about them. Then we'll create a story for them and a world for them to live in."

"Okay." Samantha was nodding impatiently. "Who's our first character?"

"Let's start with the professor who comes from Oxford to Yosemite to investigate the new modern version of our monster."

"What's the character's name?"

"You tell me," Josie said.

"Well he's British, right? Veddy veddy British."

"Right." Josie looked off, thinking. "He has a name like Oliver. Oliver Broadstone."

"And they call him Ollie." Samantha was raising her voice.

"Yes, of course they do. How old is our professor?"

"Ollie is really old. Sixty. No, seventy. A total geezer. He's got those big bushy eyebrows and that gross hair growing out of his nostrils."

"That's all?" Josie said dryly.

"Well, he doesn't see very well, which is why he can't trim his nose hair, so he wears these eyeglasses that are about as thick as vodka bottle bottoms. And his nose is red from drinking all that vodka, and he walks with a limp, and he carries a cane made out of bamboo that he got when he was in Thailand studying the jungle monsters who eat fourteen-year-old boys. That's how he got his limp because one of those boys tried to sell him guide service into the jungle, and that boy got eaten, and Ollie got the lower part of his foot bit off when he tried to save the boy."

Josie was laughing, giggling. "You're pretty good at dreaming up this stuff."

"I'm going to be a rich romance novelist," Samantha said. "I'll write bodice rippers and sell millions."

"Will old Ollie Broadstone be in these bodice rippers? And

anyway, how do you know about bodice rippers?"

"It's Ollie's gorgeous granddaughter Lucille who will be in the novels. She is in love with a handsome Thai Prince named Tanner."

Josie was laughing. "I'll have to retire from UCLA so I have time to spend all this money you're going to earn."

Samantha giggled, and Josie laughed some more. As Samantha laughed louder, she bounced up and down on the coffee shop chair. Unknown looked at both of them with a little bit of enjoyment mixed with a great deal of confusion.

Eventually, they'd made notes about several characters who were involved in the search for Grendel, and they'd made a plan to create a believable Grendel monster in Yosemite.

After they got home, they sat side-by-side on the couch and wrote on their new dumb computers that weren't connected to the internet and thus couldn't be hacked.

A couple of hours later, they'd written the first articles they could give to Cumberland to post on various websites.

EIGHTEEN

That evening, for their Private World beach walk, they took their laptops and paper pads, and Josie took her burner phone. They once again left their regular phones and the badge at the condo as before. For a bit of change in routine, they left the TV on so any monitoring would be filled with voices to deconstruct.

Sam walked Unknown on the leash.

"How are your articles coming?" Josie asked.

"I'm not sure. I found out I'm not real good at this."

"The Ollie and Lucille Broadstone bodice ripper isn't done yet?"

"Not quite. How are your articles?"

"I think one or two are done, but I want your critique," Josie said.

"What do you mean by critique?"

"Feedback. Comments. What you think works and what you think falls flat. If you like, I can critique yours as well."

"I'd be embarrassed, Mama. You should go first. Then I'll see how this works. Maybe later, I'll have you critique my articles."

"No pressure, Sam. I'll only look if you want."

Samantha nodded. "Where will your article appear?"

"I don't know. Someplace on the web. It probably doesn't matter where. As long as Cumberland can get it posted on a website, a Facebook page that isn't connected to us, and a blog or two, Google will find it. Then, if anyone searches on a term that is in the article, Google will bring them to it."

"Okay. I get it."

"My target audience is someone who's heard something about Grendel being in Yosemite. If they get curious and wonder what it's all about, they'll maybe go to Google and type in the words, 'Grendel in Yosemite' or something like that."

"Right. So if you think people are going to search on 'Grendel in Yosemite,' then those words should be in your article, right?"

"Exactly," Josie said. "Let's go out on the sand."

Samantha put Unknown in her backpack. Samantha pulled off her sandals so she could walk barefoot on the sand. They walked toward the surf, sat down, and Josie opened her laptop.

"I'll just read this aloud. The first heading is, 'As seen in Criminology Quarterly,'"

"Wait," Samantha said. "Is that one of the places you want to post this on the web?"

"No. This is just part of my creation. I don't think there is a Criminology Quarterly. I just made that up."

Samantha nodded. "My super devious Mama is back. Okay, keep reading."

"Next comes another heading, kind of like a newspaper headline. It says, 'Bizarre Details Emerge About Climber's Horrific Death.'"

Josie paused and then read.

"Questions remain about Hans Ludwig, the German climber who fell to his death from Yosemite's El Capitan fourteen months ago. At the time of his death, the assumption was that Ludwig was attempting a free solo climb, which means climbing the wall with no aids or ropes or safety equipment. Very few climbers have attempted a free solo climb anywhere, even fewer at El Cap. No one witnessed Ludwig's climb or his subsequent death.

"Because Ludwig's body was found at the base of the wall, because he was wearing climbing shoes and clothes, and because he showed substantial blunt force trauma, the county sheriff's office stated that his death was caused by a fall from up on the face of the rock. The story of Ludwig's death was widely shared on social media, likely due to the dramatic news that his left arm was torn off in the fall."

Josie could sense Samantha cringing at her side.

"Presumably, Ludwig caught his arm in a wedge or crack of

some kind as he plummeted to Earth. It would require falling at a high speed to cause dismemberment, meaning the climber fell from a hundred or more feet, which is not much compared to the three-thousand-foot wall of El Capitan. Multiple climbers familiar with the routes above where Ludwig's body was found have said they've seen no sign of the missing arm. Although all agree that such an injury, while unlikely, is possible."

Samantha held up her hand. "Wait. So how much of this actually happened?"

"None of it," Josie said. "This is all fiction designed to read the way a journalist would write it for a real newspaper."

"So this is world building. It seems real, Mama."

"Anyway, I can go on to talk about how Ludwig had just been released from prison after being sentenced to twenty years for murder. His early release for good behavior outraged many people who felt that justice had not been served." She paused. "You get the idea."

Samantha said, "And a year later, there is new interest in Hans Ludwig's death from Oxford University Professor Oliver Broadstone!"

"Yes, exactly. Broadstone has uncovered multiple murders over multiple centuries that all have unusual similarities. The victims were all murderers. And they were all branded with the letter G."

Samantha interrupted again. "So all this stuff about the professor's research is made up, too?"

"Yes. It's all fiction. We can say that Broadstone said people have suggested that the vicious monster Grendel from the epic medieval poem Beowulf has been reincarnated. And then, Broadstone explains that Grendel tore his victims to pieces. So Broadstone has recently traveled to Yosemite to continue his research."

Josie closed her laptop. "What do you think?"

"It's amazing, Mama. I had to keep reminding myself that this is all made up. Even so, it seems so real."

"Can you think of any improvements?"

Samantha was silent for a minute. "Not in your writing.

But it would be good if the article had links to related stuff. Like, you could link to Wikipedia articles about Grendel and Beowulf. Same for if Professor Broadstone has a website or Facebook page."

"Excellent, Sam. I never even thought of that."

Samantha said, "Should we put stuff on multiple websites?"

"We should ask Cumberland to do that, yes."

"It would be easy to put up a fanblog on blogger dot com. It's free and easy. It could be all about Grendel. People love monster stuff and fantasy stuff. The blog could quote your article from whatever website Cumberland posts it on. Then the blog could fill in the stuff that Professor Broadstone is reluctant to say."

"What do you mean?" Josie asked.

"Just that the prof is so kind of stuffed-shirt about the subject, which is great of course. He wants people to be rational and not believe in superstition. But the monster fanblog would be the opposite. It could talk about how the reason they couldn't find the guy's arm is that Grendel ate it."

"Oh, you are good." Josie grinned. "What else would the fanblog say?"

"The fanblog could make stuff up like what you did with the professor. But where the prof is all scientific and reserved, the fanblog could make up freak-out ghost story stuff. A little boy who saw tracks and followed them into the woods and was never seen again. Then the police found out that the little boy had done real bad stuff. Torturing cats or something. Then you have a gang-banger car that was found off the highway in the woods. When the car was found, the windows were all broken, the seats were covered with blood, and the only sign of the gang bangers was a hand that was bit clean off. Everything else had been eaten."

Samantha looked at Josie with a big grin.

"How do you think of this stuff?" Josie said. "Okay, here's an assignment. You write the Grendel Monster fanblog articles. Maybe you can find some photos to put on it. Or some kind of monster artwork. But I don't know how one gets permission to use copyrighted images."

"There's lots of websites for that, Mama. Copyright-free images. The photographers and artists post their stuff to be used by anyone in any way."

"Why do they give away their work?"

"It's like all those free Kindle books on Amazon. The authors hope that if you like a free book, you might buy others by the same person. Same for artists and photographers."

"You really know this new world," Josie said.

"Maybe my knowledge will help keep me from going to prison on the smuggling charge." Samantha's tone was dark.

"I hope so. While you're writing the monster fanblog articles, I'll write the stuffed-shirt articles. Is that a good plan?"

"Yeah, Mama. Perfect. So when do we go to Yosemite?"

"I'm thinking it'll take me at least a day to write some more articles and more time to talk my dean into helping me get time off. How 'bout you?"

"School isn't too bad. If we work while we eat dinner, I can try to have a Grendel Monster fanblog done by then."

"Then we'll need to ask Cumberland to upload our articles to the web." Josie said. "Let me call him and ask how long he thinks that will take." She pulled out her burner phone, turned it on, and dialed his number.

"Hello?"

"Hi Cumberland. It's Josie calling."

"Who? Oh, Professor Strong. What do you want?"

Josie wasn't surprised at his brusqueness. It was part of Cumberland's personality, people who were smart with math and verbal skills but had a poor grasp of social skills.

"I'm wondering if you've had any luck figuring out how to study Yosemite for the movement of people in the forest?" she asked.

"Yes. I have. I'll be contacting you about that soon. Maybe tomorrow."

"Great," Josie said. "Samantha and I will be going to Yosemite soon. But first, we're creating a story structure that we believe will draw the attention of the man we're after. We want to post this story online somehow. On websites, blogs, Facebook, and similar places that would..."

Cumberland interrupted, "So that when your quarry hears about it and searches for it online, there are plenty of information sources for him to find. You'll be manipulating him, and he won't realize it."

"Yes, that's exactly it. I didn't know how to explain it so succinctly. Can you do that for us? Posting articles online? And how long do you think it will take?"

"A day or two. But I'm not a good typist, and I don't have editing skills. I could just read it out loud, but my voice recognition software has glitches. So if you can put your stuff on a memory stick, then I can easily copy it and upload it."

"Will do," Josie said. "And, of course, I'll pay your going rate for this kind of work."

"I don't have a going rate. I just want to help you and your daughter."

"I insist."

"Then you'll have to figure out what my going rate should be."

Josie hesitated. "Okay, thanks. I'll call you when we have our material," she said.

"Okay." He hung up.

Josie turned to Samantha. "It sounds like Cumberland can do it fast. As soon as we get our articles to him, he uploads it. Do you think you could get away from school for a few days?"

"Yeah. I haven't used any of my AP vacation days. As long as my grades are As, I get two days per month. I'm up to five."

"More than I can get from UCLA," Josie said.

NINETEEN

That evening, they worked on their articles back at their condo.

By their next morning walk, Josie and Samantha had the first few articles to upload. Josie once again used her burner phone to call Cumberland. He answered almost immediately.

"Hi Cumberland. Josie Strong. I'm lucky to catch you and not get your voicemail."

"That's because I have no life."

"But you're still going to school, right?"

"Yeah. UCLA morning classes on Tuesdays and Thursdays. Maybe I'll quit and just live off hacking. But it's boring."

Josie thought it best not to comment. "We've got articles to post. Can we pick a time to bring them to you?"

"Anytime you want. I'm here. If you want to come when I'm at school, I'll skip classes."

"Would this afternoon work?"

"Yeah. I've got stuff to show you. See you whenever." He hung up again as he had in the past, no goodbye or see-you-later signoff.

Josie was home when Samantha came from school. They were usually in Normal World mode at their condo, the better to lull Mosconi into thinking that Josie and Sam were unaware of the Bureau monitoring their life.

They moved back into Private World mode, leaving their phones and Josie's badge and ID as they left.

Josie wanted to obscure their connection to Cumberland. She wore her folding sun hat with the broad brim. Samantha wore a hoodie and brought a baseball cap. They walked with Unknown down to the street and took the bus on the longer, two-transfer route. At each transfer, they changed looks before they got off the bus. Samantha pulled back her hood but kept her cap on. Josie took off her hat, rolled it up, and stuffed it in her shoulder bag. Samantha picked up Unknown, put her in the backpack, and closed the top. At the second transfer stop, they reversed the process. They always kept their heads down so their faces were not easily observed by the traffic cams. They knew it probably made no difference. But it couldn't hurt. And, it was possibly good practice for remembering that cameras were everywhere.

An hour later, they got off in Beverly Hills and began walking up the steep street to Cumberland's house. He opened the door just seconds after they knocked.

Without saying hello, Cumberland turned and led them through the house, past the large glass doors to the swimming pool, and down the stairs to his studio/bedroom.

The room was as before, unmade bed in the darkest corner, tables messy with papers and computers, shelves with electronic gear and power strips, all sparkling with red and green LED lights.

Cumberland sat at a computer. "What do you have to post online?"

Josie handed him a memory stick. He plugged it into the computer.

"There are two folders," she said. "The folder named J has articles I wrote. They take a serious, journalistic approach to discussing the history of Beowulf and the monster he slayed."

"The medieval poem, right?" Cumberland said. "The monster was Grendel."

"Wow, you're good," Samantha said.

Josie could understand Samantha's focus on the young man. He was distant and strange and awkward and brilliant, and also beautiful.

"Beowulf was just school stuff," Cumberland said. "Some class I took." He frowned, then looked toward Josie. He didn't meet her eyes, but looked down toward her feet. "Was it your class, Professor Strong?"

"I do go over Beowulf a little. But you probably studied it

in a literature class."

"The other folder is named S," Samantha said. "That's my stuff. Kind of in-your-face, racy, check-out-mag style."

Cumberland clicked on the folders, arranging files. "I see," he said. "S is for Samantha."

Samantha grinned, pleased that he remembered her name.

"Our premise is this," Josie said. "After Beowulf killed Grendel, Grendel was reincarnated. The new version of the monster wasn't evil and, in fact, was somewhat good. He has reappeared now and then over the centuries and across continents."

"His new good deeds make up for his old bad deeds," Cumberland said. "What's he do that's good?" Cumberland was lining up articles on the computer screen.

"Maybe good isn't the best word," Josie said. "He's a vigilante executioner. He kills murderers who were unpunished or insufficiently punished. He leaves marks at the crime scenes. The letter G burned into his victims or on nearby objects. He dismembers the victims."

"A fiction designed to unnerve the killer you're after," Cumberland said.

Samantha was smiling.

"Right," Josie said. It was clear that Cumberland didn't miss anything. "The articles I wrote take a scholarly approach. They have a conservative style and they appear to avoid sensationalizing the idea that Grendel has surfaced in Yosemite."

"Which means people will probably assume you're covering up the truth, which is that the big monster is coming to chomp bad guys."

"Yes, I suppose so," Josie said. She turned to Samantha. "Sam, do you want to explain the focus of your articles?"

"My articles are pretty much monster trash talk. Real outrageous. Gory details."

"Speculation rendered as gossip," Cumberland said. "The reader thinks, no way could this be real. But you nevertheless plant the outrageous ideas in their head."

Samantha nodded. "We figured Mama's stuff could be put

on a serious-type website or two. And my stuff could go on Facebook and in a blog. Some kids at school have blogs, so I was thinking about that blogger dot com site."

Cumberland shook his head. "We should keep you under the radar so no one can find out who really writes it. I can do that real quick. We need a false identity and a catchy name for your blog."

Samantha thought about it. "How 'bout, Frogtown Girl Sez, with sez spelled S E Z."

Cumberland said, "Frogtown is that neighborhood just north of downtown."

"You know where it is? Cool."

Josie was surprised. "How do you know Frogtown, Sam?"

"Kids at school say it's hip."

"And your pseudonym…" Cumberland said.

Samantha looked at Josie then back at Cumberland. "Let's call me Kikelomo Torres, the African Latina. From Jalisco, Mexico."

Josie's surprise turned to shock. "More information you got from school?"

"We had a class on different ethnic names. Kikelomo means a cherished child in Western Africa."

"And that's you."

"I don't know," Samantha said. "Am I cherished?"

Cumberland was holding his fingers above the keyboard, still waiting to type.

"I'm not interfering," Josie said. "I'm just interested. You can type, Cumberland."

"I'm waiting, Mama."

"What? Oh. Yes, you're cherished. That's all I do. Cherish you."

Samantha turned to Cumberland. "Lots of cherishment going on in our family." She bent down and hugged Unknown, who stood unmoving and tolerant.

"Right," he said. "How do I spell Kikelomo?"

Samantha told him.

He typed and clicked and dragged what looked like

templates. He searched on the name Kikelomo, went to some websites, and sampled some images.

"Okay, look at this, Samantha. Here's a blog setup. The colors are bold. They come from the Yoruba people in West Africa. The blog title, Frogtown Girl Sez, is at the top. Your name is over here on the left panel. Kikelomo Torres, the African Latina. The right panel is where you'll archive your posts."

"And the center panel is where my writing goes?" Samantha asked.

"Yeah. I'll show you how. You click on the New Post button, choose a label and pick a date for publication, then paste in your article. You can also upload photos directly into your article and move them around and size them however you want."

"Monster photos!" She bent over and picked up Unknown, then set her down. "Hear that, Unknown? I get to post monster photos."

"Whatever," Cumberland said.

Josie couldn't see Cumberland's face because he was in front of his computer, but she got the sense that Samantha's outburst gave him a little smile.

Cumberland typed some more, then said, "Does it make sense how to do this?"

"Yeah." Samantha turned to Josie. "Mama, I have a blog."

"Yes, you do, Frogtown Girl."

Cumberland glanced at Josie. "Professor Strong, I think your articles should go on some kind of scholar site. It might take me some time to find a good one. Or maybe I'll just make a new website. A real boring name like Medieval Times or something."

"Okay," Josie said. "I was thinking Criminology Quarterly. But the name Medieval Times is probably perfect." As Josie said it, she actually felt a small bit of envy for Frogtown Girl Sez.

"That's all I need," Cumberland said. "I'll have something up in a day or two."

When they got home, Josie once again felt uneasy. There was a faint smell in their condo. Something vaguely like tobacco.

Samantha didn't comment, so it wasn't especially noticeable to her. Unknown wasn't sniffing the condo, so apparently she didn't think anything was unusual, either.

Josie thought of Mandy Collar, the older woman who lived on the ground floor on their side of the building and who was a smoker. When Mandy had her windows open, her smoke would sometimes drift up to Josie and Samantha's condo.

But this smell wasn't caustic like smoke. More like a pouch of pipe tobacco. Or sandalwood soap.

Had Theo Mosconi worn obvious deodorant or cologne? What about his colleague, José Rodriguez? Josie hadn't noticed.

Josie didn't say anything to Samantha as she looked to see if anything had been disturbed. She saw nothing that made her worry.

TWENTY

The next morning, when Josie arrived at her university office in Bunche Hall, her desk phone rang.

She set her purse and briefcase down and answered it.

"Professor Strong, Medieval History," she said.

"Good morning, professor. Theo Mosconi calling from the Bureau of Investigation."

Josie's gut clenched. It should have been no surprise that Mosconi called her UCLA office phone number. It was a public number, published in the university catalogue. But it still startled her.

"Hello," Josie said, her voice dry and with as little emotion as she could muster. "What can I do for you?"

"You haven't gone to Yosemite, yet?"

"No. However, we're getting close."

"Good. I'm calling with new information you should have. A man was found dead in Yosemite yesterday evening. We suspect our cop killer may have been involved."

"I'm sorry to hear that someone died. What makes you think your suspect is connected to the man's death?"

"First, the victim was shot to death, possibly by the same type of weapon preferred by our suspect. Second, the victim fits the same profile as our suspect. Similar age, similar socioeconomic stratum, dirty clothes, several days of beard stubble."

"I don't understand."

"Killers and victims often come from the same territory. Doctors are often killed by people in the medical field. Bartenders are often killed by people who hang out in bars. Drug dealers are often killed by other drug dealers. This current victim in Yosemite has the earmarks of our suspect. Judged by their clothes and hygiene, they could be brothers. No ID is our strongest link, as our cop killer took the IDs of both deputies after he shot them."

"Why would he do that?"

"No reason other than a personal quirk. Many killers take some aspect of their victim. Think of it as a trophy."

"Excuse me," Josie interrupted. "How do you determine socioeconomic stratum on a victim with no ID and who you can't identify?"

"There are actually many ways. Condition of teeth. Brand and age of clothes. Personal grooming habits."

"Personal grooming correlates with economic status?" Josie couldn't keep the disdain out of her voice.

"You'd be surprised," Mosconi said. "You can predict a man's education and income by how often and how carefully he clips his nails. There are exceptions of course, but the correlation remains strong. It may seem counter-intuitive, but very often, killers and their victims come from similar backgrounds. This information might help you find the killer."

Josie was silent on the phone as she thought about it.

"Any indication of motive in this new shooting?"

"No. We'd guess it was a dispute of some kind. The victim was probably living in the forest in a similar way. Maybe he knew his killer for some time."

"How do you think this will impact my search?"

"Maybe not at all. But if you learn about it, I don't want you to be blind-sided by the news. The takeaway is that the man you're searching for should be considered very dangerous, so be very careful."

"I understand. Anything else I should know?"

"No. Stay in touch." Mosconi hung up.

Josie sat for some time and thought about what Mosconi had told her. She had many questions, but came to no conclusion. She didn't think this new death dramatically changed her plan other than to reinforce the notion that she should leave Samantha in Santa Monica and go to Yosemite herself.

But she'd already told that to Samantha, and Samantha was adamant that she would come with Josie, no matter what the risk.

Josie turned to her desk work, which, for a professor, was never-ending.

After two hours, she got out her new dumb laptop that wasn't connected to the internet so she could work on more articles about Grendel without worry that someone could monitor her. She realized that some or all of the articles they'd given Cumberland the day before were probably already posted online. She thought about how much illusion could be created by stories and articles. Undoubtedly, a great deal.

But there were few things as convincing as bits of physical evidence. If the man they were chasing saw Grendel's mark, or if someone he knew reported to him that they'd seen Grendel's mark, that would be very compelling.

As Josie thought about obtaining a branding iron, her first decision was whether this pursuit was part of their Private World or their Normal World.

Josie and Samantha needed to present a significant portion of their activities as part of their Normal World so that anyone monitoring them would know that they were working according to the Bureau of Investigation deal.

But Josie didn't want to show all her cards. If there was a leak in Theo Mosconi's world and the murderer learned that Josie and Samantha were making Grendel brands, their cover would be blown. That could be a deadly mistake.

So she decided that presenting physical evidence would be in their Private World. No need for anyone to know.

UCLA had dozens of libraries and research centers, most small and devoted to specialty collections. Josie left her badge and phone in her office desk and walked out of her office. She went over to the Charles Young Library and found a computer that wasn't connected to her.

She looked up branding irons and learned that many different types could be ordered online. However, most were electric, something that would not work in the forests of Yosemite. To have an old-fashioned branding iron made would likely require a blacksmith. It was an ancient profession, yet she found several in the Los Angeles area. Two were near the City of Industry. One was called Ralph Ellison Blacksmith.

It was, of course, the name of a famous author. But something else about the name seemed familiar as if she'd seen or read about the business before. She called the number using a library landline phone that was maintained for faculty use. She got an outgoing message recorded by a rough, older voice. "Ralph Ellison. I'm usually here eight to three. Closed for lunch and all day Friday through Sunday."

Josie wrote down the address.

Josie went back to her office and found an old paper map of Los Angeles. After studying it, she thought she could probably take light rail and then buses and eventually get close to where she wanted to go. But she'd still have to take a cab for the final distance. Uber was out, because it was powered by credit cards and the internet and thus was trackable. Either way, transportation without using her own car might take most of a day in transit. She didn't have that much time.

Cumberland had said that they could put a tracking device on her car.

If they had, and if the subject of where she went was a problem, she'd look for a more likely destination, like a store that she might logically shop at. She could park near there and walk to the blacksmith shop. If she didn't bring her phone, the disparity between the badge, phone data, and car info would be a giveaway that she was hiding her activity.

She decided to leave the badge in her desk. That could seem like a reasonable oversight. But she would bring her phone. They could read any of the location pings and feel reassured that she wasn't hiding her activity. A careful balance between their Private World and Normal World was critical to make them think she didn't deserve any more careful observation.

Josie left with her phone, got cash at an ATM on the UCLA campus, and went to the UCLA garage where she parked her Prius.

She took the 10 freeway east, past Los Angeles, and stayed on the road where the name changed to Highway 60. Thirty miles east, she came to the City of Industry. She made a few wrong turns, but eventually found an old warehouse district behind a shopping center. The buildings were made of brick and were probably 100 or more years old. They appeared to have never been updated from when they were built. The parking area was gravel and dirt with weeds poking up here and there. There were no street lights.

Josie drove over to the shopping center and parked, then walked back.

The doors of the building that housed the blacksmith were rusted, dented metal that blended in with brick walls that were painted rust-red. The signs above the doors were hand painted. Each section of the building had a small single garage door that was not nearly tall enough for modern trucks. The garage doors weren't the multi-panel kind that raised up on tracks. They were heavy solid doors coated with rusted sheet metal that hinged up as a single piece. Each garage door had heavy padlocks on both sides. Half of the doors were open, letting much-needed light and air into dark workshops. Some of the walk-in doors were also propped open.

The address Josie was looking for was on metal numbers nailed into the mortar between the bricks. 4352 - B.

There was a sign made of sheet metal with painted words, also nailed into the masonry. The sign was forest green, the words were painted with sky blue.

Ralph Ellison - Blacksmithing - Metal Fabrication

Josie walked up and stepped inside the open garage door. A ding-dong doorbell sounded, triggered by a light beam across the garage opening. Josie stood in the shadows. The inside of the building was very dark compared to the blinding sun outside. She waited for her eyes to adjust.

An incessant hammering came from farther back in the space, the sound like metal on metal. A gravelly voice called out, "Be there in a minute." The hammering continued for another thirty seconds, then stopped.

A man walked out from the darkened shadows of the shop. He looked a bit like a primitive spaceman, covered in strange garb. He was pulling off heavy leather gloves that reached up to his elbows. He set the gloves on a long workbench that was made of metal. Next, he pulled off safety goggles with very dark lenses. They hung from a cord around his neck. He reached up and pulled off a heavy leather hood that had a built-in collar. He put that with the gloves.

He walked forward toward the front of the garage where the incoming light made him more visible. Josie saw that he was a tall, beefy black man, mid-seventies, with curly white hair cut close, and a little white moustache. He wore a heavy long-sleeved work shirt that was mostly covered by heavy blue denim overalls. Josie thought it an improbably hot outfit considering that the temperature in this part of Los Angeles was very hot in the summer and quite warm in the spring and fall. But she imagined that he worked with hot metal and needed the clothes for heat protection.

"What can I do for you?" he asked. He frowned as he looked at her, up and down slowly. Josie knew that his look wasn't about assessing whether she was attractive. She was an out-of-shape professor. When people told her she had a pretty face, she always suspected those comments were a kind of counter thought to a negative assessment of her physique. And she had already witnessed feeling invisible when she went anywhere with Samantha. Josie decided it was her clothes that made the man look her over. Like most professors, she wore clothes that were unsuited to physical labor. Lightweight cotton pantsuit. Dress shoes. Probably this man's typical customer was a farmer wearing jeans and boots, someone who came in for horseshoes or custom-made tractor parts.

"Are you Ralph Ellison?" Josie asked.

"Yeah."

"My name's Josie St... Stillman. I'm hoping you can make a custom branding iron."

"To brand cattle?"

Josie hadn't thought of it that way. But it only took a moment to realize that if she wanted to be incognito, she needed to not stand out any more than necessary. "Yes, please."

"Does your ranch have a design? A logo?" The man looked skeptical, as if he couldn't believe Josie would have cattle.

"I… We don't have a custom logo. Yet. I'd like to use a capital G for the brand."

"This ranch around here?"

Josie hesitated. She obviously hadn't thought this through carefully enough. If she were going to lie, she should do it boldly. "No. It's in Nevada. But I'm in L.A. on some other business. So if you could just make a large G." She held up her fingers for size. "About like this. Two inches high. That would be great."

The man pulled out a work order pad and a small metal ruler. He set the ruler on the work order and sketched out a capital G. He turned the pad around to face Josie. "Like this?"

"Yes. Maybe just a little bigger. Two and a half inches. But three inches would probably be too big for a brand, don't you think? And I want it to look old-timey and dented up. Like the brand was made back in the nineteenth century and it's been in use for a hundred and fifty years."

He made some notes. "With a standard handle?"

"I suppose. But here's the tricky part. The reason I came to you instead of just ordering it online is I'd like to be able to disguise the branding iron. So I could carry it with me without it being obvious that it's a branding iron."

Ralph Ellison stared at her. "So you can sneak onto someone else's ranch, find cattle to steal, and if you're caught, no one will realize you were going to brand them with your mark."

"No, not at all!" Josie said. Then she wondered if the man was joking but keeping a straight face. "I mean, that's a good joke. So I suppose you could think of it that way. I just want it to be disguised somehow. I have no idea how you'd do that."

The man continued to stare at her as if hesitating because he had an ethical problem working for criminals.

The man turned the work pad around and said, "Name?"

"Josie. Stillman."

"Phone?"

Josie recited the phone number for her burner phone.

"Address?"

Josie gave him the address for her UCLA office without including the letters UCLA.

"I can't say how much this is going to cost," he said, "until I figure out how I would disguise the iron. But I'll need a deposit check. Normally, I give an estimate and ask for fifty percent down. In this case, it's just a guestimate. Let's say three hundred dollars for a deposit."

Josie was surprised. If that was his estimate for a half-down deposit, Josie wondered why there weren't blacksmiths on every corner. Then again, she had no idea how much work was involved in making a custom branding iron.

"Cash okay?" she said.

"Preferred," he said.

Josie paid him. She was glad she'd stopped at the ATM. She normally didn't carry cash. The man made a note on the work order, then looked at her.

"May I have a receipt?" she asked.

He scribbled out a receipt and handed it to her. It was barely legible.

"Thank you. I'm hard to reach, and my phone is unreliable. When would be a good time to check back with you?"

He looked at his calendar. "Try Thursday. I'm not saying it'll be done. I'm just saying when to call."

"Got it. Thanks."

Josie turned and walked back out into the blazing sun.

TWENTY-ONE

On Thursday, during their Private World morning walk, Josie pulled out her burner phone and called the blacksmith shop. Before the phone was answered, she remembered that she hadn't used her real name.

"Ralph Ellison," the man answered.

"Hi, Josie Stillman calling." She saw Samantha jerk her head and stare at her. She had forgotten to explain that she'd used a fake name. "You said I should call today and see how the branding iron is coming."

"Oh, lady, you're gonna love how I did it. It's all done. Come by any time. I'm here until four."

"Great, I'll be there around three-thirty." She thought that would give her enough drive time. Josie said goodbye and hung up.

"Josie Stillman?" Samantha said. "That's cuz this is Private World stuff?"

"Yes, it is. Sorry, I forgot to tell you."

"No sweat. Can Unknown and I come along?"

"You'd have to come home after school to leave your phone so they can't track where we go. I wonder if there's enough time."

"I can leave my phone at home all day. I'll be ready by two. Will that work?"

"Yes. Perfect."

That afternoon Josie and Samantha took Unknown in the car and drove to the shopping center near the blacksmith's shop. By prior agreement, they did not speak of any Private World subjects during the drive.

"School going okay?" Josie asked as they headed east on the

10.

"Yeah. We did have a scary thing happen. One of the boys, Tommy Johnson, had a seizure."

"Has he had seizures before?"

"I guess so. Tommy's younger brother Leo said he's epileptic. He gets seizures every few months or so, even though he takes pills for it."

"Is Tommy okay?"

"It seems like it. The teacher called nine, one, one, and an ambulance came and picked him up. But Tommy was already getting back to normal by the time the ambulance got there. Leo said that Tommy goes totally unconscious, and, after it's over, he can't remember what happened. Leo said it normally takes half an hour or more for Tommy to regain consciousness. And then he's usually kind of spacey for half a day."

Unknown was sitting on Samantha's lap. Samantha pet her as she stared out the car window. "Do you know what causes seizures?" Samantha asked.

"I don't know much about it. I've heard there are different kinds of seizures. I know some people with epilepsy have them, and most epileptics get by okay. I've also read that some children with epilepsy get better as they get older."

"You're born with it?" Samantha said.

"I think you can be. But sometimes a brain injury can cause it. Like an accident. Or a stroke. Either way, it's probably scary to witness."

"The scariest thing was how everybody reacted."

"What did they do?"

"They just kind of freaked out. Tommy had fallen to the floor, and he was doing this jerking thing. Leo said it's called convulsions. His back was arched, and his arms were jerking. His eyes were white, like they were sort of rolled back, and he was kind of foaming at the mouth. The kids couldn't handle it. Some were yelling, 'Oh, my God,' and a couple were crying, 'He's going to die!' Even the teacher was yelling, 'Everybody get back!' It's like they couldn't think straight. And all the time, Leo was saying to stay calm and that Tommy would be all right."

"Did the ambulance take him away anyway?"

"Yeah. Probably a cover-their-ass kind of thing. So no one can blame the school for not doing everything possible."

"Cover their ass?" Josie said.

"Basic life info, right, Mama? What's that called? Liability. Something lawyers do?"

"You're probably right. Although I don't know that they do it, so to speak. They try to prevent liability."

Twenty minutes later, Josie parked at the shopping center near the blacksmith's shop.

It was too hot this far from the ocean to leave Unknown in the car for any length of time. So Samantha took her by the leash, and the three of them walked over to the shop. Samantha frowned as they approached the dark garage door opening.

"Don't worry," Josie said. "This man seems safe."

Ralph Ellison walked out of the dark area at the rear of the space.

"Hi. Josie Stillman here to pick up my branding iron."

The man looked at her, then at Samantha. He walked over to a wall with various hooks holding decorative pieces of iron. He lifted a piece off a hook, brought it over and set it on the counter.

"Here's your branding iron." He glanced at Samantha. "The Big G stands for Goodness, ha, ha," he said.

Josie thought it seemed a strange joke. Samantha didn't speak.

The man said, "You're too young. When I was a kid back in the fifties, the Saturday morning cartoons often had commercials featuring cereals made by General Mills. Their ad line was The Big G stands for Goodness. They still have the G on some of their packages." He touched the iron G as if feeling for flaws. "I designed this branding iron based on their Big G."

He lifted it up. "You said you wanted it to look rough and old-timey. So I nicked the edges here and there and hit it with a hammer to deform it a little. I also filed off a bit of the curve. I've tested it on different kinds of leather. Works well. The G image is rough but legible."

Josie picked it up and looked at it up close. She tried to visualize using it.

"That's what you wanted, right?" The man sounded insecure.

"Oh, I'm sorry, it's perfect. Just perfect. Thank you very much."

"I gave it a twenty-four inch handle. Long enough so you don't get burned or inhale smoke from burning flesh. Short enough to put in a travel bag. The G at the end unscrews. You also said you didn't want it to be recognized as a branding iron if someone saw it. Figuring out a way to disguise it was the trickiest part. So here's what I did." He went back to the wall and took an umbrella and a leather belt off another hook and brought them over. "The handle on this umbrella unscrews." He twisted it off. "The handle on the branding iron also unscrews from the G." He did the same on the branding iron. "You screw the branding handle into the umbrella top, making the branding handle the umbrella's new handle. It just looks like an ordinary umbrella!" He demonstrated. "Disguising the big G was harder. Not only is it big, but once I'd tried it a few times, it got blackened with smoke and char. So I created a belt buckle that will be the perfect disguise for a branding iron."

He lifted up the belt. Josie could see that it had an iron buckle that consisted of letters. It looked like they said ranny. The man worked a catch and slid the G onto the buckle. It clicked into place. The blacksmith held it up and grinned proudly.

The belt buckle spelled out Granny, with the G much larger than the other letters.

"Granny?" Josie said, incredulous. First he thought she was too young to know old advertising lines. Now he thought she was old enough to be a granny.

"Yeah, isn't it great? I put nicks and dents and char on all the letters so they would go with the G."

"Granny?" she said again.

Samantha started giggling at her side.

"But I'm not a granny," Josie said. "I'm barely old enough to even be a granny unless my lineage featured women who were fecund in their teens."

"Fecund," he said. "Haven't heard that one in a long time. Just remember the fact that the granny buckle is obtrusive is what makes it a perfect disguise. And anyway, one would never think but nobly of a grandmother, right?"

"What?" Josie was too distracted by the granny concept to pay attention to what he was saying.

The man continued, "You can go out to any ranch while you're wearing your branding belt and carrying your umbrella and no one will ever realize what they are. Once you find your cattle, you assemble the branding iron, get them branded, then reinstall the branding G on the belt buckle." He spread the belt out across the counter. "See, I even used an embossing machine to print the word 'granny' on the belt leather. You'll be a walking granny advertisement. I guarantee that no one would ever think this is a branding iron."

Samantha had her fist at her mouth, trying to muffle her laughter. It sounded like she was having trouble breathing.

The man stared at Samantha.

"Hi," she said. "I'm Samantha. I'll get her to appreciate the sense of the whole granny belt thing."

"Good," he said.

Josie inhaled deeply. She had nothing against grannies and even thought that she might one day look forward to being a grandmother. But being called a granny at her age was even worse than being called ma'am. Not that he'd called her granny. But still… Josie took another breath. Focus on the task at hand, she thought.

"How do I heat this up?" she asked.

"Easy. Just build a charcoal fire and rest the branding iron in it."

Josie realized that would be unworkable in many locations in the Yosemite forest. "Is there a way to do it without so much production?"

"Sure. Just use a propane torch," the man said.

"Where do I buy one?"

"At any hardware store or one of the big home improvement

stores. Home Depot or Lowe's."

"Is there a certain kind of torch?"

He went over to a workbench, picked up a propane torch, and brought it over. "Get one like this."

"Do I just point the flame directly at the G?"

"Yeah. Move it around a little, and heat it until the G starts to turn red hot. If you want to be real careful, wear safety goggles."

"Why? What might happen?"

"Sometimes a little piece of hot metal can spark off the iron. You wouldn't want that in your eye."

"No, I wouldn't. Thank you."

"When the iron is hot, press it into the skin of the cow or steer and hold it there for about three seconds. Don't breathe the smoke. I don't know how one restrains the steer and keeps him from kicking you. But your ranch men will know all that."

"Of course," Josie said, wondering what she was getting herself into.

Samantha giggled some more.

"It takes several minutes after using the brand for it to cool down. I don't want you to burn yourself when you clip it back onto your belt buckle."

"I could maybe cool it faster in water. Would that be okay?"

"Sure. With a branding iron, we're not very concerned with tempering or quenching issues. The iron will remain strong enough for its purpose."

As Josie pulled out her wallet and removed her credit card, she mumbled 'granny' again. Then she remembered about credit card tracing. So she put her card back in her wallet and paid the balance with cash. Of course, the Bureau people could find out how much cash she was withdrawing from her bank account. But it wouldn't be so easy to find out what she bought with the cash.

She thought the cost of the branding iron was a large fee. But then she was getting actual useful items. She wasn't sure she could say that for her teaching at UCLA, and they paid her a large fee as well.

Josie thanked him and picked up the belt, trying to roll it so the granny embossings were on the inside and didn't show. Samantha picked up the Big G brand, and they left.

They walked over to the shopping center. After Samantha put Unknown in the back seat and got into the front, she started laughing again. "Mama, I've never seen you so bent out of shape about age."

Josie raised her finger to her lips. She started the car. Samantha turned on the radio. A girl group came on with a catchy song. Samantha dialed the volume up loud. "Anyway," Samantha continued in a soft voice, leaning over toward Josie so she could be heard, "I don't think you look old. But it's funny to see you get so agitated."

"Just you wait," Josie said, still upset. "A few years from now, someone's going to call you ma'am, and you'll be bent out of shape. That's when you can start counting the days before someone asks if you have grandchildren."

"Mama, calm down. He was just trying to think of a disguise for the G brand. I think his solution was perfect."

"You think I'm actually going to wear that belt?"

Samantha took a moment to reply. "If you swallowed your pride and did wear it, it would be perfect. Everything about the granny image would communicate to the killer that you were no threat at all. And if I'm near you, then I would seem like I'm no threat at all, either."

Josie drove to a hardware store, and they bought a propane torch, a sparker, and some safety goggles. She couldn't think of a way to disguise the torch or sparker or goggles.

She thought of asking the employee about a good way to disguise them but decided that the effort of disguising a torch might raise eyebrows. She didn't want to end up on any kind of arson watch list.

Before they got back into the car, she asked Samantha. "Do you have any idea of how to disguise a propane torch?"

Samantha picked it up and turned it around in her hands.

"We could find a cloth bag to carry the propane tank. With

the bag rolled up, the tank would fit across the bottom of a backpack."

"Then we need to find a backpack. But not one of those canoeing packs like we used in the Quetico wilderness."

"A Duluth pack? No, Mama. We need to blend in when we get to Yosemite. No one uses Duluth packs except for canoe trips. Camping clothes, hiking boots, hiking backpacks. There's an REI on Santa Monica Boulevard."

"Is that a sporting goods store?"

"I can't believe you don't know what REI is. It's kind of an outdoor adventure store. Camping, hiking, biking, kayaking. They'll have backpacks. We should each get one for Yosemite."

As Josie drove home back to the coast, Samantha said, "I was surprised by that old guy."

"Why?"

"Because when you went all professor on us and used that word fecund, he knew what it meant. I didn't. When you said fecund, you were referring to people like me making babies. That would be bad."

"At your age, yes. It's very simple to avoid."

"Right, Mama, no sex. If you knew the boys in my school, you wouldn't worry about me. Talk about geeky weirdos and jocks who think they're God's gift to women. They're not at all attractive."

"And when you're older," Josie said as if Samantha hadn't even spoken, "you always make sure you carry birth control."

"So if I lose control one way, I have control another way."

The subject made Josie exquisitely uncomfortable. She simply nodded. The girl group song had been replaced by a song where the singing sounded like it came from a kazoo that was filled with oil.

"Oh, I love this song," Samantha said.

Josie thought the world might be approaching its end.

A minute later, still speaking in a low voice that could barely be heard over the noise on the radio, Josie said, "What I said at that guy's shop was probably too revealing of me. But he came back with the word obtrusive." Josie knew they were in Private

World mode, but she didn't think she'd said too much.

"Obtrusive is kind of in-your-face in a bad way, right?" Samantha said.

"Correct. So he was being somewhat professorial too. And what was that other thing he said? That it would be bad to think but nobly of a grandmother. I think that comes from Shakespeare."

"So the blacksmith dude has some literature chops," Samantha said. "Makes ya wonder."

"It was different phrasing, at any rate."

"Or just kinda weird."

They went to REI and bought backpacks, olive for Josie and khaki for Samantha.

"These are good for blending into the forest," Josie said. "But there's no skull and crossbones on this pack, Sam. Do we need to go someplace to get stickers or something?"

"No, Mama, I think I'm past the Goth phase. I kind of like this muted tone. This pack won't distract from me."

"You're now in the me phase?"

"I've always been in the me phase."

TWENTY-TWO

Before they got back in the car, Josie realized that they needed experience in using the branding iron. She said, "I want to go test the branding iron. Do you want to come along?"

Samantha nodded with enthusiasm.

At the car, Josie gathered the belt, the umbrella with the enclosed branding iron handle, the propane torch and sparker, and put them all in her new backpack. She added the water bottle that she always kept between the seats.

Josie drove over to Pacific Palisades. She turned on Sunset Boulevard, headed to Will Rogers State Park, and parked near the polo field.

After they were out of the car, Samantha said, "Where are we going to test the branding iron, Mama?"

"I'm not sure. We need seclusion, so no one sees us and wonders if we're trying to light a fire. We also need to find a log or two with defensible space around it."

"What're we going to defend?"

"I just mean a bare area around the log so no spark could start a fire. Then we can test the branding iron on a log."

"Can you carry the pack, Cap'n?" Josie asked.

"Aye, Matey, and I'll hold Unknown's leash, too." Samantha said. "You set a course and plan the pyrotechnics."

Samantha swung the pack up on her back. After they'd walked a short distance, Samantha said, "This is a lot of equipment to carry, Mama. Are you thinking we'll haul all this stuff through Yosemite?"

Josie said, "I don't know. That's why we're doing a test to see what works and how hard the process is."

As they headed out one of the trails past the Will Rogers ranch home, Josie said, "Where did you learn a word like pyrotechnics?"

"It's a current boy thing at our school. They're into anything that blows up."

"What a reassuring thought," Josie said.

"But the girls aren't into those boys."

Josie thought this was probably not a good subject to probe. But she couldn't help herself. "What kind of boys are the girls into?"

"Rappers, mostly."

The answer came much too quickly for Josie's comfort. "You're not serious," Josie said.

"Of course I am. Why wouldn't I be?"

Josie inhaled a deep breath and held it. She didn't know how to deal with subjects like her daughter being interested in rappers.

After they'd hiked a half mile or more, Josie pointed to a side trail. They followed it and worked their way over a ridge and down into a small ravine that was bare dirt. The forest stretched below them. The Pacific shimmered in the distance.

"This might be secluded enough," Josie said.

Samantha looked around. She said,

"A space defensible
Makes the place commendable
So the fire that's good for branding
Can't burn down the hood where we're standing."

Josie started laughing. "You really are skilled with words."

"Maybe being a rapper would be better than writing a horror novel."

Josie was appalled. First, Samantha said she'd write romance novels. Then horror novels. Then rap. Where had she gone wrong?

"What's wrong, Mama? I can tell you don't like it. What's wrong with rapping?"

"Nothing's wrong with the part of rapping that's all about words. I think that is a kind of poetry. Performance poetry. It's the other aspects of rapping that bother me. Rappers treating women like chattel, calling them Hoes, women treating rappers like gods, acting like mindless groupies."

"You're all about respect, Mama."

"Yes, I guess so. The only so-called respect where I grew up was for the gang bangers who ran the hood."

Josie set the propane torch on the dirt so it stood up straight. She unhooked the Big G from the granny belt buckle and screwed the handle into it. She bent over and opened the valve until she heard escaping gas. Then she held the sparker near the end of the torch and squeezed it. It produced an impressive shower of sparks. On the third squeeze, she managed to get the sparks to fly toward the escaping gas, and the torch lit. Josie picked up the brand and held the Big G in the flame.

Josie spoke as she heated the branding iron, "I can visualize the horror movie credits. Samantha Strong. Writer. Producer. Director."

"But what's the horror movie title?" Samantha asked. She looked at Josie's propane torch.

"Nightmare on Strong Street?"

"Um, I don't think so. That's kinda lame."

"How about The California Propane Torch Massacre?"

"Or," Samantha said slowly as she watched Josie working the torch, "The Night of the Burning Dead." Samantha started giggling.

Josie was so pleased to hear her daughter's mirth.

"No, wait, I've got it." Samantha began jumping up and down like she was training for volleyball. "Remember the shark movie? Jaws?" She pointed at Unknown and yelled, "PAWS!"

"Oooh," Josie moaned. She put on her most demented face and spoke like a TV announcer. "Just when you thought it was safe to go back to the dog park..."

Samantha started shrieking. "YES!" She picked up Unknown, turned two circles, and set her down. "Isn't that cool, Unknown? You can be the canine monster that terrorizes Southern California. Oh, Mama, that decides it. I'm gonna write horror movies."

Josie returned to her task of heating the branding iron.

After a minute, Samantha said, "If someone sees you doing this, it won't look good, will it?"

"No, Sam. But we're away from fuels. If anyone asks, we'll just tell them the truth. We're testing a branding iron." Josie looked around. "We need some kind of old log. Can you find something?"

Samantha and Unknown walked off.

Josie continued to hold the Big G brand in the flame.

The fire was blue, and where it wrapped around the brand, the flame turned yellow.

"Got a log," Samantha announced as she and Unknown returned. She dropped it on the dirt. It was a large dead branch, about six inches in diameter and six feet long. The bark had fallen off, leaving some smooth wood that would show a brand.

Samantha looked at the branding iron. "How do you know when it's hot enough?"

"I'm not sure. I think Ralph Ellison said it should be red hot."

"You can't tell when the sun is shining on it."

Josie shifted around so she was blocking the sun and shading the branding iron.

"Does it look to you like it's hot?" she asked.

"I can't tell."

"Is that smoke coming off it?" Josie asked.

"Can't tell, Mama. But I just got a whiff. It smells bad. Bad and hot. Like burning metal."

"How do you know what burning metal smells like?"

"Same as pyrotechnics I suppose. From the boys who play with fire."

Josie was appalled. "Boys teach you what burning metal smells like?"

Samantha was staring at the brand. "Shouldn't you be trying it?"

"Okay." Josie pulled the brand from the blue torch flame and pressed it against the log. Nothing happened. After ten seconds, she pulled it away. There was just a hint of a brownish

G in the wood.

"You didn't burn it, Mama. You just toasted it a little. You gotta burn it."

Josie put the brand back in the flame. She held it there until it was glowing bright red. Then she pressed it against the log.

Smoke rose up.

"Now we're talkin'," Samantha said.

Josie pulled the brand away from the wood.

A blackened G shape was obvious.

Samantha bounced up and down on her toes. "Mama, look. It's totally great. The monster Grendel just flew in on a time-travel flight and gave that log a hot lip lock."

Josie stared at her daughter. "What does that mean, lip lock?"

"You know. Like how boys start out when their real goal is a body grab."

"Sam, what are you saying? What exactly happens with a lip lock and a body grab?"

"Just… You know. Kissing and such."

Josie looked at the black Big G mark. "I don't think I like you growing up."

"Don't worry, Mama, I got Unknown to protect me."

"At school? And, anyway, it's 'I have Unknown to protect me.' You can't say 'I got' and..."

"Expect to get into college," Samantha interrupted. "I know that. It's just trash talk. Don't professors ever talk trash?"

Josie stopped to think about it. "I don't know, Sam. Maybe some do. But the ones I hang out with don't."

"You hang out with professors? Really, Mama? Who do you hang out with? Do you go to the coffee shop with them and talk movies or music? Do you trade jokes about the dean? Or is it just serious conversation about your current medieval research?"

"I…" Josie stopped. She was going to protest and explain. But then she realized that Samantha was right. She didn't hang out with anyone. There was no trash talk in her life. She didn't even know what trash talk was. She had no close friends. "I guess I don't have…"

Josie turned away as her eyes moistened with tears.

"I'm sorry, Mama. I didn't mean to upset you. I shouldn't have said that."

Josie swallowed and wiped away tears. "It was good you said it. I need to face the fact that I have no life outside of you and my work. I'm like Cumberland. In the big picture of relationships with other people, I'm a failure. I only got to where I am through constant devotion to my work. And so I conflate work and success. So many of the kids I grew up with didn't care much about school because the schools treated them with no respect. Meanwhile, I was being the perfect little student. If I hadn't been so obsessive about it, I'd probably have friends and be poor. Which is better? At least they have a life outside of their daughter and their work." Josie looked at Samantha and blinked back more tears.

"What you did is better, Mama. What you did was really making something for you and me. It didn't make friends, and that's too bad. But it's not the end of the world."

"Maybe it is."

"No, Mama. You can always make friends."

Josie shook her head. "I don't know how. I don't have a clue about that. What would I do? Call someone I've met and ask if they want to have coffee with me?"

Samantha walked up and touched the side of Josie's face. "Yeah, Mama, that's exactly what you would do. Maybe it would take a little courage. But you could do it."

"I've tried it once or twice. But no one ever wants to have coffee with me."

"Then try it again, Mama."

TWENTY-THREE

Cumberland called on the burner phone. He said he had something to show them.

Josie drove back to their condo, left the Prius in the garage and their phones and badge in the kitchen drawer. Two bus rides later, Josie and Samantha and Unknown got off a good distance from Cumberland's place in Beverly Hills. Their hats were pulled down low as they walked up to the house. He opened the door. He didn't speak, but just brought them downstairs.

"I've found some decent ways of looking at Yosemite from space," Cumberland said.

"That's great," Josie said, trying to sound cheerful and appreciative.

Cumberland walked over to a table and picked up some papers. "I've been sampling infrared satellite photos of Yosemite. One every thirty seconds. Then I run them through comparative data software. Basically, it looks for changes from one photo to the next. Like how astronomers search for things that move against the backdrop of the stars. Then it assigns lines to those movements and tracks the times and frequencies of repetition. I applied a filter that causes it to recognize multiples of the same movements and trace those with a bolder line."

"You mean like movements you'd find at campsites and hotels?"

"Right." He handed a paper to Josie. "These red lines are likely the movements of one or two people in the forest, far from campsites and popular hiking trails. Same with these lines over here."

"Could they also be bears?"

"Probably not," he said. "I noticed that there are frequent lines that go to dumpsters and cabins and through the parking lots. I think those are bears. So I filtered the significant characteristics of those and took them out of the mix. I also made a decision to give more weight to movement during the low light of dusk before dawn and after sunset, because someone in hiding would tend to avoid being out in bright light when he could more easily be identified. The lines that remain on the map are probably a lone individual." He pointed to the paper. "Like this one, here. I think this is a guy who spends most of his time out in the woods a long way from other people."

Cumberland pointed to sheets that he'd spread out on a table.

"This first one is the master map. The scale is distant. It shows all of Yosemite park, which is roughly forty miles north to south, thirty miles west to east. It has a faint topo line overlay. Not easy to read, but if you look carefully, you can figure out the mountains and valleys."

Samantha was standing behind Josie, looking over her shoulder. "The park's shaped like a pear standing up on its narrow end," Samantha said.

"Yeah, I guess so." Cumberland pointed. "I've put a grid on the master map. Each square is labeled, A, B, C, etc."

He picked up a stack of paper and spread some of the sheets out on the table. "These are twenty-four sub-maps, one for each square on the master map. Much closer scale."

Cumberland ran his finger over the maps. "The sub-maps also have grids printed on them, but those squares are labeled with numbers."

"I get it!" Samantha said. "If you tell us to go look in, like, R twenty-two, we'll know to look on sub-map R and square twenty-two, and we'll know exactly where you mean."

"Yeah." Cumberland nodded.

"How will you learn our target's location?"

"The U.S. military has a series of thirty low-orbit satellites called USX-Three Zero that look for infrared emission. They're very good at picking up movements of anything warm. Like machinery with hot exhaust. The military uses them to watch military bases all over the world. Of course, the infrared sensors also pick up the movements of animals."

"When you see a line way back in the woods, how do you tell if you're looking at the guy we're after, or if you're looking at a mountain lion?" Samantha asked.

"People move differently than animals. Think of a person who's walking a dog off leash. As they go down a trail, the dog wanders here and there, sniffing everything. The person walks more in a straight line. Each species of animal has its traits. I've learned it's called a gait signature. The movement type reveals the animal that made it. Most animals are furtive. They sneak around trying not to be caught and eaten. Or, if they're the predators, they sneak around trying not to alert their prey as they prepare to attack it."

Samantha winced.

"Humans are among the most distinct in movement," Cumberland said. "They walk down trails. They don't wander back and forth except in certain situations. That's because they know their next meal is going to come from a restaurant or grocery store. They don't have to be on the prowl for food. And they usually don't worry that they're going to be some other animal's food."

"You think you can find this man?" Josie said.

"I don't know," Cumberland said. "If he's holed up for winter in a log cabin or a cave, and he's got a large stash of food, and he doesn't go out much? Maybe not. Same for if he always stays under really heavy tree cover."

Samantha said, "But even in a log cabin, he'd have a wood stove or something for cooking, and that would make heat the satellite can see."

"Maybe." Cumberland typed on his computer, brought up some images, then pointed to the screen. "I was wondering that very question. If you have a cook stove inside a cave, there would be no appreciable heat visible from above. Or the satellite could see a warm spot, but it looks like a geothermal hot spot because it never moves."

"Are there geothermal spots in the Sierra?" Josie asked.

"Yeah. All over. Some are well-known hot springs. Others

are just warm places that people might even walk by without ever knowing it."

"So what should we do?"

"Go to Yosemite with your Normal World gear. Use it for normal stuff. Talk on your phones, but be guarded about what you say. That way the Bureau will see that you're in Yosemite. They'll see you're doing your job. But you won't give away your trade secrets."

Samantha grinned as she looked at Josie. "See, Mama? We have trade secrets. We're like real spies."

"But also take your Private World stuff," Cumberland said, "these maps and your burner phone. Keep your burner phone on mute. If it shows a message from me, leave your Normal World stuff in your tent, the badge and ID card, your regular phones. When you're sure you're clean, take the burner phone over to a whitewater river and call me back. The river sounds will make enough white noise to cover, and I'll tell you what I've learned."

"Oh, I almost forgot." He walked over to a shelf, pulled off a paper bag, and set it on a table. It was a double grocery bag, two bags, one inside the other, the four paper handles lined up. He reached inside with both hands and lifted up four black cubes, each about two inches on a side. He set them on the table, then reached into the bag and pulled out a key fob.

"I thought you'd want your monster to make, well, monster noises."

Samantha's eyes were wide.

"Yeah, that would be cool!" she said.

"These are speakers," Cumberland said. "They have built-in batteries. Each speaker has an on/off switch and a timer. If the switches are turned on, either the key fob or the timer will activate the speakers. If all the speakers are close enough to the key fob, it will make all of them sound at once. Which you probably don't want. I'm thinking the best thing would be to set the timer to go off in the middle of the night."

"What's the sound?" Samantha asked.

"Your monster. What I did was get a recording of an

elephant making its trumpet sound. It seemed too treble in pitch. I thought a monster should have a much deeper sound." He looked at Josie. "You said you wanted a groaning, moaning sound. So I lowered the elephant sound way down and made it more of a bass pitch."

"Can we hear it?" Samantha asked. She sounded excited.

"Yeah, of course. But the thing is, it's only one volume. I figured it would have to be loud to be heard through the woods. We can listen to it, but I better wrap it up so it doesn't alert all the neighbors."

Cumberland took one of the speakers, switched it on, set it on a corner of the blanket on his bed, and rolled it up. Then he took a comforter and wrapped that around the previous bundle. When he was done, he put the package in his closet and shut the door. He handed Samantha the key fob.

"Wait," he said. He looked at each of the other three speakers, checking the switches, apparently to be certain they were all off.

"Okay," he said.

Samantha hesitated, then pushed the key fob button.

A deep groan rose from within the closet. It got louder, went up in pitch, grew louder still until it was a roar. Samantha backed up, her eyes wide. She started giggling.

The roar continued to increase until it was a deep, throbbing sound like in a horror movie. Josie thought it sounded like an alien creature being tormented.

The roar lessened, dropped back in pitch until it was more like a tormented moan, then gradually died out.

"My God, that's perfect," Josie said.

Samantha was still giggling. "I need this at Halloween!"

Cumberland made a single nod. "The range the key fob works will vary depending on temperature and weather and topography. Even humidity affects radio waves. But I tweaked the output for the maximum distance. Probably fifty yards is the farthest, if the air is clear and you have a straight sight line from the key fob to the speaker. That's another reason to use the timers instead of the key fob. So you can be far away when they go off."

"You can also place the speakers in different places during the day and be far away when they go off. They moan for ten seconds, then stop. If they're set on their timers, you'll have to reset them to get them to howl again. But the ones with the timers turned off will go every time you hit the key fob. Another thing I should tell you is that the speakers aren't real waterproof. I ran a bead of silicone caulk along the seams. But if they sit out in a humid environment, I'm pretty sure they'll go bad after awhile." He unwrapped the blanket and put all of the speakers and the key fob in the paper bag along with the paper maps.

"Thank you so much," Josie said as she picked up the bag.

Cumberland walked with her and Samantha back upstairs to the front door.

"Can I ask a question?" Josie said.

"Yeah." For a moment, Cumberland looked at her. Then he looked back down at the floor, then up and out the window, his eyes always restless, betraying his discomfort with the world.

"I don't want to intrude, but I can tell that things aren't right in your life, Cumberland. I'd like to help. I can do more than just teach medieval history."

"I'm fine," he said.

"I'm serious. When things get difficult, a little help can make all the difference."

"It's just, I don't know, family stuff."

Josie said, "You can tell me. I'm supportive. I know of many resources."

Cumberland glanced at Samantha.

Samantha said, "If you want, I'll go outside, and you can talk to Mama in private."

"No. It's not… It's just that I found out something bad about my dad."

"I've never heard you mention him," Josie said.

"There's not much to mention. He lives in San Jose where he runs a business that isn't real legit. He and mom are divorced. Six years. She got to stay in this house. He pays the mortgage. And he pays alimony and child support. But what I learned…

well, I think I should tell the cops. It would be the right thing to do. But if I do, they'll dismantle his gig. The money will dry up. He'll probably go to prison. No more checks for mom."

"Does she work?"

"Not a regular job. She has... She has some mood problems. She goes to a psychologist every week. But I don't think it helps. She stays a lot at her friend's house in Little Armenia. But if this house has to be sold to pay my father's debts, that's going to make mom's problems a lot worse."

"That's terrible," Josie said. "I'm so sorry. You can probably get your own place, right?"

"Yeah, but I have a younger brother and sister. Aiden and Cara."

"Oh, I'm so sorry," Josie said. "I didn't know about them."

"Aiden's eleven, Cara's nine. They spend half their time with dad. I guess they haven't been around when you've been here. Without the house, Mom and Aiden and Cara will be out on the street. Me, too."

Josie had trouble breathing. She'd taken the wealth of Cumberland's family for granted. "What a terrible dilemma," she said. "If you do the right thing, you put everyone out on the street."

Josie wanted to reassure him, hug him. But she knew that he was not physical like that. She asked, "What does your mother think? What is her plan?"

Cumberland gave Josie a long look. "She doesn't know about this."

"Cumberland, you're all alone in this? Is there no one who can help?"

He shrugged.

"We should help in some way," Josie said.

"We have the condo," Samantha said. "Cara could stay in my room. And Cumberland, you and Aiden could sleep on our fold-out couch." Samantha quickly shot a glance toward Josie. "Was it okay to say that?"

"Yes, Sam," Josie said. "I agree. Cumberland is helping us so much. We should do anything we can. Maybe Cumberland's mom can stay at her friend's house for the time being."

"I haven't decided if I'm going to tell the cops," Cumberland said. "Although, if I don't, maybe I'm committing a crime myself. A moral crime. And it might even be a legal crime to not report it. I don't know how that stuff works. We're not out on the street, yet. And anyway, Samantha's problems with the investigation bureau are way worse. Homelessness is nothing compared to prison."

The three of them stood awkwardly, Josie and Samantha looking at each other and Cumberland looking vaguely at the floor. To his side, leaning against the wall, was the war hammer Josie had given him after he helped them catch the murderer of Samantha's friend.

Samantha stepped forward and hugged Cumberland. "You saved me last month, swinging the war hammer at just the right moment. I'm going to do what I can to save you."

Cumberland stood stiffly, not responding.

Unknown walked over next to Samantha and Cumberland.

Josie stepped forward and hugged them both, a huddle of three. Unknown stood and looked up at the three of them.

Josie and Samantha said goodbye, adjusted their floppy-brimmed hats for maximum coverage, and walked with Unknown down the streets of Beverly Hills to the first bus stop.

They spoke of Cumberland and his siblings all the way home but didn't think of any clear way to help.

"You already told Amelia she could stay at our place," Samantha said.

"Yes. We're going to have to figure out what to do about that."

When they were back home, Josie made a dinner of vegetarian stir-fry.

"No white rice, Mama?"

"I'm trying to lose weight. Anyway, you like brown rice and wild rice."

"It's good, Mama," Samantha said as they ate. "Maybe not as good as McDonalds, but still good." Samantha kept a straight face as she said it.

Josie shook her head in mock disbelief. She pulled their pad of paper closer and wrote the word 'The Blacksmith' on it and turned it toward Samantha.

Samantha nodded.

Josie wrote, 'Remember he said how one should think nobly of a grandmother?'

'Yeah. But I forget the exact words,' Samantha wrote.

Josie thought it was okay to switch to talking. "I looked up that phrase while I was cooking. It turns out it comes from a Shakespeare play called The Tempest. There is a character named Miranda. She's talking to her father Prospero, and she says, 'I should sin to think but nobly of my grandmother.'"

Samantha frowned and said, "That wording is kind of funny. What exactly does it mean?"

"It just means that one shouldn't speak badly of a grandmother. I suppose because grandmothers are important and they're usually good people."

"Like your Bibi was." Samantha added, "What's The Tempest about?"

"Prospero and his daughter Miranda and their two servants are shipwrecked during a tempest."

"That's a storm?"

"Right," Josie said. "They become marooned on an island. The play's about betrayal and revenge and magic."

Samantha frowned as she ate. "I wonder how it is that the blacksmith guy knows about Shakespeare."

"I wonder too," Josie said.

"I think of people who know Shakespeare as, you know, professor types, not blacksmith types."

Josie nodded. "What does it make you think of, a Shakespeare-quoting blacksmith?"

Samantha took her time answering.

"Smart," Samantha said. "Well read."

Josie nodded again.

TWENTY-FOUR

Josie had been to Yosemite once before, back when she was in college. She and two classmates had borrowed a tent and some camping equipment. One of the girls had an old Ford sedan, and they all drove together for three days of camping and hiking. It immediately became—and still remained—the most fun trip Josie had ever been on.

For this trip, Josie found an online outfitter that rented equipment. She picked out a tent and cooking gear. The outfitter offered home delivery, and the equipment arrived the next day.

As Josie and Samantha sorted and packed, they were in Normal World, speaking freely about going to Yosemite. They knew that Mosconi and company expected them to go, so it seemed okay if they were being monitored. By prior arrangement—and hand-written notes to each other—the only area they didn't discuss out loud was their plan for the Grendel universe. The concept of trying to unnerve the killer, the articles Cumberland had placed online, and the branding iron were all kept private, at least for the moment. Josie didn't have a clear idea of what advantages would accrue from keeping that part of their plans private. But her instinct told her it was smart. And all would be made public soon, anyway.

Their packing day was Tuesday. Josie was able to get another professor to help with her classes. And they had arranged with Samantha's school and her volleyball coach for her to be gone Wednesday through the following Wednesday, for a total absence of eight days. Samantha's math teacher protested and told Josie he didn't approve. But he agreed not to make a formal protest with the administration as long as Josie agreed to tutor Samantha during her absence. Josie didn't tell him that she was uniquely unqualified to teach trigonometry to anyone, never mind a girl who thought math was a scourge visited on students only to teach them hardship. But Josie figured that Samantha could make up lost time somehow.

The next morning, Wednesday, Samantha woke agitated. She wanted to talk. So they left their electronics in the condo and took their beach walk in Private World.

"I'm worried, Mama. What if something bad happens in Yosemite?"

"I don't imagine it will."

"You'll need backup," Samantha said.

"You're my backup."

"But what if I can't help you in some way?"

"What do you want me to do, Sam?"

"I think you should make copies of everything. Your Bureau ID, your badge, and every bit of info you can find about what got us into this situation."

"I don't have anything. Remember? Theo Mosconi said he wouldn't give us copies because he thought that would be a security risk to him."

"Then you can write down what you remember. Names, dates, times, locations."

"Then what?"

"You make copies, fold them up, and put them in an elastic bandage that goes around your leg above your knee."

Josie paused. "Is this something you saw in a movie?"

"So what if it is? It's a smart precaution, right?"

Josie didn't immediately respond, then said, "I agree it would be smart."

When they got back to the condo, Josie wrote down everything she could remember. Samantha made copies on the desktop printer. Then Samantha figured out the best way to fold the papers and get them into an elastic bandage.

"Happier?" Josie asked.

"Yes, thank you."

They left Santa Monica and headed up the 405. Their route took them north on I-5, then to progressively smaller roads,

99 to 41 and eventually to Yosemite Valley. The day was one of those sunny fall days that makes California's weather reputation known around the world.

The beach breeze in the L.A. area had been cool and smelled of salty sea spray. The Central Valley was warm and filled with the scents of fall harvest, grapefruit and lemons, nectarines, beets and bok choy, cilantro and cucumbers, lettuce and peas, peppers and plums and wine grapes.

Eventually, they headed into the foothills and came to Fish Camp. From the first meeting with Theo Mosconi, Josie decided not to talk to Samantha about the deputies who were murdered nearby. Their trip already had enough of a dark component. Josie saw no reason to color it darker.

The elevation of Fish Camp was 5000 feet above sea level, higher even than the valley floor of Yosemite. Despite the hot sun, the air in the shade of trees was crisp to the point of cold. The camping gear website had claimed the rental sleeping bags would keep them warm down to freezing. But Josie worried that they hadn't brought enough clothes and extra blankets to stay warm at night.

A few miles past Fish Camp, Josie turned off the small highway and followed a sign that pointed to the Mariposa Grove of Giant Sequoias.

"Where're we going, Mama?" Samantha said as she happened to look up from her phone.

"To see the giant sequoias."

"Trees."

"Yes. Very large trees," Josie said.

Samantha wrote on the pad of paper and held it up for Josie to read while she drove.

'Why trees? Does this have to do with being monitored?'

Josie made a big nod.

"I've seen big trees," Samantha said. "Just look outside the car window. These are way taller than anything at home." Samantha had been looking at her phone. She went back to it.

"Right. But these are toothpicks compared to what we are about to see."

Josie found the parking area.

She wrote on the pad. 'We want anyone monitoring to think we're doing some tourist stuff on our trip. Makes us seem normal.'

It was Samantha's turn to nod.

Samantha was thumb-tapping her phone, sending texts to her friends.

It gave Josie two thoughts. First, it seemed such a waste of focus to go to such a beautiful natural wonder and not even notice, so entrancing was the wonder of a phone.

Her second thought was a kind of sadness, something that also approached envy of Samantha. For even if Josie wanted to text someone about what she was doing or seeing, she didn't have anyone to text. She had many colleagues and acquaintances to whom she could send a text. But there was no one other than Samantha with whom she'd want to share a story or a photo of the world's largest trees, some of which were already hundreds of years old back during the Roman Empire.

They came around a curve in the trail.

"You might want to look up," Josie said.

Samantha lifted her gaze from her phone, glanced at the forest, went back to her phone.

"Did you notice the tree?"

"There's trees everywhere. Are we going to that building?"

"What building?" Josie asked.

Samantha looked up and pointed. "The building with the weird siding… Oh, my God, that's not a building. Is that really a tree? I can't believe it. It's too big."

Josie parked the car.

Samantha put her phone in her pocket and ran to the tree. Unknown followed. She did the tentative trot that was her fastest speed.

Samantha stood before the tree, her head tipped back, her mouth open in exclamation. "Mama, this is the most amazing thing I've ever seen! You look up and it just goes up and up through other trees. It doesn't even have branches."

"It actually has many huge branches. But they come out of

the trunk up above the tops of the other trees."

Samantha trotted around the base of the tree. As she came around, she was beaming. She pulled out her phone and started taking pictures. Josie loved seeing her daughter be entranced by something that wasn't man-made. And she loved that Samantha was sending off thoughts and photos of trees instead of thoughts and photos of celebrities.

After an hour of wandering through the grove, they walked back to the Prius and drove to Yosemite Valley.

As they came into view of El Capitan and Half Dome, Samantha exclaimed again.

"Mama, why haven't we come here before? This place is amazing. First those trees. Now these cliffs… I've never seen rock like that. And that one has snow on top."

Samantha pointed to the right. "Over there is a skinny little waterfall."

"It's not flowing much because it's been so long since they've had any rain. In the spring the waterfalls all gush with snowmelt. This valley has numerous waterfalls, and some are among the tallest on Earth."

"Where's our campground?"

"A few miles up ahead."

Samantha stared as Josie drove. Josie found the North Pines Campground and pulled in. When they got out of the car, the scents of pine and fir and Incense Cedar were intense. The Merced River was next to the campground, and, despite the dryness of fall, was flowing and making musical burbling sounds.

Unknown trotted over to the river, walked down the bank, and lapped water.

"I want to live here," Samantha said, glancing down at her phone. "Except I've got bad cell reception. Can't have that."

"No, of course not," Josie said, feeling like she was jerked back to reality. "By the way, now that we're within the park boundaries, dogs have to be leashed and never left alone."

Samantha looked frustrated.

Josie was about to speak when Samantha said, "I know, you

don't make the rules."

They found their campsite, set up their tent, and organized their gear.

When they were settled, Samantha wrote on a pad of paper and handed it to Josie.

'When do we start our Big G plan?'

'Now?' Josie wrote back.

They shifted into Private World, locking their regular phones and Josie's badge and ID in the Prius.

Josie put the pack with the branding gear on her back and carried the umbrella.

Samantha put Unknown on the leash, and they headed out.

TWENTY-FIVE

The campground had few campers at the end of October. Nevertheless, there were several people around, setting up tents, lighting campfires in preparation for evening cookouts.

After Josie and Samantha walked away and were alone and couldn't be overheard, Samantha said, "Where are we going to do our branding thing?"

"I don't know," Josie said. "My idea is to create two or three brands in areas where people wouldn't normally see them but where they would be easy to find if they read about them."

"Like on the websites where Cumberland put our articles."

"Right. Once we make some branding marks, we can make the locations public."

Samantha said, "And our articles would describe where the Oxford professor supposedly found them."

"Exactly."

"Is it bad to burn a brand in a park?" Samantha asked. "Is that vandalism?"

"I suppose it is. But charring some wood in the forest isn't hugely different from burning wood in a camp fire. And we're trying to catch a killer..."

"And we're trying to keep me out of prison. So the end justifies the means?" Samantha said.

"I think so."

Samantha looked off at the forest. "Do you really think there's a killer hiding in these woods?"

"Maybe."

"That's creepy."

Josie nodded. "Yes, it is. But no more creepy than the tentacle creature feeling your body in the middle of the night."

Samantha grinned.

Josie turned to look at the river and then toward the Ahwahnee Hotel in the distance through the trees.

Samantha said, "The brand locations should be close to where lots of people go," she said. "Near the main trails that lead from the hotels to the popular places in Yosemite." She looked at Josie. "What are the popular places?" Then, "Wait, they're on the map they gave us at the park entrance."

Samantha pulled out the map. "Okay, number one popular spot is El Captain."

"Capitan," Josie said.

"Right. Spanish. Where is it?" Samantha looked around.

Josie pointed. "Do you see that huge wall of rock? It's one of the most important climbing places in all the world."

"People climb that? They must be crazy."

"Maybe they are," Josie said. "Tourists go to take pictures and look with their binoculars at the climbers up on the wall."

"Well, I guess if anyone could climb it, that would be a big deal. That rock looks higher than skyscrapers."

Josie nodded. "More than three thousand feet. It takes days for most climbers to climb it."

"How do they do it?"

"They hook safety ropes into special spikes called pitons, which are pounded into the rock. Then they climb up farther, haul up their ropes, and hook them into the next set of pitons."

"If it takes days to climb, do they come back down each night to eat and sleep?"

"No. They stay up on the rock, hanging in specialty hammocks up on the rock wall."

"They sleep dangling from the rock?" Samantha sounded appalled. "How do they go to the bathroom?"

"I don't know the particulars," Josie said, smiling. She realized she was glad not to know the particulars. Partly, it would change her vision of the brave climbers up on the rock. But it would also mean she'd have to explain it to Samantha, and things like that were always uncomfortable for Josie to explain.

Samantha was still looking at the wall. “I can’t imagine hanging from the rock while you sleep. Living up there on a wall. How do they grip the smooth rock?”

“I think they find little cracks they can get their fingertips into, and they pull themselves up bit by bit. I’ve read that many climbers go much faster now than they did only a few years ago. They go all the way up in a couple of days. And one climber set the new record by climbing the wall in just a few hours.”

“How could you do that, carrying gear and all?”

“I guess he didn’t really carry gear. He did what’s called free solo climbing. No safety ropes or anything. That’s what I wrote about in my article.”

“Oh, our article about the guy whose arm was supposedly ripped off when he fell from the rock, but it was really ripped off by the monster Grendel, which is actually just a made-up horror movie before they had movies.”

“Certainly. Something like that.”

“There’s no way to put a brand mark or one of the monster groan speakers on a wall of rock.”

“No, there isn’t.”

Samantha looked down at her map. “Okay, the next main attraction after El Capitan is Yosemite Falls.”

Josie pointed. “There isn’t much water now, but it’s one of the tallest waterfalls in the world.”

Samantha looked up and stared. Then she held up the map. “There’s a picture of the falls. It must be springtime when they took this photo because there’s a lot of water in the picture. We couldn’t make use of monster groans anywhere near the noise of the waterfall. No one would hear it.”

Josie nodded.

Samantha looked back down. “The next attraction is Half Dome.”

Josie pointed the other direction.

“I see where they got the name,” Samantha said. “What an amazing shape. Makes you wonder how it formed.”

“Indeed,” Josie said.

“I suppose people climb that, too.”

"No doubt."

Samantha looked at the map. "There's a bunch of other waterfalls and cliffs and something called Glacier Point."

Josie pointed toward the sky. "Glacier Point is up there, almost directly above us. But I don't think we would put our Big G brands up there because we'd have to drive or ride a bus. It would be more convenient to just work down here in the valley."

"What if the killer is camping up there someplace?"

"Theo Mosconi made the point that he would likely be close to the campgrounds so that it would be easy for him to steal food and such. I think that makes sense. So in the absence of contrary information, I think we should assume he's closer to the valley floor. We should put our brands where it's relatively easy for him to find them."

"We want other people to see the brands, too, right?" Samantha said. "The more people who see the brands, the more likely it is that the killer will hear about it." Samantha looked off toward the forest. "So we should put our brands near the trails."

"Excellent thinking," Josie said. "You've got the map. You choose our route."

With Samantha's guidance, they hiked the trails and picked out possible locations. They considered how to describe the locations in an article and how easy it would be for someone to find them. Last, they considered how easy or hard it would be to heat up the branding iron and burn it into wood without being discovered during the process.

"We also need the creep factor," Samantha said.

"What's that?"

"Like, if you found a Big G brand, would it creep you out?"

"I don't understand," Josie said.

Samantha stopped walking and looked at Josie. "Mama, you need to watch more horror movies."

"I don't watch any horror movies."

"That's the problem." Samantha pointed toward a parking lot. "Okay, pretend you just found a brand burned into a piece of wood in the middle of that parking lot. The sun is bright, and there are people and dogs walking around, and you can see the hotel not too far away."

"Okay," Josie said.

"No creep factor." Samantha pointed toward the forest. "Now look over there in those trees. See where it's really dark? And there's a boulder about the size of a house, and it's draped by trees and stuff like moss or vines or something. On one side of the boulder is a hole that goes back. Let's say you read that the Big G brand is back in that hole. To see it, you have to get on your hands and knees and crawl through a little opening under the mossy stuff. It's so dark in there that all you can think of is what the article said about the half-eaten body parts they found in that hole. And then, when you reach forward with your hand, you feel something wet and warm and squishy. And just at that moment, you hear a sound above you, and when you look up to see what it is, a tarantula drops onto your face and its hairy legs are sticking into your mouth, and..."

"Okay, okay," Josie said. "I get it. I'm totally creeped out and I'm nowhere near the place."

"That's the creep factor, Mama."

"Got it. Consider me sold."

An hour later, as darkness was descending over the valley, Samantha and Josie had burned only two branding marks. But they were in great locations. One was something like what Samantha had described, inside a cavernous hole in a huge fallen tree trunk. The entire area was overhung with heavy tree cover, fir tree boughs that created a nearly secret room, not unlike the forest hiding place they'd found in the Canadian wilderness the month before. They burned a brand into a dried piece of light-colored wood. They rubbed dirt over it until it looked old and natural, and placed the wood far back in the hole. Samantha took photos of it, using the flash to get a sense of just how hidden it was in the rotting tree trunk.

They took a different approach for the second brand. There was an old trail sign that marked a little-used trail. A tree had fallen on it and broken the post that held the sign. The sign was nearly impossible to see, obscured by the tree that had broken and other trees and brush that draped it.

Josie and Samantha burned a brand into the back of the sign. The brand was hard to see but legible once one saw it.

Unknown pulled toward something off the trail. Samantha walked away with her as Josie was putting her branding gear back in the pack. In a minute, Samantha was out of sight.

"Sam!" Josie called out.

Samantha didn't call back.

Josie started jogging toward where Samantha had gone.

"SAM!"

"I'm right here, Mama."

Josie came up to Samantha and hugged her. "You scared me."

"Don't be so worried. I was just seeing what Unknown found. Look. There's tufts of fur on the ground. Gross. It looks like leftovers from when something killed and ate an animal. It's perfect for what we need."

"You think it looks like Grendel did that?"

"It will when I'm done. Here, hold Unknown's leash."

Josie and Unknown watched as Samantha walked over to a little trickle of water that appeared to be the beginning of a creek. She reached down and scooped out a double handful of mucky dirt. She carried it over and rubbed it on the sign, front and back and across where they'd burned the Big G.

"Now we give our brand some serious punch," Samantha said. She found two sticks, put them together side-by-side, and used them like pincers to pick up several of the fur tufts. She took the fur tufts and stuck them into the mud on the sign, moving them around to make it look like the animal had been slaughtered on or against the sign instead of on the trail.

"Perfect, Sam," Josie said.

TWENTY-SIX

"What's our next port of call, Matey?" Samantha asked.

"Speakers, Cap'n," Josie said in a low voice. "We have to place our speakers."

Samantha nodded. She looked around at the forest. "If the moaning comes from someplace near our brand marks, it would make sense because when the guy eventually finds the brands, they're gonna be near where he thinks he heard the monster."

They hiked into the forest behind and a little above where they had placed the brands.

"This would be a good place," Samantha said.

"Should we set the speakers on timers or use the key fobs?"

"Two of each."

They hid all four speakers in the woods, inside tree hollows, under rock overhangs, beneath piles of pine needles. The two on timers were set to go off in the middle of the night.

"We probably shouldn't test the key fobs," Samantha said.

"No. I think Grendel is nocturnal. We'll wait until it's dark and no one is about. Then we'll sneak out and do the deed."

TWENTY-SEVEN

When they were done hiding the speakers in the woods, they went back to their campsite. Josie walked over to the river and stood next to a section of whitewater that made enough noise to cover her voice. Their other electronics were still in the car, but she had her burner phone. She dialed Cumberland. He didn't answer, so she left a message leaving the map coordinates of both places where they'd burned their brands. According to their previous agreement, he would insert the locations into articles they'd written and post them online.

After leaving her message, Josie thanked Cumberland and hung up.

"Do you think it's bad that we put out our speakers when we don't yet know where the killer is?" Samantha asked.

"I think it's fine. When Grendel moans, he's probably going to be heard all across the wilderness. But either way, once we know where the killer is, we'll be able to focus on that location."

Josie and Samantha had put their food in a bear locker. They pulled out several items and cooked a meal of vegetarian brats and canned beans on their rented propane stove.

Long after they'd eaten and it was time to climb into their tent, Josie said, "Ready to let Grendel moan and howl?"

"That bad boy gonna roar once he outta his cage," Samantha said.

Josie made a little shake of her head. Samantha always surprised her. "Okay, Cap'n, lead the way."

"Aye, Matey."

They hiked with Unknown off into the near darkness, staying on the seldom used trails, but not using their flashlights. When they got within 30 or 40 yards of one of the speakers, Samantha whispered, "You think this is close enough?"

"Yes. Should we hide? If the moan comes as we intend, then we can act shocked and scared in case we see someone."

Samantha looked up and down the path. "It makes sense that we don't even hide. We're just walking when he howls, right? We should kind of act freaked out at the sound. I don't see anyone else out here. But someone could come down the trail at any point. We shouldn't play it cool when Grendel does his thing, because that would be a sign that we know all about it. Don't want that. And no one's gonna know we have the key fobs in our pockets."

Josie nodded in the dark. "I agree." She took Samantha's arm. "We're just walking along, out for an evening stroll, when we hear a monster..." A terrible shrieking, howling erupted from the forest. "You pushed the fob!" Josie said, shocked at the result.

The result was impressive.

Samantha started running back toward their campsite, high-stepping, her legs and feet going up and down like jack hammers. Unknown trotted after her.

The moaning rose from the depths of the woods like an alien creature. It grew in pitch and volume until it was a full-throated roar. Josie put her hands over her ears. The monster moan had the same impact as when a fire truck drove next to her, siren wailing. Samantha's foot pounding seemed to increase. Josie ran after her, falling farther and farther behind.

The howling sound was so loud, Josie had no doubt it could be heard from one end of the valley to the other. It was astonishing, like a monster in unbearable agony and torment.

And then it stopped. Samantha was still running, her feet hitting the ground so hard that Josie could hear them pounding from a distance. Samantha had her hands clenched into fists, and she held them next to the sides of her face.

Samantha stopped. Josie caught up to her and whispered. "Don't push that fob again! Once is enough!"

Samantha made an exaggerated nod.

They hurried down the trail, away from the monster sound.

Unknown came with them, looking back as if to see if some creature would chase them down.

"We're still in Private World, right Mama?"

"Yes."

They jogged over toward the river, then went to their campsite.

Other people were standing up. Some had gotten out of their tents.

One man called out to Josie and Samantha, "Do you know what that was?"

"No!" Josie yelled back.

"What a horrible sound!" he said.

"Yes. It was like some kind of monster or something."

"Maybe it was an alien," the man said. "I've heard that when they get out of their spaceships, something about our air burns their skin off. Maybe it's just a story, but that's what I heard."

Two men came running from the direction of the Ahwahnee Hotel.

"Did any of you hear some kind of howling?"

"Oh, my God, yeah," Samantha said. "It was in the forest over there." She pointed.

"We heard it from inside the hotel. Do you think someone fell or something? Maybe injured themselves?"

The man near his tent said, "No way that was human. It was a monster. Maybe an alien. I'm not going anywhere near that area."

It was a cold night, and they woke up shivering. They draped their extra clothes over their sleeping bags and managed to get back to sleep when the monster moaning came again. Josie was instantly awake, remembering that they'd set two of the speakers on timers. She lay there in the dark, amazed at how horrible the monster sounded even from within the insulation of their sleeping bags. And right after the first monster started howling, a second one started up, a kind of duet of extra-terrestrial agony.

Samantha and Unknown were just inches away, separated from Josie by sleeping bag fabric. Josie could tell that Samantha had wrapped herself around Unknown in an effort to reassure the dog. And to comfort herself.

This time, being farther away and snuggled in their sleeping bags, the sound wasn't so atrocious and scary. But there was no doubt that everyone within miles would be talking about the moaning come morning.

As the sun rose, Josie and Samantha warmed up with coffee and a campfire.

At 11 a.m., Josie's burner phone vibrated.

Cumberland left a message with his phone number. Josie's ID, badge and normal phone were still in the car. She walked over to the Merced River, went upstream until she came to a bit of white water that produced noise, and used the burner to call Cumberland back.

"I got your message," Josie said. "But first, how are you doing? Have you made any decision about your situation with your father?"

"No. Mostly I just lie awake trying to think my way through it. But I haven't figured out any answers."

"You remember our offer to help."

"Yeah, I remember. I think I found the man you're looking for."

Josie had always noticed Cumberland's tendency to go from one subject to another with no pause or segue.

"You have a location?" she asked.

"Yeah. The square labeled Seventeen on map H. You know the main valley in Yosemite, El Cap and Half Dome?"

"Yes. That's where we're camping."

"I think he's in that valley but kind of on the edge and up above the valley floor. Pretty much straight under Half Dome."

"Where you guessed he'd be the last time we talked about it."

"Right. My software logs the time of any movement that I identify for tracking. He moves in the middle of the day and also late at night. What I did was apply an algorithm filter to the movement of people over time. I had the computer map out people movement using red lines. I got a thousand squiggles all over Yosemite, mostly in the valley, a little bit elsewhere. Then I applied a filter that looked for changes in the patterns after your Grendel stories went live. The first day, nothing. The second day, yesterday, a few changes. This morning there was a bunch of new movement, little red squiggles that went to your two Big G locations. It's almost like something major went down last night."

"Something did. It was your speakers broadcasting the Grendel roar. They were beyond amazing. The entire park is riveted by what they heard in the middle of the night!" Josie paused, suddenly worried that she might have said something she didn't want Theo Mosconi to hear. Then she remembered she was on her burner phone and her other electronics were in her car.

"So the Grendel roar worked."

"You can't imagine," Josie said.

Cumberland expressed no surprise or delight. It was as if he knew the roar he created would work. He said, "Most of the new movement came and went from places like the Ahwahnee Hotel and the main campsites. But there was one group of squiggles that came and went from a place where there is no lodging or park building. It's a place up above the valley floor and in the middle of heavy forest. I think that's where he hangs out. Some kind of backwoods campsite. I counted the visits from that spot to the Big G brands. Four trips over last evening and this morning. He didn't go anyplace else. Just the branding spots. And just an hour ago, there was another trip. Real short. It's like he wanted to see the brands one more time. Or maybe he was looking for signs of the monster howling last night."

"Can you tell how far his campsite is from the brand locations?"

Cumberland took a moment to consider it. "I'd guess about a mile. Maybe a little less. Sometimes he appears on one of the main trails like he walked some distance through heavy forest cover and then popped out on the trail. It's hard to see his path when he's in the heaviest forest cover. And then there's times he moves very fast in a straight line. I think that means he's got a mountain bike. Anyway, his main trail goes through grid H Sixteen and H Fifteen, toward the main campsites. On the satellite photos, I can see that most of it is a broad trail. He moved fast on his bike this morning. I'm guessing that daytime movement allows him to scope out the territory when there are tourists around to provide some cover. When he goes out at night, he moves like a bear, going slow, prowling around the campsites, probably looking for supplies to steal."

"Can you tell where his campsite is on the map?"

"I think so. I'd look at H Seventeen, maybe right on the edge of G Seventeen. But I don't know what his shelter is. The reason is because it's under heavy forest canopy. The daytime photos don't show any cabin. The trees are too thick. Based on the topo lines, I think he's partway up a real steep slope. I'm guessing he's under some kind of overhang that gives him shelter from the rain and snow. He might have a view through the trees down toward the valley floor. So he could, you know, see anyone coming."

"Thanks. This is great information. Please call if you learn anything else."

"Okay, bye." Cumberland hung up.

If Josie didn't know Cumberland, she'd think he was very rude, hanging up before she could even say goodbye. Instead, she knew it was just his way.

Josie went back to Samantha, who was sitting in a spot of sunshine on a folding chair outside of their tent. Unknown lay next to her. Josie pulled their other chair nearby and spread out the map sheets on her lap as she spoke in a soft voice. Josie told Samantha what she'd learned.

"Cumberland found him?!"

"Shhh," Josie said in a whisper.

"Oh, sorry."

Josie spread out the maps on Samantha's lap. They found the grid squares that Cumberland had talked about. Based on the topo lines, it looked like what he'd described. A steep slope that rose toward Half Dome above.

TWENTY-EIGHT

"It must have snowed overnight," Samantha said. "The top of Half Dome and the Captain are white."

Josie looked up at where Samantha was pointing. The aromatic smoke from campfires mixed with cold air swirling down from the high country. A layer of haze cut across the middle of El Capitan, yet the air was completely clear at the base of the monolith. And the sky at the top was so blue that if a photographer had taken a picture of it, viewers would think it had been photoshopped. The sun was warm, but the late October air was chilly.

They ate a breakfast of cereal and fruit as they studied the maps Cumberland had printed for them. They fed Unknown her dog food flavored with a vegetarian brat from the night before. As always with a tasty meal, Unknown ate it without any of the speed that other dogs demonstrated. It was as if the dog was careful about everything. Whether she was brought treats or affection, she regarded them slowly, not necessarily with suspicion but with the prudence and caution that she'd acquired in her previous life.

Josie and Samantha had met Unknown's most recent owner, Bill, the man who was murdered in the Canadian wilderness the month before. Bill had seemed very kind and courteous to Unknown, doting on her. So they suspected Unknown's harsh life lessons of caution had come from an owner previous to Bill.

They plotted out a hiking path, figuring the best route to and from the area where Cumberland thought the killer was camping.

"You think we'll be safe?" Samantha asked.

"Yes. We'll stay on the main trails where there'll be other

people. We're just tourists, right? A mother and daughter from L.A. Nothing could be worrisome about that." Josie said it in a breezy manner, trying to set a casual tone. But she didn't feel that way. The reality of what they were doing in the park felt like a crushing weight. Find a killer and report his location. Maybe even figure out how to arrest him. The whole concept seemed crazy. And her sweet innocent daughter was relying on Josie to make smart and safe choices. Josie wondered if she was making the biggest mistake of her life.

When they were done eating, Samantha asked, "Is today Private World or Normal World?"

"The California Bureau of Investigation will have certainly tracked us to Yosemite. They'll expect us to walk around. So I'm thinking Normal World."

"Bring phones and be careful what we say," Samantha said.

"Yes."

They got all their electronics from the car, packed a lunch in their packs, left their campground, and headed out to explore the places that Cumberland had mentioned. Josie noticed that Samantha had wrapped Unknown's leash around her hand, shortening it, keeping the dog close at her side.

The first trail they followed took them back to where they'd burned a Big G brand on the broken trail sign. There were two men looking at the brand. One was taking pictures with his phone. Josie and Samantha walked on past, not slowing, acting as if they had no idea what the men were looking at.

The trail went through a very dark section of forest. Josie looked at the sun's angle. Despite the approach of midday, the sun was low in the sky, the shadow of Half Dome seeming to cover half the forest. The short days of winter were approaching. Josie realized that sunlight would rarely hit the forest floor for months.

A deep, pulsing bird sound came through the forest. Samantha made a little jerk at the sound. Unknown stared off through the dark trees. Josie wasn't sure what kind of bird made the call. A Pileated woodpecker? She couldn't even tell if it was a friendly call or a warning call. At that realization, Josie had a profound sense that her life in academia, her endless hours spent inside university buildings, hadn't prepared her for life in a different environment. She was a literal example of ivory tower isolation, cloistered, ignorant of all that wasn't her academic interest, and even helpless in the wilderness.

She reminded herself that they'd thought this through. Helpless or not in the woods, they could still put on a convincing tourist act.

A couple approached on the trail. An older man and woman. The man held binoculars. The woman held a bird book. They looked off through the trees. The man pointed at something, spoke in a low voice. Then they moved on, nodding acknowledgment as they went past Josie and Samantha.

Josie realized they'd made a significant oversight in not bringing binoculars. Too late now.

The trail wound back far enough that the sounds of people seemed to disappear, and all they could hear were distant sounds of falling water and the calls of various birds. There came a loud, deep, scratchy call, followed by another from a different direction. They were unattractive rasping sounds. Then came two huge black birds flying through the woods, their slow wing beats making whooshing sounds through the air. Josie noticed to her own pleasure that even an ivory tower academic like her could recognize ravens, perhaps because of her affinity for Poe's poem.

The sound of children came from behind. Soon, they were overtaken by two women, an older man, and four young children. They were noisy but reassuring. More people probably served to inhibit the actions of a killer. Josie and Samantha paused to let the children, and their noise, go on past them.

When they resumed walking, the trail became deserted. They came to a fork. There were wooden trail signs like the one on which they'd burned the brand. The distant sound of the children indicated that group had taken the left fork. Josie consulted her map.

"We go right," she said in a low voice.

They hiked on. Half Dome had grown much larger and

loomed nearly straight above them.

When they'd gone a good distance farther, perhaps a half mile, they came to another split in the trail. This fork wasn't marked. The left route was a broad trail, well-traveled. The right route was narrow and little used.

Josie paused to study the ground but tried not to be obvious in case anyone could be watching.

"What are you looking for, Mama?" Samantha said in a near whisper.

"Footprints," Josie whispered.

"I don't see any," Samantha said. "But look at that depression. It's kind of like a wide groove."

"You think it means something?"

Samantha nodded. "At school, sometimes kids ride mountain bikes over our volleyball court. It drives our coach crazy. This groove in the dirt looks like the ones at our volleyball court."

"You think this is a mountain bike trail."

Another nod.

Josie stopped moving. Turned her head. Listening. She held her finger to her lips. After long seconds, she started walking. She didn't turn off on the narrow trail with the groove. Instead, she went down the main trail, looking off to the side, both right and left.

They walked for a minute. Josie stopped.

Samantha whispered again. "Do you see something, Mama?"

Josie pointed to the left, away from Half Dome, which was up to the right. Josie spoke softly. "See how this area goes back and then slopes up a bit? I'm thinking that if we go back there, we might be able to get up high enough to see over the trees and across to the base of Half Dome. Maybe we can see where the man has his campsite."

Samantha looked in both directions.

They left the trail and started into the forest.

The trees were dense.

"You could get lost in here," Samantha said, her voice sounding worried. "But at least we have a compass in our phones."

Josie unfolded her maps. "We should be about here." She pointed. "Over there, the trail heads toward Mirror Lake. Here's what we'll do. This slope is gentle, so it's easy to go up the most direct way. We won't go sideways. Just straight up. When we decide to return, we'll come back down the most direct way. That way, we'll come back to the main trail."

"No detours," Samantha said. "Just up and down. Easy to not get lost."

They hiked slowly. It seemed as easy for Samantha as it was for Unknown. Josie was quickly breathless. She took small steps. Samantha got ahead of her, turned around, saw her panting, then stopped and waited.

They eventually made their way up the slope and stopped where there was an open area. Josie sat down on a boulder to rest. Samantha and Unknown stood.

"We're up high enough to see across toward Half Dome," Samantha said. "That's what you wanted, right?"

"Yes. Can you see any sign of a person over there? You have better eyes than I do." Josie took off her glasses, wiped the lenses.

"I can't see anything from up here," Samantha said. "Too many trees. Too far away. It looks like it's a real steep slope going up to the base of Half Dome."

"So no campsite, obviously," Josie said.

"He'd have to have an orange tent to be visible. Ain't no way he fly 'nuff to cop a dayglo crib." After a moment, she added, "And yeah, ain't no college gonna let me talk whack. I'll jus' get bent, grab my biscuit, 'n bust a cap in they ass."

"Am I really that bad?" Josie said. "Do I judge you so much?"

"Kinda," Samantha said.

"I'm sorry."

"It's okay, Mama. I know you mean well. I was just talking hip hop for fun."

"What's whack mean, anyway?"

"Real bad."

"And fly?"

"Cool," Samantha said.

"And the thing about a bent biscuit?"

"It means, I'll get intoxicated, grab my gun, and shoot them."

Now Josie started laughing. She couldn't seem to stop. Samantha joined in. Unknown looked at both of them, her brow furrowed.

Eventually, Josie got her breath and said, "If we can't see his crib, I'll just have to climb up close and take his biscuit 'fore he can cap my ass."

Samantha bent over giggling. She collapsed to the ground, pulling Unknown down with her.

When they calmed and walked back down to the trail, Josie sensed movement. A man on a bike. Josie worried that Samantha wouldn't see him, as she was holding her phone.

"Careful, hon," Josie said as a man flew by on a mountain bike.

Samantha jumped back to get out of his way.

"You okay?" Josie asked.

"Yeah. He didn't come that close."

Josie stared after the man. "It didn't even occur to me to take a good look at him. What a shame if he turns out to be our guy. We never had a chance to get his picture."

"Sure we did, Mama." She held up her phone. "I'm fast on my spy app."

TWENTY-NINE

"You took his picture?" Josie was amazed and delighted. "What does he look like?"

Samantha held up her phone for Josie to see. The picture was blurry, but it revealed the man's face. Brown hair cut medium length, beige baseball cap, dark shading on his face as if he had dark stubble, brown pants and shoes. His nose seemed large, his eyes close together, his ears were mostly under his hair.

"I never even saw you raise your phone."

"That's what the spy app is for. You don't have to raise your phone. There's this little attachment over the front lens. You can take a pic with the phone lying on its back."

"Do you have a cell signal here? We could email the picture to the Bureau and see if this is the man who was seen by the employees at the hunting store."

"I've got two bars. Do you know the email or text address?"

Josie pulled out her old-fashioned pocket notebook. She read off Theo Mosconi's address while Samantha entered it.

"What should I say?" Samantha asked.

"'This man might be our target. Can you confirm?'"

Samantha tapped out the words. "Okay, done."

Josie and Samantha and Unknown left the area near Half Dome and were walking back toward their campsite when they saw a large Black man leaning against a rust red pickup that was parked next to their Prius. The pickup was really old. Josie didn't know vehicles, but she would have guessed it was from the 1960s. The emblem on the front said Ford. The man was older still. Probably in his 70s. He looked like a cowboy in a magazine ad, a rugged guy with a big jaw, faded blue jeans, red flannel shirt, an open leather sheepskin jacket, cowboy boots, and hat. Not quite a cowboy hat. A khaki, broad-brimmed hat like Josie had seen in a movie. He was thick with just a hint of belly. His weight was on one leg. The boot of his other leg was crossed over the boot he was standing on. It was a picture of repose. The man watched them as they approached.

"Josephine Strong?" he said. His voice sounded familiar. As they got a bit closer, he looked familiar, too.

"Who's asking?" Josie said.

"Mama," Samantha whispered at her side, "that's the blacksmith guy!"

"Ralph Ellison," the man said. "You came to my shop. Got the Big G brand. The Granny belt."

Josie stopped ten feet away. She held her hand out to the side to stop Samantha as well. She was aware that Samantha's phone and Josie's badge were picking up all sounds. But maybe this was a time when it was okay to be in the Normal World. If Mosconi was listening in, he needed to know that Josie was trying to fulfill the mission he'd sent her on. And maybe it was good to be overheard if this man meant them harm.

Josie realized she'd told the blacksmith her name was Josie Stillman, yet he knew her real name was Strong.

Josie's internal sense of warning was on high alert. "How do you know my name?"

"After you and your daughter picked up the branding iron and left my shop, I saw that you hadn't parked in my lot. Same as when you placed the order. I was curious. So, I followed you over to the shopping center and saw you get into your Prius." He gestured toward their car. "I wrote down the license number. A cop friend of mine looked it up and told me your real name. That was very intrusive on my part. I'm sorry about that. However my Army training has made me spend my whole life looking out for those in danger."

"You're stalking us." Josie was very worried.

"Not stalking. Concerned. The former is not in your interest. The latter is." The guy hadn't moved. He still leaned back against the pickup. He looked relaxed.

Josie looked around to see if other people were nearby. There was a couple sitting on folding camp chairs outside of their tent.

They were reading paperback novels in front of a campfire. If this guy tried anything, the couple would hear Josie scream. Samantha and Unknown would help. Josie took a deep breath, tried to calm herself.

"What do you mean, danger?" Josie asked.

"It's a sixth sense. You showed all the indicators."

"That's ridiculous. Tell me what you're doing here in Yosemite," she asked. She was about to call the police.

"It's not a short story," he said. "Can we talk?"

"That's what we're doing. Keep doing it."

Samantha looked at her. Josie realized that it was unusual for her to sound brusque. But she didn't mind. That some blacksmith guy from L.A. had found out her real name and then found her in Yosemite made her want to flee back to Santa Monica. Was it a coincidence that he was in Yosemite at the same time they were? If not, if he'd tracked them there, that suggested either he was a criminal or a psycho or both.

"As a young man I spent six years in the Army," Ellison said. "Green Beret. Among other things, I worked eighteen months on an undercover mission. Part of our training was focused on psychological issues, how to spot a person who is under the stress of worrying about being attacked as opposed to a person who's under the stress of planning an attack. You displayed all the markers of the target victim. Inadequate attempts at disguising your name and your plan for the branding iron. Awkward moves like parking in the shopping center as if to be incognito when in fact it only drew more attention to yourself."

Josie saw Samantha's eyes narrow.

"What is a Green Beret?" Samantha asked.

"An elite branch of the Army. The name comes from British commandos in World War Two. Maybe you've seen movies about Special Ops. We're like that. Only it wasn't called Special Ops back in the day."

"So you're like the Navy Seals?"

Ellison gave Samantha a smile that seemed part tolerance and part earnestness. "Kinda. My group always said that the Seals work out harder, but the Green Berets work harder."

Ellison looked back at Josie. "Anyway, when you came to my shop you might as well have worn a sandwich board saying 'look at me and guess what strange activity I'm involved in.' So, I looked you up, found out you're a prof at UCLA. Not long after, I saw an article on the Merced Register website. They ran this weird account of a professor from Oxford University searching for the medieval monster Grendel in Yosemite. One of the things this new Grendel supposedly does is mark his crime scenes with a brand in the shape of the letter G. They showed a picture of one of the Gs. Imagine my surprise when I took a close look and realized it was the Big G brand I made for you, complete with the little tweaks and dents. My first thought was that I didn't want to be implicated in some strange perversion of a twisted professor. On the face of it, one would think you and the Oxford prof are running some complex scam." He gazed at Josie, long and steady. "But then I remembered the worried look on your brow when you were in my shop, the forehead wrinkles that are a second cousin to what a person shows when they're about to cry, or worse, fall apart. So my second thought was that this professor is under attack, in serious danger, and is creating an elaborate cover to save her ass."

Josie felt like a fool. She'd made every mistake possible, and they were all obvious to this old Green Beret blacksmith. Even so, it seemed clear that she should not reveal anything. Maybe she could make a vague statement that would not give away information. Or she could ask a reasonable and straight-forward question. "Why are you here?"

Ellison shifted his stance, put his elbows back and leaned them on the top edge of the pickup's bed rail. "I usually close the shop for a week in the fall. I go camping someplace so I can be outside, away from the crush of L.A. The Grand Canyon or Bryce Canyon or Joshua Tree or Point Reyes up north of San Francisco. Probably more than anyplace else, I come here to Yosemite and hang out beneath these cliffs. It's like church with a Miwok Indian vibe. The air here is restorative, as are these mountains. I didn't expect you to be here. But then I'm not surprised, either. Perhaps I can be of help."

Josie was trying to think of something noncommittal.

"Doing what?" she asked.

"I could help you clarify just who and where your enemy is. Of course, I don't know if your dragon is metaphorical or literal. But I might be able to help you draw him out of the forest. Or protect you if he comes gunning for you."

Josie felt her world tilting far away from level. "It sounds like you're on some kind of fantasy prowl for damsels in distress."

Ellison shrugged. "We each find purpose and meaning in different ways. Are you and your daughter damsels in distress?"

Josie ignored the question. "And why would you do this?"

"Matters of the heart are hard to explain. You came into my shop wearing the fine threads of a professor. You were earnest and sweet and confused and stumbling. Then you brought this young girl when you picked up your branding iron." He only briefly glanced at Samantha. "When you left, I thought this woman and her daughter are in over their heads. I didn't know the size and scope of the ocean you'd dived into. But I thought I could take my getaway in Yosemite because, well, you never know where someone will show up. And the article connecting Yosemite to a brand that I designed… It seemed that you might go there. I thought, if we should cross paths, maybe I could help build a life raft and prevent you from drowning."

Josie didn't know what to think. Too much surprise from a man whose motives were unclear and whose words sounded suspicious. After a moment, she had a thought that might reveal the man's character. "Tell me about your name."

"Yes, hard to escape the impact of the author Ralph Ellison. My mother was very taken with the novel Invisible Man. She thought it perfectly described the world she wrestled with, a life where black people were invisible to much of society. The novel came out in nineteen fifty-two. I came out the same year. What with her last name being Ellison, she couldn't help herself. I would have rather been named after a ball player. Jackie Robinson Ellison. Or, Willie Mays Ellison would've had a nice ring. Hell, I would've settled for Tony Oliva Ellison. But I didn't have a vote in the matter. Ralph Ellison, the author of Invisible

Man, tried to point out how people can be ignored, be cast out, be adrift. I've seen it in others. I've experienced it myself."

"So you saw the article on the Merced Register website."

"Except for your involvement and my brand, it was just a curiosity. Some prof from Oxford investigating weird deaths. But the other stuff on the web was more specific. There was this blog from some writer called Frogtown Girl. It's some kind of fantasy blog about fantastical creatures. It had a post about how the monster Grendel has come back to life as a vigilante killer, targeting murderers and robbers, and he's taken up residence in Yosemite. Sounded like a bunch of hokum to this blacksmith. But it was provocative, and I was curious. So I decided to, once again, make my foray to Yosemite. I made my normal campsite reservation, came up here like I've done for years. Then, in this very campground in the middle of the Grendel BS, I see the professor lady who was so scared she parked in a crowded shopping center lot instead of in the lot outside my blacksmith shop. Of course, I can leave you two to your business. I'm not sure what that business is. But I'm guessing it involves you going around burning Big G brands in the local landscape, stirring up the stories that the Oxford prof is writing about. Of course, the Oxford prof may be as ephemeral as most fiction, existing to satisfy your needs, then to fade away."

Josie realized she had her hand on Samantha's arm, gripping it so hard her fingers dug into Samantha's flesh.

She started to talk, stopped, couldn't find words. "How does a Green Beret blacksmith know the word ephemeral?"

"My mother read Invisible Man to me when I was six. By eight, I'd read it myself. The adult stuff went over my head. I wasn't much of a school boy. But I had a background that included reading, and thus a broad vocabulary."

Josie stood silent. Her cover had been blown. Her world was unmasked by this blue-collar soldier. Was he an imposter? Had Mosconi and his Bureau of Investigation counterparts followed her to Ellison and then recruited him to spy on her? Did they instruct him to help her? Was he a lost soul who had no life and was looking for an adventure?

"How long are you staying in Yosemite?" she asked.

"I didn't have a plan. If you want me to stay around for a bit, I'll take that into consideration. Same for if you want me to leave. Judging by your stiffness, Point Reyes might be a more restful spot. I could have my tent set up, and be looking over the ocean, in five hours."

"I think so," Josie said.

"Does that mean you want that?"

"I think yes." It was a mild statement, not representative of her strong desire for this man to leave them alone.

Samantha was shaking Josie's arm. "Mama!" she whispered.

Josie turned to Samantha, saw the intensity in Samantha's eyes, felt the vibration of disagreement as the girl made an intense-but-minimal shake of her head. Josie turned back to Ralph Ellison. "My daughter and I would like to talk," Josie said. "Can you give us an hour?"

Ellison said, "It's the time of day to pull a beer out of my cooler. I'll wander over to the river and listen for the Miwok spirits. If you look long enough up at Half Dome, you hear both the coyote Trickster and the coyote Creator. Once, I even heard the coyote Diver from beneath the flowing water."

Josie nodded, not knowing how to respond. She respected Native American mythology. But when someone who wasn't Miwok spoke of actually hearing their spirits, it was too far outside of her world for her to connect to it. It would be the same as if she imagined she were connected to Hutash, the Chumash goddess that she and Samantha had learned about from the artist Shulu Ojai.

As they were about to leave, Samantha said, "Does the hotel allow dogs?"

"I don't know," Josie said.

Ellison reached out his arm. "I'll take him."

"Her," Samantha said. "Her name is Unknown, and she doesn't like being mistaken for a boy."

Ellison's eyes opened wide.

He stood in front of Unknown and made a little bow as he took her leash. "Pleased to meet you, girl."

THIRTY

Josie pulled out her phone and pointed to their tent. Samantha nodded. They put all their electronics in the tent. Then Josie pulled on Samantha's arm and steered her down the trail toward the Ahwahnee Hotel.

"You think talking about Mr. Ellison is Private World stuff?" Samantha asked.

"I don't know. When in doubt..."

It was as if they both realized that they needed a small space where they could sit and talk undisturbed.

They walked in through the huge front door that was surrounded by a granite proscenium. The lobby was the size of a medium theater. Over on one end was a crackling fire made of large split logs.

Josie and Samantha found two huge leather chairs. But when Josie sat in one, Samantha passed up the other chair and joined Josie in the same chair, scrunching in next to her. It was tight, but Samantha was a skinny girl. It was cozy and comforting.

"What do you think of Ralph Ellison?" Josie asked. She had her arms around Samantha's narrow waist, holding her in a gentle embrace.

Samantha was slow in answering. "It's kind of strange, him showing up in Yosemite."

"Do you trust him?" As Josie asked it, she marveled that she relied on the judgments of her 14-year-old daughter. But Samantha had an unerring sense of things, better, Josie often thought, than her own.

Samantha said, "Yeah. I mean, I guess he could be an actor or something, trained to seem trustworthy. But why? I think he's probably what he says he is. A guy who sensed the weirdness of you getting a branding iron and the whole Grendel story that he saw online. Obviously, it worked like we wanted it to. People noticed. But he would think that was totally out there. And because he made the branding iron, he would wonder how we're involved. He'd naturally be interested. So I think he's what he says he is. Plus, he's, like, thinking this is more interesting than watching football on TV. That's a good sign for us, don't you think?"

"You may be right. What about his offer to help us?"

"I don't know, Mama. Probably, he's doing it because of the damsels-in-distress thing. He certainly would know how to help. He's an Army guy. He must know all kinds of stuff that we don't have a clue about. We're trying to track a killer who will probably see us coming and will maybe snuff us out like he was squishing bugs. This Ellison guy might know how to fight back."

"What about the fact that a killer might easily sense that Mr. Ellison is a trained soldier, even if he's old. The killer could shoot him dead. Whereas the killer would just think we're a couple of tourist women who pose no threat."

"That's a good point."

Josie nodded.

Samantha suddenly grinned. "Do you really think of me as a woman? Your baby girl is now a woman?"

"Look, girl, you still do some major adolescent stuff. But when it comes to your judgment? Yes, I've come to think of you as an adult. A sensible, smart woman. Even if you do talk whack."

"Wow, thanks, Mama. That's real… That's fly."

"Just don't disappoint me."

"Yes, professor," Samantha said. She raised her hand to her brow in a salute.

"What I'm wondering is this," Josie said. "If we let Mr. Ellison help us, how much do we tell him about our mission?"

Josie watched Samantha's face from the side as her daughter stared at the crackling fire. It was as if Josie could see Samantha thinking.

"Well, first of all, maybe we don't tell him about my

smuggling," Samantha said.

Josie understood that news of the smuggling arrest would be embarrassing. It would also reveal more than necessary. "We could just tell him that we were hired by the Bureau of Investigation to help find this guy because we caught that killer last month, and because I know about medieval history, and there is the medieval history component to the case."

"A component," Samantha said, "that we created with the Grendel story."

"Right." Josie nodded. "But Mr. Ellison doesn't know that."

"But he knows we created the Big G brand."

Josie said, "He can think the brand came after we read about the Oxford professor and the Grendel story, so we tried to use it to our advantage."

"Like, we were adding to it in ways that might make the killer come out of his cave?"

"Yeah," Josie said. "Something like that."

"Do you think he'll believe it?" Samantha asked. "That the Bureau of Investigation would hire two women with no cop experience to go after a killer?"

"It is a stretch. But it's the truth. The ID and badge prove it. I could show him the handcuffs and shackles. It all adds up to credibility."

Samantha seemed doubtful.

Josie said, "Right now, Mr. Ellison's confronting crazy stuff. A history professor is burning Big G brands in the forest in support of an Oxford professor who is pursuing a time-traveling, continent-hopping monster. It seems completely nutso. But once Mr. Ellison knows that we're simply trying to come up with a way to unsettle the killer and get him to reveal himself, then all our activities seem much less crazy."

"And a critical part," Samantha said, "is that the cops and Bureau people have tried to find the guy and they haven't succeeded."

"Right."

"In other words," Samantha said, "the truth, strange as it

seems, is more believable than the fiction he's now focused on."

"Well said. All we'd leave out is the hold the Bureau has on us."

"That they've got a legal vice grip on me, and I'll go to prison if we don't do what they say." Samantha said it in a low voice filled with distress and dejection. Samantha hung her head. "I'm so sorry, Mama. I created so much trouble for us." Her eyes teared.

"Don't worry about it, Sam." Josie reached up and wiped Samantha's cheeks. "You didn't know. Now you do. It won't happen again."

Samantha made a single nod. "So what are we going to tell Mr. Ellison?"

Josie was slow to answer. "I'm thinking we go back and tell him the truth about the Bureau hiring us to search out a killer who they can't find. We explain why and how we're trying to unnerve the killer. We tell him a little about our satellite information, but without mentioning Cumberland. We explain that our goal is to identify the killer, then tell the authorities."

They were quiet, both thinking.

"Does this plan seem plausible to you?" Josie asked.

"Yeah, I think so," Samantha said. "But..."

"What?" Josie had learned in the past that Samantha's hesitations had value.

"But shouldn't we first look up Mr. Ellison? You know, check him out? Make sure he doesn't have some kind of psycho past?"

"Good point. See, Sam? This is why I need you. I miss the obvious, but you often notice the important things." Josie turned her head and looked around at the hotel lobby. "Hotels often have computers for their guests. Maybe we could use one of them."

They stood and walked through the hotel.

"We could ask at the info desk," Samantha said. "What are those called?"

"Concierge. But that might alert them to us. Let's look around first."

They walked the various corridors on the ground floor.

"Mama," Samantha said in a low voice. "Down that hall on the right." Samantha didn't point, but just moved her head a little.

Josie looked where she indicated. They walked down the hall. There was a small office center with two computer desks and a printer. A woman was working at one of the computers. Josie tried the door. It was locked. There was an access lock with a reader for a room key card.

Josie turned and walked down the hall several feet.

"We'll just wait here and see if that woman leaves anytime soon. We can walk in when she comes out. I didn't see an access lock on the computer."

The office door opened, and the woman came out quickly. Samantha took two quick steps and grabbed the door before it clicked shut. They walked into the office.

The computer was still on. Samantha went to Google and typed in Ralph Ellison. Up came endless hits about the author and the novel. Next, she used quotes to indicate required words and typed, "Ralph Ellison Blacksmith."

Up came just a few hits, links to click-bait sales pages for info about Ralph's address and phone number. One link showed that his birth date was in July of 1952. Another referenced a City of Industry business catalog and a listing for Blacksmiths. Ralph Ellison had been in business since 1992. One review popped up. It was a five-star review that said, 'Job was done as advertised, quality work, quality guy.'

"He seems pretty normal," Samantha said.

"A blacksmith who listens to Miwok spirits and uses words like ephemeral is not normal."

"How would you know, Mama? I've heard people say that professors live in unreal worlds and talk funny. Those people would never think you were able to fight an assassin in the wilderness."

"For with judgment I pronounce I will be judged?"

"Yeah, I guess. What's that from? The Bible?"

"The Book of Matthew, somewhat misquoted."

"But you said the Bible was mostly just a collection of amazing stories. Not something you follow. Yet now you're quoting it?"

"One should know the important stories regardless of whether or not one thinks they are sacred."

Samantha pointed to the computer screen. "So are we satisfied that Mr. Ellison isn't a psycho who's going to cut us into pieces?"

Josie stared at her. "Where do you get these thoughts? The movies?"

Samantha grinned.

"It was your idea to check him out. If you're satisfied, I am."

Samantha nodded. She closed the tab on the computer browser, pushed open the door, and walked outside.

On the way back, as they walked down the trail, Samantha said, "Tell me about the Invisible Man book."

Josie took her time responding. It was difficult to describe the book.

"First, I should point out that the science fiction writer H.G. Wells also wrote a novel called The Invisible Man back in the eighteen nineties. It was about a scientist who invented a way to be literally invisible. Fifty years later, the author Ralph Ellison wrote a novel with the same title minus the word 'The.' But it was about how Black people are metaphorically invisible to many people in society."

"What does that mean?"

"My take on the novel is that as the author Ellison grew up, he noticed that people would often see Blacks in terms of stereotypes. The poor rural Black farmer. The intellectual Black lawyer or judge. The compassionate Black doctor. The Black jazz musician."

"So they wouldn't really get to know the individual," Samantha said. "It was more about seeing Black people in terms of which box to put them in, and all of the boxes were about them being Black?"

"Exactly," Josie said. "The specific individual person

was subordinated by their job or status. The individual was invisible."

"You're doing the professor thing again, Mama."

"What? Oh. Subordinated? Sorry. That just means putting something at a lower level than something else."

"Like a woman whose opinions are subordinated by her husband's?"

"Sadly, yes. That's one kind."

They walked in silence for a minute.

"So what box would a Black girl like me be in?"

"Let me think. I don't think it would be about being black. More like, hip, in-your-face movie critic, chronicler of social trends and, very recently, writer of a cutting-edge fantasy blog?"

"Wow. That's me? That doesn't sound too bad."

"But if you wear the full black Goth outfit and put metal piercings in your lips and nose, then the box would be different."

"I'd be in the angry, troublemaker box?"

"Perhaps."

"But angry troublemaker isn't all bad."

"No, it's not," Josie said. She reached her arm around her much taller daughter's shoulder and squeezed.

"They said Rosa Parks was a troublemaker," Samantha said.

"She sure was. Lucky for us, too."

THIRTY-ONE

Ralph Ellison was sitting in a folding camp chair near the river, holding Unknown's leash. He had his hand resting on Unknown's back. He seemed to be looking up at the sunset sky and talking to Unknown about it. On the chair next to him were a bird book and binoculars. He turned as Josie and Sam walked up.

"This girl and I were watching a large raptor that was riding a tight thermal," he said. "I could only guess what kind of bird. Golden Eagle? It was very high. 'Turning and turning in the widening gyre.' It probably climbed a thousand feet before it left the thermal and headed toward El Cap."

Josie was struck by his quote of the line from Yeats. She didn't get to comment because he spoke again.

He paused. "Make a decision?"

"We'd like to talk."

"Okay," he said.

Josie leaned in close to him and spoke in a whispered voice. "Not here. Over by that cataract where the water makes white noise. And we'd like you to put your phone and any other electronics in our tent. You don't need to worry about it, we'll be able to see it from the river."

Ellison raised his eyebrows. He looped Unknown's leash around the arm of his chair, pulled out his phone, walked over and put it inside his tent. He came back, picked up his chair and, still holding Unknown's leash, walked toward the cataract.

Josie and Samantha had already put their phones and Josie's badge in their tent. They carried their folding chairs over to a place where the water noises were loudest. They all sat. Samantha seemed to study how Unknown responded to Ellison.

"You probably think I'm paranoid," Josie said in a low

voice.

"Either that, or you're in an extraordinary situation," Ellison said.

She said, "I've been asked by the California Bureau of Investigation to hunt a bank robber and cop killer."

Ellison showed surprise. "The professor is an L-E-O?"

"LEO?" Josie repeated.

"Law Enforcement Officer."

"Obviously not," she said. "I didn't know the phrase."

"But you're employed by the Bureau of Investigation."

"Maybe employed isn't quite the right word. They think my knowledge specialty will help find this guy. So they gave me an ID and deputized me."

"Then you are an L-E-O."

"Only in principle. I know nothing of the career. Nevertheless, they want me to find this killer."

"How're you gonna do that?"

"We're still working on it. But the Bureau is serious. They issued me handcuffs and shackles. They're monitoring me. We found out that the ID they gave me has an RFID chip in it."

Ellison frowned. "What's that mean, RFID?"

"Radio Frequency..."

"Identification," Samantha finished. "There are RFID readers that send out radio waves. If a chip comes near, the radio waves bounce off it. Like the machines that read your credit card chip. By the information in the bounced waves, the reader can tell which particular chip it is."

"Thanks, Samantha," Josie said. "That was a very good, succinct explanation."

"Where are the readers?" Ellison asked.

"Practically everywhere," Samantha said. "FasTrak toll booths, parking lots, mass transit, airports, government buildings."

"They also gave me a badge," Josie said. "That also has an RFID chip. In addition, it has a battery and an active recorder. It's sound-activated. It records all conversations and then uploads them whenever it is in range of an RFID reader. So we leave our phones at home or in our car whenever we want to be private."

"Big brother lives," Ellison said. "How do you know your phones and badge listen to you?"

"A tech-savvy friend."

"Ah. What do you know about the suspect you're after?"

"He robbed some banks and stole a pickup in Merced." Josie almost mentioned he'd killed police officers but stopped herself. "Now the Bureau believes he's hiding in the Yosemite forest."

"Why would the Bureau want you to help if you have no law enforcement background?" Ellison asked.

"They think the suspect has the knowledge to evade the searchers and trackers who follow standard protocol. The Bureau thinks that someone who takes a different approach would have the best chances of finding this man. That's our biggest advantage, taking a different approach."

"Did you apply for this job? Or was it on your wish list?"

Josie paused.

Ellison said, "So they didn't actually hire you. You're a UCLA professor. It's not like you need a second job. Which means they coerced you. You've got some skeleton in your closet, and they threatened you with exposure or something."

Josie stayed silent. Ellison was a little too smart for her liking.

"What kind of sidearm did they give you?" he asked.

"None. I wouldn't want one. I don't know how to use one."

Ellison regarded Josie and Samantha, then looked over at the river and stared at the water. He reminded Josie of a math professor she knew who would stare at the blackboard trying to make sense of inscrutable equations.

"This doesn't make sense," Ellison said. "If they want you to help them, there's a lot you could do where your expertise would come in handy. But how are you going to find a murder suspect when you don't have law enforcement background and you don't even know how to use a gun?"

"We may have already found him."

Ellison's head made a little jerk. "Oh?"

"We used an unorthodox method."

Ellison paused, waiting.

Josie didn't respond.

"You don't want to brag about your methods. I respect that. Don't reveal your cards until you have to. I remember from looking you up that your gig is medieval history. Maybe something about medieval history made it so you could find the guy when the cops could not. And the branding iron you had me make fits into that somehow. Naturally, I'm wondering what brought you to the Bureau's attention. They could have approached lots of other people who have skeletons they'd like to hide. But I suppose it's none of my business."

Josie paused, thinking. Ellison seemed trustworthy. His questions seemed sincere, not like someone who was trying to trick her into trusting him. Josie looked at Samantha. Samantha gave her a look that contained no warning or worry.

"Five weeks ago," Josie said, "Sam and I took a canoe trip into the Quetico, a Canadian wilderness just north of Minnesota."

"I've heard of the Boundary Waters Canoe Area Wilderness. Near there?"

"Yes. Right next door. It was supposed to be a vacation. Sam and I didn't know that we had seen something incriminating in L.A., something that made some men send an assassin to follow us, kill us, and leave our bodies in the North Woods."

Ellison's eyes showed surprise. It took a moment for him to respond. "Obviously, that didn't work," he said. "How'd you stop an assassin?"

"In my Introduction to Medieval History class, I get the students engaged by teaching them about medieval weapons."

Ellison grinned. "You used your medieval weapons expertise to make weapons and kick the assassin's ass." Maybe he meant it as an exaggeration. Maybe not.

"Something like that," Josie said.

Ellison turned to look at Samantha. "You were part of this?"

"Yeah," Samantha said. "We built an Onager and used it with Greek Fire. And we nailed him with sling bullets. We definitely kicked his ass and burned him up pretty good, too."

Josie stopped herself from correcting Samantha and saying, 'pretty well, too.'

"Sling bullets?" Ellison said. "Like David fighting Goliath?"

Samantha nodded. "Yeah. I'm pretty good at it."

"Apparently," Ellison said. "Where is the assassin now?"

Samantha looked to Josie, maybe wondering how much to tell.

Josie said, "He's in jail awaiting trial. His accomplice is dead."

"Am I prying too much if I ask how the accomplice died?"

"He shot me through the leg, and when I fell, he went to shoot me in the head. So I shot back."

"I thought you said you don't know how to use a gun."

"I don't. I killed him with a homemade crossbow."

"When you say homemade, do you mean a crossbow you made yourself?"

"Yes. A medieval design. Part of my Ph.D. dissertation."

Ellison's eyes widened. "Okay, consider me properly chastened," he said. "I'm in the presence of modern day warrior women who could probably vivisect me in some horrible way if I do them wrong."

"Not likely," Samantha said.

"That's a great qualifier," he said. "You won't likely vivisect me. Implying that you probably could."

Josie shook her head. "It's not like that. We're exactly what you see. An out-of-shape professor and a smart kid who worked together to thwart some bad guys. Our lives were threatened. We had no choice. Now we're faced with doing it again. And we've decided to accept your offer of help."

"Does this mean you'll explain why you had me make the Big G brand?"

"Yes." Josie took a deep breath. "After the man killed the two sheriff's deputies, he abandoned the pickup and escaped into Yosemite Park. He's been in hiding for over a year. The Bureau and other agencies have sent in trackers and dog teams and none of them have found him. They think that a different approach is appropriate. So, Samantha and I created a story about the medieval monster Grendel who's come back to life over the centuries in order to kill murderers who've gone unpunished."

"You mean Grendel as in the poem, right? Beowulf was the warrior who killed Grendel."

Josie nodded. "Our goal was to unnerve the killer to the point that he would come out of hiding. Or, that he would change his patterns enough that he would reveal himself."

Ellison seemed doubtful. "I'm surprised someone would believe that a fictional monster from the past has come alive and is burning G brands into the landscape."

"I agree. But I spoke to a psychologist about this. He said I should consider how many people believe all manner of things that aren't true. Conspiracy theories. The holocaust never happened. Bigfoot lives. Your astrology sign reveals your personality."

"Good point," Ellison said. "I've met people who believe some of those things. This monster would fit right in. Probably David versus Goliath would too, huh?"

"Actually, the monster slayer mythology is common in cultures all over the world," Josie said. "The Navajo have a complex origin story involving monster slayers. It's the same for Hindu people, the Ancient Greeks, the Vietnamese, the Inuit, the Iroquois."

"How does this connect to you?"

"Just that we recognized the power of story. So we created one to serve us."

Ellison nodded. "Then what?"

"Once we decided that Grendel was an appropriate monster, we reincarnated him as a time traveler. Unlike his original version, he has cleaned up his act, and he only kills murderers."

"A vigilante Grendel," Ellison said.

Josie nodded.

"How did you get from that idea to finding the killer?"

"Our partner is good with computers. He hacked into a satellite network that picks up infrared emissions, and he used that to watch the forests of Yosemite."

"Because humans give off infrared energy."

"As do animals and geothermal hotspots. Two days after our Grendel story went live, our friend saw unusual infrared movement in the forests. The movement was consistent with a person leaving a cave of sorts and visiting the locations where we'd created our Grendel evidence. It seems as if the suspect must have some kind of internet access, and he read about the Grendel story and went to look at the places where we'd left the brands. Last night, we used special speakers to play a Grendel roar in the forest. It was very loud. So we posed as tourists and wandered near his hangout. We think we bumped into him on a trail, and Samantha got his picture with a spy camera attachment on her phone."

"What's a spy attachment?"

Josie looked at Samantha.

"It's a hidden mirror over the lense," Samantha said. "You hold your phone like you're texting, and you can take pictures of whatever's in front of you. We sent that photo to the Bureau. We're hoping they'll confirm he's our suspect."

She turned to Josie. "We should get our phones. See if the Bureau wrote back about the photo I sent."

Josie nodded. "Okay. But then we can't mention the monitoring or the badge and ID. We'll be back in the Normal World."

"Right." Samantha ran to their tent.

Josie said to Ellison, "If he's where we think he is, we just need to drive him out of his cave and catch him."

"How do you plan to do that?"

"We haven't gotten that far. In principle, we would make him feel unsafe or uncomfortable to the point that he voluntarily leaves."

"Is there a medieval way to do that?" Ellison asked.

"Probably lots of ways. One way would be to attack him in his fortress. It seems like he probably lives on a very steep slope, almost like a cliff. He might be in a small cave or a recess under an overhang that projects out. We think he sleeps in there. We could climb up above his lair and drop an incendiary device down on him. Or a wasp nest. I saw a large one not far from here."

Samantha came back. "No email, yet." She handed Josie her phone and badge.

Ellison said, "If this guy doesn't willingly come out of his hiding place, do you have a medieval way of catching him?"

Josie shrugged. "We could use snares. Or maybe a net. Nets can be set with tension similar to a large mouse trap and triggered by pulling on an invisible monofilament line. It doesn't have to be foolproof. If we can tangle him up, maybe we can get handcuffs on him."

"You two seem dangerous. I hope you don't ever think I'm your enemy," Ellison said.

"Medieval weapons can be very effective. But he could just be an innocent homeless guy. So, if possible, we shouldn't do something cruel and unusual. And there is another approach that might work even better, anyway."

"What's that?"

"Talking. His hiding place has limited access in and out. It appears there's only one main approach path. Although I have to assume he has some kind of an escape route. If I can get close enough to call out to him, I can possibly convince him to come out."

Ellison looked skeptical. Samantha looked surprised.

THIRTY-TWO

"I think," Josie said, "that the typical law enforcement approach to a suspect is heavy with aggression. I imagine they have good reasons for that. But simple conversation could be the best way to entice this guy out of his lair." Unknown was still sitting next to Ellison. The dog had her jaw lifted up and resting on his knee. Josie wondered if Ellison reminded Unknown of her former owner in the Boundary Waters.

Samantha's phone chirped.

Josie watched as Samantha looked at the screen.

"Email," she said. She tapped on the screen, looked at it for a moment, then handed the phone to Josie.

Josie saw the email.

It said, 'Visual confirmation affirmative. The photo you sent is our man. Proceed with caution. - Theo Mosconi'

"That's the Bureau of Investigation," Josie said. "We have confirmation that our suspect is the man the Bureau is looking for."

"They tell you his name?"

"No, they have no idea of his identity. They only have a police sketch they got from some hunting store employees. The employees who saw the man who stole the pickup. Presumably, the Bureau emailed the photo we took to those witnesses."

"Is this all you have to go on?" Ellison asked. "Some witnesses who saw a guy in a hunting store?"

"Right. It's because of this situation that I have doubts about what we've been told."

Ellison frowned.

"Think of this situation from a typical suspect's point of view," Josie said. "Imagine you're a cop killer. You're hiding in Yosemite. The police know you're out there somewhere. What do you do? Keep hiding until they find someone who knows you and can give them something to scent dogs on? Or do you wait until fall when the mountain snow from the previous winter has melted, and you can hike up and over the Sierra Crest and down to the Nevada desert. The mountains here are high, something like thirteen thousand feet. But I've heard that you can hike over that elevation if you're in shape. Once down the eastern side, you hike to one of those towns, Lee Vining or Mammoth Lakes. You figure out a way to steal a car. Three or four days later, you're in Florida or Maine." Josie paused as if considering her scenario. "That's what I'd do if I were a cop killer, someone that the police would want to shoot on sight. But this man didn't run. Why?"

Ellison said, "You're saying, if he's really a cop killer, he'd be in Florida or someplace. He wouldn't be hanging around here waiting to get caught."

"Right," Josie said. "So maybe he isn't a cop killer."

What Josie didn't say was that before they'd headed north from L.A., Mosconi had called her office number to say another man had been killed, and he thought that the man they were after was the likeliest suspect. But something about Mosconi's news made Josie doubt Mosconi's theory of how the man died. In addition to her doubt, she hadn't wanted to cause Samantha to have more worries about any additional fallout from her smuggling. If there came a time when Mosconi's speculation seemed more truthful, she would tell Samantha about the phone call.

Ellison was picking his teeth with a long pine needle. "One possible reason he hasn't run is that he sees the benefits of hiding in plain sight. Yosemite is comfortable. There's easy food to steal. There's flowing water. The climate is relatively comfortable. A homeless person can exist nearly anywhere. However, homeless are fairly visible most places. But not in Yosemite. There's lots of cover. And if he feels threatened, it's just a day's hitchhike to L.A. or San Francisco. Or he can steal a car here."

"I agree. I think there's something else involved."

"What's your guess?" Ellison asked.

"Maybe he's not the guy the Bureau is looking for."

"But you just said they IDed him."

"Maybe they made a mistake," she said. "They do make mistakes sometimes."

"Or maybe there's some other reason he wants to stay put in Yosemite," Ellison said. "Maybe he's got buried cash from the bank robberies. He wants to haul it out when he gets the chance. And he won't do that until the police focus loses steam."

"Either way, I want to talk to him first. I don't want to light his lair on fire like a medieval assault."

Ellison said, "I understand your idea. So I have to ask the question, what if you go to talk to him, and he runs and escapes. Or worse, he shoots you."

"It's a risk to be balanced by the risk of what happens if we go in with aggression."

"The way the cops would," Ellison said. "You're right. That would probably entail just as much risk or more."

They were all silent. The river white water made the constant sound of rushing water. Downstream, where the water was smoother, the river burbled musical tones.

"How do you want to proceed?" Ellison asked.

"I'm going to talk to him. If I can find him, that is. First thing tomorrow morning. If I go early enough, I can maybe get to him when he's still sleeping."

"How would you like me to help?" Ellison asked.

"I'm thinking that you and Samantha could station yourselves down below his hideaway. You could be behind trees but make enough movement that if he looked down he might see you and think you were cops. LEOs as you said. If you both wear dark clothes and baseball caps, that might add to his picture. From a distance, Sam could look like a young, thin Bureau agent. You fit the bill perfectly, Mr. Ellison, the senior agent guiding the rest of us in a law enforcement activity."

"Senior," he said.

"Hey, you made me a granny belt. So don't go all age-sensitive on me."

He made a little nod.

"If I'm able to talk to the suspect, I can probably reference the agents who have him surrounded. He might look down and find corroboration when he sees your presence."

Josie and Ellison talked out the potential details. Samantha brought up some good points. Then Josie left her phone and badge with Samantha, walked away, and used her burner phone to call Cumberland and explain what they were going to do. Afterward, they all walked the trail toward the cliff slope where Josie believed the suspect had his hideaway.

Josie watched Samantha as she, in turn, watched Unknown. Samantha was no doubt trying to understand the dog's mind, trying to divine her past. The dog's body seemed to work fine. She didn't appear to have arthritis. But her wounds, psychic or emotional or not, made it so that she still never ran, never played. Sometimes, Samantha tossed a stick for fetch, but Unknown just watched it.

When they got back to the campsite, Josie and Samantha and Mr. Ellison spent the hours before dinner time walking out into the parking area, looking up at Half Dome, roaming the nearby woods, making plans, finding sight lines, running through possible scenarios.

Later, they made a campfire, and Ellison sat with them. He was quite the raconteur, telling them blacksmith stories about fitting horseshoes on impossibly frisky horses and working with rich Mexican ranchers whose roots in Southern California went back before the Mexican American War to a time when Mexico owned the western part of the U.S.

After they said goodnight, Josie put all their electronics in their car, then lay awake in the tent, thinking about how the morning would play out. She listened to the comforting sound of Samantha breathing. Then Samantha started making whimpering noises and her breath caught. She began to call out in her sleep.

Josie rolled over in her sleeping bag and put her arm over Samantha.

Samantha's cries got enough louder that Ellison might have

been able to hear them from his tent 100 feet away.

"It's okay, Sam," Josie whispered in her ear. "Everything's all right. I'm right here. You're safe." Josie rubbed Samantha, trying to wake her up from her nightmare.

Eventually, Samantha woke and calmed a little. Then she started a gentle crying.

Josie hugged her. The tent was small. But even so, Unknown seemed to crowd Samantha from the other side. Maybe she was trying to comfort Samantha, too.

Samantha spoke through her tears. "I'm so sorry, Mama. I caused all of this. I screwed up so bad, and now you're here sleeping in a cold tent, trying to find some cop killer. It's terrifying. We should be home in Santa Monica. We should be walking on the beach in the sunshine."

"We'll get through this, Sam. I'm just glad I have you. You're my only friend. We need to be strong for each other."

"Yeah, that's our name," Samantha said, her regular joke.

"It certainly is."

THIRTY-THREE

A few hours later, still dark in the middle of the night, Josie called Cumberland as was their plan. It was 90 minutes before dawn. Josie was still in her sleeping bag. She'd been lying awake partly because it was so cold and partly because she was stressing about the details of her potential encounter with a criminal suspect, someone suspected of murdering two sheriff's deputies.

"Any recent movement?" she asked Cumberland when he answered.

"No. But it can take several minutes for movement to propagate through the software system. But based on the past few days, he doesn't move before dawn."

"Thanks much."

Josie got up and pulled on extra clothes. Even from inside the tent she could tell it was very cold outside. She pulled on her thin knit gloves with the Norwegian pattern. Surely, serious hikers would laugh at her for not having a pair of custom back-country gloves. But you work with what you have.

Josie crawled out of the tent.

The ground had a layer of frost. The only light came from a quarter moon high up in the sky and from a security light at the far side of the campground.

Josie lit the cooking stove to boil water for coffee. Then she lit the second burner and held her hands above it for warmth. When the coffee was done, she poured a mug and carried it to her tent.

Samantha had recently taken to drinking coffee. She didn't like it strong. But she liked it. It had become a great morning ritual at home, mother and daughter drinking coffee together before they faced the day.

"Sam, hon, I've got coffee."

Her daughter groaned and moaned and sat up in her sleeping bag, and took the coffee.

Josie poured herself a mug, sat on a folding chair, and sipped. El Capitan was a dark looming wall to the west. It was impossibly huge, much wider and taller than any building on Earth. To the east was Half Dome, less imposing but even more dramatic as an outcropping silhouetted by the stars. With its top blanket of moonlit snow, it looked like a white-topped helmet. Even with the moonlight, it seemed that Josie could sense the glow of the Milky Way.

Her coffee steamed in the darkness, its warmth an ancient comfort against the cold of the mountain air. She felt a connection to the Miwok Indians who'd been drinking their own hot beverages in this very place, 4000 years before, 2000 years before the Roman Empire.

When she finished her coffee, she poured another mug and carried it over to Ellison's tent.

"Ralph?" she called out in a loud whisper. "Are you awake? I have coffee here for you."

"Um. Great. Thanks. Yes. I'm awake. Sort of. Not lucid. But awake. You get to my age, sleep is not a given but a gift, a gift that goes away by three in the morning even when it continues to fog your brain until dawn." His tent zipper raised up. His hands reached out.

"The handle is toward you," Josie said.

He took the mug, his fingers cradling its warmth, and pulled it into his tent.

"Give me ten," he said. "Then I'll be out. Fifteen minutes. Maybe twenty. Soon."

Forty-five minutes later, the three of them had eaten and were walking through the dark. Samantha held Unknown's leash. They used no lights for fear of alerting their quarry, even though he was nearly a mile away. They had left their electronics locked in their cars, although Josie had taken the burner phone just in case she needed to check in with Cumberland.

They walked through the parking lot toward the trail.

There weren't many other vehicles, as it was the slow season. The world was dark and quiet and mostly asleep. Although Josie noticed that someone had lit a small campfire at the edge of the campground. Another person had already walked into the parking lot, a dark figure leaning into the side door of a dark van, one of the extra tall models.

They went down the trail. The forest was redolent of night aromas, the powerful, wonderful scents of pine and fir and Incense cedar, the softer aromas of musty dirt. The wind was calm, yet there were many sounds. The scurrying of night creatures and the occasional whooshing flap of owls searching out prey.

The eastern sky began to glow a soft rose hue beyond Half Dome. With the additional light, they were able to find the smaller trail they'd walked the evening before. They followed a plan Ellison had developed, found some reference marks and viewing locations.

Josie and Samantha left Ellison at the first view spot. From there, they walked a short distance to a place where Samantha and Unknown would stay in a second view spot. Samantha was able to look out and down a bit to see Ellison behind them. The visual connection was strategic in that they could communicate with some hand signals Ellison had taught them. The connection was also a reassurance. Samantha had made it clear that when Josie headed off alone into the forest, she wouldn't feel frightened as long as she could see Ellison.

Both Samantha and Ellison had trees that gave them partial shelter from the suspect's view in the event that he happened to look out and down toward them. They also had a view to the route that Josie planned to use to hike up toward the location where they thought the suspect had his campsite.

Josie said goodbye to Samantha and wished her good luck. She reached down and gave Unknown a pet. The dog leaned against Samantha's leg. She looked up. Her brow was furrowed.

"Don't do that, Mama," Samantha whispered.

"What?"

"Don't do that thing where you say goodbye and good luck.

It makes me feel like I'm never going to see you again. Just say, you know, 'see you later,' like you're going to walk up there a little bit where we can see each other the whole time."

Josie kissed Samantha. "See you later, girl. I'll just walk up there a little bit. Where we can see each other the whole time."

Samantha grinned and gave her a hug. "Way better," she said.

"This will take me some time," Josie said. "The air is thin, so I have to go slowly to breathe. Be patient."

Josie walked down the trail, then turned off where they'd found the mountain bike track. She worked her way up through the forest, following the route she'd memorized from the map and from what she had observed when they'd gone up the opposite slope and looked across at the base of Half Dome. She'd studied the topographical lines on the map and gauged the best approach up the slope to the point where she believed the suspect had a trail of sorts to his hideaway.

The moonlight had lessened as it moved toward the horizon to the west. But the coming sun had lit high clouds, and there was a growing glow that penetrated the forest canopy.

Josie's hike went up at a gradual angle. The exertion made her breath very short. The elevation was somewhere over 4000 feet above sea level. It was nothing like really high country, but there was, nevertheless, a significant reduction in oxygen compared to what she was used to in L.A. She had to breathe much more than if she had been hiking in the forested canyons north of Santa Monica.

The path she'd planned involved two switchbacks. First, she angled to the right, moving toward a point directly below where she thought the suspect had his camp. The topo map indicated that she was about three hundred feet below him. However, she came to an abrupt rise where the forest floor got too steep to climb. She reversed direction, angling to the left. The forest became more dense, blocking her view of the valley below. She kept her bearings by the lay of the land and her sense of where the sun was going to rise. After a hundred yards of uphill hiking, she came to an area of house-sized boulders. There was no clear way up through the rocks. So she again turned and headed back to the right. Her route became more of a zigzag than she had anticipated.

As her path up the slope diverged from her plan, Josie worried that she would lose track of where she believed the suspect's hideaway was. She knew that his trail in and out would be nearly impossible to detect. He would have been very careful not to leave a well-tread track. Her sense of where he was derived more from Cumberland's description of what the satellites had detected than from Josie's sense of the forest.

The suspect wouldn't access his hideaway on a steep slope, either going up or down, because that would leave marks from his boots digging in or even sliding on a steep slope. Instead, his path would roughly follow a topo line on a map, a path across the slope where he could step gently and not leave prints or broken branches or disturbed rocks that would indicate his presence.

Yet again, Josie was forced to make an unplanned switchback. Because the forest was so dense, she couldn't tell where she was. She paused to breathe, moving very slowly back and forth, looking for a view through the trees. There was one potential viewing place. But she'd have to be a little higher. She climbed straight up the slope. It was hard work. But doable. She glanced back below. A little higher. Perfect. She could see down toward the valley floor. Somewhere in the trees were Samantha and Ellison. She turned to look, then leaned one way, then the other. Then she slipped.

Josie's feet went out from under her. She landed on her butt and slid down the slope. It took concentration not to cry out. Focus. She grabbed at the trees and shrubs. Caught a branch. She came to a stop, but not before dislodging a small boulder.

The rock rolled and bounced, hit other rocks with a loud clattering. Then it slammed into a tree trunk, making a loud thud. Then silence.

Josie held still. She breathed deep breaths. In and out. Willed herself to stay calm.

The skin of her hands and her right forearm burned from

sliding down the slope.

The noises had been loud enough that she was certain they could be heard by the suspect. Maybe even Samantha and Ellison, too.

Josie hoped the suspect was sleeping. She hoped that Samantha and Ellison would stay still and not assume something was wrong. The only way to sneak up on the suspect was for everyone to stay silent. Josie had failed by that measure.

She heard no sounds. Maybe all was well.

There was no path for Josie to follow. She hiked back up the slope, going at a shallow angle, turning, hiking at a different angle, turning again.

She came to a more open area. The ground was rocky, but it was possible to go across the slope without difficulty. Not just possible, easy.

Was this where the man came and went? Across this slope? Josie bent down and examined the ground in the growing predawn light. She looked for broken grasses or crushed pine needles. There was nothing that indicated the passage of man or animal. But she was aware that she had no informed idea of what to look for. Yet, the lay of the land suggested that if she went across the slope, she would come very close to where she thought the suspect's hideaway was.

Josie looked down toward the valley floor. Here and there were view windows through the trees. She studied the territory. Her eyes had never been good at picking up stationary detail. But she could see movement well. She raised her arm in a gentle wave.

There. A motion. A return wave. It was Samantha. In her hoodie, no one could tell who she was or even if she was a she. She could have been a skinny guy with a dog.

Josie looked to Samantha's side. She couldn't see Ellison. But, presumably, he was there in the trees.

Josie resumed hiking. Across the slope. Toward the suspect. Toward what she assumed would be a confrontation. She came to more boulders and trees. They blocked the slope. There was no easy way forward.

There was a narrow passage between two huge rocks. It might be possible to squeeze through. What was beyond? Josie thought she was very near the suspect's den. If she got through the passageway, she might be at his doorstep. If so, he'd be surprised, maybe angered. He might shoot.

Josie looked up. The sun's rays were touching the treetops. The suspect was probably awake. Maybe already gone.

Josie called out in a voice that was clear but not very loud.

"Hello? Anybody here? Hello? I don't want to intrude or surprise. It looks like I'm approaching a campsite. Is anybody around?"

She paused, waiting, listening.

"Hello? I'm coming through. I hope it's okay. Please say something if I shouldn't."

She walked up to the narrow passage between the rocks, turned sideways, and started to squeeze through.

"Stop right there," a man's voice said.

THIRTY-FOUR

Josie froze. She could see nothing.

"Who are you? And what are you doing here?" the man said. His voice came from behind the rocks.

Josie was leaning to the side, her hands against the rock, taking some of her weight, stabilizing herself in an awkward position. She slowly turned her head a little. She sensed a vague dark shape to her side. A man. Holding something like a stick.

Josie's arms shook with strain. "I can't hold myself in this position any longer. Is it okay if I move a little?"

"Move very slow," the man said.

Josie shifted, moving in slow motion, turning a little. She managed to step out of the narrow passage in the rocks. She held her hands up so he could see that she held no weapon.

He was in the shadows of an overhang. He had a broad-brimmed hat, camo brown, pulled down low, shading his face. The hair projecting from below the sides of his hat was brown and medium long. He was tall, over six feet. Not thick, but he seemed muscular. He wore brown denim pants like the evening before. Only now he had on a brown leather motorcycle jacket that was so worn it looked like a camouflage jacket. He wore heavy, leather hiking boots. The man had no beard or moustache, but it had been several days since he'd shaved. The stick he was holding turned out to be a rifle. His left hand held the barrel, his right was down near the trigger.

He said, "Who are you and what do you want?"

His tension was obvious. He reminded Josie of a compressed spring, a man who was ready to explode at anyone who got in his way. Josie thought that the only reason he hadn't had a violent reaction to her was that she was a middle-aged woman who couldn't look threatening if she tried.

Yet she realized that if she didn't telegraph complete honesty when she answered his question, he might shoot her.

"My name is Josie Strong. I'm a professor from UCLA. My daughter committed a crime, so we're in severe trouble with the authorities. The California Bureau of Investigation made us a proposal I couldn't refuse. They wanted me to help find some man who is hiding in Yosemite. If I didn't, our lives would be ruined. I have no knowledge about you. I don't even know your name. I have no desire to see you get in trouble. All I'm trying to do is save my daughter from going to prison. Maybe you're the man they want. Maybe not."

"How did you find me?"

"I have a student at UCLA who is a computer hacker. He used satellite cameras to look for movement in the forest. Some kind of infrared vision. He told me that, in the last couple of days, there was a lot of movement near this spot."

The man frowned. "Something weird is happening in the woods. I heard some people talking about strange burn marks."

"You can hear people up here?"

"Internet news. On my phone. Headphones. So I went to look. I found some burns. Like the letter G. Then there was some kind of moaning, roaring sound in the trees. Late last night. Like a monster or something. I'm ready to pack up and move back to Florida. I'd rather deal with alligators and pythons."

The man made a furtive look toward the valley floor. "What's the hacker's name?" he asked.

Josie didn't want to take a chance and betray Cumberland.

"Garcia," she said. "Antonio Garcia."

"Let's say I'm the guy you're looking for," the man said. "What were you supposed to do when you found me?"

"They had this ridiculous idea that I would somehow bring you in. They even gave me an ID and handcuffs and shackles. How I would bring you in, I don't know. It's not like I know anything about cop stuff. And I don't have a gun. But the cuffs are in my pack if you want to check. I thought it was unlikely that I could even find you when they hadn't been able to. It was clear to me that, even if I could find you, all I could do was talk to you. Maybe convince you that they'd go easy if you turned yourself in."

"Are you alone?"

"Up here, yes. But my daughter and friend are down in that open area. They're worried about me. So I told them they could come with me to the base of this slope, but no closer."

The man seemed to think. "Let me look in your pack."

Josie raised her arm to slip it off.

"No, don't move," he said. "Just turn around and stay perfectly still."

She did as asked. She sensed him come up behind her. "What did the Bureau of Investigation tell you I did?" he asked.

Josie felt a tug on the pack's shoulder straps.

She said, "They said you stole a pickup and robbed a bank and then you killed two sheriff's deputies."

The man made a snorting sound as if scoffing.

"And they recently found another shooting victim. They think you are behind that killing as well."

Josie felt the backpack straps twist her shoulders as he reached into the pack and felt around.

"I helped rob a bank," he said in a low voice, his mouth close to Josie's ear. "Another guy stole the pickup and shot the cops. I ran for cover. The other guy didn't come with me. Later I found out he framed me for the murders. Aside from right and wrong, killing cops is stupid. And I haven't heard of any other killing. It sounds like BS to me. If they want the guy who killed those cops, they should..."

His voice was interrupted by a strange sound, a wet, squishy popping sound as if one threw a ripe tomato at a wall. Warm liquid splashed against the side of Josie's neck. Then came a crack in the air.

Josie turned to see the man's hat blow off. The man was lurching away from her, sideways, arcing through the air, back toward the overhang. When he fell and hit the rocks, his head turned. Josie saw that his temple was blown open in a jagged crater, as red as a Valentine rose.

Josie screamed.

THIRTY-FIVE

There was another crack that felt sharp in Josie's ear. The man was already dead. One bullet wasn't enough?

Josie couldn't think. Couldn't breathe. She sagged down until she was sitting on the rocks. She reached up, touched the back of her neck, looked at her fingertips.

Red with blood. The man's blood.

The man was just ten feet away. On his back, his shoulders twisted, head turned sideways. Probably dead. Undoubtedly dead. He was still the way a fallen tree is still. No breathing. No lingering tremor or jerk. His brains had been blown apart.

It was obviously the work of a sniper. The bullet came faster than the speed of sound. The sound of the rifle cracks came after the sound of the bullet hitting his flesh. Josie thought that indicated that the sniper was far away.

Josie pulled out her burner phone. She couldn't call Samantha or Ellison. Their phones were in the cars or tents.

She dialed 911.

"Nine, one, one dispatch. Please state your name and address."

Josie felt in a fog. "My name's Josephine Strong. I'm in Yosemite Park."

"What's your emergency?"

"A man has been shot. He's up above the valley floor somewhat. Below Half Dome. I don't know how to say where. Maybe a mile from the campground parking lot." Josie was shaking violently. "There's no rush to get to the victim. He's dead. But the sniper who shot him will probably be trying to leave the park. Vehicles leaving should be checked. Just before dawn, I saw a man in a dark van. One of those extra tall vans. He was out when everyone else was still asleep. He could be the sniper."

"Stay on the phone, ma'am. We'll have the park police en route to you in a minute."

"Tell them to head out the trail that goes toward Mirror Lake and the base of Half Dome."

Josie took a quick glance at her burner phone. The battery indicator was low. "My battery's dying. I'll watch for them on that trail."

She clicked off. She crawled on hands and knees over to the body. If she stayed low, maybe she'd be out of sight even from someone with binoculars. Josie tried not to look at the man's face. It was too horrible to contemplate.

She felt his front pants pockets. It wouldn't be easy to insert her gloved hands into the pockets. But she didn't dare take off her gloves because she could leave fingerprints. And she didn't want to disturb a crime scene. Clearly, she was involved in something much more complicated than she anticipated. If she could at least find out who the dead man was...

Josie could feel some coins through the fabric of the man's pockets. She felt a small tool, a pointed object. Nail clippers maybe. Nothing that felt like a wallet or ID.

She reached under him, trying to feel if there was anything in his back pockets. Nothing for the first one. The other pocket was squarely under him. She'd have to roll his body. She tried to lift up on his belt. He was much too heavy. It wasn't possible.

His thick leather jacket had empty pockets as well.

Josie crawled over to the depression behind the overhang. Pebbles felt like dull picks stabbing through her jeans and into her knees. The dawn had given brightness to the sky, but the forest was still in shadow. There was very little light under the overhang. She had a flashlight in her pocket. She turned it on only to discover that it was very dim, not at all bright enough to illuminate the depression under the rocky overhang. Why hadn't she brought one of the extra bright flashlights?

Josie peered into the recessed space. There was some bunched-up fabric. A sleeping bag? Farther back was more fabric, camouflage-colored like what hunters use. There was a glint of something metallic. The frame of a backpack. There would probably be useful information to be found in that pack. Josie began to crawl toward it, then stopped.

Crawling in there would contaminate the scene with her presence. The bigger reason was that she didn't have the nerve to venture back into that dark enclosed space.

She crawled away, over to the narrow opening in the rocks where she'd come through. She stood up but stayed bent over as low as possible in case people were watching. After squeezing through the rocks, she hurried across the rocky slope. When she came to a section of heavy forest, she went into the trees and began to work her way down the slope.

She stayed in the heaviest area of tree cover. It only took a few minutes to go down a slope that had taken her a long time to hike up. When she reached the valley floor, she was breathing hard. But she began jogging. Josie knew that her jogging was like a fast walk for many people. But she kept it up, her breathing increasing to a fast gasping pant.

It didn't matter to her that she was running away from a dead man and possibly toward a sniper. She just wanted to get to Samantha. And Ellison.

She saw movement through the trees ahead.

"Samantha!" she shouted.

Her daughter ran to her. Unknown was at her side. They hugged hard.

"Are you okay, Mama? I heard gunshots! What happened? Are you hurt?"

"No. The man we were after was there. He was shot and killed. It was horrible. But I'm okay."

Ellison came to them.

"You okay?" he said.

"Yes. The man was shot as he talked to me. I called nine one one. They said the park police would come."

As Josie said it, she saw flashing lights in the distance through the trees. Blue and red strobes. No siren, something she immediately appreciated, as sirens would do nothing but upset sleeping people all over the valley.

"Mama, you have blood on your neck. Oh, my God, it's all over you!"

Two vehicles appeared to turn off from the parking lot road and drive up the broad trail. As they approached, Josie stood in the middle of the trail, held her arms up, and waved. Samantha and Ellison were next to her.

The vehicles stopped. They were black cars with white Park Police lettering on the sides. Four cops got out, three men and one woman. Two stayed behind their open doors as if they were shields. Two came forward toward Josie. All the officers wore uniforms, black pants and jackets, with badges and emblems.

"Did one of you make a nine-one-one call?"

"I did," Josie said. "A man was killed up on that slope." She pointed up through the trees.

"Your name?"

"Josephine Strong."

"Where are you from?"

"Los Angeles. I'm a professor at UCLA."

"May I see an ID."

Josie pulled her purse out of her pack, removed her driver's license, and handed it to him.

He looked at it. "Do you know the victim?"

"No."

"His name?"

She shook her head. "No idea."

The officers asked many questions, and Josie answered them as best she could.

A few minutes later, two of the officers walked with Josie toward the slope below Half Dome while the other two cops stayed behind.

Josie called back to Samantha. "Stay here, hon. You'll be okay with Mr. Ellison. I'll be back soon."

It took her some time to find her way. The police seemed frustrated having to go slow, waiting for Josie as she struggled to get enough air to make it up the slope. But she eventually guided them to the dead man's hideaway.

They did an initial processing of the crime scene, got on

their radios, and made reports.

Josie stood off to the side.

An hour later, two more cops appeared.

One of them appeared to be in charge. One of the other cops referred to him as 'Sergeant.'

"Take us through the event from the beginning," the sergeant said to Josie. He held a small dictation recorder.

Josie explained her movements from the time she began hiking up from the valley floor before dawn through to the moment the man was shot and she rushed back down the slope.

"What was the reason you came up here?"

"I was assigned the job by the California Bureau of Investigation. They hoped I could find a man they wanted, a man they believed was hiding in Yosemite, a man they haven't been able to find."

"You're a Bureau agent?"

"No. I'm just a professor helping out the Bureau. They deputized me. But they made it clear that I'm only a deputy, not an agent with power. It's a single mission."

The cop made a single nod. "Why did they want you to find this guy?"

"They told me the suspect shot two deputies who pulled him over by Fish… Fish something. They've been searching for him for a long time."

The cop made a perfunctory nod. "Fish Camp," he said. He obviously knew about the case. "How did you end up working for the Bureau of Investigation?"

Josie explained who she was and how she'd come to the park at the request of one of the CBI agents. She left out the part about Samantha being caught as a drug mule at the border near Tijuana, Mexico.

"You have something to verify this?"

Josie reached into her pack and pulled out her Bureau ID and her lapel badge, and she showed them the handcuffs and shackles in her backpack.

"Why did the Bureau hire you and deputize you?"

"They heard that my daughter and I had found a murderer in Santa Monica. They thought I could take the same approach to finding a murderer in Yosemite."

"Which you apparently did," the man said.

"Yes."

"How did you find him?" he asked.

"To my knowledge, police normally search for a guy by tracking him through the woods. I looked for him using satellite imagery."

The officer looked at Josie for a long time. "Satellites," he said.

"Yes. Infrared sensors. It was explained to me as an ant-in-the-forest mission. It's pretty high tech. But it worked."

"You figured it out because you're a professor?" he said.

"Not at all. One of my students is a computer expert." Josie said. "He figured it out."

"The Bureau never told you the suspect's name?"

"I don't think they ever knew."

The sergeant turned to one of the other cops. "You find an ID on the victim?"

"Yeah. Guy named Hadley Painter."

The sergeant looked at Josie. "Ring a bell?"

"No. I've never heard the name before."

"Did you get a good look at the man before he was shot?"

"Yes. I'd never seen him before, either."

"Do you have any idea why he was killed?"

"No. But he told me he was framed for the murders of the deputies. So maybe that had something to do with it."

The sergeant turned to his colleagues. "You guys finish up here. Full treatment. Every possible photo. Bag every possible bit of evidence. I'm heading back down with the woman."

One of the other cops made a hand motion, almost like a salute. The other was on his hands and knees. He was wearing latex gloves and was picking up items and bagging them. He didn't even look up.

Josie walked down with the sergeant and the fourth cop. They passed a couple of EMTs carrying a stretcher up the slope.

There were more officials, police and park personnel, with Samantha and Ellison.

She hugged Samantha once again.

"Are you okay?" she asked as she pulled Samantha off to the side.

"Yeah," Samantha said in a low voice. "I've answered their questions. There's some Private World stuff where I didn't say anything more than I thought I had to."

Josie nodded.

A voice behind Josie said, "Lieutenant. What gets you out from behind your desk?"

Josie turned to see one of the uniformed officers talking to an approaching man who wore plain clothes, a light blue shirt and over it a brown tweed jacket.

"Murder in the park will do it," the plainclothesman said. "The local ISB guy is on his way. I'll be his stand-in for the time being."

The uniformed cop frowned. "I guess I'm too new to know about the ISB."

"Investigative Services Branch of the Park Police. Murder in the park gets their attention."

The uniformed cop nodded. He gestured at Josie. "This is the witness."

The plainclothes lieutenant nodded and turned to Josie. "They probably told me your name..."

"Josephine Strong."

"You've undoubtedly answered lots of questions," he said. "I have more."

"Of course."

"First, your ID."

Once again, Josie got out her driver's license, her Bureau ID, and her Bureau badge. She also pulled out the card Theo Mosconi had given her and handed all the documents to the lieutenant.

"The phone number on the card is the one that Agent Mosconi asked me to call if I found the man they were looking for."

The man looked them over, then put them in his jacket pocket."

"Wait," Josie said. "I need those IDs."

"I have to check them out," he said.

He turned sideways to Josie and began walking. His demeanor and gestures made it clear that he expected Josie to walk with him. They moved some distance away from the others and then stopped. The man had Josie go over what had happened once again. The uniformed cop stood about 20 feet away, at attention like a guard, his hands clasped in front of him. Samantha and Ellison walked toward the guard cop then stopped, so not to intrude on the space around Josie and the lieutenant.

"You said you were present when the man was shot?" the plainclothesman asked.

"Yes. The victim was looking in my pack while it was still on my back. He was suspicious of me, and I was afraid of him. So when he wanted to look in my pack I agreed. Then I heard the bullet impact. A short moment later, I heard the crack of gunshots."

"Let me clarify," the cop said. "You're saying you heard the sound of the man being shot, but it was the bullet impact you were hearing. You didn't actually hear the crack of gunfire until after that point?"

"Right."

"I'm a former Army Green Beret," Ellison called out from where he stood. "I know a little about firearms. I heard the shots from down here. It sounded like a high-powered, medium-caliber round going overhead. I'd guess a six millimeter Remington or something similar. The gunshot crack came after." Ellison pointed. "From back that way. The shooter was likely in the parking lot. If he took the shots from, say, fifteen hundred yards out from his target, the round would have found its target maybe a half second or more before Ms. Strong or I heard the rifle crack. The shootcr obviously had sniper experience. Probably military background. At the minimum, he's an experienced hunter. The shot wasn't easy. But the wind was calm, and the air was clear. It was doable for a pro."

The plainclothes cop stared at Ellison with the universal look of discomfort at having a layperson insert their opinion into an official matter, never mind whether or not the layperson's opinion suggested expertise.

Josie was thinking about what Ellison said. She wasn't surprised that he knew about bullets, the sound and such. What surprised her was his thought about the bullet being a 6 millimeter Remington. She never would have thought that a regular person would have such expertise.

The plainclothesman spoke to Ellison with an irritated voice. "You got a theory on why someone would shoot the guy up on the slope when your lady friend was up there with the victim?"

It sounded like he was insecure regarding Ellison's knowledge.

"I have no idea other than what seems like the likeliest explanation," Ellison said. "Someone had been tracking her and was expecting her to make contact with the target. The lady drew the target out. The shooter took the shot."

"You know the target?"

"No."

"You're here why?"

"I was camping in the park. Bumped into the lady and her daughter. I recognized them from when they'd been customers of mine in my blacksmith shop down in SoCal. When I asked why she was in Yosemite, the lady said she was looking for someone who was camping out in the backcountry of Yosemite. She asked if I'd accompany her and her daughter when she went to possibly meet that person."

The plainclothesman turned to Josie.

"Stay here while I call the Bureau."

"Sure," Josie said. "Ask for Agent Theo Mosconi. He's the… I guess you'd call him my boss."

The man walked away. He reached into his pocket and removed the business card Josie had given him. He pulled out his phone, dialed, talked, walked farther away, then turned to face Josie as if to keep watch while he talked on his phone.

Josie walked over to Samantha and Ellison. Samantha wrapped her arms around Josie. Unknown stood near them, looking unsettled.

The plainclothes lieutenant came back. "I'd like to look in your backpack."

"Sure." Josie took it off and handed it to him.

He opened it, looked inside, reached in and felt the corners. He pulled out the handcuffs and shackles and Josie's purse. He looked at them, then put them back in the pack and set it on the ground.

"Where is your sidearm?" he asked.

"You mean a gun?"

"Of course. The Bureau issues sidearms to all of its agents."

Josie was shocked. "I'm not that kind of agent. I'm a deputy. I have no gun. I've never had a gun. Did you talk to Agent Mosconi?"

The plainclothesman narrowed his eyes. "I was told you were issued a sidearm."

"That's not true! Agent Mosconi specifically said I was a deputy, not an agent with power. They don't hand out guns to deputies like me."

The man shook his head as if he was disgusted with Josie's lies. "He even looked you up in the computer to double check. They issued you Glock Forty-two instead of the usual Glock Twenty-six. Smaller weapon for a smaller person. His notes said that you were familiar with the six round, single stack mag."

"I don't know what you're talking about! They didn't give me a gun. I don't even know how to shoot a gun!" Josie was aware that she was nearly shouting. She added, "Ask for Theo Mosconi's subordinate. I can't remember his name. José something. José Rodriguez."

The man looked at Josie as if he found her very irritating. "I got the information I needed."

Josie sensed something very wrong with the man's tone.

"Tell me how long you've known Hadley Painter," he asked.

"I don't know him. I'd never seen him until this morning."

The man gestured toward Ralph Ellison. "And how long have you known this Army man?"

"I only just met him several days ago. A week maybe." Josie felt confused. The man's questions seemed strange. The situation didn't feel right.

"How did you meet this man?"

"I went to his blacksmith shop to get a custom branding iron."

"What was the purpose of the branding iron?"

"It was part of my investigation on behalf of the Bureau of Investigation. I was using the brand to unnerve Painter and draw him out of his hiding place."

"You said you didn't know that Painter was the victim's name."

"Correct," Josie said, trying to be clear. "It wasn't until your man found his ID that I heard his name was Painter."

The lieutenant paused as if wondering whether Josie was telling the truth. "How was your brand going to draw Painter out of his hiding place?"

"It was part of a ruse about the mythical monster named Grendel. From the poem Beowulf."

The lieutenant looked very doubtful. "How did this… this ruse work?"

"I suppose you could say it was a psychological experiment. The idea we promulgated was that the monster looks for murderers. I thought that when Painter heard about the brand and the monster, he would investigate."

"And this was at the direction of the California Bureau of Investigation?"

"Yes. Well, no. Not the Grendel part."

The man looked hard at Josie. "Why not the Grendel part?"

"We were keeping that information from the Bureau," she said

"Why?"

"Because we didn't trust... We didn't think that the Bureau was being straight with us."

"So you weren't being straight with them." The man's voice was thick with condescension. "You dreamed up this ruse in order to help the Bureau, but you didn't tell the Bureau how you were helping them."

"I suppose you could say that."

"How were you going to discover if the ruse would work?"

"We knew it was working when his movements showed up on satellite scans. He rode his mountain bike to the brand locations."

"How do you know that?"

"We saw him on his bike last evening."

The plainclothesman frowned and squinted as if he had smoke in his eyes. "But you just said you'd never seen him before this morning."

Josie couldn't breathe. She stammered, "I… I just meant I hadn't seen him up close in daylight until just before he was shot."

"Yet you saw him close enough last evening to identify him on his mountain bike. How could you claim to know it was him, if you hadn't known him previously? He would have just been an unidentified mountain biker to you."

Josie started to feel panic. The man was twisting her words. "You're missing my point. I believed it was him because his movements on the satellite scans suggested it."

"Where did you see these satellite scans?"

"I haven't seen them. They were described to me by a…" Josie felt trapped. "I hired a computer investigator to do a search of satellite databases."

"Josephine Strong, turn around and put your hands on your head so I can pat you down."

"But I've done nothing wrong. I'm working for the Bureau of Investigation!"

"I said, turn around and put your hands on your head!"

Josie did as he asked.

She felt the cop run his hands down her sides, over the small of her back, down the inside and outside of her legs, her ankles. He didn't seem to notice the elastic bandage she had around her knee. Perhaps the fabric of her jeans was thick enough to obscure the thickness of the bandage. He also didn't look in her bra. She still had her burner phone. And they didn't look in her boot, where she had cash hidden under the insole. Josie realized that the purpose of the pat down was to discover if she had a gun. To that end, the pat down revealed all it needed to reveal.

"Mama, what's happening?" Samantha called out.

The plainclothesman said, "Josephine Strong, I'm detaining you for questioning in the murder of Hadley Painter. You will come with us to our station."

"You can't do that!" Josie said. "I've done nothing wrong! All I..."

"Ms. Strong!" The man's voice was loud. "Resisting me is grounds for arrest! Turn around."

"I'm not resisting! I'm just being emphatic."

"I said turn around!"

The man put his hand on her shoulder as if to rotate her.

Josie was terrified. She turned.

"Put your hands behind your back," the cop said.

Josie lowered her hands and held them behind her.

The cop put something on her wrists. He pulled. It made a zipping noise.

A zip tie.

"You can't handcuff me!"

"Yes, I can, and I just did. One more word and I will arrest you for resisting an officer. Push me further, I might also arrest you for the murder of Hadley Painter."

THIRTY-SIX

"Mama!" Samantha shouted. "Mama, they can't do this! This is wrong!"

The plainclothesman turned to one of the uniformed cops. "Officer Bittner, take Ms. Strong to the station."

"Sure, boss."

The man named Bittner led Josie away.

Samantha tried to follow, tried to grab Josie's arm.

One of the cops pulled Samantha back.

When they were some distance from the lieutenant, Josie spoke to the officer named Bittner. "I'm not going to run from you. You can take these cuffs off. You can't handcuff me if you're not arresting me."

"Yes, we can. Handcuffs are not exclusive to arrest. They are to prevent danger to officers and the general public."

"But I am not dangerous! I want these cuffs off."

"It doesn't work like that. Consider yourself warned. As the lieutenant said, if you even verbally protest, then you are resisting an officer's order, which is grounds for arrest itself."

They came to a black Park Police patrol SUV. Bittner opened the rear door and pushed her down so she was sitting on the back seat. Josie looked toward Samantha, seeing desperation on her daughter's face. Josie didn't know what to do.

"It's okay, Sam!" she yelled. "I'll be okay!"

Samantha tried to run toward her. A cop held Samantha. Ralph Ellison stepped forward. A third cop raised his baton in warning. Ellison stopped and put his hands out to his side like an umpire calling a runner safe. Samantha tried to get out of the cop's grip. He pushed her hard. Samantha tripped and went down, hitting the ground on her side, with one of her elbows digging into the dirt.

Bittner pushed Josie's legs into the SUV, and shut the rear door of the patrol vehicle, locking her inside. He got into the driver's seat and drove away, taking Josie away from her daughter and Ralph Ellison.

Josie couldn't breathe, couldn't think. The Park Police had gotten it all wrong. Had Mosconi or someone else at the Bureau purposely lied about her? Or did they assume that because she was in the Bureau's computer, she must have been issued a gun?

For whatever reason, the cop decided she knew something about Hadley Painter. It made no sense. Josie struggled to see out the rear window of the patrol SUV. She looked back at Samantha. The view receded. The SUV went around a corner. Samantha was gone from Josie's sight.

Josie's heart was beating as if to crack her ribs. She tried to take deep breaths, tried to find small calm.

Ellison would take care of Samantha, wouldn't he? Josie desperately hoped that Ellison wouldn't be arrested, too, because that would leave Samantha abandoned in the park.

Josie felt rage as the cop drove through the park. People stared at her in the back seat of the SUV.

"Where are you taking me?" Josie asked Bittner. "What is your evidence? I've done nothing but try to help the Bureau of Investigation."

"Save it, lady."

"But I'm telling you the truth! If that lieutenant is working on some kind of hunch, he's wrong. If he's working on some information from the Bureau, then they were mistaken. Maybe they lied."

"Right. Us cops, we always lie. We just make up stuff. Like that dead body up on the slope. Like that blood that splattered on you when you shot him. Like your gun that has suddenly gone missing. What'd you do? Toss it down the slope? We'll find it, you know."

"I've never shot a gun in my life."

"It sounds like you know about guns. Who else would

even understand that a bullet could hit before the sound of the gunshot got there? You even got your friend to talk about hearing a rifle bullet. That doesn't fool us. You should know that it's impossible to tell what kind of gun was used until we either find it or find the casing or the round."

He shook his head as he drove. "People never realize, you shoot someone at close range, the blood splatters on you. And you've certainly got your victim's blood all over you.

Josie's rage grew until she couldn't breathe.

Gradually, her anger morphed into a great sadness. She'd been used in some way that she didn't understand. Samantha's mistake bringing a bag over the Mexican border had presented the authorities with an opportunity. They realized they could make Josie do nearly anything. Now she was enmeshed in some scheme, the size and shape of which she couldn't comprehend.

Josie tried to turn sideways on the back seat so that she didn't lean back so hard against her arms. The zip tie bit painfully into her wrists.

Josie knew she lived a privileged existence. But being handcuffed and hauled away from her only family was more upsetting than anything she'd ever experienced. She couldn't imagine enduring it for any longer. She had to get them to realize she wasn't a criminal.

As Bittner drove, she tried to calm herself and think about the situation from the police perspective.

A murder had been committed. Josie was the closest person when it happened. She and Samantha were the only people who knew that the victim was wanted by the Bureau of Investigation. But Josie wasn't going to mention Samantha's name. The cops would assign great importance to the fact that Josie was the one person who could be connected to the murder, no matter how remotely. It would look very bad from their perspective.

Josie also realized that the very reason to detain someone for questioning was because they were a suspect. Detaining them was a legal way to hold them for a day while they tried to acquire enough information to charge them with the crime.

Josie's best defense would be to have the Bureau of

Investigation back her up and tell the truth about her involvement. Instead, intentionally or not, they provided false information that made her look guilty. If they didn't support her, it seemed that it would just be a matter of time before she would be arrested for Hadley Painter's murder. After that would come arraignment and a trial. Unless Josie could get Theo Mosconi to tell the truth about her involvement with the CBI, she had no reason to think she would be acquitted in a trial. She'd seen far too many examples of innocent people being convicted of a crime they didn't commit.

That left her with a sickening conclusion. If Mosconi didn't put the correct information in the computer or tell the park lieutenant the truth, there was no way for the lieutenant to know she was innocent. Without a strong advocate in the CBI, she'd have to find another way to uncover the truth about what happened. But she couldn't do that from wherever it was that they detained people for questioning.

Which meant she'd have to think about escaping.

Josie didn't think these park police were crooked. It didn't appear that they were manufacturing evidence against her. But they were certainly operating on bad information.

She had a lawyer in Los Angeles. If she called him, he would try to help. But although he was smart and eager, he was young and inexperienced. He'd helped her in several small matters. But if the police arrested her for murder, she'd need a tenacious criminal defense lawyer. Josie was confident that her lawyer did not fill that description.

Without sufficient defense expertise, bad information from the Bureau could stay attached to her until she was convicted and incarcerated. Josie understood informational inertia. The more people hear that someone is a killer, the more likely they are to believe it. That applied to the police as well as potential jurors.

But if she could take control of the situation and find out what was really happening, she could possibly unravel any bad information that cast suspicion against her. To do that, she needed two things. One was freedom. The other was immediacy.

She couldn't wait to track the killer of Hadley Painter, she had to pursue it now. The legal system operated very slowly. It could take days if they arrested her and arraigned her. It could take more days getting bail posted and being released. And there was always the possibility she wouldn't be released on bail. She needed her freedom now.

Of course, escaping from police detention might be very much like escaping from jail. For all she knew, the way they detained her might be by putting her in a jail cell.

How could she escape? Samantha had probably seen how escapes were done in movies. But Samantha was nowhere near.

Thinking about Samantha gave Josie an idea. At first, it seemed ridiculous. But being locked in jail with no guarantee of release was even more ridiculous.

Josie called out toward Bittner. "Do you have my purse up there in the front seat?"

Bittner didn't respond.

"Do you hear me?! Do you have my purse? I haven't had my midday pill. If I don't have my medication, my brain goes off."

"Sorry, lady. I don't have any purse up here."

"How can you take me and leave my purse! People need their medications!"

The man glanced down toward the seat. "No purse, here. So whatever your brain does is probably gonna happen."

"I mean it," Josie said, her voice louder, her pitch higher. "I have to have my pill. You need to call your boss. Or radio, however you communicate. We need to go back. Or have your colleagues send my purse to wherever we're going."

"Lady, we're just cops. We don't have colleagues. Cops don't use fancy talk like you professors."

"It doesn't matter how you talk! If I get a brainstorm, I lose it." Josie tried to put desperation into her voice. "I'll have seizures. I'll soil your car. If I aspirate, I'll choke and die. You don't want that on your shift!"

"Stay cool, lady. We'll be at the jail in five minutes. You can calm down there."

The man drove for some time.

"I'm starting to get the aura," Josie called out. She inhaled audibly as if beginning to panic. "That's the ocular disturbance that comes first. I have to have my pill."

Bittner didn't respond.

"I can't believe you're not taking this seriously," Josie shouted. "I could die."

The officer eventually turned off the road and pulled into a small parking lot in front of a concrete block building.

He parked, got out, and opened the rear door. "Time to get out," he said.

Josie had a hard time scooting across the seat with her hands behind her back. She got her legs to the door, inched forward until her feet were out the door, dangling over the ground.

"I can't see," she said. "My aura is affecting my visual field."

"Out of the car," he ordered.

"It's coming!" Josie said, her voice filled with dread. "I haven't faced this without my medication in... in..."

Josie let herself fall back on the seat, her cuffed hands under her back, her legs still projecting out the open rear door.

She did her best to roll her eyes up as far as possible. She arched her back as if to an inhuman degree and then started jerking her body. Her head went up and down, banging on the seat cushion. She clenched her hamstrings, bending her legs hard. Her feet were still outside of the rear door, so her calf muscles slammed against the doorsill. Josie did her best to flutter her eyelids. She opened her mouth and forced her tongue in and out. The motion made it so she could get some saliva. She tried to make it bubble and foam at her lips.

Through her fluttering lids, she had a partial view of the upside-down world out of the rear window closest to her head.

The door next to her head opened.

Bittner had walked around to the other side of the patrol vehicle. He stood just outside of the open door. Josie's bucking head was near the opening.

"Oh, Christ," the cop said.

He pulled out his cell phone, tapped some buttons.

"Clark Bittner, here, Park Police, Patrol Four. I just pulled into the station. I'm transporting the potential suspect in the Half Dome shooting. She's having some kind of seizure. Better rush a bus over. What? Yeah, I'd say so, from the looks of it. Foaming at the mouth. Eyes rolled back. She warned me she'd croak without her pills. I don't know where they are."

The cop clicked off. His upside down figure in Josie's vision retreated across the small parking lot. He opened a door and disappeared into the building.

Josie relaxed her movements a bit, still arching and bucking, but not so much that she'd have traumatic brain injury by the time the officer came back.

Bittner came back a minute or two later. He stood at the vehicle door, looking down at her as he made another call.

"Our suspect is still seizing. She's still alive, but it's not looking good. I called nine, one, one. I've never seen a seizure up close. Scary stuff. What? I have no idea. It looks like she's breathing. No, I'm the one who never got the CPR training, remember? Take a video? Okay." He tapped on his phone, then pointed it at her.

Josie resumed her most vigorous movement.

After a half minute, a siren grew in the distance. The cop turned and walked out of Josie's line of sight.

The siren was suddenly loud. Tires crackled on little stones in the parking lot.

The siren turned off. Josie heard a vehicle door open, then shut. Then another door.

"What have we got?" A woman's voice.

"This suspect is having a seizure," the officer said. "Said she needed her medication, which we don't have."

Josie felt hands on her legs and hips, turning her.

Josie squinted through her eyes even as she kept fluttering her eyelids. She sensed a person in her field of vision. Smaller than the cop. A female EMT. Josie remembered what Samantha had described. The kid named Tommy was coming out of the seizure as the EMTs arrived. Josie slowed her jerking.

Two women leaned over Josie.

"Now you'll put everything you learned from the classes

into practice," said one of them.

"Okay. Okay. I'm thinking," said the other. "Airway seems clear. Patient is breathing."

Josie felt hands touching her, throat and wrist.

"Seems like she's got a decent pulse."

"Good," the first woman said. "That's your ABCs. Airway, Breathing, Cardiac. Now the DCAP-BTLS. Letter by letter."

"Right. Deformities? I don't see any. Contusions? The same. Abrasions. Penetrations. None are present. Burns? None. Tenderness? No way to tell with an unconscious patient. Lacerations. Swelling. Nothing stands out. And we can't get a history until she wakes up."

One of the women thumbed Josie's eyelids back, shined a bright light, spoke in a loud voice as if she was talking into a recorder. "Female, mid-forties, tonic, clonic seizure. She appears to be coming out of it. Her airway seems clear. Let's get her in the bus."

Josie couldn't tell who the woman was talking to.

The woman called out in a loud voice, "How long has it been since the seizure started?"

Bittner answered. "Two, three minutes."

"Would you say four minutes is the outside?" she asked.

"Yeah."

"Good," the woman said.

The officer continued, "But I could be wrong. Frankly, I was distracted because she was hysterical. A real outburst, it was. Women get so bent out of shape. But, of course, why am I telling you women?"

Lying on the car seat, still pretending she was having a seizure, Josie could easily imagine that the EMT was insulted by Bittner's comment.

Josie heard noises come from the ambulance. A gurney being raised on supports, metal braces clicking into place, wheels rolling.

Hands gripped her.

"Officer! This patient has zip tie handcuffs on. We need these off!"

"The woman is a potential murder suspect."

"The woman needs treatment!"

"She could escape."

"A small, middle-aged, unconscious woman? You think we can't handle an unconscious patient? Or maybe we'll get too hysterical?"

"I didn't mean to imply..." the man stopped talking, probably realizing he'd already said too much.

Josie kept her eyes rolled back. She felt hands tipping her sideways, more hands working at her wrists. There was a snipping sound and the zip ties came off her wrists. Josie's hands were pulled around to her front. The relief in her arms was huge, but she tried very hard not to react. She continued to pretend she was unconscious. Then came another zip as her hands were once again bound in front of her.

"What are you doing?" one of the women said. "When we get to the ER, those cuffs'll make it very hard for the nurse to find a vein."

"Sorry," the cop said. "I should ride with her. But I'm flying solo until my partner gets back here. You're in charge, ladies," the man said. "Something goes wrong, you'll be glad she's cuffed."

"What's the patient's name?" one EMT asked the officer as they put Josie on the gurney and strapped her down.

"I don't know. I didn't get the clipboard or her ID. Call her Jane Doe for now. We'll have the information very soon."

They rolled Josie to the ambulance, loaded her in the back, and locked the gurney in place. They stretched an oxygen mask over Josie's face and put a monitor over the tip of her finger.

"Whoa, heart rate is elevated," the woman said. "One twenty-five. That's fast."

"Yes and no," the other woman said. "She's been having a seizure. That's like major exercise."

One of the EMTs took a scissors and slipped the point into the fabric of Josie's jacket and shirt. She cut a large X near Josie's elbow and slipped a blood-pressure cuff around Josie's upper arm. The zip tie made it difficult. The two women tugged on the zip tie, tried to straighten and rotate Josie's arm until the pressure cuff was in the correct position. The woman inflated the pressure cuff. She let the pressurized air escape.

"One seventy over one ten. Very high. But maybe not too bad considering what she's been through, right?"

"Possibly. Put it on the chart." One woman went around to the driver's seat, started the engine and drove off.

The woman spoke back through the passageway as she drove. "I once took another EMT on her first ride. She couldn't focus. Said the siren made it so she couldn't think."

"Kind of screws me up, too. They should do siren exposure in training."

"Traffic is slow, the patient will likely live, so I'll leave lights on and siren off except at intersections."

The woman on the seat next to Josie leaned toward the passageway to the driver's cabin. "I've never seen a seizure. Aren't there drugs for it?"

"Yeah. I've heard of a drug called Diazepam. It's basically Valium. No matter for us, though, because drugs need an IV."

"Paramedic stuff."

"Yeah. EMTs can't break skin."

The ambulance hit a bump. Careened left. Then right. Josie wanted to tell her to focus on driving instead of EMT talk. But she managed to stay silent.

A minute later, the ambulance made a hard turn, then accelerated to high speed.

Josie opened her eyes half way. She tried to look dazed and uncomprehending. She waited a minute and then spoke.

"Where are you taking me?"

"To the ER in Mariposa. Just stay calm. You're in good hands. You had a seizure. But you'll be fine."

"Can I talk to you women frankly?"

"Of course. But you should stay quiet and rest."

"I'm okay. I have a bit of a story to tell you. It will probably make you angry. But I'll make it profitable to your company."

"What are you talking about?"

"I'm very sorry to tell you this. But I didn't have a seizure. I faked it."

THIRTY-SEVEN

"What?! You scammed us?!" It was the driver, the more experienced EMT who was talking. "Oh, lady, you are in so deep! You're bringing a pile of bad legal crapola down on yourself. Not to mention pissing us off."

"I'm very sorry. But please, hear me out. I beg you to let me explain."

"It better be good," the driver said. She slowed the ambulance. "It better be damn good."

Over the next half hour during the ambulance ride, Josie explained everything she could think of that seemed germane to her predicament. She gave them names and phone numbers and email addresses of people at UCLA who could provide references. She directed them to internet links to news stories about the killer she and Samantha had captured weeks before.

As Josie talked, the driver pulled up one of the stories on the ambulance computer. A past TV news story from one of the biggest Los Angeles stations played on the ambulance screen. The story also featured a video interview with the reporter talking to Josie. Following that was a short clip of TV coverage from the LAPD event where Professor Josephine Strong was awarded a medal for citizen action and courage.

When the TV interview was over, Josie told the EMTs about Samantha's detention as a drug mule and how the California Bureau of Investigation approached her. Josie explained that she had documentation in the elastic bandage around her knee. She pulled up her pants leg, and the woman in the patient compartment took the elastic off and pulled out the copies of her California Bureau of Investigation ID, badge, and the sheet that documented everything that brought Josie and Samantha into their relationship with the Bureau of Investigation.

The two women asked lots of questions. The one in the back handed Josie the copies of her ID and other information, and Josie used the elastic bandage to rewrap them around her knee. Then Josie asked where in the ambulance they stored tools such as a wire cutter or stout scissors.

The EMT driver looked up into the rearview mirror and traded a glance with the EMT next to Josie in the patient compartment.

The woman near Josie opened a storage tray.

Josie reached and lifted out a wire cutter. It was difficult to manipulate the cutters with her hands bound at the wrists, but she managed to use it to cut her zip tie, then put the wire cutter back.

Josie asked for a pen and paper.

The EMT handed her a Bic pen and a pad.

"How much does it usually cost for ambulance transport from Yosemite to the ER where you are taking me?" Josie asked.

The woman next to her shrugged. "I have no idea. But it's real expensive, I know that."

"Five thousand dollars," the driver said.

Josie nodded and wrote:

'I, UCLA Professor Josephine Strong, found myself detained and handcuffed, the result of a misplaced directive by the Yosemite Park Police. There had been a murder in the park, and the victim was a man the California Bureau of Investigation asked me to find. I believe that the CBI gave the Park Police bad information, whether willfully or not. When the police ignored my explanation for the events that tangentially involved me and then took me into custody as if I were a suspect in a murder, I faked a seizure. The policeman holding me dialed 911, and I was picked up by your ambulance service. After some searching, I discovered where the ambulance tools were kept. So I borrowed a wire cutter to cut the zip tie on my hands. Please know that the EMT women in the ambulance were extremely professional and were focused on my health and comfort. They are a credit to their employer as well as to their profession. In a few minutes, I am going to ask that they stop the ambulance and let me out. I realize that all of these events are a breach of the rules. I take full responsibility. Your EMTs have no control over my decision. They also have no authority to hold me against my will.'

'In appreciation of your ambulance services, I will mail your company a check for $10,000, which should cover your normal fee and leave extra for you to use as you like, perhaps to distribute to your EMT crews as a tip.'

'I hope to intervene with the authorities and arrange it so no one has any problem with your ambulance company.'

'Thank you for your ambulance and EMT service. Sincerely, Josie Strong.'

Josie tore the sheet off the pad and handed it to the woman next to her in the patient compartment. The woman read it.

"Tangentially?" she said.

"Oh, sorry. My daughter is constantly telling me to stop talking like a professor. It's a hard habit to break."

The woman looked skeptical.

"One more thing I'd like," Josie said. "For obvious reasons, I can't pay you two for being so helpful to me. That would be inappropriate and look like a bribe. But if you give me the name of someone in financial need or a struggling charity or business unrelated to you, I can send some anonymous financial thanks to them." Both of the women stared at her. The woman next to Josie in the patient compartment looked confused and questioning, no doubt feeling on uncertain ground with such an unusual event happening during one of her first official rescue missions. The driver looked in the rearview mirror, a deep frown creasing her forehead.

"Please," Josie said. "It's the least I can do. A quid pro quo for your help, which, of course, your employer will never know you provided. A poor person you know or some student who is deserving. I can't even reference you when I send a check. You may eventually find out about it, but that knowledge will remain between you and me."

Eventually, the woman next to her gave her the name of a neighborhood kitchen that provided meals for the homeless. "I don't know the address number, but it's on Porterpull Street in Merced."

"I'll find it," Josie said. She looked up at the driver. "And you?" Josie said.

"There's an old guy who goes to my church. He gets his groceries at the corner market because it's too far to walk with his walker to the supermarket. The corner market helps him get by each month. You could send them something to put on a credit in his name. His name is Craig Johnson. He lives in the Starshine Shores apartments on New Bethel Street in Fresno."

"Thank you." Josie made some notes and put the papers in her pocket.

Josie said, "Before you get to the ER, I'm wondering if either of you know a person I could hire to give me a ride."

"There's a cab company that shuttles people from Mariposa to the Amtrak station in Merced. They also go up to Yosemite."

"I'd prefer to stay away from official transport, if possible. It's best if I stay under the radar for the next few hours."

"Right," the driver said. "Let me think."

"I bet Lenora Jones would do it," the other woman said.

"Peach Jones's kid? I think you're right. She's always trying to scare up baby-sitting jobs and such. This would be perfect for her. Plus she's got that newer blue Toyota. They're reliable. Do you know her number?"

"No, but Peach takes calls at her salon. Let me call her."

"Would it be possible to not mention my real name? Maybe refer to me as... Sally?"

"Understood," the woman said. She pulled out her cell and dialed, talked to Peach for less than a minute, wrote down a phone number, then thanked her and clicked off. She dialed the number Peach gave her.

"Hi Lenora, this is Tammy Nathan. I'm a friend of your mother's. She does my hair. What? Right. I'm an EMT. Hey, I've got a question for you. I know a woman who needs a ride. She'll pay, of course. Where? Let me ask." The woman turned to Josie.

"Hey, Sally, where do you want to go?"

Josie thought about it. Misdirection was sometimes as necessary with good people as with bad. "Yosemite. Yosemite Valley."

Tammy Nathan relayed the information to Lenora.

"How much?" Tammy said and then looked at Josie.

Josie said, "How about four hundred dollars? Cash."

Tammy repeated the amount.

"Right," the ambulance attendant said. "Cash. Not bad for a ninety-mile round trip."

Josie heard the young woman exclaim over the phone.

Tammy spoke into the phone. "You could pick her up at the Mariposa transfer station in fifteen minutes. Will that work? Okay, good." Tammy looked at Josie as she spoke. "She's easy to spot. A sweet lady wearing jeans and a windbreaker jacket with a big ol' hole cut in the fabric by her upper arm. She's got the prettiest dark chocolate skin you ever saw and a short, L.A. updo that looks real 'phisticated."

Tammy smiled at Josie, obviously pleased with her description.

Josie held up her index finger, signaling she wanted to say something. The woman gave her a questioning look.

"Can you tell Lenora not to talk about this? Tell her I want to... surprise someone with a birthday party."

Tammy explained to Lenora. "Okay, she'll be waiting for you." The woman clicked off.

"Yosemite," Tammy said, making a little shake of her head. "Back into the frying pan, huh?"

"Yes. Thanks very much. If you can make a quick stop near the transfer station, I'll jump out."

The women nodded. The driver said, "After we drop you off, there are a couple of things we can do to delay the moment when we show up and reveal that our patient managed to disappear on us. That should help you."

Josie reached out and touched her on her shoulder. "Thank you both very much."

Five minutes later, the driver came to an intersection, turned right, drove several blocks.

The driver gestured. "We're getting close. The transit station is on the next block. Lenora should be there shortly."

Josie was briefly thinking about what she'd learned from Cumberland. She said, "Probably the ambulance company is able to watch your location in real time. So you'll want to head off immediately. Oh, one more thing. When it comes out what happened, be sure to tell your boss and the authorities that I commandeered this ambulance. You had no choice."

The driver nodded.

"You two are good people," Josie said.

She reached for the back door of the ambulance, then paused and raised her hand to her hair. "Is this really called an updo? My hairdresser calls it top curls."

"Oh, honey, top curls is fine." Tammy said. "But Peach is one of the world's experts, and updo is what she calls anything where the action is on top. I even saw them in her portfolio. She's got a whole section of updos. And there's these women in Merced, some kind of doctor and nurse group, I guess. They all come up to Mariposa to have Peach do their hair, and they all get beautiful updos like yours. I'd get that look myself if I didn't have this limp, stringy pretend hair."

Josie gave her a warm smile. "Thank you both again."

THIRTY-EIGHT

Josie stepped down out of the rear door, shut it behind her, and the ambulance drove away.

She walked over to the transit station, which was little more than a sun canopy that shaded a bench on the sidewalk. On the street in front was room for vehicles to pull over. The place was deserted. She sat down on the bench and took off her boots. She straightened her legs and rotated her feet, stretching them. She leaned forward, stretching her back, hoping it would disguise her movement as she reached into her left boot, lifted up the insole, and pulled out the baggie with cash in it.

A minute later, she had her boots back on and the cash in her pocket.

She remembered that she'd been splashed with blood. She didn't want her hired driver to see that.

Josie found a tissue, used her tongue to moisten it, and scrubbed the side of her face and neck in an effort to remove the blood.

For a moment, Josie's thoughts went to Samantha. Josie's breath caught. She was about to start crying when a blue Toyota hatchback pulled up. The passenger window rolled down.

"Are you Sally? The woman who wants a ride to Yosemite?"

Josie waved and grinned. "That's me. Thanks so much." She opened the passenger door and got in. The driver was a red-headed, green-eyed white girl even skinnier than Samantha. She had one of those striking, angular faces with a sharp jaw line and wild eyebrows that some people would think is homely but agents might think is the face of the next super model.

"You must be Lenora. I'm Sally. I really appreciate you giving me a ride." Josie fanned out four $100 bills, and handed them to the girl.

The girl grinned and stuffed the bills in the front pocket of her jeans, then drove off. "We'll be in Yosemite in just an hour or so."

"Actually, I just got a phone call that changes my destination. Can you take me to Merced, instead?"

"No problem," Lenora said. "I'm all, you know, at your service," she said in a kind of teenaged slang. "Merced is about the same distance but a faster highway."

After they'd driven for 20 minutes, heading west toward Merced, Josie thought she was safe. She breathed deep, slow breaths, striving for calm. She thought that when the ambulance women reported her missing, they would probably say that she was heading back toward Yosemite. If the police were thorough, they would talk to Peach, who would possibly report that her daughter had been hired to give a woman a ride from Mariposa to Yosemite. Meanwhile, if they communicated with the Yosemite authorities, the Park Police would be watching Samantha. They'd be aware of Josie's Prius and the tent. They'd possibly be aware of Ellison as well. They'd watch for any indication of Josie returning to the park.

"Do you live in Merced?" Lenora asked.

"Yeah. I had car trouble in Mariposa. Gotta get to my night job at the bakery."

"Oh, I always thought baking would be an awesome job. Yummy pastries."

"It is awesome. But as you can see looking at me, there's about twenty-five pounds worth of downside to eating them."

Lenora drove fast, taking the corners like she'd watched too many car races on TV. Josie was glad to gain distance from the police even though the fast turns threatened to make her car sick.

As Lenora was looking to the left and pulling into a tight turn, Josie reached into her collar opening and pulled her burner phone out from her cleavage.

She didn't dare call Samantha. She knew Samantha's phone was compromised. So she dialed Ellison.

He answered on the second ring.

Josie realized she needed to be thoughtful about her wording so as not to draw too much of Lenora's attention. "Hello, Ralph? Our connection sounds strange. Is my voice clear enough? This is Sally." Josie held the burner phone tight to her ear so Lenora couldn't overhear Ellison's response.

"Sally," Ellison said in Josie's ear. "I get it. You can't talk freely."

"Right. I'm looking forward to seeing you again, Ralph."

"So I'll just talk softly and casually," he said, "and answer your unspoken questions. Samantha is fine. She's a tough kid, that one. Sees you get hauled off, and instead of falling apart, she gets mad. I won't hand the phone to her. That might alert anyone watching us. Samantha is watching me talk to you, so I'll just let her know not to react, and I'll say that you're fine. That's correct, right?"

"Yeah, sure," Josie said, trying to sound normal, aware that Lenora was listening. She wanted desperately to talk to Samantha, but now was not the time.

Ellison lowered his voice. "I called my cop friend. Don't worry, he won't blab. He looked at the computer reports and said you had a seizure and were taken away from the jail by ambulance. He also said that you escaped from the ambulance not long ago, and you're now an official fugitive. Arrest warrant to prove it. Exciting life you live, Professor Strong. Because you sound fine to me, maybe that indicates that you faked the seizure and used that to get an ambulance ride, which led to your escape."

"That pretty much sums it up," Josie said, glancing at Lenora. It seemed she was focused on her driving.

"My kind of woman," Ellison said. "So now you've got the coppers chasing in circles while you put your plan into action. Speaking of which, can you indicate your plan without giving away critical info to whomever is near?"

"Well, I had car trouble in Mariposa, so I'm getting a ride to my job in Merced." Josie was thinking fast, trying to anticipate how Lenora would interpret the conversation. "They've switched me over to the graveyard schedule at the bakery, but we could meet this evening before I go to work or in the morning when I get off. Would that work?"

"Certainly. I'll bring Samantha and Unknown in the truck. If they scrunch down on the floor, I can cover them with a pile of clothes and my sleeping bag. And if the coppers haven't posted a description of me and a BOLO at the entrance gate, we might be able to get out of this park. We'll just leave your wheels here."

"Okay. Thanks so much," Josie said.

"So we'll see you in Merced. I'll call your burner when we get there. If we don't have trouble, we'll be there in, let me think, about two hours or so."

"Thanks. Save room for some donuts."

"Donuts?"

Josie clicked off. Because Lenora might notice, Josie put her phone into her pocket, rather than back in her bra.

"Your boyfriend likes donuts big time, huh?" Lenora said.

"He's not really a boyfriend. But yeah, if you bring donuts, he's, like, all over 'em," Josie said, hoping the casual slang would sound authentic. "Yours, too?"

"I don't have a boyfriend, either. But my brother, he says, 'I don't do beer and pot like my friends, I do donuts.'"

Josie nodded. She and Lenora made a little additional small talk here and there but mostly rode in silence.

As they approached Merced, Lenora said, "Where should I drop you off? Am I taking you to the bakery? Is it downtown?"

Josie immediately realized the pitfalls of not knowing the territory. If she couldn't mention a street, she'd reveal that she was a kind of imposter. "I don't go to work for some time. So maybe just drop me anywhere that's convenient for you."

Lenora nodded. "I don't know Merced very well. My friend goes to the university, so I know that area some."

"Tell you what," Josie said. "Could you take me there, if you don't mind? I know someone there, too. He could help me figure out how to get my car towed."

"You paid for the ride, so I'm happy to take you wherever." Lenora drove toward the center of town, then turned north on one of the cross streets. "I even thought about going to that school myself. It's a nice campus. Even that big metal sculpture, all shiny, is kind of cool. But I don't know what I'd study. My friend majors in history. Imagine that. What in the world will she ever do with history?"

"Yeah," Josie said. "Are there history jobs, or what?"

"I guess she could teach it if she gets desperate," Lenora said as she made another turn and accelerated.

"Ah," Josie said. "I never think of that."

"But who'd want to be a teacher..."

"Right," Josie said.

In the distance was a shiny, metallic sculpture in the vague shape of a U. It was as tall as a multi-story building.

Lenora said, "My friend says that metal sculpture is called 'Beginnings.' How's that for weird?"

"Pretty weird," Josie agreed.

"Where should I drop you?"

"How about near the sculpture."

"Perfect." A minute later, Lenora pulled over to the side of the street. "This good?"

"This is good. Thanks again." She opened the door and got out. "Thanks, Lenora. You make the best driver ever."

"Thank you, Sally."

Josie shut the door, and Lenora drove away.

Josie felt exposed standing on the big open area of grass that surrounded the Beginnings sculpture. She didn't imagine the police would be looking for her in Merced, but...

Josie walked toward one of the closest buildings. She found a place where she could sit and not be so obvious. She pulled out her burner and dialed Ellison again.

"Yup?"

"It's Josie."

"Good. I think we've made it," he said. Then, "Oh, crap, maybe not. More cops ahead. I'll call back." He clicked off.

Josie waited, worrying. Imagining Samantha trying to hide by curling up on the floor of the pickup, holding Unknown, covered in a sleeping bag and clothes. Maybe there was a road block. Or a check point, with the police checking all drivers, looking into vehicles. They'd probably wonder why Ellison had a big pile of clothes on the floor next to him.

After ten excruciating minutes, her phone rang.

"Ralph?"

"We're out of the park," he said.

"Thank God," Josie said.

"Samantha and the hound are still hiding under clothes. I want to make more tracks before she emerges. But I thought I should call so you would know we're okay and you can relax."

"Thanks. I was so worried..."

"It was touch and go there for a bit. The police were interested in my business. They were looking at this sleeping bag and the pile of clothes. I told them my friend Will Southern manages the vacation rentals for Wavoka Real Estate, and they had a wedding party coming to stay in the three Sequoia Grand units, and how they found a ton of mouse droppings and even some roaches in the loft bedding and one of the closets, so I was making a run to the laundromat in Mariposa. The cop said it was good I didn't put the bedding in the truck bed because it would blow away. But he still stared at the pile and frowned like he was uncomfortable. So I joked that if they wondered if I was smuggling something over the mountains from Nevada, I'd be happy to haul it all out onto the parking area next to them, but that the dust from mouse shit carries bubonic plague, and it blows in the slightest breeze. So the cop shook his head and told me to be on my way."

"Do you really know a vacation rental manager?" Josie asked.

"No. That's about as real as your Grendel BS."

"I see. But good details. It was the details that sounded convincing. Can I talk to Sam?"

"I'll slip this phone to her."

Josie heard some muffled noises.

"Mama, you escaped! I'm so happy. We escaped, too."

"Hi, hon. I'm glad you're okay."

"Mama, Mr. Ellison is as devious as you. He had us leave

both our tents and other stuff so it looks like we're still at the park. He even got some of his underwear and socks wet, then hung them up to dry. He said no one would leave underwear hanging out if they were going to leave."

"Smart."

"Where are you?" Samantha asked.

"I hired a woman to drive me to Merced. I'll wait for you here. If you give the phone back to Mr. Ellison, I'll tell him where to go."

When Ellison was back on the phone, Josie explained that she was at the university campus in Merced.

"That should be easy to find," he said.

"When you get to the campus, look for a huge U-shaped sculpture. It's shiny metal. Probably forty feet high. If you drive on any of the perimeter streets, I'll see you."

"Will do," he said. "I'm guessing we're an hour out. Give you time to find some donuts."

Josie looked around. "Sorry, that reference was to make it seem real to the woman who was driving me."

"Conversational verisimilitude," Ellison said.

"Something like that. Thanks so much, Ralph." Josie said.

"Now that we're on the subject, I almost don't notice Ralph. In my brain, my name is Ellison."

"Mister or just Ellison?"

"My friends, few as they are, just call me Ellison. I'd like you to be a friend, so..."

"Just Ellison it is," Josie said. She clicked off. She started to slip the burner phone back into her pocket when she remembered that Samantha's suggestion of hiding the phone in her bra was the only reason she still had the phone after the lieutenant patted her down. So she tucked the phone back in her bra.

THIRTY-NINE

When the old rust-colored pickup appeared on the street across the commons, Josie stood up from the bench where she was sitting. She raised both her arms above her head and waved. Then she thought about how Cumberland had explained that street cameras were ubiquitous. She quickly lowered her arms and looked around to see if any cameras were obvious.

The pickup turned onto an intersecting street and drove closer. It stopped as it came to the closest point. The passenger door opened, and Samantha ran out. Unknown trotted next to her.

"Mama!" Samantha called out.

Josie walked fast. She and Samantha hugged. Unknown stuck her nose between them. "I was so worried, Mama!" Samantha said.

After a long embrace, Josie whispered in Samantha's ear. "Your phone?"

"Completely turned off and tucked into a compartment in the rear bed of Mr. Ellison's pickup."

"Good. Thanks."

"What about your ID and badge?" Samantha asked.

"Still in the Prius with my regular phone, as far as I know."

"So we're safe," Samantha said.

"Are you okay?" Josie's voice was choked with emotion. "Did the police hurt you when they pushed you down?"

"I'm okay, Mama. I didn't get hurt. Mr. Ellison called somebody and found out you'd been taken to jail. He said he wouldn't leave us until you and I were back together."

Ellison walked up. He reached out both hands, took Josie's hand, and held it. "Sorry you had to go through that charade, or whatever it was. It certainly seems like a miscarriage of justice."

Josie leaned toward him and whispered. "First I should ask if you have your cell phone on you."

"After I spoke to you and we made plans to meet here, I pulled over to help Samantha out from under the clothes and sleeping bag. At that time, she made me check my phone to make sure the locator was off and then I shut it all the way down. Then she told me that phones that are powered down still phone home, so she made me hide it in the cubby in the rear of the truck. Hers went in there, too."

"Really, Sam? You forced him to hide his cell?"

Samantha grinned. "I'm a good student. I learned what Cumberland taught us."

"Even though it's likely the coppers still don't know who I am," Ellison said. "But they will soon. And your daughter is persuasive. Don't wanna get on her bad side. Anyway, this Mosconi dude seems corrupt. What do you think?"

"Let's sit on the grass and talk about this."

They sat. Josie and Samantha linked arms. Unknown lay at their side. Ellison was across from them.

"They treat you all right?" Ellison asked.

"Considering they detained me for questioning about the murder, I suppose so."

Josie gave them the details of her ambulance escape.

She looked at Ellison. "Anyway, thanks, Ral... Ellison, for staying with Samantha and then coming to rescue me. I don't know what we would have done without your help."

He nodded. "Can't let a girl be abandoned in the woods. I moved my tent close to yours in case you were gone for the night. Like I already said, Samantha's a tough kid. It was obvious that having you hauled off was distressing. But she didn't complain or cry. I think you should keep her." He made a little grin, then reached out and patted Samantha on her shoulder.

"What do we do next, Mama?" she asked.

Josie looked at both Samantha and Ellison. "I'm open to suggestions. First, it seems that Theo Mosconi is either evil and set me up, or he's incompetent. If he's evil, he'll be looking to capture me. With both the Bureau of Investigation and the Park Police after me, I'll have a hard time escaping. Sam?" Josie said. "What do you think?"

"They treated you totally rotten, Mama. The only reason I can think of why they would do that is if Mosconi is rotten and he pressured them to think you were the murderer. Now that I think back on it, the search we did for the cop killer doesn't feel right. It's like Mosconi wanted Hadley Painter found. But his reason seems bogus. Do you even know if cops were killed at Fish Camp?"

"I think so. The local police knew about it, so that seems true. But I don't think it's clear who did it. Right before Hadley Painter was shot, he admitted to robbing a bank but said he was framed for those murders."

Samantha's eyes got very wide open. "No!"

"Yes." Josie nodded.

"Maybe Mosconi wanted Painter dead for some reason," Samantha said. "But he or the other cops couldn't find the man. So he got you to find him. Theo could have had someone follow us, and as soon as you found Painter, he was killed. I think you're… What's it called?"

"A fall guy?" Ellison said.

"Yeah," Samantha nodded. "I think we need to get out of the area. Get back to L.A. as fast as possible. Remember what Cumberland said. It's easier to hide where there are lots of people."

"I don't have a clue what we should do or where we should go. The day is mostly gone. Where will we spend the night? And what about our tents and our car, all back in Yosemite?"

"You want my input?" Ellison asked.

"Please," Josie said.

"First of all, forget about the tents. The grounds people will collect our gear and put it in their lost and found. It will end up donated to some cause. As for this Mosconi fellow, you want to expose him, right?"

"Yes." Josie nodded, as much to herself as to Ellison.

"But to do that you need freedom. Which is, of course, why

you escaped. In light of that, your car and other stuff is of no importance at all. In fact, having the car in the park will make law enforcement wonder if you're staying near or coming back. So your freedom will be found elsewhere. Back home in Los Angeles."

"Except that we can't go home," Samantha said. "They will look for us there, right?"

"Right," Ellison said. He paused as if considering something. "You can stay with me."

"We couldn't impose on you like that."

"Yes you can. It's my idea."

"They will look for me at your place as well."

"Eventually. But they might not figure out who I am for another day or so. They didn't ask my last name. Which I'm sure was an oversight. But to them, I was just a bystander who happened to have met you in Los Angeles. Of course, they'll see that my tent was left near yours. Eventually, they'll find their record of me entering and leaving the park. They've probably got video. Maybe someone will remember seeing me near my truck. The policeman I told about going to Mariposa to do laundry will communicate with the police who came to the crime scene. But that will take some time. Once they figure out that I was the guy in that pickup, they'll get my license plate and get my identity from the DMV. They'll put a BOLO on my truck. So we'll need to stay off the interstate and other main routes as much as possible. That's hard to do while driving to L.A. Hopefully, they won't start that search until we get back home."

"The DMV records will tell them where you live."

"It'll give them my Post Office box," Ellison said. "But it won't be easy to get my home address because my loft is owned by my limited liability company. The LLC name is not my personal name. Like I said, they'll figure it out. But it'll take them some time. I have a friend with a minivan. He'll let me borrow it. As long as I don't drive my truck to my home, we'll have anonymity for at least a couple of days."

"An LLC is a limited liability company," Josie said slowly.

"I'm curious why you have an LLC to own your house?"

"It's not a typical house. It's an old warehouse building that was remodeled for artist lofts. I bought the loft to use as a metal foundry space. I was going to move my business there. So I put the title for the loft in the name of my business. But once I moved in, I realized it would make a nice living space. So I left my foundry business in the rented space, sold my little house, and moved into the loft. Bottom line is that my personal name is two steps removed from my home."

Josie nodded. "Handy for privacy's sake."

"Yeah. I actually learned about it in training as a Green Beret for our tours in Southeast Asia. They spent a lot of time on how to build a fake identity for infiltrating enemy groups. They didn't talk about LLCs. I don't even know if LLCs existed back then. But they talked about not having one's real name on records that hostile governments have access to. Of course, that is useful in dealing with our own government as well. Anyway, I'll call my friend with the minivan. But, of course, that will require a phone. I doubt mine is currently monitored, but..." He looked at Samantha.

"Mama has her burner phone."

Josie nodded. She began to reach inside her shirt, then hesitated because of self consciousness.

"Just give him your phone, Mama. It's not like Mr. Ellison is going to have a problem with, you know, your storage technique."

Josie made a solemn nod, reached into her bra, and pulled out her phone. She wiped it on her jeans and handed it to Ellison. "Sorry my burner is kind of sweaty."

"No problem," Ellison said. Josie saw him turn the slightest bit toward Samantha and give her a wink. Maybe Samantha had already told him about their hiding places. There was no privacy with these two!

Ellison dialed. He listened for a bit. The "Hello" of the person answering was loud. "Ellison here. Is Homer in?" Pause. "Right. This is a burner. I'm just wondering if I can borrow his minivan." Pause. "Call back this evening? Will do. Thanks."

He clicked off and handed the phone back to Josie.

"Your friend doesn't have a cell phone?" Samantha asked.

Ellison shook his head. "There's a few of us left."

"But you have a cell."

"Only because I use it with one of those credit card readers to take payments from my customers who like to pay with a card. If I didn't need that, a cell phone would seem to me the way a leash seems to a dog. A way for others to control more of my time. And at my age, I'm aware of my remaining time slowly draining away."

Samantha made a slow nod, her hand stroking Unknown.

"How long do you think it will take to drive to L.A.?" Josie asked.

"Five hours. But it's gonna be real cramped with three of us and the hound all in the seat of my truck. And it's already late and we've been up since before dawn. We could use some sleep."

Samantha said, "Let's drive a good distance from here and find a motel where we register under a false name and pay cash so they can't identify us."

Josie looked at Ellison as if with an unspoken question.

"I agree. Your kid's got brains. Let her figure this out."

"But I used most of my cash hiring the ride to Merced," Josie said.

"I don't have cash, either," Ellison said. "And motels get uncomfortable with cash customers. Makes them think of drug dealers."

"I can't use a credit card because Mosconi could be monitoring my cards."

"I can pay for a motel room," Ellison said. "If they're watching you, that would prevent your name from raising a red flag in the system."

"Thanks, but if they succeed in figuring out your name, they can track you as well."

"True. But, I have a credit card in the name of P.T. Elison. First initial wrong and only one L in the last name."

"You have a fake credit card?" Josie didn't want to feel

alarmed, but she was sensitized.

"Not fake. Just not spelled accurately. Twenty-five years ago or so, when I ordered a new landline phone, they got my name misspelled. That name ended up in databases. Not long after, I got a credit card come-on in the mail. It had my name misspelled like on the phone bill. I sent it in just to see what would happen. They issued the card. I still pay the rent on that P.O. box where the bill goes. I collect some mail there even though I moved ten years after that. I recognized at the time that the credit card name mistake presented lots of possibilities for obfuscation. Shades of my Green Beret training. So, I continue to use the card now and then to keep it current, and I always pay my bill on time. The only drawback is that I can't use that card in a big name hotel because they always want to swipe your driver's license as well. But the card is great everywhere else."

"You're sure this is okay."

"Of course."

Ellison had a duffel bag tucked into the truck bed cubby. He took all the clothes from the front seat, crammed them into the duffel, and tossed it into the truck bed. Although the duffel was heavy enough that it wouldn't easily bounce out, he lashed its drawstring to one of the hold-down hooks.

Then the three of them squeezed into the front seat with Samantha in the middle and Unknown on her lap. Ellison started the truck, drove through Merced and turned south on 99.

As they drove, Ellison spoke slowly.

"When the man in Yosemite was killed, you said you heard two gunshots."

"Correct."

Ellison turned to look past Samantha toward Josie. "You told the cops that one of the shots hit the man in the head."

Josie nodded, looked across Samantha toward Ellison, trying to understand what he was getting at.

"When did you first realize that the man had been shot?"

Josie thought about it. "He was behind me, looking in

my pack. I heard the sound of a bullet hitting him. It was… Grotesque. Blood splashed on the back of my neck. He fell away from me." Josie felt Samantha shudder.

"And when did you hear the sound of the gunshots?"

"Immediately after he'd been shot." Josie took a deep breath. The memory made it hard to breathe.

"The sound of the gunshots clearly got to you after the sound of the bullet hitting him. Not before."

"Yes, clearly."

Ellison frowned. "What did you do the moment you heard the bullet hit him?"

"I don't know. Nothing, I suppose. He had his hands on my backpack. Then he sort of jerked away from me. Maybe he gave me a little push or tugged at me as he fell down."

"So you moved almost immediately after he was shot."

Josie began to feel very uncomfortable. "What are you getting at?"

"Why do you think there were two gunshots?" Ellison asked.

"I assume the first bullet missed him and the second bullet was the one that killed him."

"You said you heard the gunshots almost immediately after the bullet hit the man. Can you try to remember that? Maybe get a clearer sense of the time delay between the sound of the shot hitting him and the sound of the gunshots?"

"I don't know. I think the first crack came almost immediately. Less than a second. The second crack was maybe a second after that."

"Did the man move much when he looked in your backpack?"

"I don't think so. But he was behind me, so I don't really know."

"But you moved after he was shot. I think the second gunshot sound took too long to be the bullet that killed him."

"Oh, God," Josie said, her voice quaking. "You think it was the first shot that hit him. And the second shot was intended for me."

FORTY

"Mama!" Samantha exclaimed. She turned to look Josie directly in the face. Samantha's eyes were huge. "I can't stand it. Mr. Ellison, you think someone is trying to kill her?"

"Let's play it safe," Ellison said. "I think we should be very careful to keep you two away from your regular haunts," Ellison said. "Your house, grocery stores, your office, the university."

"My school?" Samantha said.

Ellison glanced at her as he drove. "Yeah. Probably."

Josie looked at him. "So we go to your loft. But what if someone comes after us there?"

"If necessary, we'll make a fast exit."

"But what could you do? I mean you no offense. But..."

Ellison took his right hand off the steering wheel, unsnapped his sheepskin jacket, and opened it up. On the side of his chest was a gun in a holster. "I'm old, but I can still shoot."

Josie felt a shock. "Oh, my God. You have a gun?"

"It's called a Colt Government, a forty-five caliber pistol."

"I can't believe you carry a gun."

"A Colt Government was the type first issued to me in the Army. It's an ancient model, but it works well. So after I got out of the service, I bought my own. I've had lots of experience with it. I'm quite competent."

"What's it for?"

"Blacksmith customers often pay with cash. My shop is in a rough part of town. The sheriff was happy to give me a concealed carry permit." He glanced in the rear view mirror.

"You really think someone is targeting me?" Josie thought it was the case, but she wanted confirmation.

"Yeah. Tonight, we'll find a safe place out on Ninety-Nine

and get some sleep. We'll head home tomorrow."

"Ellison, you're being so kind and helpful. We'll be okay. You don't need to babysit us."

"I'm not babysitting you. I'm trying to keep you alive."

Just outside of Visalia, Ellison pulled into an independent motel that was not affiliated with any chain. He parked and got out. He walked around to the passenger side and tapped his knuckle on the window.

Josie found the old-fashioned window crank and turned it, lowering the glass.

"You okay with this place?" Ellison asked. "A no-brand motel has less security on their computers and fewer security lights in their parking lot," Ellison said. "And they're more grateful for the business. Will you feel comfortable enough to sleep?"

"Yes," Samantha answered without even looking over at Josie. "But they need to take dogs."

"Got it." Ellison patted his hand on the roof of the pickup and walked toward the office. Josie noticed him scanning the area. He was especially focused on the street.

Ellison came back out ten minutes later.

"We're number two-ten and two-eleven on the second floor." He pointed. "The outdoor stairs are over at the end."

"Did they ask questions about who you're with?"

"Yeah. I said you two were my baby sister and niece and we were on our way back from a gathering in Tahoe. This motel is a family place, mom behind the counter, dad doing maintenance. They were happy for the business. They didn't even ask my license plate number. This is perfect for our needs. It even has old-fashioned metal keys. And they take dogs."

He handed them a big wooden key fob with a key dangling from it. Samantha took it from him. Unknown immediately sniffed the fob with interest.

"After we get settled, we can go out for some food," Ellison said.

Two hours later, they'd had a fast-food taco dinner that Josie could barely tolerate, but which Samantha and Ellison gulped down. Unknown didn't eat with enthusiasm, but it appeared she liked it more than Josie did. Back at the motel, Ellison spent a few minutes in his room, then came into Josie and Samantha's room. He had changed to a large hooded sweatshirt, a wrap that was cooler than the sheepskin jacket but that still covered his gun and holster. The sweatshirt was more appropriate for the Central Valley weather, which, in early October, was much warmer than up in the mountains of Yosemite.

Ellison pulled a can of beer out of each of his sweatshirt pockets. He held one out to Josie. "Want one?"

"No thanks."

"Mind if I have one?"

"Not at all."

Ellison put one beer back in his pocket and opened the other.

"You probably drink red wine," he said.

"Mostly white, but not a lot. How did you guess?"

He shrugged. "Seems like a woman of refined tastes would drink wine."

Samantha had one hand on Unknown. With her other hand, she gave Josie a soft, slow slug on the shoulder.

Ellison said, "I used the motel phone to call my friend with the minivan. His roommate said he's out until tomorrow night or the next day. There won't be any reason for anyone to trace a call from a motel to my friend's phone. Nevertheless, I revealed no information to the roommate. Anyway, I can't get the van until then. And I still think my place might show up on this Mosconi dude's radar sooner than I'd like. So, I'm wondering if you have a friend where you can stay tomorrow night, someone you can trust to keep quiet about your presence."

Josie saw Samantha shoot a sideways glance at her, the kind of look that said, 'This is the kind of problem that comes from your isolated life.'

"I, uh, can't think of anyone like that," Josie said.

"Just tell him, Mama. You don't need to be embarrassed." Samantha turned to Ellison. "Mama doesn't have any friends. She's, like, the lonely professor lady trapped in the ivory tower."

"No sweat," Ellison said with a casual voice, as if everyone was in the same predicament. "How about you, Samantha? You probably have lots of friends. Could you stay with them?"

"I do have friends. But the problem is they're kids. And kids can't keep secrets. They'd probably post my whereabouts on Facebook. Wait, I know who can keep a secret!" She turned to Josie. "Mama, Cumberland can keep a secret, right? Maybe we could stay with him."

"Oh..." Josie stopped. "I can't imagine it. He's nice but..."

"Loosen up, Mama. We should operate on the assumption that someone's trying to kill you. With that perspective, it shouldn't be a big deal to give him a call and ask."

"No, I suppose not."

"But you should call him now, Mama, so he has time to, you know, prepare for two people and a dog. Our phones are in Ellison's pickup. So we're in Private World mode."

Josie nodded. She dialed Cumberland with her burner phone.

"Oh, hi, professor," Cumberland said when he answered. "Did you find the ant in the forest?"

"What? Oh, yes. Thanks to you, we did. I'm calling about something else."

She explained her dilemma.

"Tomorrow night? You could sleep here," he said. "Mom's gone. And Aiden and Cara are at dad's until the day after tomorrow."

"Are you sure it's okay?"

"Yeah. Um. I don't really have any food except pizza, if that works for you."

"Yes, of course, Cumberland. We're at your mercy. Maybe we can stop and pick up some food. What would you like us to get?"

"Well, I'll probably eat the pizza tomorrow, so maybe another pizza would be good."

"I'm guessing we'll be there late morning. Is that okay?"

"It doesn't matter. I'll be here."

"Thanks," Josie said. Then she thought she didn't sound very earnest. "Thanks very much."

"Yeah. Bye." He hung up.

Josie went back into the motel room and told Samantha and Ellison that they would be okay at Cumberland's the following night. She added that it would be good if they brought food.

"Then we'll stop at a market near this guy's place. Where does he live?"

"Beverly Hills."

"You don't have friends, but you can just call up a guy in Beverly Hills and stay with him," Ellison said.

"He's a former student. It's kind of a reach for him and the two of us to have Sam and me show up at his door. But it should work. He's the guy who used computer mapping to help us figure out how to find the man in Yosemite."

"Computer mapping?" Ellison said.

"Something like that. What would you call it, Sam?"

"I'm not sure. Map data analysis, maybe."

"That sounds good."

Ellison nodded. "Okay. In the morning we'll get some food and I'll drop you in Beverly Hills. Then I'll talk to my friend whenever he gets home, and I'll borrow his minivan. The following morning, I'll pick you up in the van and take you to wherever you decide. Theo Mosconi and company shouldn't be able to figure out your whereabouts."

Ellison sipped beer. He said, "After I leave you in Beverly Hills, what will you do?"

"I'm going to see what my student can find out about the man who was killed, Hadley Painter."

"How would he do that?"

"Computers. He's a hacker."

"How does that work? This hacking stuff?" Ellison asked.

"I don't really know the best way to describe it. Samantha? How would you describe it?"

"All information goes into computers, right?" she said. "Big company computers and small individual computers. The computers pretty much all have passcodes. Kind of like door locks. When you lose your house key, you call a locksmith because locksmiths know how to open up locks, right? Computer hackers are like locksmiths."

"I've never heard anyone explain that so well," Ellison said.

Josie watched as Samantha nodded. Samantha didn't grin at the compliment. Josie realized that Samantha was developing the technique of playing things cool. Get a compliment? Act like it's no big deal, like your expertise is to be expected. Josie just hoped that, as her daughter discovered the power of her intelligence, she wouldn't get arrogant.

"The trick," Samantha added, "is to know which house to unlock. And once you're inside, you still have to know where to look to find the info you want."

"I'll remember that if I decide to segue from blacksmithing into hacking."

Ellison stood, raised his hand in a kind of salute, and said goodnight.

"Lock this door behind me," he said as he went out.

The next morning, they were headed south on 99 by six a.m. An hour south, Ellison slowed and turned into a gas station.

"I can pay," Josie said. "My purse and credit cards are in the Prius. But I still have some cash.

"Conserve your remaining money," he said. "We'll put it on P.T.'s card."

He swiped his card in the gas pump and filled his pickup.

"What a nice guy, Mama," Samantha said in a low voice.

"He certainly is. He's kind of an old-fashioned gentleman."

When Ellison was done and got back in the pickup, Josie said, "I'll pay you as soon as I can get more money."

"I'm not worried. My greater concern is your next move."

"What do you mean?"

"You're going to ask this hacker dude to help you. What if the Bureau agent can find out what the hacker is doing?"

"My assumption is that this hacker can operate in stealth mode. He's the kind of expert the Bureau hires."

Ellison nodded. He pulled out of the gas station and headed

back down 99. As they approached Los Angeles, he said, "You wanted to stop at a supermarket before we go to Beverly Hills."

"Yes."

"I know a place in Thousand Oaks. They won't think to look for you there."

A few hours later, Ellison came south down the 405, past the Getty Museum looming above the freeway. He exited the freeway and drove east on Sunset.

"Is this Bev Hiller north or south of the tracks?"

Josie knew he was referring to the old days and the rail line near Santa Monica Boulevard. "North," she said. "Past the flats north of Sunset and into the hills."

He nodded and followed her directions as he drove.

"This is so weird, Mama, not to be going home. Will we ever be able to go home?"

"I think so, hon." Josie burrowed her hand beneath Unknown and squeezed Samantha's knee.

Ellison cruised east between the Bel-Air Country Club and UCLA. Not long after they went by the Beverly Hills Hotel, Josie said, "It would be good if you turned left on the next street."

Ellison did as she said.

"Now turn right and then take the next left."

Ellison glanced at her and frowned. "Seems like we're going through a labyrinth."

"I'm trying to avoid a traffic cam that reads license plates. I forget what it's called. The hacker told us about it."

"ALPRS," Samantha said. "Automatic license plate recognition."

"Smart." Ellison made more turns as Josie directed him. A couple of minutes later, he turned into Cumberland's driveway.

"Want me to come in? Haul the groceries?" he asked.

"Actually," Josie said slowly, thinking, "it might be better not to show your face, just in case there are other security cameras at nearby houses."

"And you think someone could hack into them..."

Samantha answered quickly. "We don't think it, Ellison, we

know it. Cumberland explained. Security cameras are monitored by companies. Their video data can be mined by artificial intelligence programs. They can all be hacked."

Ellison made a little jerk of his head.

"Sorry I was brusque," Samantha said.

"No, it's good I learn these things."

After Josie and Samantha and Unknown got out of the truck and lifted their groceries out of the back, they paused at the open passenger window.

"I know you're not going to ignore what happened with those Park Police and the Bureau guy," he said. "You'll be making plans. I'm hoping you'll let me help."

"You've already helped us more than enough," Josie said. "So we're mostly going to see what ideas Cumberland has. Talking more than anything."

Ellison shook his head. "I know better than that. You two are more like action heroes than sit-at-home-and-talk ladies. I'd like to tag along and watch. It'll be like re-visiting my Green Beret glory days."

"I hope there won't be any of that."

Ellison shrugged. "Then I could at least be nearby when you kick their butts. So you go strategize with Mr. -- what was it -- Cummerman?"

"Cumberland Durand."

"Got it. I'll go borrow the minivan and let you know when I get it."

"If I need to get ahold of you before that, I'll call you with my burner," Josie said from outside the passenger window. Samantha was standing next to her, still holding Unknown.

Ellison reached across the cab, out the window, and gave Unknown a pet on the head. "I won't leave until you're inside."

Josie and Samantha walked to the door. Samantha rang the bell. Cumberland opened the door and beckoned them in. Josie turned to look back at Ellison and made a little wave.

He nodded, shifted into gear, and drove away.

FORTY-ONE

Cumberland led them to the kitchen and watched as they put their groceries away, opening cupboards, exploring, finding appropriate places. Josie couldn't decide if it didn't occur to him to help or if he didn't know where things should go.

When they were done, she sat at the little kitchen desk, put her elbows on the cold granite surface and lowered her head to her hands. It was hard not to feel overwhelmed.

Eventually, she collected her thoughts, lifted her head and said, "Thanks, Cumberland. We can't tell you how much we appreciate you taking us in. How are things in your world? Are your siblings okay? Where are you with your father?"

Cumberland shrugged and looked down at his feet. "Not much has changed. Aiden and Cara are in San Jose with him. They come back in two days. Mom will come back then, too. If I call the cops on my dad, I'll do it after they're back."

"Where is your mom?"

"She's at a friend's house in Little Armenia. She's under a lot of stress, so she kind of escapes to there whenever possible. Her friend got divorced from a man who wasn't good. I think her friend gives mom emotional support." He glanced up at Josie, then returned his gaze to the floor. "You found the guy in Yosemite." It was more statement than question.

"Yes, but he was killed."

"I read about a murder on the internet news. I wondered if it might be your guy. I also saw that you were questioned about the murder. Anyway, it's obvious now that the cops let you go."

"No. I escaped."

"Oh, wow. Your life is like a comic book. Lots of drama."

Josie nodded.

"Too much drama," Samantha said. "We've gone from the

Normal World/Private World stuff to hiding in Secret World. We can't even go home."

"'Cuz the cops will look there," Cumberland said.

Samantha made an exaggerated nod. "I don't even know where to take Unknown for a walk." Unknown was lying on the floor. At the sound of her name, she looked up at Samantha.

Samantha squatted down and pet her. "Did you see that, Mama? Unknown recognized her name!"

"You could take her around here," Cumberland said. "When I was young, I knew a bunch of trails that wind behind the houses. No cameras. The trails are probably still there. The only concern would be if you can keep your dog from barking."

"Unknown doesn't bark."

"You mean doesn't like can't? Or doesn't like doesn't?"

Samantha shrugged. "We don't know. We've just never heard her bark. Maybe that means she can't. She did make a little growl that time when you and Mama saved me from the murderer. So something in her throat works."

They ate a small lunch, then headed out. Cumberland led the way, out past the backyard pool, through a hole in a hedge. The opening was wide enough for Unknown to easily walk through. Cumberland and Samantha went through by turning sideways. But it was too narrow for Josie. She got stuck, branches poking uncomfortably into her in several places.

"You can do it, Mama! Just like squeezing through that cabin window in the Quetico Wilderness last month. Here, I'll pull these branches. Cumberland, you pull those."

"This is so embarrassing," Josie said. "I'm supposed to be a dignified professor. Instead, I'm hiding from the authorities and getting trapped in the brush on a secret trail."

"It's okay, Mama."

Cumberland led the way through overgrown foliage similar to a jungle. Occasionally, they got a glimpse through to lush backyards and more swimming pools. The twisting trail climbed up a slope, looped around, and headed back down. Josie had no idea where she was. She tried to think the way she imagined

Samantha would think. Give herself over to the spirit of adventure, follow the guide, and don't worry about everything.

An hour later, they came to yet another pool.

"This pool's a lot like yours," Josie said to Cumberland.

"It is ours. We came through the hedge a different way."

"A bigger opening where I wouldn't get stuck," Josie said.

Cumberland shrugged.

"I'm hot," Samantha said. She turned to Cumberland. "Would it be okay for me to go swimming?"

"Sure." He pointed toward a small building at one end of the pool. "That's the pool house. You can change there. There's also a shower if you want."

"But I don't have a suit," Samantha muttered.

Cumberland frowned. "You could... I've got some shorts and a T-shirt. Would that help?"

"Yeah, that would be great. Can I, Mama?"

"Of course. You're all sticky with the hiking, so you should shower and wash first."

Fifteen minutes later, Samantha was swimming.

Josie was so pleased to hear her shriek and laugh. It had been a rough time since her arrest as a drug mule.

Samantha splashed water on Unknown.

"She can go in, too," Cumberland said.

"But she's dirty," Josie said, looking at Unknown.

"I think it's okay. The pool has a good filter."

"Did you hear that, Unknown? You can swim. Do you know how to swim? Of course. You used to live in the Boundary Waters. You must know how to swim."

Samantha pulled on Unknown's collar. The dog resisted. Samantha picked her up, carried her into the water and let her go. Unknown swam to the pool steps, climbed out, and shook herself off, water spraying everywhere. Samantha's grin was huge, and that pleased Josie very much.

That evening, Josie cooked a vegetarian spaghetti dinner in Cumberland's kitchen. Without asking, she found a large mixing bowl and put some spaghetti in it for Unknown. The dog ate it at a measured pace. Josie served the rest to Samantha and Cumberland.

"When your mom and siblings are gone, you can come and go as you please?"

Cumberland seemed to think about it. "I suppose. But where would I go?"

"Out with your friends?"

"I don't have any friends."

"I'm sorry to hear that," Josie said, immediately thinking that as strange and awkward as Cumberland was, he shared characteristics with Josie.

"Have you talked to your father about his situation? Or your mother?"

Cumberland was silent for a moment. "I'm kind of in a holding pattern. I haven't decided what to do next."

"Keep me informed, please?" Josie said. "I can help. I can be supportive. But only if I know what you're thinking about."

"I can help, too," Samantha said. "I'm good at talking through stuff."

Cumberland paused, then said, "So how did it, you know, go? In Yosemite? Finding the guy."

Josie immediately thought of her detention by the police and Ellison's belief that whoever shot Hadley Painter also wanted to kill her. Josie didn't want to burden Cumberland with that information. "Yosemite went very well by most measures. Your help with the websites and the articles and the speakers was fantastic. We burned some brands and put the speakers in the woods. Late at night, we walked to different points in the forest and hit the key fobs."

Samantha spoke loudly, "Oh, my God, Cumberland! You should have heard it. The monster roar was amazing! Everyone was talking about it."

Josie said, "Later, the man we found commented on them. I could tell the whole package unnerved him. Because of the brands and the roar, he had left his lair to go look. And your analysis from the satellite information was perfect. The man was camped out right where you said he'd be. I was able to go right to his hiding place and find him. He told me that the Grendel monster unnerved him so much, he had decided to leave Yosemite. But he never got the chance."

"Because he was killed." Cumberland's voice was subdued.

"That was very sad, yes," Josie said. "I'm so sorry it came to that. But his death and your tracking information were two disparate things. You helped me. You provided critical info. And I guarantee you that when this is all done, good things will have come from this, and it will trace back to your contribution. Samantha will be in a safer place because of you."

Cumberland didn't respond for a long moment. "I also read that there was an arrest warrant for you." He sounded sad.

"Yes, that was unfortunate. There seems to be some major confusion. I haven't sorted it out, yet." She said it in a breezy way that didn't match how she felt at all. They were silent for a minute. "I have a question," Josie said to Cumberland.

"Yeah?"

"Is there a way to search on a variety of subjects where each subject might bring up thousands or millions of hits, but multiple subjects would narrow those hits down?"

"Sure," Cumberland said. "Of course, you can Google words in quote marks, and the search engine will look only for those words. But there are other ways of going through databases that Google doesn't have access to."

"I thought Google had access to everything."

"No, not at all. For example, Google can't look inside company records. Think about UCLA. The school has internal files, right? As an employee, you can access certain files with your user name and password. You have access to a world that Google does not."

Josie asked, "Can you hack into those records?"

"Sometimes. It may be difficult, but with some effort, it can often be done."

"Like military satellites," Samantha said.

"Yeah. Pretty much," he said.

"What I'm looking for," Josie said, "is a confluence of subjects. Maybe you can tell me what you think."

"Hold on, let me get a pen and paper." He got a pad out of a drawer below the kitchen desk.

Josie said, "The first subject is the man named Theo Mosconi. Maybe Theo is short for Theodore. He's probably worked for the California Bureau of Investigation for some time. Prior to that, he may have been in law enforcement in some other capacity. A second subject would be the murders of two sheriff's deputies in Fish Camp near Yosemite. Third would be a stolen pickup and three bank robberies near Merced. Fourth is the man who was killed in Yosemite. His name was Hadley Painter."

Josie paused while Cumberland wrote.

"Yet another subject is firearms. Specifically, Theo Mosconi talked about rifles that shoot thirty-aught-six ammunition. The man who made the branding iron and later happened to come to Yosemite heard the shot that killed Hadley Painter. He thought it sounded like a six millimeter Remington. So we want to keep both kinds of bullets in the mix. Thirty-aught-six and six millimeter."

Josie waited as Cumberland made notes.

"What do you think?" Josie asked. "Is there a way to find any info that would connect to several of these subjects?"

Cumberland paused. "I'll do some experimenting."

"If it's too difficult, don't worry about it."

"I don't think it's complicated. I'll try different Boolean operators and let you know if I find anything."

Josie nodded. She'd learned long ago to stop asking casual questions about complex subjects.

That night, Josie and Samantha and Unknown slept in a guest room that overlooked the pool and the jungle growth beyond. The bed was king-sized, and Samantha laid out a large beach towel for Unknown to lie on.

In the morning, Josie found coffee grounds. She and Samantha were both drinking coffee outside by the pool when Cumberland walked out.

"I've found some stuff," Cumberland said. "And I think I figured out a way that you could get the guy who did this."

FORTY-TWO

At that moment, Josie's burner phone rang.

"Hey, professor," Ellison said when she answered. "I got a van. You got a plan?" He said it like a rap rhyme, the way Samantha might have said it.

"I will shortly," Josie said. "Cumberland is just briefing us on what he's found. You said you wanted to help. I recall your words were something like re-enacting Green Beret action."

"I'm, ah, often guilty of excessive verbiage, but my sentiment was heartfelt."

"Do you want to meet?"

"Yeah."

"Hold on and let me coordinate." Josie covered the phone and told Samantha and Cumberland that Ellison had gotten transportation in the form of a van that didn't connect to him in the event that the ALPRS license plate recognition cameras picked it up. "Ellison is willing to help. Cumberland, would it work for you if Ellison comes here to your house and you tell all of us what you've found?"

Cumberland nodded.

Josie uncovered the phone.

"Ellison, why don't you come back to Cumberland's place. That would be a safe place to meet, don't you think?"

"Probably safe as any other place," Ellison said. "Name a time, and I'll be there."

"Soon would be good. How long would it take you to get here?"

"An hour?"

"Perfect," Josie said. "Humor me and leave your electronics behind?"

"You are a stickler for details," he said. "And your daughter read me the rule book yesterday. Probably'll make a great professor like you," he said. He hung up.

Josie, Cumberland, and Samantha went inside and cobbled together a breakfast from Cumberland's nearly non-existent supplies. Then Cumberland disappeared downstairs.

An hour later, the doorbell rang.

Josie walked to the door, looked through the peephole, and saw that it was Ellison. She stepped outside and shut the door behind her.

"Thanks for coming," she said. "I really appreciate it. I also want you to know that Cumberland, the young man who lives here, is a little different, not socially adroit. So don't let it put you off."

Ellison nodded. "When a military commander assembles a raiding party, you recognize that he chose each participant for their specific talents not their social skills."

"What makes you think I'm assembling a raiding party?"

"It's my specialty, and you asked me to help, ergo... Anyway, I don't expect highly-skilled participants to be my beer buddies. If they were, they probably wouldn't be in the raiding party in the first place."

"Thanks," Josie said.

They walked into the house and out the glass doors to join Samantha and Cumberland by the pool. The sun dappled the water in a few places, but most of the area was shaded by a huge Magnolia tree. With the shade and breeze, the day was cool.

Ellison and Josie sat down on lounge chairs. Unknown walked over and sat on the terrace next to Ellison's lounge chair.

"What?" he said to her, leaning his head slightly toward her, staring at her intently. She moved her tail as if hinting at a wag, then lowered her head and rested her jaw on his thigh, her eyebrows lifted as she looked up at Ellison.

He rubbed her neck.

"Cumberland, this is Ralph Ellison," Josic said. "Hc's hclping us. He made the branding iron and helped us in Yosemite." Josie turned to Ellison. "Cumberland is the computer expert who found the fugitive in Yosemite by using satellite imagery."

Cumberland didn't move. He sat stiff as a wooden figure, uncomfortable with her introduction, apparently uncomfortable seeing a person he didn't know. He gave the briefest glance at Ellison, then looked away with what seemed like alarm as if Ellison were a bull with horns and looking directly at his eyes might trigger a dangerous reaction.

Ellison lifted his hand in greeting.

Samantha, sensing discomfort, reached across and, with two fingers, briefly rubbed Cumberland's knee, an act of reassurance. Josie watched as Cumberland looked at Samantha's hand like it was an unusual life form, a starfish that had crawled out of a tide pool. Cumberland didn't say anything. Josie realized that this much socializing was far beyond his comfort level.

Cumberland had a sheaf of papers in his lap. "I looked up the guy who talked to you at the Bureau. Theo Mosconi. I printed some stuff out. Because, you know, it's safer than emailing."

"Right," Josie said.

"I found some things that aren't all, um, alarm-bell stuff individually. But together, they kind of add up."

"I'm eager to hear."

Cumberland looked down at the papers as he spoke. "Some of this comes from databases. But I also found some county and city crime reports that I think apply."

He folded the top sheet in half, then unfolded it, an unconscious nervous movement. "Fifteen years ago, there was a guy in Florida named T. Willem Moscone."

"Just to make sure I understand," Josie said, "Moscone is spelled with an E at the end, not an I like Theo Mosconi."

"Correct," Cumberland said. "Moscone was charged with robbery and with impersonating a police officer and wearing a uniform to interrogate people and confiscate their belongings. He pled guilty to lesser charges, got a five-year sentence, was let out on probation after two years, but skipped town before his probation was over." Cumberland put his index finger on his paper as if finding his place.

He continued, "Moscone's mother had a second husband

named Tal Painter. Which is how Moscone ended up with a stepbrother named Hadley Painter."

Samantha inhaled so loudly that Unknown lifted her head off Ellison's leg and looked at Samantha's face.

Josie said, "You think that T. Willem Moscone is Theo Mosconi."

"I'm pretty sure," Cumberland said. He continued, "Hadley Painter was briefly married to a woman named Theresa. Theresa and Hadley Painter lived in Tallahassee. They were visiting Hadley's stepbrother T. Willem in Miami, staying at Moscone's apartment, when Theresa died in a bathroom fall. The death was ruled accidental. The newspaper article said she'd died from accidental blunt force trauma. Basically, she slipped and her head hit the bathtub faucet."

Cumberland looked up at them for a moment.

"Theresa had a term life insurance policy that had been taken out by her father when she was a kid. The insurance company was Florida General Life and Accident Insurance. Theresa's father paid the premium until Theresa turned twenty-five. After that, Theresa paid the premium each year. The policy had a double indemnity clause in case of accidental death."

Josie interrupted him. "Whoa, Cumberland, I can't breathe. Let me think for a moment." After a moment, she spoke. "Who was the beneficiary of the insurance policy?"

"In the beginning, it was her father. When he died and Theresa started paying the premiums, she changed the beneficiary to her husband, Hadley Painter."

"Do you know what the payoff amount was?"

"The policy was for one hundred fifty thousand. The double indemnity clause for accidental death made the payout three hundred thousand."

Josie couldn't speak. It felt like a poisonous fog had descended over her. She was vaguely aware of Samantha at her side, and Unknown and Ellison on Samantha's far side. Josie looked across the pool at the thick plantings as she thought about what Cumberland had said, revisiting the salient aspects.

The man in hiding in Yosemite, the man Theo Mosconi

had set her up to find, was Mosconi's stepbrother Hadley. And the implication of the Theresa Painter's death was that Hadley Painter and Theo Mosconi conspired to kill her and split the insurance money.

Josie stared at the leaves of the Magnolia as she visualized a young woman in a Florida bathtub, her skull cracked, her scalp torn, and copious blood draining into the tub.

"Professor Strong, are you okay?"

Josie looked back at Cumberland. "Yes. Sorry. I'm okay."

Ellison asked Cumberland, "You get all this stuff off the computer?"

Cumberland looked uncomfortable. "I don't understand the question. Everything comes off the computer."

Ellison nodded.

Cumberland looked over his notes, turning the page over, then continued. "Hadley Painter took the insurance money and moved to California. I think I said that T. Willem Moscone skipped his probation and disappeared right around the same time that Hadley Painter moved."

Josie saw Cumberland look up at her face as if to see how much he should explain. She nodded to show that she was following. And Josie could see the shock in Samantha's and Ellison's faces.

Cumberland consulted his notes. "The slightly different name Theo Mosconi is in the records as receiving a criminal justice degree from the University of Nevada Las Vegas four years later. After graduating, Mosconi moved to California. Seven years after graduation, the name Theo Mosconi shows up in the databases as an intern at California's Bureau of Investigation. Later, he was listed as a full-time employee who became an agent. Maybe it's the same person?" Cumberland looked from Josie to Samantha, then gave the briefest glance at Ellison.

Cumberland turned over the note paper and looked at his writing on the back side. "Maybe this is of no consequence, but I found out that the Bureau of Investigation issued him a vehicle, a Ford Explorer. The DMV address for his driver's license is a house near San Bernardino. The house is a three bed, two bath ranch in a small canyon. There are no close neighbors. But on the ridge up above the house, two neighbors have filed noise complaints about the house hidden down below them. They say that they hear loud music at all hours, and they often hear gunfire, both day and night. A San Bernardino crime log report shows that police visited, and the occupant of the house, Theo Mosconi, claimed he had a legal right to engage in target shooting on the canyon wall behind his house. He showed the police his multiple weapons and permits. The police report showed that one rifle was chambered for thirty-aught-six ammo. The rifles were registered to Theo Mosconi."

"Oh, my God, Cumberland. You've hit pay dirt," Josie said. "I can't thank you enough."

Cumberland ran his fingertip down the paper. "There's other stuff if you want it."

"It's hard to imagine there could be even more."

Cumberland looked back down at the papers. He pulled out a different sheet.

"A couple of months ago, federal agents raided an illegal gambling house. They caught several men who were connected to organized crime. With them was Theo Mosconi. Apparently, he had a gambling debt with those guys, and he had convinced them he could use his position with the California Bureau of Investigation to help them. After he was caught, he was fired from the Bureau and charged with multiple crimes. He posted bail and then disappeared."

"Wait, wait," Josie said. "Are you saying that when Theo Mosconi made the deal with us to find Painter, he had already been fired and was a fugitive?"

Cumberland nodded.

Samantha stood up as if jerked to her feet by shock. She stood with her legs straddling the lounge chair. She had her hands balled into fists, as if ready for a fight. "That scumbag." Samantha was shaking, bouncing as if boiling over. "So Mosconi knew who to call in the San Diego Sheriff's Office to convince them to hand me over to one of his friends? Did the sheriff's office think he was still working for the Bureau? And then he gets Mama detained for questioning about Painter's murder? I can't stand this! This is unbelievable! I want to catch that jerk and stomp on his head after what he did to me! To us!"

They all were silent, absorbing the implications.

Josie said, "When Theo Mosconi had me come to his office in the Bureau's Annex building, that was all faked?"

Cumberland shrugged. "I suppose. He'd already had experience impersonating a police officer. So after working for the Bureau, he would have known how their systems worked. He would have known how to install malware in Samantha's phone and give you a forged RFID badge and monitor it. Maybe the building you went to was basically empty and he set up some furniture in some of the office rooms to fool you into thinking it was official. If the electricity was off, he could have brought in a portable generator."

Cumberland looked back at his notes.

Josie shook her head in disbelief.

"There's more," Cumberland said. "Beginning two years ago, there were three unsolved bank robberies in the Central Valley over a period of eight months. Shortly after the third bank robbery, a Mercedes dealer in Burbank sold a black Mercedes Sprinter van for seventy thousand dollars. The van was paid for with cash, and it was registered to Hadley Painter."

"What's a Sprinter van?" Josie asked.

"They're the tall ones, Mama. You can stand up inside."

"I just remembered," Josie said, her eyes wide. "That morning when we got up early when it was still dark and we walked toward Half Dome so I could go up to Hadley Painter's hideout?" Josie said.

"Yeah?" Samantha said.

"In the parking lot there was a man at a dark van, maybe a black one. But it was definitely one of the tall ones. He had the slider open and was leaning into it."

"Bingo," Ellison said. He looked at Josie, his eyes intense but distant as if he was thinking of far away places. "Maybe Theo Mosconi and his stepbrother Hadley Painter did the bank robberies together, and somehow the last one went bad. Painter escaped into Yosemite. Maybe Painter purposely went into hiding with the bank loot. So Mosconi cooked up a plan to use the two of you to find him. Maybe Mosconi thought that was his best chance to get the bank loot. Or..." Ellison trailed off, thinking. "Or maybe Mosconi already knew where the money was stashed, and he wanted Painter dead so he didn't have to split the take."

"Sam and I were careful not to leave too much of a trail," Josie said. "But Mosconi could've had someone watching us as we tracked Hadley Painter."

Ellison said, "Could be, when you went up to his hideaway at dawn, Mosconi had Painter shot. Maybe Mosconi did it himself. Then he tried to cover his tracks by taking a second shot, this one at you. Thankfully, he missed. Then he acted as a Bureau bigshot and got the local cops to detain you."

"I wonder why he would be motivated to kill me," Josie said, "when he's already in so much trouble."

Ellison said, "You probably demonstrated more skill in tracking Painter than Mosconi expected. He might have worried that you would turn that same skill to figuring out why Painter was shot, which would come back to Mosconi. So Mosconi tried to kill you with that second bullet. When he didn't succeed at that, he got you brought in by the Park Police. He probably suggested to them that you were a suspect for Painter's murder. The question now is how you want to pursue this. If Theo Mosconi wasn't afraid of you before, he certainly is now. Which means he will be more dangerous than ever."

"I want to expose him on the Painter murder," Josie said. "And the kidnapping of Sam and the conspiracy of sending me after Painter. I want to destroy him. But I have no idea how."

"I know how," Samantha said. "Cumberland figures out how to find him, then you and I go in and kick his butt the way we did with the assassin in the Quetico Wilderness."

Cumberland raised his hand like a student in class.

"Yes, Cumberland," Josie said.

"I have some ideas about that."

"Great. Let's hear them."

FORTY-THREE

Cumberland said, "Remember how you created the idea of Grendel in Yosemite, and that drew Hadley Painter out of his hideaway?"

"Yes, thanks to your expertise."

"I think you could do something similar with Theo Mosconi."

Everyone waited.

Cumberland continued. "Instead of creating a story about Grendel in the woods, you put a different story on websites, the story about Theo Mosconi being rotten and a bank robber and murderer." Cumberland glanced at Samantha. "Maybe we post it anonymously on the Frogtown Girl site. It could be like an insider scoop and explain about a Bureau imposter who committed bank robberies and was likely involved in Painter Hadley's murder."

"Yes!" Samantha nearly shouted. "And we post Theo Mosconi's name!"

"Couldn't he claim defamation?" Josie asked.

Ellison spoke up. "Technically, I think that you can say anything about someone as long as it's true. Of course, they could still pursue you in court. But the law would be on your side."

"Also," Cumberland said. "The anonymous way I did the Frogtown Girl website makes it very hard for anyone to find out who is making the claim."

"And anyway," Samantha said, still nearly shouting. "We'll nail him before he knows what happened." She stopped and frowned. "But how do we do that?"

"You set a trap," Ellison said. "We just need a way to pull the bad guy into it."

Cumberland said, "I think you can make like you're telling someone about it, and you do that with Samantha's cell phone nearby."

Samantha said, "And Mosconi overhears it because he's monitoring my phone!"

Unknown again lifted her head off of Ellison's thigh and looked up at her.

Cumberland looked startled. "Yeah. Maybe you have the badge nearby, too."

"I can't. I gave it to the lieutenant in Yosemite."

"Okay. Then Samantha's phone will have to be enough. You wouldn't want to be too specific and clear because then it would seem like you're hoping your message is intercepted. But you could use some key words."

"Is that a general concept?" Josie asked. "Or is it specific to this project?"

"Monitoring software can be set to listen to certain words. So you think how he thinks. He'd want to know if you said his name, right? He'd want to know if you mention the Bureau of Investigation. Whatever words he puts into the system, if the software picks it up, it will alert him."

Cumberland paused and looked at Josie.

"Please go on, Cumberland," she said.

"Let's say he gets an alert," Cumberland said. "The system picks up your voice saying, 'I've figured out how Theo Mosconi was involved in Painter's death.' If he heard that, I think he would be seriously focused on how to stop you."

Ellison spoke. "I think this idea is brilliant. Mosconi would imagine lots of dark scenarios once he knows you're onto him. Men who do dark deeds imagine dark deeds. He'll be thinking you might be bringing in a posse. He'll imagine a SWAT team descending."

"But I probably wouldn't be able to get police department on my side considering I'm a fugitive and I might be charged with murder."

Ellison frowned. "Probably not. But Mosconi can't count on the cops bringing you in and effectively silencing you. He'll want to take drastic action first by killing you."

Josie flinched at Ellison's words.

"Sorry, I didn't mean to come on too strong," Ellison said.

"No, I need to face the reality, no matter how harsh." She looked away, thinking. "So I have to catch Mosconi because he's trying to kill me, and I also have to get him to confess to his crimes or at least implicate himself in the crimes."

"If you do," Ellison said, "then you'll have unequivocal evidence he's the bad guy and you're the good."

Josie felt overwhelmed with darkness. Bleak thoughts made it hard to concentrate. She couldn't think of possibilities that might neutralize Mosconi. "Cumberland, you've obviously thought about this a great deal. Do you have an idea of how I would put this to work?"

"Well, one way would be to pretend you're going to a place where you'll meet someone who's going to help you. Mosconi might think he can surprise you at that meeting."

"And I would lure him to this trap by simply talking about it near Samantha's phone? Because mine is in Yosemite."

"Yeah," Cumberland said.

Ellison said. "But if he realizes you're setting him up, then he's likely to bring several men and hit you with a lot of firepower. Or he could tip off the police and hope they'll bring you in."

Josie thought about it. "Much better if he thinks I don't suspect him, then he can come by himself and shoot me with a single, well-placed bullet."

"Exactly."

"So you keep it innocent," Ellison said. "Choose your words carefully to make them seem like they weren't chosen carefully. Let them think you never considered that you'd be overheard. You just want advice from a friend."

"If this idea works," Cumberland said slowly, "and he picks up your conversation, Mosconi comes after you. He thinks he's got the drop on you. But the reality is you've planned it all, so you've got the drop on him." Cumberland paused, frowning. "The only thing that's missing is a location."

"It's important that you don't break into his world, because that would make it seem like you're the perpetrator," Ellison said. "But if he breaks into your world, then he becomes the perpetrator. No matter what goes down after that, you're pretty much in the clear because you were just defending yourself."

Josie said, "I'll be the bait in a trap, and he'll be the prowler."

"I've got an idea," Ellison said. "A friend of mine has an A-frame cabin on five acres. Fifteen miles or so from Big Bear Lake. It's at seventy-five hundred feet near the San Gorgonio Wilderness. Very remote. Just one dirt road goes through the forest and past the cabin. Easy to monitor if you know the terrain. It's run by solar panels. Completely off the grid. Not even any cell phone signal."

Josie shook her head. "I don't want Mosconi breaking into a stranger's cabin because he thinks I'm there."

"I'm thinking of my friend's shop, not his cabin. It's an old garage about two hundred feet from the cabin. The place used to be a storage garage and hunting shack. It still has Pronghorn Antelope antlers mounted above the garage door. There's an oil-barrel wood stove in one corner. My friend used the garage to rebuild classic cars. He's got a sixty-six Mustang in there, a project he started maybe fifteen years ago. He had a stroke seven or eight years ago, and the A-frame and garage have sat unused. I volunteered to check on the property in return for being able to stay there and ski in the winter. I can give you a set of keys. As Cumberland said, you could be overheard talking about meeting someone there. Me, for example. I can talk to you over the phone and pretend to be a reporter doing an undercover story on rotten apples in law enforcement. So, I'm meeting informants in a secret location, which, of course, I'll tell you on the phone. Maybe I'll explain that I might be a little late. That way he thinks he'll be able to get you alone. If he's the sicko we suspect, he might just fall for it."

"This is a good idea," Cumberland said.

Josie looked at Ellison. "Are these just exploratory thoughts?" she asked. "Or do you really think we could pull this off?"

"I think it would work. I've known men like this. Smart-but-twisted psychopaths who are amoral and see other people as nothing more than potential prey. Financial or otherwise."

"Can you talk out how a scenario might play out?"

"Sure." Ellison turned to Cumberland. "You want to take that question?"

Cumberland shook his head. "I only know computers."

"Okay, I will," Ellison said. "Mosconi gets the alert from…" He looked at Cumberland. "What did you call it? Monitoring software?"

Cumberland nodded.

Ellison continued. "It triggers a chime on his computer or something that signifies his name has been used." Ellison looked at Cumberland. "That's similar to what happens, right?"

"Pretty much," Cumberland said.

Ellison continued. "So Mosconi listens to the recording, picks up just enough to convince him that you are going to a clandestine meeting with a reporter in the wilderness near Big Bear. You say something that makes him think you'll be there early in the morning. Mosconi realizes that, if he hurries, he can get there before you and ambush you as you arrive. You've already served your purpose in finding Hadley Painter, so Mosconi will have no problem taking you out. He'll probably hike to some high ground where he can get a view of you approaching, and he'll shoot you like he probably shot Hadley Painter."

Josie felt another flinch as Ellison said it.

Ellison saw the flinch. "Sorry, is this too graphic?"

"No," Josie said. "I want it graphic. I want the hard truth of what I'm doing. That will help me be prepared for whatever comes."

It was a moment before Ellison spoke. "When you first came into my blacksmith shop, I thought you were out of your element. But I could tell you were sensible. What you just said shows that."

Cumberland said, "I think it's better if she's inside the garage. Making Mosconi break in would establish the framework of how cops will look at this afterward, right?"

Samantha said, "I agree with Cumberland. And I can show

Mama how to get everything on video with my phone."

"Okay," Ellison said. "We construct it so Mosconi thinks you'll be there right before dawn. That way, he knows it will be dark as you arrive. The beauty of that is if it's dark, he can't snipe you from a distance. And I can be nearby in the woods," Ellison said, "ready to run out of the trees."

"I can bring my war hammer," Cumberland said. Then he looked embarrassed. "Not like I'd know what to do with it."

"I saw you swing it before," Samantha said. "Like a Viking or something."

Cumberland turned red. As if to change the subject, he glanced in the direction of Ellison without actually looking at him. "Do you have GPS coordinates? Or the property parcel number? I can get a map for Professor Strong." Cumberland pulled out his phone.

Ellison looked at Josie and muttered, "Your request was that I don't bring my phone."

Josie said, "Right. Sorry. Those restrictions don't really apply to Cumberland. He's our privacy guru, the guy the tech people go to. So we don't need to worry about Cumberland's phone."

Cumberland's face got red again. And once more, he glanced at Ellison.

"I don't know about GPS," Ellison said.

Josie looked at Cumberland. "If there's no cell signal at the property, than what good are GPS coordinates, anyway?"

"Different system," Cumberland said. "Cell signals mostly come from utility towers. GPS works off of satellites. But satellites that provide cell signals are coming, so it's all changing."

"I don't have the parcel number, either," Ellison said. "Any chance you could use an old-fashioned address?"

Cumberland frowned and then nodded, as if addresses were so retro that he had to think about what do with one.

Ellison gave him the address.

Cumberland held his phone with one hand and entered the address with just onc thumb, and at a speed that made all of them notice. He swiped and tapped a few times, still working one-handed, then lifted his backpack off the pool terrace. He reached in and pulled out a black device that was smaller than a small laptop. He pushed a button and fed in a piece of paper. There was a whirring sound, and the paper was pulled through.

"That is so cool!" Samantha said. "I've never seen such a small printer. Battery powered and wifi, too! But..." She paused. "Why not just use your printer inside?"

Cumberland shrugged. "I kind of have a security fixation. Every connected device has its own IP address. Phones, printers, tablets, cars. Those little Kindle book readers. I use a different name to register each device. And I have other ways of disguising their connections to me. Kind of like the T-shirt that fools the facial-recognition software. It makes me a little less like an open book. Not that anyone is interested enough in me to poke into my life. But now that I'm working with..." He stopped talking and handed the paper to Josie.

He said, "That shows Mr. Ellison's friend's garage at a scale of fifty feet per inch. I'll zoom out with other maps so you can see how to drive in." He printed out several maps.

They all leaned over the maps and discussed options.

Josie looked at Ellison.

"Ellison, how early do you think I'd need to get there to be ready before Mosconi might show up?"

Ellison shrugged his shoulders. "In the military, we'd head to our position just after twilight the night before. The idea is that typically, if an enemy thinks you're planning a morning assault, they would assume that you'd assemble before dawn, not lie in wait the entire night before. So, instead, you get there the evening before."

"If we plan this for the morning after tomorrow, I should be in position tomorrow night," Josie said.

"We'll be in position tomorrow night," Ellison said. "I'll come back tomorrow with the borrowed van, pick you up, and we'll drive up there." Ellison pointed to the map. "We'll drop you off here, near the garage. I'll help you get your bearings. Then I'll drive Samantha and Cumberland..." Ellison stopped and looked at Cumberland.

"Yeah, I'll come," he said.

"But I can't have Samantha in harm's way," Josie said.

"Mama, I'll be careful."

"You were careful when you got kidnapped. I can't imagine going through that again. No matter how smart and capable you are, you're my cherished child. In your mind, you might think you know better. But it's my job to keep you away from unnecessary risks."

"Okay, then I'll be a lookout. Mr. Ellison can drive me and Cumberland to some high ground where we can hide in safety."

"I don't need to hide," Cumberland said. "I've got my war hammer. Even if I'm a scaredy cat and no good at swinging it."

Ellison looked from Josie to Samantha and back. "You two need to make this decision. We can leave Samantha at home."

"Mama, I can hide in the woods. I'm sure I can be useful! But more than that, I'm not going to sit home while you're off risking your life because of a stupid thing I did." Samantha shot a glance at Ellison as if she remembered that he still didn't know about her smuggling charge. "And where would I stay?" she continued. "We can't even go home!"

Josie nodded, wondering if she was making a terrible mistake. "Only if you stay far away."

Ellison was looking at a map and a satellite photo. "Here's what we'll do," he said. "We'll head up this dirt trail that goes through the trees to this ridge. I can drop Cumberland at a good observation point above the road leading in." Ellison ran his fingers over the map as if feeling for a good place. "Then I'll drive the van along this ridge that goes above the garage and the A-frame cabin. There's an open area without many trees, and it's arid, so I don't think there's much ground cover. If I can switchback up this slope, I can leave Samantha locked in the van, and she'll have a view down below. If there's shrubbery in the way, I have a hatchet I can use to chop it out. Once I leave Samantha, I can hike through the forest and take up a position near the cabin." He used the thumb and index finger of one hand to point to two spots on the map simultaneously. "Samantha looks down from here, and Cumberland will look down from there. My lookout position will be above the road leading out, in case he comes from that direction." With his other hand, Ellison pointed to the garage. "These three points make a triangle of sorts, one hundred yards on a side. When any of us sees Mosconi coming, we'll contact you."

"You said there was no cell signal," Josie said. "How can you contact me?"

"I've got owl flutes. We used them in Vietnam. When you blow on them, they make a hooting sound."

"You think we can communicate like owls?"

"Absolutely. We can use hoots as warning sounds. Like Tolkien described in The Hobbit. My owl flutes sound like Great Horned owls. Great Horned owls make lots of sounds, but three hoots is most common. At the first sign of trouble, we'll be owls."

"Trouble in this context meaning that Mosconi is approaching me where I'm hiding in the garage," Josie said.

"Right. When any of us see him coming, we hoot three times on our flutes. After several seconds, we repeat."

"Are these owl flutes audible at a distance?"

"If the wind isn't too loud in the trees, you can hear them two hundred yards away. We'll all be able to hear any hooting any of us makes."

"What about me in the van?" Samantha said. "How will the sound of my flute carry?"

"The van has swing-out side windows. If you point the flute out the opening, we'll be able to hear it."

"But what if Mosconi were to sneak up on the van with Samantha in it?" Josie said.

"I don't think he could find her. Nevertheless, Samantha will have the doors locked. I'll leave my hatchet with her. If Mosconi were to try to break the door glass and reach in the window, she cuts off his fingers. Same for if he reaches in one of the swing-out windows."

Josie was uneasy, but his logic seemed sound.

Ellison added, "I really don't think you need to worry about Samantha. It would be very unlikely for anyone to come upon her up in the ridge trees. And my friend's van is brown. Perfect for blending in at night."

Cumberland was tapping on his phone. "The weather forecast for Big Bear tomorrow night is for light breeze. It shouldn't interfere with hearing the flutes."

"I'll bring my flutes tomorrow and show you all how to hoot. It's easy to hear at a distance, and it is calming. It won't agitate our target in the event he's got his car windows down and he hears it."

"This is very scary," Josie said. "Just imagining myself as bait in a trap."

"You don't have to do it, Mama," Samantha said.

"Yes, I do. For me. And for you. We need to catch this criminal." She pointed at the map and turned toward Ellison. "How do I get into the garage?"

"There's a deadbolt lock on the garage. I'll give you a key."

"Once I'm inside, where do you think I should hide so I'm not obvious when he breaks in?"

"In the Mustang."

"But how would I defend myself? You can't move in a car seat."

"Normally not. But my friend's sweet little ride is missing a windshield. So if you wear dark, non-reflective clothes, sit on the passenger side, pull the visor down, and have your weapon ready, pointing out the windshield opening, you'll be fine. Ideally, you should wait until you know he has a weapon. It's possible he already has it out when he breaks in." Ellison paused a moment. "Any chance you have a gun?"

"No. But I have my homemade crossbow."

"I mean no disrespect, Professor. But I think you need a serious weapon. Not something that shoots an arrow. You can take my gun."

Samantha spoke up. "Mr. Ellison, her homemade crossbow is a pretty major weapon. And it shoots a bolt, not an arrow."

"Oh, that's right. You told me about it. You used it to take out Sam's kidnapper."

Josie nodded. "I don't know how to shoot a gun, anyway."

"You can probably poke the crossbow out through the Mustang's windshield opening and prop it on the dash."

Josie tried to visualize doing that. The plan seemed very tentative.

Ellison continued, "Assuming this trap works, Mosconi will break into the garage thinking that he'll hide there and surprise you when you show up. But you'll already be there."

"I'll be a sitting duck." Josie felt despondent. "Like Hadley Painter."

"You'll have warning from us. If any of us see him, we'll start our hooting. With luck, I'll be near as he breaks in."

"And if you're not near? If nobody sees him approach? Then what?"

"Once he breaks in, you take him down either way." Ellison seemed to think about it. "An alternative would be that I hide closer to the garage. But I wouldn't be able to see him coming in advance."

Josie shook her head. "That doesn't feel as effective. We lose your ability to see him coming from a distance. And we increase the chances that he senses your presence nearby and decides to abandon his assault on me. But what if you hid in the garage with me?"

Ellison shook his head. "There's no good place for a second person to hide. I could duck down behind the rear of the Mustang. But he'd see me there the moment he kicked the door in. The only real good hiding place is inside the Mustang, in the passenger seat so the windshield corner post obscures the view. Once he breaks in, you've got him."

Samantha said, "Unknown and I will be all alone at our lookout. How long do you think we'll have to wait? In the dark all night? No way to communicate but hooting like an owl?" Her voice was plaintive and full of worry.

Ellison said, "He will think Josie and I are coming to meet at dawn. So he will come during the night. Probably the hour when there is the least traffic. Three or four a.m. By the time he arrives, you will have been in place for several hours. Get lots of sleep tonight so you don't get drowsy."

"Trust me," Josie said. "I'm not going to fall asleep when I know a man is coming to kill me."

Ellison made a somber nod.

"I'll be fine in the garage," Josie said. "You said three hoots is for warning. But how do I call you when I want backup?"

"Two hoots will be for backup. He comes in, you disable him, then you blow two hoots. You pause, then repeat."

"Got it," Josie said. "Three hoots is a warning to me. Two hoots is a backup request from me."

They were all silent for a moment.

Josie thought about the situation. "Okay, I'm comfortable with this plan. The problem is that if he talks to me and I respond, I'll immediately give away my location inside the Mustang."

"Not necessarily," Cumberland said. He looked at Ellison. "What's the garage like?"

"Just a normal old garage," Ellison said. "Barely big enough for two small cars, a workbench, and a bunch of tools. The Mustang is in the center." Ellison closed his eyes, visualizing. "There are metal shelves along one wall, a bunch of miscellaneous hardware, a rolling rack of wrenches and such, a drill press, an engine hoist, two wheels without tires, an air compressor, some electrical conduit pipe. Stuff everywhere. You have to step carefully to move without tripping on something."

"Where would someone logically think a person is hiding?" Cumberland asked.

"Someone who's never been inside the garage would probably think a person would hide in one of the rear corners. Although there's barely enough room. The left corner has the drill press, the compressor, and the engine hoist. A real skinny person could maybe squeeze in behind them. The right rear corner has the barrel stove. A person could possibly get behind that as well."

Cumberland said, "Professor Strong, you remember those speakers you put in the Yosemite forest to make the monster moans."

"Of course," Josie said. "A miracle of theater. I feel terrible that we left them in Yosemite."

Ellison said, "Let's hope someone finds them and takes them

home."

Cumberland kept talking. "I've got more speakers. I can give you a mic and two of those speakers with a wireless connection. When you get there, you put the speakers back in a corner. If you separate them by a few feet, they will create a stereo perception of your voice. You'll have the wireless mic pinned to your jacket. There's a little switch on the mic. When you turn it on and talk from the Mustang, you will seem to be back in the corner behind all that stuff."

Ellison was nodding vigorously. "More brilliance." He looked at Josie. "Where'd you get this kid? He's amazing."

Josie glanced at Cumberland. "He's a Beverly Hills hacker who took my medieval history class."

Cumberland didn't react.

"How long do you need to get this type of equipment?" she asked Cumberland.

"I've got the stuff in my bedroom studio. Ten minutes to hook it up and show you how to use it."

Josie looked at Ellison. "Do you think there's a downside to me getting to this so-called meeting place before Theo Mosconi? A downside to acting as bait?"

"Well, things can always go wrong. And it would be scary. But if you have your weapon, and I have mine, we should be able to control the situation. If there's a way to slow him down, that would make it even better."

"There are medieval ways," Josie said.

"Such as?"

"Well, most of them are too wicked to use. Sharpened stakes and such. But a classic, relatively-harmless one is a net with weighted edges. He breaks in the door, steps inside, and a net falls over him."

Ellison raised his eyebrows. "I hope you're always on my side. A net would be great. It would hobble his effort to move, to pull a gun, to run away. But how do you set it up to fall at just the right time?"

"One way is a trip wire," Josie said. "A mono filament line attached to a prop that holds the net up near the ceiling. He hits the line with his shin, the line pulls out the prop, and the net falls. Another way is to have the line run to a place where the person waiting can pull on it at the right time."

"Like inside the Mustang," Ellison said. "It would take some time to set up a net trap. But I can imagine doing it in that garage."

"We already talked about me getting there early," Josie said.

"But once you're there," Ellison said, "you'll want your full attention on watching and listening while you wait. So here's what I'll do. I'll try to get a net and some weights and line, and I'll head up there this afternoon. I might be able to set up a net and trip line and be all done before night. Do you know where to get a net around here?"

"No idea," Josie said.

"I'm thinking about fishing nets," Ellison said. "Did medieval nets have any qualities in particular?"

"Not that I know of. It doesn't even need to be especially strong. It just needs to tangle someone up for a few minutes. With time, the trapped person could free himself from the net or maybe cut himself free with a knife. But by then, the trapper is in control of the victim." She hesitated. "In theory, at least."

Ellison nodded. "I imagine I can figure out something. I'll call your burner tonight and let you know if I was successful. Then I'll be back here at, say, noon tomorrow, and we'll all drive up to Big Bear." Ellison looked at Samantha and Cumberland. "Does that work for you two?"

Cumberland nodded.

"Sam?" Josie said.

"Definitely, Mama. I think it's a good idea. But it's terrifying. You being there in the dark, waiting for him to come after you. Hoping to drop a net on him. I can't imagine it!"

"Unfortunately," Josie said, "that's the best plan we've got."

They were all silent for a minute.

Ellison gave Unknown a pet, and stood up. "I'm off to find a fishing net."

He made a little salute toward the rest of the group, then left.

FORTY-FOUR

Josie tried to focus on the plan, but had no success. Staying in Cumberland's house a second night was as distracting as the first. Samantha tried to do homework with the same result. They ate an early dinner. They watched a Netflix movie on Cumberland's streaming service. As twilight approached, Cumberland once again joined Josie and Samantha to take Unknown out for a walk.

At 8 p.m., Cumberland said goodnight and went down to his bedroom studio. Ellison still hadn't called. So Josie used her burner phone to call him.

"I was gonna call you," he answered. "I got the net installed. Now I'm driving back. Turns out they don't just sell fishing nets everywhere. But I know a guy who knows a fisherman, who has a damaged cast net. Holes too big to catch four-inch finger mullet. But not too big for catching men."

"I hope it wasn't too expensive, for your sake." Josie said. "You've already spent a lot of money on my behalf."

"The net is borrowed. If we can get it back to him in one piece, there'll be no cost. It took me a little bit to develop my net support technique. I improvised weights from scrap in my shop. Once I got the hang of how to prop the weights up in the roof trusses of the garage, it was easy. The trip line runs to the rearview mirror of the Mustang. I tested it three times. Even though the car jostles a bit when you get in and out, it doesn't release the net. The only downside is that the net is very obvious if you flip on the light and look up when you walk in the door. But I'm quite proud of the apparatus. It should do what you want."

"Thanks so much," Josie said. "Are you still willing to be my theatrical partner for the revealing phone conversation in the morning? A conversation we hope will be overheard?"

"Oh, you can't imagine how we Green Berets practiced our oratory and our stage personalities each morning. Elocution. Diction. Enunciation. I'll feel like I'm back in the action."

"You are so full of it," Josie said.

"Ha, ha. You and I will put on a great performance."

Josie and Ellison went over how the conversation would go. They even practiced a few lines.

Josie said, "I think it would be best for you to call my burner from a phone that isn't connected to you. We don't want them to be looking into your identity."

"But my phones connect to me. Wait. I can go to the San Bernardino VFW hall and use their phone. But they don't open until eight in the morning. Would that work for you?"

"Sure. But I have to admit I'm having difficulty focusing on the details."

"Why do you say that?" he asked.

"I feel like my fate is sealed."

Josie heard Ellison breathe. He said, "I remember reading something a big-cheese writer wrote. French, I think, Voltaire maybe. He said that while we don't get to choose the cards in our hand, we do get to choose how we play them."

"You surprise still," Josie said.

They went over a few more details and hung up.

Before bed, Josie and Samantha sat together on one of the couches in Cumberland's living room, Josie on one side of Samantha and Unknown on her other side. They turned off the lights, so the only illumination was the blue glow coming in from the underwater lights in the swimming pool.

"Mama?"

"Yeah?"

"Are we crazy? You're going to be bait for a bad guy with a gun while Mr. Ellison and Cumberland and I are being lookouts up on a mountain. In Yosemite, we were sort of chasing a phantom idea. Now the idea is real. We think someone tried to kill you in Yosemite. This is more dangerous. You're tempting this man to kill you."

"Maybe we are crazy, Sam. But what's the alternative? I go to trial on a phony murder charge? And you go to trial on the drug mule charge. We could both end up in prison. There are uncountable stories of innocent people who are prosecuted by zealous DAs and then get convicted by a jury that doesn't see their innocence."

"It seems like we have no choice," Samantha said.

"Then consider this. If our trap for Mosconi goes bad, what's the worst that can happen?" Josie said.

"You could get killed."

"Which, in my opinion," Josie said, "wouldn't be as bad as going to prison for thirty years on a false murder charge."

Samantha seemed to clench her jaw. "Put it that way, we have no choice but to kick some California Bureau butt."

"I'm with you on that, Cap'n," Josie said.

"Aye, Matey."

FORTY-FIVE

Josie's burner phone rang at 8:15 the next morning.

Before she answered, she made certain that Samantha's phone was powered on. She hoped it would pick up the conversation designed to bait Mosconi into coming to their trap.

The burner phone rang a second and third time while Josie reminded herself of the main points she wanted to make during their little theatrical play.

"Hello?" she answered.

"This is the reporter," Ellison said. "Our names are unnecessary."

"Right."

"Have you decided to talk on record?"

"Yes. I've decided to give it all to you. Theo Mosconi is bad. I know his history, his crimes, his fellow crooks."

"Do you have evidence?"

"Yes. You won't believe it. He'll be prosecuted for at least two murders, one in Yosemite and one in Florida more than a decade ago. There are multiple bank robberies. I'll give you all the evidence. Just tell me where and when."

"There's an A-frame cabin with a garage near Big Bear Lake in the San Bernardino Mountains. It's old, out of the way, almost hidden near the San Gorgonio Wilderness. We'll meet at the garage tomorrow morning a half hour before dawn. We can talk in that garage. No chance anyone can overhear us. No Wi-Fi there."

"Where is the garage?"

"I'll call back with the GPS coordinates this afternoon. If you're in the area, you'll have plenty of time to get there before dawn."

"I'll wait for your call," Josie said.

"Theo Mosconi's crimes will be in the late edition of tomorrow's paper, and front page news the next day. His life as he knows it is over."

They hung up.

While the phony meeting between Josie and the "reporter" was "stated" to be early the next morning, Ellison showed up in a little over an hour, and they left at noon.

Cumberland's last move before getting into the van was to pick up the war hammer from near the front door. He hefted it as if to gauge how it would swing, then got into the borrowed van with the others.

With Ellison driving, Samantha and Unknown sat in the front passenger seat of the van, and Josie and Cumberland in the rear seat. Their goal was to be in position up in the mountains near Big Bear by the time twilight descended.

As they'd arranged in advance, Josie and Samantha had packed sandwiches along with peanuts and water. They also had a supply of dog food and water for Unknown. They brought Samantha's phone, which had the monitoring software Mosconi had installed.

Ellison's first stop was at UCLA. Josie told him where to park. She left them all in the van and walked quickly across to Bunche Hall. She worried that Mosconi might have someone watching her office. She pulled a large sun hat down low over her forehead, went inside and up to her office, where she kept the homemade crossbow on display in one of her bookshelves. She had no bag large enough to hold it. But she had an overcoat on the rack. She wrapped the crossbow in the coat, put the extra bolts in her small bag, and left. There were lots of students walking across campus. Mixed in were several professors, a qualification that Josie could determine simply at a glance. There were no specific identifying characteristics. But they still stood out from the students the way American tourists stand out to locals in Europe. Josie was relieved that none of the students or professors recognized her, which meant a lower chance that someone would ask what she was carrying wrapped in a coat.

Back in the van, Ellison pulled out and headed to the 10 freeway. He turned east and headed across Los Angeles.

Josie interrupted their silence. "Maybe while we drive, you can give us a lesson in how to use the owl flutes."

"Oh, crap, I knew I forgot something." Ellison glanced at his watch. "No problem. We have plenty of time, and we're driving near my place. We'll stop and pick them up."

Samantha looked back toward Josie in the rear seat.

"It'll be okay," Josie said.

Josie saw Ellison looking in the rearview mirror. But he wasn't looking at her.

Josie turned and looked out the back window. There was a black-and-white CHP vehicle behind them, not far back, keeping pace with Ellison.

Like Ellison, Josie didn't comment. It was probably nothing. But she was a fugitive. She desperately hoped they hadn't found her.

Ellison kept watching the mirror.

Periodically, Josie glanced behind them. The CHP was still there. Josie thought about how they would handle it if the patrol pulled them over. Ellison would have to handle talking to them. He'd have to explain why the van's registration wasn't in his name. Should they be discussing his response in advance? Josie decided that Ellison's real-world experience would give him a better instinctive approach than she would have. She knew the university environment. Ellison knew the military and business environment. It was clear which world was closer to the world of most law enforcement.

A moment later, the CHP vehicle rushed up on their left. Its light bar turned on, colored strobe lights flashing, and its siren squawking. It raced on past and left them far behind in a few moments.

Josie saw Ellison rub his hand across the back of his neck.

No one spoke.

East of L.A., Ellison got off the freeway and drove into Montebello. A few miles and several turns later, he pulled up to an old building that might have once been a warehouse or school. Or, Josie thought, a monastery. The building was four stories high and, like Ellison's blacksmith shop, made of red brick. The building had large windows comprised of many smaller panes. He parked near the door.

"This is where you live?" Samantha asked, surprise and a hint of disappointment in her voice.

"Home sweet home. We've got plenty of time. You may as well all come in. See how a blacksmith lives."

"What about Unknown?" Samantha asked.

"A VIP as far as I'm concerned," Ellison said.

They walked up to the front of the building to a double wide door with no windows and made of metal. It looked like it would withstand a battering ram. In place of steps, there was a broad concrete ramp suitable for hauling pianos or heavy equipment.

To the side of the doors was a small sign made of metal with the letters cut out as if by stencil. It read, 'Artemesia to Zorn, loft d'artiste.' Josie thought that Ellison had probably made the sign in his blacksmith shop.

Inside was a wide hallway that went far back. The floor was concrete, coated with gray epoxy paint. To the side of the hallway was a long, wide staircase, with concrete steps on a metal framework. Josie was about to comment about an elevator, but she stopped. This was no different than her condo. It was healthier to take the steps.

"This is a strange place to have a home," Samantha said.

Ellison grinned at her.

They went up the steps, Samantha trotting with Unknown beside her and Cumberland following, taking the steps two at a time. Ellison went next, at a slightly more sedate pace. Josie was last.

"Exercise," she muttered to herself as she huffed.

Ellison's place was on the fourth floor. By the third flight, Josie realized that it was much more exercise than her condo, as each floor was twice as high. She tried to maintain a pace of one step per second. Not fast, but steady. Despite her heavy breathing, she was grateful that it was easier than hiking up under Half Dome during her search for Hadley Painter.

At the top floor, Ellison walked over to a huge, gray, metal door that hung on rollers from a large metal track.

Ellison put a key in the lock, and the giant door rolled sideways, moving up at the slight incline of the track it hung from. A counter weight came down on the side. It was attached to a cable that went up to a pulley and across to the door.

"Veuillez entrer, chers amis," he said. He stepped to the side of the warehouse door and gestured toward the entrance with his arm.

"Oh, my God," Samantha marveled as they walked into a cavernous space with an 18-foot ceiling that was mostly skylights. One outer wall was mostly windows. The space was a basic glass-and-brick box with some furniture and an old butcher-block table at one end. The portion of the walls that was brick instead of windows was painted white, giving the space a light, airy feel. Along one side was the kitchen area, which was created by two long stainless steel shelving units. Both units were on rollers. One had a built-in sink and dish-drying rack on one end. On the other end was a cook top. The other unit contained shelves and cabinets. They were like something Josie had seen in restaurant kitchens. On top of one set of cabinets was a microwave.

Samantha nearly ran into the space and turned around, her arms held out, like she was performing on a movie set. "This is so cool! Look at all the skylights." Unknown trotted in after her, stopped, and looked up at Samantha's face as she exclaimed. "The windows and skylights make it seem like you're outside."

"The benefit of the top-floor unit," Ellison said. "Except the skylights also let in a lot of heat. So I get a little exercise working the chains to let heat out in the summer." He pointed. At regular intervals were long loops of bicycle chains that draped down to about six feet above the floor. By reaching up and pulling on them, one could open or close the skylights.

Samantha looked over at a long, straight staircase, also made of metal with see-through grid work for steps. "Do you sleep up there? Can I go up and look?"

"Sure."

Samantha ran up the stairs. Unknown went to follow, then stopped to look at the see-through metal grating that made up the steps. She set one paw on the first step, pushed up, put the other paw down, and stopped. She backed off the steps and looked up toward where Samantha had gone.

"Metal grating is uncomfortable on a dog's paws," Ellison said. "Maybe the grating hurts, or maybe it's just unsettling. Whatever it is, dogs don't like it."

Samantha nearly shrieked when she got up to the loft.

"Cumberland, you have to see this. You can see out the windows all the way to downtown. There's Disney Hall! It shines like a spaceship."

Cumberland went up the steps two at a time. He wasn't effusive like Samantha, but he seemed intrigued at a living space so different from what he was used to.

"C'mon in," Ellison said to Josie, who was still standing at the entrance door.

"I agree with Samantha," she said. "I love your place."

"It's great as long as you don't care about an oven or washed windows. I thought about getting ladders and scaffolding and making a window-washing attempt once. But I realized a proper washing would take me three months and that's just to do the inside. Life is too short. And the light still comes in through the dirt."

Josie walked over to a huge metal sculpture of a woman. The sculpture was seven or eight feet tall. It was rendered with welded steel, mostly polished but with the rough areas left black. Although it was intentionally coarse in design, the beauty was apparent. She was a regal figure.

"Say hello to Thena," Ellison said.

Josie walked around the sculpture twice, once up close, once at a distance to take in the height.

"I like this very much. Is Thena short for Athena?"

Ellison nodded. "Goddess of wisdom, named, supposedly, after her city of Athens and not the other way around. But it's the height of bombast for me to tell this to a history professor."

"Not at all, Ellison. My period, the Middle Ages, began around five hundred Current Era, a thousand years after the era of this goddess. I know very little about ancient Greek history. Where did you get her? An artist in the building, perhaps?"

"Yes. Thena is my work. And my muse."

"You sculpted this? How wonderful! It's impressive."

"A guy who earns his bread making gates and light fixtures needs a loftier pursuit. And if that pursuit results in living with a goddess, well, hard to beat that, don't you think?"

"Absolutely." Josie called up toward the loft. "Sam? Did you see this sculpture?"

Samantha looked over a railing. "The grand woman? Yeah, it's cool."

"Ellison made this."

"Really? Cumberland, come look at this."

He leaned over the railing and looked down.

"Meet Athena," Josie said. "Goddess of wisdom."

Samantha trotted down the stairs. She looked up at the sculpture, and then turned to Ellison. "Wowie Kazowei. You made this, Mr. Ellison? That's so cool you're a sculptor."

Maybe Josie or Ellison showed a bit of surprise at Samantha's statement.

Samantha said, "Was that the wrong thing to say? I meant it as a compliment."

Ellison was grinning. "It's perfect. Like what Roy Lichtenstein wrote in one of his paintings. 'Whaam! Pop! Wowie Kazowie! Soon I'll have all of New York clamoring for my work!'"

"An artist wrote that on a painting?"

Ellison nodded. He walked over to a bookshelf, pulled out a large volume, flipped through pages, turned it toward Samantha.

"Cool." Samantha grinned. "That's like a panel in a newspaper comic strip. It even has those dots, whatever they are."

"Half-tone dots. Part of the printing process."

"Real fly, huh," Josie said, looking at Samantha.

"Mama, you're so hip. You remembered."

Josie was looking at the sculpture.

"You see what's on her shoulder," Ellison said.

Josie said, "I'm thinking the two circles are the eyes of the owl and the curved lines represent its wings."

"You're too smart," Ellison said, a duplication of what Josie had thought about him in Yosemite when he figured out that the Bureau had coerced her into helping them. "Yes, the Owl of Athena sits on her shoulder, symbolizing Athena's wisdom."

"We have a sort of neighbor who's a painter near Santa Monica. She's Chumash Indian. She paints the Chumash goddess Hutash and represents her as a Great Horned Owl. She even gave Samantha a small owl painting after Samantha was kidnapped."

Ellison smiled. "That's a nice use of classic imagery."

He opened a drawer and pulled out four wooden flutes that were polished with some kind of varnish. They looked to Josie like a type of Native American flutes she had seen in the past.

Ellison blew on one of the flutes. The note that came was airy and resonant, very similar to the hoot of an owl. "You can make different pitched notes by covering the various holes with your fingertips. But leaving them all uncovered produces a sound closest to a Great Horned Owl." He blew three times on the flute, mimicking the slight syncopation of a hooting owl. "You can all practice this while we drive. Once we get to the site, we shouldn't blow again until we are sending the signal that Mosconi is approaching."

He handed each of them a flute, then turned toward the door. "We should get going. We've got a two-hour drive ahead of us."

FORTY-SIX

When they were once again driving in the van, Josie said, "Cumberland, you brought the speakers that I will use inside the garage, right?"

"Yeah. They'll make it so the bad guy can't tell where you are."

"Maybe you could show me how to use them before we get there."

"Sure." Cumberland pulled two speakers and a clip-on mic from his backpack and gave them to Josie.

"These speakers have switches just like the ones you used in Yosemite. Once you turn them on and also turn on the mic, they broadcast whatever the mic picks up. They're not set to high volume like the ones in Yosemite. But they're pretty loud. So talk softly."

He turned on the speakers.

She set the speakers on the floor of the van and then spoke, "Testing, one, two, three." Nothing happened.

"The switch on the mic," Cumberland prodded.

Josie turned on the mic and spoke again.

Her broadcast voice was loud and clear.

"Perfect," she said. "Thanks so much." She turned everything off and put the speakers and mic in her pack.

An hour later, they had wound their way far up into the mountains. The view stretched down to the wind farm near Banning. In the distance were the green patches of golf courses in Palm Springs, 30 miles away and thousands of feet below.

Ellison glanced at his phone. "Good signal, here," he said. He pulled the van off the road and stopped at a slow-traffic pullover.

He looked at Josie in the rearview mirror. "Ready for our

next bit of theater?"

"Yes. You call my burner while I have Samantha's phone nearby so that it can pick up what I say."

Ellison turned around. "Hey, Cumberland, which would be better? I call Josie's burner from my own cell or she calls me?"

"I don't think it matters, but I think you should use one of my phones," Cumberland said.

Ellison frowned. "You have more than one phone? A burner like Josie's?"

"I always carry multiple phones." He said it as if anyone sensible would do that.

"Because... Sorry," Ellison interrupted himself. "I'm not judging, just curious."

"For, you know, times like this," Cumberland said. He reached into his pack, moved his arm as if stirring the contents, and pulled out a phone. "Use this. It will give you more privacy."

Ellison nodded and took the phone. He stared at it as if it were an alien creature. Then he shrugged and slipped it into his shirt pocket.

They all got out of the van.

Cumberland said, "You should separate from Professor Strong, so you don't get feedback from my phone to hers."

Ellison nodded. Josie took her burner phone out of her pocket. Ellison hiked up a short incline above the road. Josie walked 50 yards down the road.

When Josie's phone rang, she answered, "Josie Strong."

Ellison spoke in his reporter voice and gave Josie the GPS coordinates of the garage and added some details about the turns in the dirt road. Their conversation was short by design.

They clicked off.

"Good?" Ellison said after he'd returned the phone to Cumberland.

"Good," she said, her mood getting a bit somber. They were getting close to the time when she would be locked alone in a dark garage, bait for Theo Mosconi.

Ellison said, "Cumberland? When do you think Mosconi

will be getting an alert that we were talking about him?"

"He probably already has," he said.

Everyone stayed quiet as they got back into their van. Ellison pulled back onto the highway and continued to head up into the mountains.

When they came near Big Bear Lake, Ellison stopped again. They spread out their maps on the tailgate of the van and memorized locations and discussed their final plans.

As Ellison pointed at the maps and made comments to Samantha and Cumberland, Josie's concentration drifted.

She looked around at the surroundings. In all directions, there was nothing but the forest and mountains and valleys of the San Gorgonio Wilderness. Nowhere could Josie see any sign of human habitation. Not a single building. Not a single road other than the one they were on. To the west, the sun was blindingly bright. But it was lowering toward the San Bernardino Mountains and, west of that, the San Gabriel Mountains and the Pacific beyond. For a moment, it seemed that Josie could barely visualize the beautiful wide beach in Santa Monica, just steps from the safety and privacy of their condo.

They got back in the van, and Ellison drove even farther up the mountain.

The afternoon light was waning as he turned onto what seemed like a non-existent road, drove several bumpy, twisting miles, then turned down a faint dirt trail and came to a stop near his friend's garage. He parked in a shady spot where the van wouldn't be obvious.

"We should err toward silence," he whispered as they got out.

Ellison gave Josie the garage key.

She used it to unlock the deadbolt.

"Remember not to bump the net overhead," he said.

Josie carefully opened the door and stepped inside the garage. She looked around the dark, dusty interior, getting her bearings. Ellison leaned in next to her. He pointed up at the net and the trip line that went to the Mustang.

Ellison gestured toward the right rear corner. "Just so you're aware, there's a second side door over there. But there's so much stuff stacked nearby that it would be hard to even get to the door.

Josie went back to the van, put one of the owl flutes in her pack along with her food and the extra bolts, then unwrapped the crossbow and carried it and her pack to the garage. She set the weapon on the hood of the old car, then went back outside to say goodbye to the others. Samantha gave her a long hug.

"Will you be okay, Mama?" Samantha's voice was thick with emotion.

"I will, hon. I promise. And you'll be careful as well."

Samantha nodded. Her face was tracked with tears. "I need you, Mama."

"I need you more, Cap'n."

Ellison, Samantha, and Cumberland got back in the van, and they left.

Josie waved goodbye, then turned and surveyed her surroundings. The garage was in disrepair, warped siding, broken corner trim, a simple gable roof built at a shallow angle and missing shingles. The garage door was splintered in one area as if someone had bumped into it with a vehicle. Under the peak of the roof were antlers that hung crooked and were missing a prominent point on the left side where it had broken off. Along the wall with the door were three small windows, set high on the wall, enough to let light in by day, but small enough to be very difficult to climb through if an intruder were to break the glass. Not that a person would try. It would be easy enough to simply kick in the side door.

Josie slowly swung open the door, wary of the net that Ellison had installed above. He thought it was secure and wouldn't fall unless the trip line was pulled. But there was no harm in being careful.

There wasn't enough light in the gathering dusk for Josie to easily see the inside of the garage. She stepped through the door once again, aware of how quickly it was getting dark. She moved gingerly as if stepping onto thin ice, reaching her shoe out carefully, feeling the threshold and the solid concrete floor beyond. Ellison had said there was a light switch next to the door. She reached in and felt it. But she realized she should leave it off. Although it was likely no one was around for miles, she didn't want to call attention to her presence. Best to play it safe.

Despite her fear, part of her felt safer in the darkness. She reminded herself that they had done what Ellison had suggested and gotten there over twelve hours before the time the phony meeting was to take place.

Josie shut the door behind her, and locked the deadbolt, closing herself into an unfamiliar space filled with scents of oiled metal and old paint and gasoline and insecticide.

Initially, it seemed cave-black inside the garage. Cumberland had given her two flashlights, one a blindingly bright LED, and the other a dim old-fashioned flashlight with little output, which Cumberland had further dimmed by putting masking tape over most of the bulb.

The dim flashlight gave Josie just enough glow for her to avoid walking into objects, but not enough for her to really see the interior. Fortunately, Ellison had made clear drawings depicting the location of the major tools. She had memorized the drawings.

Josie used the dim flashlight to maneuver past a group of electrical conduit pipes leaning against the wall near the door. She was careful not to bump them as they would make a loud clatter if they fell to the floor. Past the conduits was the engine hoist and drill press.

As she explored, her eyes adjusted, and she became aware of dim light coming in the windows. But as the twilight moved toward night, what little light came in was diminishing by the minute.

Josie flipped on the switches of the two speakers and then reached back and set them on a dark shelf in the corner behind the drill press. As Cumberland had instructed, she moved them three feet apart.

Once the speakers were in place, she flipped the switch on the lapel mic and tapped it with her finger. The tap was amplified in the speakers, a loud static popping noise. Josie made a very soft whispering sound.

Her voice coming from the corner was dramatic. She didn't dare actually talk for fear that it might alert anyone within a hundred yards. If and when Mosconi broke into the garage, she would have to speak with the softest possible voice.

She flipped off the mic switch, and was turning to inspect the rest of the garage when she heard a hooting sound.

Josie panicked. Her heart thumped painfully. Did she imagine the sound?

Then came two more! Hooting like a real owl. Three hoots. The warning that Mosconi was coming.

Was it the real thing?! Or were the others practicing communicating? Were they unaware she could hear it?

Their agreement had been very clear. None of them would use the owl flutes except to alert Josie that a vehicle was coming down the road toward the garage. Three hoots was the warning to Josie. Two hoots was Josie's request for backup.

There was only one conclusion. Someone, probably Theo Mosconi, was driving toward the garage.

FORTY-SEVEN

Josie froze motionless. It was 12 hours too early. Again, Josie wondered if it was a mistake. Maybe Samantha had gotten nervous and tried the flute without thinking.

Then came another hoot, very short, as if someone were doing a quick little practice note. If they were warning her a second time, there'd be two more hoots.

Josie waited. There were no more hoots.

What did that mean? Josie felt trapped. She didn't know what to do. She tried to imagine where Samantha would be at that moment.

It had been twenty minutes or more since they left Josie at the garage, enough time for all to be in position. That meant Ellison had dropped Cumberland off at one of the observation points and then driven Samantha up to the top of the ridge and left her and Unknown locked in the van, which would be hidden among the trees. Ellison would have shown them the sightlines and the rough location of the garage down below them. They'd been so careful to ensure there would be no mistakes. Then Ellison would have left them and walked to the point near the A-frame cabin where he could see the other dirt road that led into the property. All of them would be out of sight from Josie, a necessary aspect of their plan to have a good view of the roads that accessed the property. And their three-point view would give them a comprehensive panorama of the property.

It seemed clear. One of them had hooted to let Josie know that someone was driving down the dirt road toward the garage and A-frame. Josie couldn't tell which direction the vehicle would come from. But that didn't matter.

Josie had to face the likelihood that Theo Mosconi was probably coming to the meeting place 12 hours before the planned time. He was doing what Ellison said was smart, arriving far in advance of what your enemy anticipates.

But if Mosconi was really on his way, then what was the fourth, short hoot? They'd agreed that three hoots were the warning. So why one short hoot?

Josie could only think of one reason for a single, short hoot. Someone started to do another three-hoot warning but got cut off. She couldn't even bear the thought. She had to focus on her current dilemma in the garage.

She had to be in position! In the Mustang. But as the encroaching dusk had made the inside of the garage nearly black, she didn't know exactly where the Mustang was.

Josie had seen the vague shape of the Mustang as she moved through the dark. She set her crossbow on its hood, then moved to the rear of the garage to place the speakers. But she hadn't really looked at the car.

She reached her arms out farther, moving slowly, trying to feel for the Mustang's door handle. It would make noise as she opened it. It might even turn on the interior light if the car battery was hooked up.

Josie's hands swept empty space. She could turn on her dim flashlight to get her bearings. But even the smallest amount of light could probably be seen from outside.

Josie tried to think, tried to quell her panic.

She could operate in the dark. There was no crucial need to turn on a flashlight and take the risk that the light entailed.

But she couldn't get into the Mustang without opening the door. So the risk it would make noise was unavoidable.

She moved forward, still holding her arms out in the dark.

Josie took another step. Reached with her arms.

Where was the Mustang?! Had she gotten turned around? The minutes were going by. Theo Mosconi might be upon her very soon. But there were still no vehicle lights.

Josie turned slightly and took another step. She'd already wasted so much time. The garage was small. The Mustang couldn't possibly be more than inches from her fingertips.

Light flashed in through the small windows in the garage!

Mosconi's vehicle was approaching. Headlight beams washed directly over the windows.

Josie only had seconds.

She took a another step toward the center of the garage where the Mustang was parked. Her fingers hit cold metal. She ran her hands left and right, felt the edges, the corners, tried to find the passenger door.

More light flashed from outside, brighter than before. Mosconi's vehicle was pulling up close!

Josie tried to move fast. She found the door handle, pushed the button, pulled open the door.

It made a grinding squeak, like metal rubbing on rusted metal.

As she lifted her foot to step into the car, she remembered the trip line Ellison had installed. Where was it?!

At first, she couldn't remember. Then it came to her.

The rearview mirror. He'd tied it to the mirror. Just reach up and pull it, he'd said. But where did it run from? Would she bump it getting into the dark vehicle?

Then he'd said the Mustang's windshield was missing. The trip line must come from in front of the car, through the windshield opening, to the mirror.

Josie got into the passenger seat. She pulled the door, trying to shut it. It was stuck on something. The cuff of her pants.

She gathered the fabric of her pants, then pulled the door shut. The door made another screech. It seemed so loud that the person approaching the garage would have heard it.

Josie wanted to be ready with the crossbow. It would do her no good on the hood of the car. She reached through the windshield opening, feeling in the dark. She touched the crossbow, got a grip on it, carefully pulled it through the opening and into the car.

She oriented it so its front end was on the dashboard, pointing out the open windshield.

The headlights outside of the garage went off. The vehicle's engine turned off.

Josie heard the thump of a shutting door. Mosconi would be

walking up to the garage. She grit her teeth, took a deep breath, tried to be silent.

Josie gripped the crossbow so hard, her hands hurt. Then she realized she hadn't cranked her crossbow tension! The bolt was in place, but it was useless until it was tensioned.

But the crank made noise. Josie couldn't breathe. She shivered with terror. If Samantha were here, she would tell Josie to act like a professor and analyze her situation.

A moment's thought made it clear. It would be better to tension the crossbow, even if it alerted Mosconi to her presence. She simply had no choice. There was no point in having a weapon if it couldn't be used.

She started cranking it. The clicks of the tension ratchet seemed very loud. She went slowly, gradually, hoping the slow clicks would be less noticeable. Maybe if she gave no burst of noise, he wouldn't notice.

She kept cranking. Click. Click.

There was noise at the door. He was rattling the door. Shaking it to gauge how strong the lock was. No doubt, Mosconi was simply checking out the garage. Once he'd seen it, he would want to park his vehicle where it wouldn't be seen when the meeting participants showed up.

Josie cranked faster. The little clicks of the mechanism sounded to Josie like a woodpecker on a hollow log.

He pushed hard on the door.

With every sound, Josie cranked faster. Her crank hit the stop. The draw string was fully tensioned. The bolt was in its track, held in place by the stop. When the trigger was pulled, the bolt would be released.

The sounds outside stopped.

Josie remembered that Samantha had given Josie her phone and the little support stand Samantha had attached to it. Josie needed to have it ready to record. Josie fumbled in her pocket, feeling for the phone. She got it out and dropped it.

There was an explosion of sound! Breaking wood, shattered hardware.

He had kicked the door open.

FORTY-EIGHT

At the sound of the door breaking, Josie gasped. She couldn't tell how much sound burst from her throat. She clenched her teeth as the man kicked the door again, then pushed it open, wood splinters cracking.

Josie rested the end of the crossbow on the Mustang's dash.

The man lurched into the darkened space and switched on a flashlight. The beam wobbled as if he had trouble holding the light.

The flashlight seemed to be tucked under his left arm. He held a handgun in his right hand. Why was the flashlight under his arm? Did he have a second weapon in his left hand? Why hadn't he turned on the garage light? The man turned his body left and right, a movement that was accompanied by the motion of the flashlight beam peering into the depths of the garage and all its equipment.

Josie realized she'd forgotten to lower the visor. She quickly reached up and pulled it down to the lowest position.

The man swept the space with his light. If he'd heard the noises she'd made, he would know someone was inside. If not, he'd probably be satisfied that he'd broken into a vacant garage. He might be wondering if this really could be the place of the secret meeting scheduled for the following morning, the meeting between the reporter and the professor who'd found Hadley Painter.

The man stepped forward, his movements awkward like those of a man in pain. He muttered, "An ugly garage for a meeting?" he said aloud to what he thought was an empty space. "That doesn't make sense."

If he went a few more steps he'd be out of Josie's range to the side! Her crossbow would be useless.

Josie flipped on her mic switch.

"Not another step," she said, her amplified voice booming from the rear corner in the small space.

The man jerked in surprise.

He recovered quickly. "What's this?" It was Theo Mosconi's voice. "An ambush? I'm impressed. A good surprise, but probably more of your medieval silliness."

Josie wondered about his comment. He must have learned that she was behind the Grendel story.

"You didn't learn the power of the Bureau?" Mosconi said. "You have to do what the Bureau says, when they say it, how they say it. If not, you go to prison. We have the power to put your daughter away for life."

Josie spoke into the mic. "What I learned was the power of a rogue agent, twisting the state's power to his own, evil end. But now you're history. You killed the deputies up by Fish Camp. You framed your stepbrother for the murders. Then you had your stepbrother killed after I found him. Or maybe you killed him yourself."

"Crazy thoughts from a mad person," Mosconi said, though he sounded surprised by Josie's information.

"Mad is correct." She raised up her crossbow and aimed it at him.

It was clear he didn't know where she was. He turned so his flashlight shined toward the rear corner of the garage, toward the sound of her voice coming out of the speakers.

"You probably think hiding in the dark is a good plan," Mosconi said. "But I will find you and put a bullet in your head."

"I think not," Josie said.

"Face the truth, little lady. As a parent, you have to pay the debts that your daughter owes society." He lowered his voice to a harsh whisper. "I've come to collect that debt."

The words filled Josie with dread. Yet something about his words distracted her. There was a familiarity to them. And a kind of desperation. Josie spoke into the dark, her voice booming from the speakers. "I've learned that you don't collect on debt, you incur it with your reckless gambling..." For a moment she thought about Samantha, and it choked off her words.

"You snide little bitch," he said.

"A murderer and a gambler," she said. "I'll give you one chance to reverse direction. You give up and turn yourself in, I let you off easy."

Mosconi laughed. "You think you're going to scare me?" he said.

"You should be scared," Josie said. "Do you know firearms? Do you have any idea of the energy packed by a large caliber bullet?"

"Oh, yes." Mosconi was still looking back toward the dark corner at the rear of the garage, the corner where her voice was coming out of the speakers.

"Do the math, Mr. Mosconi. Think about the energy carried by a thirty-aught-six bullet from the rifle you told me about in our first meeting. What does that bullet weigh? Like a fountain pen? What if you were hit by a bullet that weighed nearly half a pound?"

"I'm not impressed. No round is that heavy. And you don't have the guts to shoot me." Mosconi swept his flashlight beam across the space, caught a glimpse of Josie sitting in the Mustang. He immediately swung his gun toward her and fired it before he'd even slowed its motion.

It was a blinding flash, and ear-numbing explosion. Josie felt numb with shock.

Mosconi's shot missed.

Josie fired. The crossbow bolt was invisible in the dark. But she could see Mosconi's flashlight fly from his side as if he'd been hit with a war hammer. He slammed against the wall behind him and collapsed, his legs sagging. Josie turned on her bright flashlight as Mosconi slid down the wall leaving a bloody trail on rough boards.

The bolt had gone far enough through Mosconi's shoulder to project out on both the front and back side of his shoulder. Mosconi dropped until he was sitting on the floor. He looked over at the bloody bolt projecting from his shoulder. His eyes showed terror.

He'd dropped his gun. It was lying on the floor next to his leg. Blood was coming out of his shoulder at a good rate. Not pulsing as if from an artery, but oozing steadily.

The man's eyes were huge. "I… I can't believe you did that." His voice was weak and airy.

Josie got out her owl flute and hooted twice for backup. She waited ten seconds, then hooted again, this time louder.

"A call for help," he said. "Clever. But I got to your helpers first. No one's coming to help you."

The statement was like a punch to Josie's solar plexus, knocking the wind out of her.

Mosconi could be bluffing, she thought to herself. Then again, there was that single hoot that was cut short as if Samantha or Cumberland or Ellison had been interrupted while trying to warn her.

Josie realized she was panting with fear. She forced a deep breath, held it, then let it out slowly. She couldn't think. If this man had gotten to Samantha... But he couldn't have found her if the van was where Ellison had planned to leave it. That meant Mosconi had gotten to Cumberland or Ellison. Rage grew inside her.

"If that's true," she finally managed to say, "you're in bigger trouble than you can imagine."

She put the flute back in her pocket and shined her flashlight in Mosconi's eyes. She realized that one of them was severely wounded. The eyeball was partly out of its socket and bulged to one side. His face looked like a fright mask. His other eye was glossy with perception. But his face was tight with a grimace of pain. The side of his head with the damaged eye had a huge purple bruise, purple enough that the injury hadn't just occurred when she shot him. She had no idea why or how he'd been injured before she shot him.

Josie moved the flashlight beam down to the bolt. The blood flow was steady.

"You said you weren't impressed by medieval silliness," Josie said. "You should be more careful with your words. And you should never fire a weapon at a woman thinking she doesn't have the guts to fire back." Josie shined her light on the rest of the man. There was a tear in his pants near his knee. Another wound bled from behind the fabric. The source of his limp.

"Fall on a rock?" she said.

"Go to hell. You're going to cry yourself to sleep for the rest of your days."

Josie pulled another bolt out of her pack, set it in the groove of the crossbow, and began cranking the ratchet, pulling the draw string back, farther and farther. When it was fully tensioned, she aimed her bright flashlight at the crossbow so he could see it. She pointed the crossbow at Mosconi's face.

"If I shoot this at your face, you will be dead before you slump over." She lowered the crossbow to aim at the man's stomach. "But of course, I won't put you out of your misery that quickly. Instead. I'll shoot it at your stomach. You will live for many minutes. Maybe an hour or more. The agony will be unbearable. Having something akin to a railroad spike driven through your stomach will concentrate all of your attention in a way you've never experienced. But if I don't shoot it, if we get you medical attention for your shoulder, you might survive."

"Don't." Theo Mosconi's words were soft. His skin was pale.

"Don't what?"

"Don't shoot me again." The words were slow and measured.

"I won't if you tell me everything you did. Every wicked thing. What you did to Hadley Painter and the deputies you shot in Fish Camp. Tell me about the scam you pulled at the Bureau. Explain your monitoring of me and my daughter by surreptitious means."

"Go to hell," he said again.

"Ah, you need more persuasion," Josie said. She opened the door of the Mustang and got out. She set the crossbow on the Mustang's hood so it pointed toward the garage door, walked over, and kicked away Mosconi's gun, which slid under the drill press. Josie flipped on the garage light and stood close to Mosconi, looking down at him, crowding him with her presence.

"You have caused my daughter and me so much anguish and fear. Now I have in mind some of the medieval silliness for which you have such disdain."

Josie paused to see if Mosconi was paying attention.

His breath was short. His eyes were intense. Despite his pain, it was clear he was registering what she said.

Josie said, "Eighth century monks developed some effective techniques to produce enough pain to convince people to talk. Those men of God were thought of as pacifists. And they were generally kind and helpful to those in need. Pacifists in most ways. But if you crossed them, they used pain with impressive success. So, I'll give you one more chance to tell your sordid story. If you don't, I'll apply those techniques to you."

"Confessions obtained by torture are inadmissible in court," he said. His words were slurred, and his voice was weak. But his sentiment was strong.

"I'm not looking for an admissible confession. I just want the details of your crimes. Your words will tell investigators where to look. They'll uncover all the evidence they need on the basis of your deeds, not your words. Are you ready to talk?"

Theo Mosconi made some mouth movements, then spit at Josie.

"Okay. That's your answer," she said. "One more bit of advice," Josie said. "What I'm about to do will cause more pain than any person can bear. You will say anything to make me stop it. Last chance."

Mosconi didn't speak.

Josie balled up one of the thick wool socks she'd brought to stay warm through the night and stuffed it into his mouth. He was unable to resist.

Josie stood clear of his hands and feet, reached down to the bolt that was projecting out of his shoulder. She gave it a jerk.

His scream, though muffled by the sock in his mouth, was a wail of agony bcyond dcscription.

"Now are you ready to talk? Or do you want more medieval silliness?"

He hesitated. She gave the bolt another push.

His shriek was even louder than before. It stretched out over long seconds, then slowly dropped down in volume until he was sobbing and sweat was rolling off his face.

Josie pointed her flashlight into the Mustang, found Samantha's phone and its stand, and set them on the Mustang's hood, just six or seven feet from Mosconi's face.

When things were in place, her phone camera ready to record, she reached again toward the bolt in his shoulder.

He started jerking his head and making mumbling noises. His eyes were as wide as eyes get.

"Do you want to talk?"

He jerked some more.

"If so, I'll take the sock out of your mouth. But if you spit at me again or cause me any trouble, or refuse to answer any of my questions, I will twist and jerk the bolt until you beg me to kill you and put you out of your misery."

She paused. "You do what I want, or you die of pain. Do you understand?"

He nodded frantically.

Josie pulled on the broken door. It swung in easily. She stood in the opening and gave two strong hoots on her owl flute. Then she shut the door, took the sock out of Mosconi's mouth, and turned on her phone recorder, both sound and video.

FORTY-NINE

"First question," Josie said. "After you shot Hadley Painter in Yosemite, you intended your second shot to kill me, correct?"

Mosconi's voice was very soft. "What second…" He stopped talking.

"I'm waiting," Josie said.

"Yeah. Sure. The second shot was intended for you."

Josie said, "You didn't know about the second shot, did you?"

There was a moment before he spoke. "Of course, I did. I made the shot."

"No. Don't lie. You said, 'What second...' Then you caught yourself."

"I can't think. My shoulder hurts so much, it makes me forget everything. I was focused on Painter."

"There was another shooter in Yosemite, wasn't there?" Josie asked.

"No. Just me. And Painter. I had to take him out."

"Why?"

"He was going to turncoat me."

"Turn you in?"

"Yes."

"What did you shoot him with?"

"My…" Mosconi hesitated. "My thirty-aught-six."

"Not a six millimeter Remington?"

"No. Maybe. I forget. I had two rifles in my van."

"Are they in your van now? Is one of them a six millimeter Remington?"

"I don't remember. Yeah, I brought the Remington, too."

Josie said, "Why did you want me dead?"

"You learned too much."

"Why did the park police detain me for questioning about Hadley Painter's murder?"

"I told them..." he stopped, started moaning. "My shoulder..."

"I'm waiting." Josie made as if to reach for the bolt.

"They wondered if you could have killed Painter. I said yes. I told them we expected you would try to kill him."

"They consented to your wishes because you used the reputation of the Bureau to intimidate them."

"Well, I..."

"The entire operation from the time you persuaded the San Diego Sheriff's Office and Immigration and Customs Enforcement to hand my daughter over to you was designed to hide and cover up your personal involvement in the bank robberies and murders including the murders of the police, correct?"

He hesitated.

Josie reached for the bolt in his shoulder.

"Yes!"

"Tell me why."

"I knew you could find Painter. Then I could learn where he buried the money from the last bank robbery."

"But you killed him."

He hesitated. "Yeah, right. I killed him."

"Why kill him? Then you would never find the money."

"Like you, he knew too much. And I decided I could figure it out. Maybe he left something in his camp. A ticket or something."

"What does that mean, a ticket."

"I meant a key. For a locker."

"You think there are lockers in Yosemite?"

"I don't know. But I thought I could find some kind of clue where he was camping. But you called the cops. So I couldn't search his camp. But I thought the cops would find something. They wouldn't know what it meant. But it would indicate to me where to find the money."

"Before you came to California from Florida, you were charged and found guilty of impersonating a police officer, correct?"

"Right."

"One more question. In addition to committing the murders of the two deputies in Fish Camp, and the murder of Hadley Painter in Yosemite, you and Painter killed his wife Theresa in the bathroom of your apartment in Miami, and then you two split the life insurance payout. Is that correct?"

"How did you find that out?"

"I want details. Every little detail. Dates, times, agreements, where you got your weapons, how you committed each murder and robbery. Addresses in Florida and California."

Mosconi was silent.

Josie reached for the bolt in his shoulder.

"Okay, okay!" His whisper was hoarse but easy to hear and loud enough to be clear on the recording.

It took forty minutes. Mosconi was thorough. When his explanations slowed, Josie reached for the bolt. Before she could touch it, he spoke with renewed energy.

Josie asked several more questions. When she'd collected the information she needed, she turned off the recording and put Samantha's phone in her pocket.

Josie once again opened the broken, splintered door, stepped out into the dark, and used the owl flute to hoot twice, the backup signal. No one had come.

She was so worried about Samantha, it choked off her breath. But she reminded herself that Samantha was almost certainly safe. It was Cumberland and Ellison who were cause for worry, because Mosconi was more likely to have found them.

Mosconi was still conscious, but blood loss had taken its toll. He could do nothing other than sit against the wall.

"We're done here," Josie said. "Time to stand up. You're going to turn yourself in." She realized that Mosconi might not be able to get up off the floor. There was a portable generator near his feet. She rolled it over in front of Mosconi, then stepped on the wheel brakes. "Put your good hand on the generator frame. You can use that to pull yourself up."

"I can't stand up."

"Yes, you can." She reached for the bolt.

"Okay! I'll try."

He grabbed onto the generator with his good hand. Josie reached down, grabbed his belt, and lifted. Mosconi strained and whimpered and panted.

They got him up on his feet. He leaned with his good hand on the generator. He shook violently, a total body tremor.

"Now turn toward the door. That's right. Move your feet. Grab the shelf next to the wall. Hold onto that. Take a step toward the door. Lift your foot over the threshold."

"I can't. I'm too weak."

"No, you're not. You had enough energy to come in here to murder me. You're going to use some of that energy to walk out the door. Otherwise, I grab the bolt."

"Don't grab the bolt!" he whisper-shouted, his desperation obvious.

"Then step outside."

"It's dark. I can't see."

"Move!" Josie shouted. She gave him a push in the middle of his back.

He stepped outside.

Lights appeared down the road.

Josie heard Mosconi make a little laugh. "I knew it," he said.

"What?"

"Doesn't matter," he said. "You're about to get dead. And your daughter is next. She'll be dead before the night's over."

Josie inhaled.

Was it possible the vehicle was the van Ellison drove? With Samantha and Cumberland inside? Or maybe it was one of Mosconi's friends. Maybe the friend was waiting for a call. When it didn't come, he came to save Mosconi.

The headlights grew brighter. The vehicle stopped about fifty feet away. Josie couldn't make out anything about it. Josie realized that police might park at a distance while they waited for backup.

A vehicle door opened. The vehicle's headlights made it impossible to see any person or what kind of vehicle it was.

Josie called out. "This man is Theo Mosconi, a corrupt CBI agent. He tried to kill me. We're both unarmed. Although he is severely injured." Josie shined her light toward the vehicle. But she could see nothing past the blinding headlights.

Josie heard sounds. Like a person getting out of the vehicle. But no one appeared. The vehicle's headlights were still on.

Josie prodded Mosconi forward. "Just keep walking," she said.

There was a loud crack, and Mosconi collapsed, dropping to the ground like a dead weight.

FIFTY

As Theo Mosconi fell to the ground, dead from a gunshot, Josie dropped as well, hitting the ground with her hands and knees. She scratched at the dirt as she turned an about-face. Her panic made it impossible to breathe. But she could crawl.

She scrambled on hands and knees toward the garage.

There came another crack. Josie cried in terror. Grit and chips of wood or something hit her in the face.

Josie's hand hit the doorsill. She went over it. Her right knee slammed into the sharp edge of the sill.

Another crack cut through the dark night. But Josie was inside.

She shut the broken door as far as it would go and reached up and flipped off the light switch. Then she crawled farther back into the dark garage. She stopped, trying to breathe, trying to quell the panic.

Who was this new shooter? Probably the shooter who fired the shot at Josie after Hadley Painter had been killed. Mosconi didn't know about the second shot that was clearly intended for Josie. So, he was covering for the actual shooter. His accomplice was probably the person outside, the person who just killed him and was intending to kill Josie.

Was the shooter going to charge the garage? If so, Mosconi's body was lying there in the vehicle headlights. The shooter knew that Mosconi had been killed by his gunshot. But the crossbow bolt in his shoulder was obvious. That might slow the shooter down if he became aware that Josie was in the garage and she had a powerful weapon.

Josie had to escape. She crawled to the Mustang, reached up on the hood, and felt around for her crossbow.

Her fingers touched its frame. It was reassuring to feel.

But it was no match for a rifle when the distance was more than a few feet.

Josie wanted another weapon, but there was none.

She tried to think like a medieval warrior. Was there anything in the garage that could serve as another weapon? Medieval warriors used daggers and swords and war hammers and pikes and…

Josie stopped her thought at medieval pikes. Very long poles with blades at the end. A pike could be thrust or stabbed and sometimes even thrown. One of the most effective uses for the pike was to push its rear end down into the ground and hold the sharp end up where a charging attacker would impale himself on it. When Josie had first come into the garage, she'd seen the group of metal conduit pipes leaning in the corner of the building.

The conduit pipes had no points like medieval pikes, just open circular ends. Josie thought they looked very long, maybe ten feet. The conduit pipes were stiff, and their circular ends had thin edges, even if they weren't sharp. It was better than nothing and light enough that she could carry one while she also carried her crossbow.

Josie knew the killer could come through the door at any moment. But she scrambled over to the wall near the door where she'd seen the conduit. She reached out, felt around, got a grip on one of the conduit sections, and tried to lift it up and out without making noise.

It clanked and banged as she pulled it free.

Josie turned and reached with her other hand for the crossbow. The conduit hit the wall near the corner. Then the other wall. The racket was very loud.

Josie grabbed the crossbow and scooted around the far side of the Mustang. She tried to slide her feet along the floor, feeling for obstructions. She managed to switch the conduit to the hand that held the crossbow so she'd have a free hand to feel for the other door in the far rear corner.

Her hand found the edge of the door. She felt up and down, trying to find the knob, a dead bolt, a slide latch. Anything!

But there was nothing. Then she realized the door must open on the other edge. She felt the other side of the door, frantically sliding her hand up and down. There was a lock. A turn knob. Josie grabbed it, twisted. It seemed frozen in place.

Then she remembered the fishing net trap.

Ellison had set the fishing net up with a trip line tied to the Mustang's rear view mirror. Josie had forgotten about it when Theo Mosconi had broken into the garage. In the end, she hadn't needed it. But now she could use it.

She took quick steps over to the Mustang. She hit the fender with her leg and leaned over the hood. She reached her hand over to the windshield opening, feeling its edges, found the rearview mirror, moved her hand gently to find the trip line, getting ready to pull it.

The door to the garage opened six inches. A hand reached in. The light switched on. The shooter was coming into the garage.

As a person came through the door, Josie tugged on the trip line. She heard the sound of cords sliding across wood as the weights fell and pulled on the net.

The net dropped down on a man. Josie couldn't see clearly.

The boom of a gunshot was deafening in the small space.

But Josie was gone out the back door.

FIFTY-ONE

Josie stumbled across the dirt, away from the rear door of the garage. She carried the length of electrical conduit in one hand and her crossbow in the other.

Josie had no idea if the net would entangle him and delay him for a few seconds? Half a minute?

All she could do was to try to escape.

But, as she ran from the garage, stumbling into the black night, she remembered what Theo Mosconi said just before he was shot. They were going to come after Samantha. But while Samantha was well hidden, Cumberland and Ellison were not.

Mosconi had a partner, and it was probably that partner who killed him. Would that reduce the danger to the others? Josie thought it would probably do the opposite. The murder of Mosconi showed how focused this second killer was.

Josie was unable to get her mind off of their intention to kill Samantha. Had she stayed locked in the van? Or was it possible she heard the gunshots and got out of the van to investigate? If so, was she still alive? Josie's gut clenched as she wondered.

When they'd first arrived in Ellison's borrowed van, it was twilight. Josie had seen the dirt drive snaking back toward the A-frame cabin where Ellison would wait. But he hadn't come when Josie hooted on the owl flute. If he hadn't heard her blowing on the flute, he certainly would have heard the gunshots, and he would have come running. But he hadn't appeared. And Mosconi had been wounded when he broke into the garage. Maybe Mosconi and Ellison had fought. Maybe all had been compromised. That would also explain why Cumberland hadn't come after he heard the gunshots.

Mosconi had surprised them, maybe injured them. Or worse...

Josie stopped running and forced herself to breathe. She resolved to believe that Samantha was still alive.

Josie couldn't simply flee and escape. She had to keep fighting. She had to try to bring down this new killer.

The lights of the killer's car still lit up the night on the other side of the garage. Josie could hear the engine running. Could she get to the vehicle? Was it unlocked?

If it was unlocked, what would she do? If she drove away, the shooter with the rifle would probably be able to shoot her in the driver's seat. Instead of fleeing, how could she get an advantage over a killer with a rifle? Could she use the killer's car to run him down? Josie felt paralyzed.

Josie heard a noise. The killer coming around the garage. He'd gotten free of the net.

Josie ran toward the dark. She didn't know anything about survival strategy. She only knew the three basics of medieval battles. Overwhelm your enemy with numbers, surround them and starve them out, and attack when and where they'd least expect it. Josie couldn't use the first two approaches. But maybe she could try the third, make a surprise attack.

How?

She had no idea.

The killer appeared around the side of the garage. The vehicle was still out of Josie's sight, on the far side of the garage. But light from its headlights washed past the dark van that Theo Mosconi had driven, then lit up the killer and the slope that rose behind him. Josie couldn't make out any details of the killer. But she could see that he was holding his rifle as he rounded the garage.

Josie thought of trying to go up the slope toward the ridge where Samantha waited. But that was far above. There was no way she had the stamina to go up a mountain at high altitude. Instead, she could run down the trail toward Ellison and see if he was alive. But she'd be in the wash of the vehicle's headlights, in full view of the killer. Neither approach would work. She was out of shape, and the killer would be upon her in seconds.

Josie tried to remember if there was any other structure where she could hide, an old shed or something. All she recalled was the slope with the tall grass, waving in the evening breeze.

She could run into the tall grass, and be certain that he observed her doing so. She could make noise or turn on her flashlight. That would force him to come and do a careful search with his flashlight.

It could take the killer many long minutes to find her hiding in the grass.

After Josie feigned hiding in the tall grass, she could continue on into the darkness and circle around to his vehicle, which was still running with its lights on.

She trudged up the slope of grass, still carrying her crossbow and the length of metal conduit.

Immediately, she was out of breath. 7000 feet of elevation. Much higher than Yosemite. Too little oxygen for a sea-level dweller. No matter how desperate she was, she couldn't run up a hill in thin air.

She tried not to inhale too loudly. Then she had another idea. She continued up the slope, but more slowly. Even the shortest steps, if regular, will make progress.

When she'd gone maybe a hundred feet up the slope, she sensed a darker area. There was no light except bounced illumination from the vehicle's headlights shining on distant trees. Josie had her flashlights, but she didn't dare turn one on.

The darker patch on the slope was probably a small stand of trees. They were surrounded by the tall grass. The contrast between the trees and grass was visible in the dim light. Josie worked her way toward the trees, forcing herself to go slowly enough that she wouldn't pass out from lack of oxygen.

Josie had to stop to catch her breath. She was largely hidden by the tall, waving grass. But she could see the killer.

He had changed direction. He, too, was heading for the slope of tall grass, a good distance away and proceeding a different direction than Josie.

As Josie trudged up the slope, her foot struck something that moved. She bent over, feeling with the hand that held the conduit. It was a large cobble. About eight inches across. She set down her crossbow and conduit and picked up the cobble with both arms. It was very heavy. She cradled it next to her body.

A crunching sound of breaking wood came from down by the garage. Josie turned to look. The killer had flung open the broken door and was walking along the outer wall of the garage. He must have wondered if she'd gone back inside to hide. He held his flashlight in his left hand and his rifle in his right. He shined his light over the area. He went around the far side of the garage, out of her line of sight. Josie saw the light beam from his flashlight jumping across the landscape.

He reappeared over near Mosconi's darkened van. The killer shined his light up the slope toward Josie, then swept it left and right across the tall grass.

Josie hoped she could time things just right...

Using both hands, she held the cobble as she watched the man shine the light. When his light went one way, she tossed the cobble the other way.

The stone made a thump, then rolled down the slope.

Josie picked up her crossbow and conduit. She ran a few steps across the slope, away from the rolling cobble, then stopped and crouched down in the tall grass.

The man jerked his flashlight toward the sound. From the motion of his light beam, it seemed that he saw moving grass before the cobble came to a stop.

The man's light swept across the slope, looking for movement. The beam settled on a point near where the stone had stopped, some distance from where Josie crouched. He held the light at that position for a long time, waiting for the resumption of movement. She crouched as low as possible in the grass. When he shifted the flashlight beam away from her, she walked softly across the slope.

The man started walking up the slope. He swept the beam left and right, always coming back to hold steady on the point where he'd first sensed movement.

Josie took a wide, curving path across the slope and down, always staying crouched, moving farther from the man and his flashlight beam. At one point, he swung his beam up toward her location. But she'd been watching, and she dropped to her knees and bent over at the last moment. His light beam went over her head, came back, then went away again. It was clear he'd seen nothing but tall grass.

He refocused his beam where she'd rolled the cobble.

Josie resumed her hike across the slope. Minutes later, she saw him searching the slope, going back and forth.

Josie came down near the garage, out of sight from where the man was searching. She peeked out to see where he was.

Still hiking across the grassy slope with his flashlight.

Josie tried to make a soft-footed run toward the rear of his vehicle, which she could now see was a pickup. It was parked behind and to the side of Mosconi's van.

As she went behind the pickup, her conduit swung and hit the back of the pickup's tailgate. It made a metallic banging sound that was so loud, it could have been heard hundreds of yards away.

"Dammit!" came the man's voice from up the slope.

He turned and started running down the slope. He'd be on her in seconds.

Josie ran around to the driver's side of the pickup. The door was open, classical music playing softly inside the cab.

Josie was panting so hard, she couldn't think. But she was aware of what would happen if she got in and tried to drive away. The man would take careful aim with his rifle and shoot through the windshield toward the driver's seat, likely killing her the way he'd killed the deputies near Fish Camp.

Without a clear plan, she dropped her crossbow and conduit on the ground, reached in the open driver's door, and tried to grab the shift lever. The pickup was so tall, she could barely reach the shift. She pulled it toward Drive. The shift wouldn't budge.

She remembered that the driver has to put a foot on the brake pedal to release the shift lever. She stepped up on the running board, hitched her hip up onto the seat, stretched her foot out to step down on the brake.

This time she could move the shift. She pulled it down toward Drive. It scooted past Drive to Low gear. Just as well.

The truck started to move. Josie stepped out of the truck.

"Damn you!" the man said.

Josie looked up. He was only a hundred feet away. Less. Sprinting fast. He was illuminated by the truck's headlight beams. She recognized him as Mosconi's partner from their first meeting. José Rodriguez. Lit by the lights, his eyes flashed as if they were aflame.

Josie shut the driver's door. The truck crawled forward.

Rodriguez stopped, aimed his rifle, and fired.

The windshield shattered, glass exploding above the steering wheel. Her ruse worked. He thought she was driving.

The truck kept rolling slowly toward Rodriguez. He fired again. And again.

He probably assumed he'd killed her.

He started running again, coming for the driver's door.

Josie knew he'd see her as soon as he got out of the headlight glare. He'd kill her in a moment.

The man sprinted forward.

Josie picked up the conduit and stepped over next to the front fender. She held out the conduit, pointing toward the man. She lowered the rear end to the ground and stepped on it.

It pointed up at a shallow angle. A medieval pike.

The truck kept grinding forward in low gear.

The man ran past the blinding headlights and hit the conduit at high speed. He struck the end of the conduit with his groin.

He made a loud grunt of pain and spun sideways. The conduit was jerked from Josie's hands as the man fell to the ground, one arm still holding the rifle.

Josie didn't know if he'd been severely hurt or not.

As if in answer to her thought, the man raised his rifle. He rotated it around, toward her, moving slowly, trying to take careful aim in the dark as the truck crawled past him.

Josie picked up her crossbow. She tried to step sideways, out of his line of sight.

As the wash of the truck's headlights went past and he was no longer blinded, he took a rushed aim and fired. He missed.

Josie took careful aim with her crossbow. She didn't miss.

FIFTY-TWO

Josie was shaky with fear and adrenalin. She stared at Rodriguez, lying on the ground in the dark. He was writhing and moaning.

She stepped toward him and turned on her flashlight, shining it in his eyes. He looked unconscious, his eyes half-open, turned up to the side. The crossbow bolt had hit him high in the center of his abdomen, up near his stomach.

Could he be faking unconsciousness? His rifle lay on the dirt to his side. His hand was near it. Planning to grab it?

Josie stepped on his hand. He didn't react. It could be a ploy. She twisted her hiking boot, grinding his hand down into the dirt. She imagined that some people could take such pressure without reacting. But not most.

She reached down and picked up the rifle by gripping the end of the barrel thinking that shooters might occasionally touch the barrel at the end, but most of their prints would be elsewhere on the weapon. She didn't want to obscure any prints Rodriguez had left on the gun.

Dragging the gun by its barrel, she took several fast steps toward some brush. The gun was heavy, so she had to use both hands on the barrel to toss it through the bushes and down an embankment.

Josie looked around, seeing that Rodriguez hadn't moved. She thought about Samantha. Was she still hiding in the van up on the high ridge? And where were Ellison and Cumberland?

Josie picked up her crossbow, lifted it up high, and set it into the back of the pickup. She ran alongside the slow-moving truck and climbed into the driver's seat. The seat was positioned back from the steering wheel. José Rodriguez was a tall man with long legs. Josie reached down but couldn't find the seat lever to move the seat forward.

She scooted toward the front edge of the seat so she could reach the controls. She shifted into reverse. She turned the truck around, and drove it away, careful not to drive over the wounded man who was still writhing in unconscious delirium on the ground. She looked out through the broken windshield and saw the rutted road in the headlights.

She wanted to find the trail that went up to where Samantha was on the high ridge. But she didn't know how to get there.

She headed away from the garage and found the dirt road that went toward the cabin. She rolled down the driver's window and called out as she drove up the road.

"Ellison? Ellison? Are you here? Can you hear me?"

There was no answer. Josie kept driving. The dirt road curved to the left. The trail was barely visible. The A-frame cabin came into view, a small building with a very steep roof.

Josie slowed further. Ellison should be near, but there was nothing to see. As she turned the truck a little, its headlights washed over the A-frame. There was no sign of movement. Josie stopped the truck but left it running. She got out and walked toward the cabin.

Ellison would have hidden nearby, someplace where he could see the road and watch for Mosconi's arrival. Josie turned on her bright flashlight and swept its beam across the landscape. There was nothing to see in the dark except an old duffle bag lying against a tree.

Ellison!

Josie ran toward the tree.

Ellison was sitting slumped, his back to the tree trunk. He was making small movements and moaning. A dark flow of sticky blood had oozed out of his temple and down the side of his head. There was duct tape over his mouth. The blood ran over the corner of the duct tape and down onto his neck.

"Oh, Ellison, You're hurt!"

Josie got a grip on the edge of the tape and tugged. It didn't want to come. "I'm going to pull off this duct tape."

She gave the tape a fast tug. Ellison's head jerked, but he

didn't say anything.

Josie shined her light and saw that his arms were stretched out behind him, pulled back to the tree trunk. Josie saw something else. Another person on the other side of the tree.

"Cumberland!"

Cumberland made some muffled groaning sounds. Josie shined the light on him. Like Ellison, Cumberland was sitting with his back to the tree. His arms were also pulled back. Cumberland's and Ellison's wrists were duct-taped to each other. They were nearly immobilized by their awkward, painful position on either side of the tree.

"I'll get you two free as soon as possible!"

Josie kneeled down beside them and went to work on the snarl of duct tape holding the men together. Cumberland moaned louder. Josie turned her light. He was gagged with some kind of fabric stuffed into his mouth and held in place with a crushed cardboard tube, folded over. The core of the duct tape. She went to pull it out of his mouth, but it didn't want to come. It looked very painful. "I'm trying to get your gag out, Cumberland, but I'm afraid I'll break your teeth. Let me get your arm free, and you can do a better job of getting the gag out of your mouth. Just hold on one more minute."

Josie tried to get her fingernail under the edge of duct tape. The fingernail tore off. She couldn't get purchase on the tape. She bent down, pushed her mouth up against Cumberland's wrist and got her teeth on an edge of tape, trying to be careful not to bite his skin. She pulled to rip it. Eventually, she got one of Cumberland's wrists free from Ellison's wrist. He reached up and got the gag out of his mouth, spitting and coughing and gasping.

Without saying anything, he crawled around to the other side of the tree and went to work at separating his other wrist from Ellison.

When the two men were separated, Josie faced Cumberland in the dark.

"Are you injured?"

"No." He rotated his arms as if to see if his shoulders were still working.

"Are you okay?"

"No. But I will be."

"Can you help me get Ellison into this pickup?"

"Yes."

Josie got on one side of Ellison and Cumberland got on the other. Together they tried to lift Ellison up. He was somewhat conscious and able to help support himself. Josie realized that she was providing very little help in lifting. If Ellison hadn't been able to help, they wouldn't have succeeded.

Rodriguez's pickup was the type with four doors. They got Ellison into the back seat. Cumberland got in the front passenger seat.

Josie climbed up into the driver's seat. "Cumberland, can you reach down below my seat and see if you can find the adjustment lever to slide the seat forward?"

He did, and Josie could finally reach the pedals.

"I want to drive to where Samantha is hiding in the van. Can you tell me how to go?"

"I'll try. Go down this trail and turn left up a trail that comes down from the slope."

Josie jockeyed forward and backward until she got the truck turned around. The truck was twice as big as anything she'd ever driven. She bumped a tree hard enough to dent a fender, and then backed over a bush that got stuck under the truck.

She gunned the engine, wheels spun, and the truck got free from the bush.

Josie followed Cumberland's directions, which, he said, were partly guesses. Eventually, she got the truck up to the high ridge trail and drove along it slowly, bouncing over ruts and rocks. "How far to the van with Samantha?"

"I don't know," Cumberland said. "I think it's down this trail, maybe on a curve."

Josie found the switch for the high beams. The mountain ridge was well lit, but there was no sign of the van.

"No, wait," Cumberland said. "I think we were supposed to turn to the right back a ways."

Josie backed up. The rear bumper dug into an embankment. She shifted forward, jockeying the truck. She came to a fork, and turned down it. There was Ellison's van.

Josie knew Samantha would be terrified seeing a big new truck. She left the truck running with the headlights on, opened her door, and climbed down quickly. She ran into the beam of the headlights so Samantha could see it was her. Then she hurried toward the van.

The door opened and Samantha ran out carrying Unknown.

"Oh, Mama! You don't know how glad I am to see you. And you look okay! I was so worried!"

They hugged hard. Samantha's skinny form felt so reassuring to Josie. Unknown pressed between their legs.

Samantha began crying, speaking through her cries. "I thought Mosconi was going to..."

"Shhh, it's okay," Josie said. "Just breathe. You're safe now. Those men cannot hurt us anymore."

"Are they...?" Samantha's words were choked.

"Theo Mosconi is dead. José Rodriguez killed him. Rodriguez is wounded and nearly dead, too. You're safe."

"What about Mr. Ellison?"

"Ellison's badly hurt. We have to get him to a hospital."

"What should I do?" Samantha's voice was shaky.

"Help Cumberland get Ellison into the van. We'll leave Rodriguez's truck here for the cops and drive the van to the hospital."

Josie wasn't able to provide much help as Cumberland and Samantha moved Ellison from the truck and into the van. They laid him down across the wide seats in the middle row. With Josie's help, Samantha got in and they propped Ellison's head on Samantha's lap. Cumberland sat in the front passenger seat with Unknown.

Josie didn't know if she should take her crossbow with them or not. She remembered she'd put it in the back of Rodriguez's pickup. She got out, ran over and retrieved the crossbow. She would turn it over to the police as soon as she met up with them. She put it in the back of the van, then got into the driver's seat.

This time, Josie was able to work the driver's seat adjustment, sliding it all the way forward. Ellison had left the key in the ignition. Josie started the van.

Samantha and Cumberland both helped to explain where Ellison had driven after they'd left Josie in the garage. Josie made two wrong turns but eventually got back to the paved road.

Josie remembered grabbing Samantha's phone off the hood of the Mustang. She pulled it out of her pocket and held it up over her shoulder.

"Sam, can you dial nine, one, one and hand the phone back to me?"

A moment later, Samantha reached forward from the back seat and handed Josie the phone.

Josie continued to drive as she called the report in, stating for the recording all the pertinent information about what happened, a sequence of events that only she knew. Before Josie hung up, she said she'd stop in at the sheriff's office when she was done with the hospital and that it would probably be several hours.

The dispatcher responded with directions for the nearest hospital, and they had Ellison to the Emergency Room an hour later. Before they left, Ellison was in a hospital bed. They had cleaned and bandaged his head wound. He used a single finger to beckon Josie.

Ellison's voice was so weak, Josie had to lean over to hear his words.

"They say they want to keep me for observation," he whispered. "Don't know what that means. Watch me sleep, I 'spose. Your place in Santa Monica is too far to drive after being up all night. Go to my loft and get some rest. I won't let them keep me here long. I'll call when you can come and pick me up. Here's my key." He handed her a single key on a ring.

Josie bent over and gave him a gentle hug.

"Thank you so much!" she whispered. "Thanks to your help, we got the bad guys."

FIFTY-THREE

Two days later, Josie, Samantha, Ellison, and Cumberland had been through multiple interviews with the San Bernardino Sheriff's Office. They'd each given their statements to different people.

They were told that José Rodriguez would live, although his left leg would be paralyzed, not from the crossbow bolt, which punctured his stomach and required substantial surgery to repair, but from the conduit, which went into his groin and severed the leg nerve.

The third day after the events on the mountain, Josie got a call from the San Diego County District Attorney's office. They set up an appointment at the California Bureau of Investigation building in Los Angeles, which was a long way from San Diego County. They requested that both Josie and her daughter Samantha come and that they would be meeting the San Diego County District Attorney Selena Guadalupe Peralta.

Josie was wary about going back to the Bureau of Investigation.

But this time, the meeting was in the main CBI building, not the vacant building nearby where Theo Mosconi and José Rodriguez had created a mock office.

The meeting room was large and had two sitting areas with upholstered furniture. There were framed paintings on the wall. It was the kind of room where high-level bureaucrats might talk to reporters at an evening mixer and try to shape media coverage.

Josie and Samantha sat down next to each other on a leather couch. Samantha held Unknown in her lap. A short time later, the door opened and two women came in. Josie recognized the older one from TV. She was in her sixties, physically petite, but radiating a powerful personality. She wore a navy suit and navy leather shoes with low heels. She had a red sash at her neck but wore no jewelry other than little pearl earrings. She had very little makeup on skin the color of varnished cedar.

Her younger companion spoke to her in a near whisper. "Anything else you need?"

"No, thanks," the older woman said.

The younger woman left.

Josie and Samantha stood up.

The woman waved them back down to their seats.

"Josephine Strong, Samantha Strong, I'm Selena Peralta, San Diego County DA. Good to meet you."

Josie wasn't sure how to respond. Despite the woman's smile and pleasant demeanor, she was a bit frightening.

"Good to meet you as well," Josie said.

Samantha nodded at her side.

"Please sit," the DA said.

They all took seats.

"I've been informed of recent events involving you two," Peralta said. "I'm here today for two reasons. First, Samantha, I want to reiterate to you that what you did as a drug mule, although unintended, was very wrong. We hope you have learned your lesson and will be much more vigilant in the future." She paused and gave Samantha a stern look.

Samantha nodded silently.

"However, we feel that what Agent Theo Mosconi put you both through creates sufficient extenuating circumstances to not bring any smuggling charges against you. The San Diego Sheriff's Office feels properly chastened at having been manipulated by Agent Mosconi. We will be reviewing our policies to ensure that this doesn't happen again."

Peralta shifted in her chair. "As for the Bureau agents who targeted you, both Mosconi and Agent José Rodriguez had recently been fired and were facing multiple charges before this current situation." Peralta took a breath as if considering what she was about to say.

"I was shown a bit of the video you took of Theo Mosconi. The information you obtained was bracing. However, it appears you committed a crime torturing the man to get the information."

Peralta looked away and took another deep breath. "District Attorneys have a fair amount of latitude in deciding which crimes to pursue. In this case, if the San Bernardino County District Attorney were to charge you for a crime up at Big Bear Lake, he would be aware that a good defense attorney could likely convince a jury that you and your daughter had been sufficiently abused and threatened and attacked, and that you had a great deal of justification for your actions. In addition, the information you uncovered helps all the California counties in their pursuit of law enforcement."

Peralta took another breath before she continued.

"I've spoken to the District Attorneys involved, and they agree not to charge you. You've done them all a service. I should probably add that we would appreciate it if you didn't share the details of your altercation with Agents Mosconi and Rodriguez up by Big Bear Lake. That would help prevent some enemies of law enforcement from trying to make trouble. I'm sure you can agree that the actions you took in self defense need no embellishment or amplification in the tabloid media. But then you are a UCLA professor. I don't need to convince you of the value of discretion."

Peralta looked at Josie with a steady stare.

"I agree," Josie said. Samantha nodded at her side.

"Incidentally," Peralta said, "As part of a plea bargain to avoid the death penalty, Agent José Rodriguez has confessed to the murder of his fellow agent Theo Mosconi as well as the murders of two sheriff's deputies up by Yosemite and Mosconi's stepbrother Hadley Painter. He also confessed to participating in multiple bank robberies that the three men committed. Rodriguez will spend the rest of his life in prison. But, of course, you know these details."

Josie could feel Samantha sitting stiffly next to her, as rigid as if she'd been frozen.

"Thank you," Josie said.

"Yes, thank you very much," Samantha said.

"Second," Peralta said, "the governor's office asked me to do the honors of apologizing for the Bureau's activities. Having those agents engaging in heinous crimes and using you to their ends is unforgiveable. We can't make that go away, and for that, the state is sorry."

"We're glad to hear that," Josie said.

"Lastly, I spoke to the Mariposa County DA this morning. He is aware of Rodriguez's confession to the murder of Hadley Painter. He has dropped inquiries involving you. And he is not going to pursue charges related to your escape from the Park Police and your time as a fugitive from the law. You will be getting an official communication from him."

"More thanks," Josie said. "These last several days have been stressful."

The DA stood up. Josie and Samantha followed.

"Do you have any questions?" Peralta asked in a tone that suggested she wanted none to answer.

"No," Josie said. "But I wish to convey our deepest condolences to the family of the police officer who died in the accident while he was chasing the woman who received the bag Samantha had carried over the border."

Josie sensed that District Attorney Peralta felt awkward, almost embarrassed.

"Thanks for your concern. However, the death of that cop was another fabrication by Agents Mosconi and Rodriguez. They were trying to scare you to death."

Josie's hand rose to the base of her throat. "Oh, thank God. That lifts a weight off us."

After a long moment, Peralta said, "Very well. Thank you for helping us catch two bad men." Peralta gave Josie a penetrating look, then looked at Samantha. "Seeing you two in person, I'm struck by the disconnect between your diminutive size and demeanor and your outsized initiative and energy. I'm going to keep your names in my book for possible future consultation."

The woman made a little nod, then left the room.

EPILOGUE

Two days later, in the late afternoon, they assembled on the beach in Santa Monica. Early winter sun reflected off wind-rippled ocean waves, scintillating like diamonds. The surf was mild and quiet enough that it was easy to talk. The only other sounds came from laughing children on the Santa Monica Pier a quarter mile to the north.

Ralph Ellison sat next to Josie. He was subdued, still weak from his head injuries. After multiple days, the bandage on his temple where they'd stitched him back together still showed signs of weeping fluid. The bruises across the side of his face remained deep blue even though the swelling had begun to recede.

Across from Josie and Ellison, forming a small circle, were the others. Unknown lay half in the backpack and half out and had her head on Samantha's thigh. Near them was Cumberland, looking as awkward and uncomfortable as ever. Between Samantha and Cumberland sat his siblings, Aiden and Cara. Although they didn't telegraph the awkwardness of their older brother, they looked like they'd rather be anyplace other than on the beach with these strangers. Both kids focused on petting Unknown.

Cumberland had asked Josie if it was okay to bring them, and she assured him that they were welcome anytime.

Josie was curious about the siblings of the genius hacker who'd become so important in Josie's and Samantha's lives.

Aiden looked about eleven years old, not quite entering puberty. A cowlick at the top of his forehead, which sent his hair straight up in a point, had been unsuccessfully gooed over with cream to hold it down. The result looked like a good surfing wave as it crested in a curl. The attempt at taming his unruly hair demonstrated that Aiden had crossed a boundary on his passage from childhood to adolescence and had entered the era of self-consciousness. He was a handsome kid with strong, dramatic eyebrows.

Cara was perhaps nine years old. Cumberland had introduced her as a talented writer, a surprising description for the simple reason of Cara's youth. Very thin and gangly and with none of the handsome attributes of her older brothers, her intelligence was obvious. But Cara seemed as uncomfortable as Cumberland.

Josie put her arms behind her and leaned back, fingers in the sand. The sun was descending toward the water. Its last rays were warm on Josie's skin. The sand still felt cozy warm on her bare feet.

She turned to Ellison. "I want to thank you for all the help you gave us. Getting Samantha out of Yosemite. Borrowing the van. Providing the venue for trapping the bad agents. The emotional support."

"Happy to help," Ellison said. "Did you get your weapons back?"

"They found the war hammer down a slope near the cabin. The San Bernardino County Sheriff's Office says I'll get both it and my crossbow back, but it will be some weeks."

Ellison nodded. "The wheels of bureaucracy and justice turn slowly."

He used both hands to massage the back of his neck. "I'm still sorry Mosconi got the drop on me," Ellison said, his voice sounding depressed. "I got off a hoot or two on the flute as he came running. It never occurred to me Mosconi would be hiding at the A-frame. But it was an obvious place for him to wait. I should have anticipated it. He tackled me and my head bounced off a tree. I must have wrestled with him a bit, but I was a goner. Luckily, right after Mosconi jumped me, Cumberland showed up out of nowhere and swung his war hammer. He blew out Mosconi's leg." Ellison turned to Cumberland. "How was it that Mosconi didn't grab the war hammer and kill us both?"

Cumberland spoke in a low voice. "After I hit him, he did grab the hammer and went to swing it at me. But he had blood on his hands from when you fought him. So the war hammer slipped out of his grip and flew down a slope into the dark. Maybe he didn't think to stomp us to death. He had duct tape, so he taped us up."

Josie worried about the children overhearing Cumberland talk about the violent details. But Cara and Aiden were talking to each other about Unknown. They seemed absorbed in petting the dog.

Ellison looked at Cumberland. "I was thinking how he took my gun and smashed my head with it. But he didn't shoot us with it. You figure he didn't want the gunshot noise to tip Josie off that he was coming?"

Cumberland shrugged even as he looked at the sand and didn't meet anyone's eyes. "He didn't even hit me with it like he did you."

"I barely remember," Ellison said. "I think I grabbed him and pulled him down with me after my head hit the tree. But I was already losing consciousness. That was all I remember."

"The pathologist figured it out," Josie said. "It turns out that the blood on your fingers belonged to Mosconi." She lowered her voice so the kids would be less likely to hear. "You gouged his eye most of the way out of its socket. And his shoulder had significant ligament tears. They said it was consistent with a severe hammerlock injury. Whatever that means."

Ellison frowned. Eventually, he said, "A lifetime ago, Green Beret training had us practice close-quarter combat until we could literally fight in our sleep. One of the instructors' techniques was to sneak up on us when we were sleeping. You'd be having a pleasant dream and wake up with someone putting a choke hold on you. The result was you learned to respond when you weren't fully conscious."

"Well, you and Cumberland put Mosconi in a bad way. He couldn't aim properly, and it enabled me to shoot him."

"Glad for it," Ellison said. He looked at the kids. Samantha was talking to Cara. Cumberland turned to Aiden as the boy said something to him. Ellison spoke in a soft voice. "Aiden and Cara and Cumberland seem to share a natural introverted demeanor. They are as different from Samantha as kids could be." He lowered his voice further so that only Josie could hear him. "Samantha telegraphs charisma and charm and social confidence." Ellison was whispering. "Cumberland and his siblings, not so much. Why? Could be genetic, of course. Nature, as they call it. But I'm guessing it's at least as much nurture. Probably because you raised Samantha with full-time heart. I doubt those other kids had that."

"I made a lot of mistakes," Josie said. "I'm still making them."

"But you were fully engaged. Always there, always caring, always supportive." Ellison said. "Critical components of good parenting. From a certified expert, of course." Ellison moved his arm and gave Josie a little elbow bump.

There was a pause in the kids' conversations.

Josie said, "It was so nice of you to bring Aiden and Cara and introduce us, Cumberland."

Cumberland seemed very uncomfortable. His siblings looked like they wished to disappear. None of them spoke.

Samantha leaned over toward Cara and said something in a soft voice. Cara shrugged. Samantha spoke again, too softly for anyone to hear. She gestured toward Unknown.

Cara slowly reached out and gave Unknown a pet.

"Are things going okay?" Josie asked, looking at Cumberland.

"Well, um, it's been a little rough."

"How do you mean?"

"I told you about my father."

"Yes," Josie said.

"I had decided to say something to the police. But before I did, he'd already been arrested by the Santa Clara County Sheriff. Just yesterday. They've charged him with multiple crimes. It's pretty serious."

"I'm so sorry, Cumberland. Is there anything I can do to help?"

"I don't think so. Today, two men came to our house. They scared my mother. I guess my dad owes them a lot of money.

They made some threats."

"My God, that's terrible. Did they know your father had been arrested?"

"Yeah. They said my dad had pledged the house as collateral, and they are going to take it."

"I'm so sorry!" Josie said. "What happens next? Do you have a family attorney you can call?"

"My mother called him. Whatever she was told made her freak out."

"I wish I could help. Is there anything I can do?"

"I don't think so. I mean, I have enough money for food. We're not going to starve. But my mother isn't real coherent. I get the idea she doesn't have much in the way of reserves."

"Can you help her?" Josie asked. "With your hacking income?" As she said it, she looked over at Aiden and Cara. They both looked like they were about to cry.

"Not really. I earned a lot last year. But my dad was in trouble. So I lent it to him."

"All your money?"

Cumberland nodded. He looked very embarrassed.

"And now you won't see it back."

"No." Cumberland looked down at the sand.

Josie saw Mr. Ellison shift position on the sand. He had a severe frown on his face.

"Your mother will try to keep the house, right?" Josie said.

"She doesn't have a choice. She has to give it up. And after those men scared her, she pretty much came unglued. She told me to babysit, and then she drove away. I think she went to her friend Milena Karayan's house in Little Armenia."

Josie looked at Aiden and Cara then back at Cumberland. "Over by Hollywood," she said.

Cumberland nodded.

Josie said, "So you're in charge at home."

"Yeah. Those men are scary. They said something about their contract with my dad and how they would have title to the house in just a day or two. They said that if we haven't moved out, they would get the sheriff and hire a moving crew to haul us out."

"I think California law requires a month waiting period before evicting someone."

"Yeah. But I think it might be dangerous for us to stay there. That's why I brought Aiden and Cara with me today. For, you know, safety. I think it might be smart for us to stay someplace where those men won't know we're staying."

"Mama," Samantha said. "Remember what we said."

"What? Oh. Yes, we should do that."

"You can stay with us," Samantha announced. "Mama and I have room. Cara, you can stay in my room with me. Aiden and Cumberland, you can stay on the foldout couch."

Aiden and Cara looked as stricken as if they'd just fallen from a ship into the ice cold ocean.

Cumberland didn't respond.

Ellison spoke up. "Josie, I haven't seen your place. And I don't want to intrude. But do you have enough space?"

"It's a two-bed two-bath condo. About nine hundred square feet."

Ellison took a deep breath. He turned to Cumberland. "You were just at my loft before we headed up to our fateful meeting with the phony agent Mosconi. So you know what it's like. A whole lotta room. Four thousand square feet. It ain't comfy cozy, but it only makes sense that you three camp at my place."

Josie inhaled.

"What's that sound mean?" Ellison asked.

"Mr. Ellison, I'm just concerned whether you've thought this through. Becoming an impromptu bed-and-breakfast host is beyond generous."

"Who said I was cooking breakfast?" Ellison asked, making a small grin.

Josie looked from Ellison to Cumberland. "What do you think, Cumberland?"

"I don't know what to say. Two offers for housing. Thank you so much." His eyes were moist. "Can I talk to my brother and sister?"

"Of course," Josie said.

Cumberland motioned to Aiden and Cara. The three of them stood up and walked down the beach, talking. Although Cumberland towered over his younger siblings, they seemed like three equals figuring out their future.

As Josie watched from a distance, she put her hand on Ellison's forearm and said, "That is so nice of you to offer."

"Yeah, Mr. Ellison," Samantha said.

"Least I could do."

After a couple of minutes, Cumberland and his siblings came back. He said, "The three of us think we should stay the next night or two at your house, Professor Strong. Because, um, it's close and then we can easily go home tomorrow and figure out our next move before those men come back. But we'd come back to your house tomorrow night. Then we could move to Mr. Ellison's. Because all of us in your house would be pretty crowded. And Mr. Ellison's got space. But I don't drive, so…"

"I'm walking distance to the Commerce Metrolink train station," Ellison said. "From there you can get most places. All the way to Santa Monica, if you want. It's not fast. But driving isn't, either."

"Good, it's settled," Samantha said. She took hold of Cara's hand and squeezed.

"Now the sun is going down, and Mama, we have a little something for you."

"What?" Josie said.

Samantha handed Josie a little white box that was wrapped with red ribbon.

"Sam, you shouldn't have."

"Mama, you saved me and my future. This is thanks from all of us."

Josie teared up. She took off the little ribbon, opened the box, unfolded some tissue and pulled out a small silver bracelet with several charms hanging from it. She put it on her right wrist, held up her hand, watched it sparkle in the setting sun. She wondered what the charms represented.

"It's beautiful," Josie said. "Thank you so much."

"Mr. Ellison," Samantha said. "Do you want to go first?"

He pointed to a silver figure shaped like a large bird. "A wise lady deserves the owl, a symbol of wisdom."

Josie touched the little silver owl, then kissed her fingertip, and touched Ellison on his cheek. "It's like the owl you created on the shoulder of your Athena sculpture."

He nodded.

"Cumberland?" Samantha said.

He hesitated. "You figured out we were in trouble and needed help. And you and Samantha offered help without even thinking about it. That was, like, the nicest thing anyone has ever done for us. We want to thank you for that." He actually looked Josie in the eye. "Oh. It's the heart that I'm talking about. Actually, I didn't put it on there. I told Samantha what I'd like, and she did it."

"Same thing," Josie said. "Thank you so much."

"The lion's from me," Samantha said. "It represents courage. You are the most courageous person I know. I can't imagine doing what you did."

"Hear, hear," Ellison said. "Stare down the enemy's gun barrel without flinching and fire back."

Josie fought to maintain her composure. She rolled forward onto her hands and knees, crawled three steps to Samantha, and kissed her.

Josie held her hand with its bracelet and its charms to her chest. "I don't know what to say to all of you. I'm so fortunate to have you. I guess I have some great friends, after all."

They all nodded.

The sun had lowered into the sea and was almost set beneath the horizon. As they sat there in silence, the sun blinked out beneath the waves. Immediately, the air seemed to cool, and the breeze picked up. Josie could sense a cold night coming. There would be lots to figure out before the sun's warmth returned. But she felt warm inside.

They stood. Samantha lifted Unknown in the pack and got it situated on her back. She again took Cara's hand and Josie took Aiden's hand. "C'mon, kids," Josie said. "Let's go to your new home away from home. We'll make some popcorn and watch a movie."

Ellison and Cumberland followed behind them.

As the party walked up the sand and then headed across Ocean Avenue, Josie felt like they were walking into a new life.

About the Author

Todd Borg and his wife live in Tahoe, where they write and paint. To contact Todd or learn more about the Josie Strong thrillers or the Owen McKenna mysteries, please visit toddborg.com.

A message from the author:

Dear Reader,

If you enjoyed this novel, please consider posting a short review on any book website you like to use, such as Goodreads and Amazon. Reviews help authors a great deal, and that in turn allows us to write more stories for you.

Thank you very much for your interest and support!

Todd

Made in the USA
Middletown, DE
09 August 2024

58382256R00208